THE VERGENCE OF TIME

THE RING OF WORLDS

BOOK THREE

C.S. HARRIS

The Vergence of Time

Copyright © 2023 by C.S. Harris

All rights reserved.

A New Reality Publishing

Paperback ISBN: 979-8-9900922-5-9

eBook: 979-8-9900922-4-2

No part of this book may be reproduced in any form or by any electronic or mechanical means, including information storage and retrieval systems, without written permission from the author, except for the use of brief quotations in a book review. Thank you for respecting the hard work of this author.

This is a work of fiction. Names, characters, places, and incidents either are a product of the author's imagination or are used fictitiously, and any resemblance to locales, events, business establishments, or actual persons— living or dead— is entirely coincidental.

Fulfilling a Vow: A Ring of Worlds Prequel

Galen Ohahakehte carries a solemn vow etched into his soul: to vanquish the malevolent necromancer, Adrienne Vorpahl. His path to vengeance, however, takes an unexpected turn as he becomes the mentor to Alexander Eldred, a fourteen-year-old prodigy brimming with immense magical potential. Galen's reasonably sure that training a teenage boy will be easier than defeating an undead monster.

Start reading: https://dl.bookfunnel.com/x0nshhkla6

Oceanus Septentrionalis

GLACIALIS

ALBION

LONDINIUM
ROMA

TÈNG EMPIRE

XIĀNGYÁNG

FRIQIYE

PERSIA

HECATOMPYLOS

ĀRYĀVARTA

PĀṬALIPUTRA

AXUM

Oceanus Australis

TENEBROSUS CONTINENS

• Vindmar
🏠 Nephilim Temple

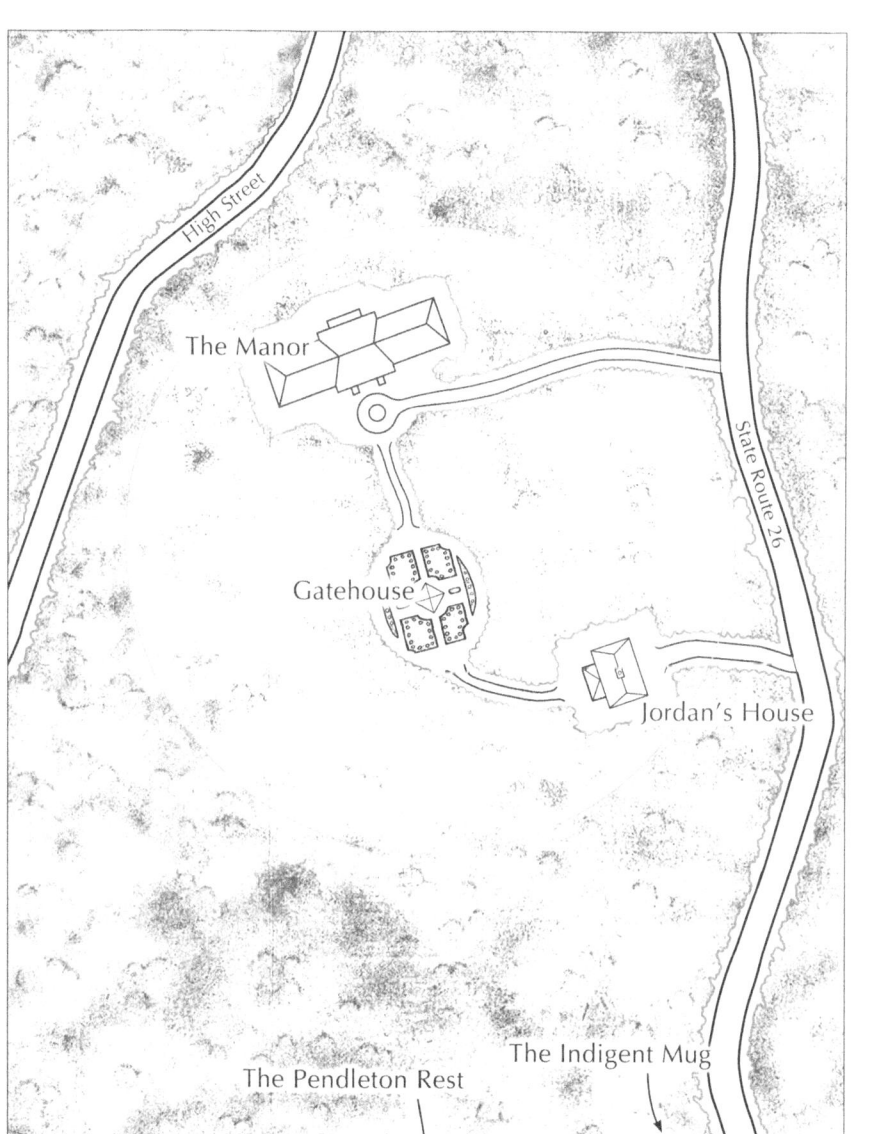

A Quick Note on Pronunciation

Whenever I dive into a new book, I'm always eager to fully immerse myself in the world the author has created, right down to the pronunciation of each word. I believe that understanding the language as the author intended adds a rich layer of authenticity to the reading experience.

To help you enjoy *The Vergence of Time* in this same immersive way, I've compiled a handy glossary of names and words you'll encounter. But, hey, I'm only human—if there's a term you're curious about that I haven't included, I'd love to hear from you! Drop me a line at chris@chrisharrisbooks.com with any terms you think should be added. Your input is invaluable, and I'm more than happy to update future editions with your suggestions.

In the meantime, for a more extensive dive into the language of the book, check out our always up-to-date online glossary at www.theringofworlds.com/glossary. Don't miss the latest version of the Ôrëńos-English dictionary at www.theringofworlds.com/conlang.

You'll find the word, the International Phonetic Alphabet entry for each term, and an approximate pronunciation for English speakers.

Words that derive from the Ôrëńos language are denoted by an asterisk (*) at the head of the entry.

Adrienne Vorpahl /ˈæd.ri.ən ˈvɔr.pɑl/ (AD-ree-en VOR-pal)
Æsir /ˈaɪ.sɪr/ or /ˈɛ.sɪr/ (EYE-sir) or (ESS-ir) (the pronunciation varies according to the source)
Aeronwen /aɪˈrɔn.wɛn/ (eye-RON-wen)
Āiláo Quán /ái.láu tɕʰy̆ɛ́n/ (eye-LAO chyehn)
Ākāśa /aːˈkaː.ʃə/ (ah-KAH-shuh)
Amaterasu /a.ma.teˈɾa.su/ (ah-mah-teh-RAH-soo)
Amlodd /ˈam.ɬɔð/ (AM-loth)
Amr̥ta /əmˈɽi.tə/ (uhm-RIH-tuh)
***Anïj Vor** /ʌˈniʰdʒ vɑɹ/ (uh-NEEJ vawr)
Auditum Peritiae Arcanae /ˈau̯.di.tum pe.riˈti.e arˈka.nae/ (OW-dee-toom peh-rih-TEE-eh ahr-KAH-nay)
Ásbrú /ˈau̯s.bruː/ (OWS-broo)
***Atülän** /ʌ.tjuˈlɑn/ (uh-TYOO-lahn)
***Ävidä Saclendra** /ɑ.vɪˈdaʰ sʌˈklɛn.dɹʌ/ (ah-vih-DAH suh-KLEN-druh)
Bifröst /ˈbɪv.røst/ (BEEV-rerst)
Bohuslava /ˈbo.hu.slɑː.vɑ/ (BO-hoo-SLAH-vah)
Calamitas /käˈlä.mɪ.täs/ (kah-LAH-mi-tahs)
Cathedra /kəˈθiː.drə/ (kuh-THEE-druh); the plural is **cathedrae** /kəˈθiː.dreɪ/ (kuh-THEE-dray)
Cernunnos /kɛrˈnʊ.noʊs/ (ker-NOO-nohs)
Chèuhngsāam /t͡ʃʰ.ɔːŋˈsɑːm˥/ (chawng-SAHM)
Conciliar /conˈkɪ.li.ar/ (kon-KIL-ee-ar)
Concilium Magorum /kɔnˈki.li.um maˈgo.rum/ (kon-KEE-lee-um ma-GO-rum)
Consiliarius /kɔn.siˈli.a.rjus/ (kawn-see-LEE-ah-ree-oos); the plural form is **Consiliarii** /kɔn.siˈli.a.ri.i/ (kawn-see-LEE-ah-ree-ee)
Cymraeg /kəmˈraɪg/ (kuhm-RYE-g)
Darhavil /ˈdar.ha.wil/ (DAHR-hah-vill)
Darhavilon /dar.haˈwi.lon/ (dar-HAH-vih-lon)
Dilşad /dɪɫˈʃad/ (dil-SHAD)

Drëndi /ˈdɹɛn.di/ (DREN-dee)
Ednyfed /ɛd.ˈnə.vɛd/ (ehd-NUH-vehd)
Eirianned /eir.ˈi.an.ned/ (AYR-ee-an-ned)
Et Alas Mercurii /ɛt ˈa.las mɛr.ˈku.ri.i/ (et AH-las mer-KOO-ree-ee)
Gaea /ˈɡaɪ.ə/ (GAI-uh)
Glacialis /ɡla.ki.ˈa.lis/ (gla-kee-AH-lis)
Gladius /ˈɡlad.i.ʊs/ (GLAD-ee-uhs); the plural is **gladii** /ˈɡla.di.i/ (GLAH-dee-ee)
Guānyīn /ɡwænˈjɪn/ (gwan-YIN)
Gulielmus Occamus /ɡu.ˈli.el.mus ˈɔk.ka.mus/ (goo-lee-EL-moos AWK-ka-moos) (William of Ockham)
Hayonhwathahonte /hɑ.ˈjɔn.hwɑ.θɑ.ˈhɔn.te/ (hay-ON-wah-tha-HON-teh)
Hrdlička /hrd.ˈli͡t ʂ.ka/ (hrrd-LEETCH-kah)
Iskariótés /is.ka.rj.ˈó.tes/ (ees-kah-ree-OH-tes)
Kalypto Hesykhia /ka.ˈlip.to he.ˈsy.kʰi.a/ (kah-LEEP-toh heh-SY-khee-uh)
Kāmla Vicchāya /ˈkaːm.laː vi͡t .ˈʃʰaː.ja/ (KAHM-lah vich-CHAH-yuh)
Kanehsatà:ke /kɑ.nɛh.sɑ.ˈtɑː.kɛ/ (kah-neh-sah-TAH-keh)
Kanienˈkeháka /kɑ.ni.ɛnʔ.kɛ.ˈhɑː.kɑ/ (kah-nee-ehn-keh-HAH-kah)
Karkheh Dam /ˈkɑr.keɪ/ (KAR-kay)
Kathreftis tou Narkissou /ˈkaθ.ref.tis tu nar.ˈkis.su/ (KAH-threhf-tis too nahr-KEES-soo)
Kr̥tyā Bījā /kr̥t̪.ˈjaː biː.ˈd͡ʒaː/ (kruht-YAA bee-JAA)
Lethargum Cantatio /lɛ.ˈtʰar.ɡum kan.ˈtaː.ti.oː/ (leh-TAHR-gum kan-TAH-tee-oh)
Lex Parsimoniae /leks par.ˈsɪ.mɔ.ni.ae̯/ (LEKS par-SI-moh-nee-eye)
Liáng Bo /lǐ.ăŋ pwǒ/ (lee-ahng bwaw)
Lucullus /lu.ˈkul.lus/ (loo-KOOL-loos)
Nādī /naː.ˈɖiː/ (nah-DEE)
Obscuratus /ɔb.skjuː.ˈrɑː.tus/ (ob-skyoo-RAH-toos); the plural form is **obscurati** /ɔb.skjuː.ˈrɑː.ti/ (ob-skyoo-RAH-tee)
Ohahakehte /oʊ.ˈhɑː.hɑː.keɪ.teɪ/ (oh-HA-ha-kay-tay)
Omejis /ˈoː.mi.dʒus/ (OH-mee-juhs)
*****Ôrëńen** /ɔ.ɹɛʰ.ˈnʰen/ (aw-reh-NHEN)

***Pāskendińoldor** /pe.skɛn.dɪ.ˈnʰɑl.dɑɹ/ (pay-sken-dih-NHAWL-door)
Phoenix /ˈpʰoî.nix/ (FOY-niks). The plural form is **phoinikes** /ˈpʰoî.ni.kes/ (FOY-nee-kes)
Phylacterium /ˌfaɪ.læk.ˈtiːr.i.əm/ (fy-lak-TEER-ee-um); the plural form is **phylacteria** /faɪ.ˈlæk.tə.ri.ə/ (fy-LAK-tuh-ree-uh)
Prāṇa /ˈpraː.ɳə/ (PRAH-nuh)
Prāṇamaṇḍala /ˈpraː.ɳə.mən̪.ɖə.lə/ (PRAH-nuh-muhn-duh-luh)
***Pritanea** /pɹɪ.tæ.ne.ˈʌ/ (prih-TA-nee-uh)
Proventus /proː.ˈwen.tus/ (proh-WEN-tuhs)
Pyxis /ˈpʏk.sɪs/ (PIK-sis). The plural form is **pyxides** /ˈpʏk.sɪ.deːs/ (PIK-si-dees)
Rilladwen /rɪl.ˈlad.wɛn/ (rill-LAD-wen)
Śāśvatavrata /ˈʃaː.ʃvə.t̪ə.vraː.t̪ə/ (SHAH-shwuh-tuh-vraht-uh)
Seiren /se͜ɪ.réːn/ (say-REEN); the plural form is **seirenes** /se͜ɪ.réːn.es/ (say-REEN-es)
Semilamia /se.mi.ˈla.mi.a/ (seh-mih-LAH-mee-uh) The plural form is **semilamiae** /se.miˈla.mi.ae̯/ (seh-mih-LAH-mee-eye)
Śiva /ˈʃi.və/ (SHE-vuh)
***Sirenī** /sɪ.ɹɛ.ˈnaɪ/ (sih-reh-NAI)
Skawen'na'háːwi /ska.wɛn.ˈná.há.ʔwi/ (skah-wen-NAH-hah-quee)
Stygius /ˈstyː.ɡi.us/ (STYE-gee-oos)
Sulwyn /ˈsɪl.wɪn/ (SILL-win)
Tèngyīn /tʰə̂ŋ.ˈin/ (tung-EEN)
Thalatte /tʰa.ˈlat̪.t̪i/ (thuh-LAT-tee)
***Thīaterīka** /θaɪ.æ.tɛ.ˈɹaɪ.kʌ/ (thai-uh-teh-RYE-kuh)
Vacuolation /ˌvæk.ju.ə.ˈleɪ.ʃən/ (VAK-yoo-uh-LAY-shun)
***Valas Amris** /væ.ˈlæs ʌm.ˈɹɪs/ (va-LASS um-RISS)
Vanir /ˈvɑː.nɪr/ (VAH-nir)
Verum Iacet /ˈwe.rum ˈja.ket/ (WEH-rum YAH-ket)
Wú Xiāng /wǔ ɕi̯.áŋ/ (woo with a falling tone shy-ahng with a rising tone)
Yllundi /iːl.ˈlʊn.di/ (eel-LOON-dee)

One last thing when it comes to the languages of the Ring of Worlds: many different beings communicate throughout my books. Your garden variety speech is contained between quotes, and telepathic communication is italicized without quotation marks. Sometimes, however, you'll encounter dialogue tucked between two / markers. This denotes nonverbal, nontelepathic speech, so if you see a backslash in the book, that's why.

"The notion of unrestrained striving and competition. Being able to go all-out and use any means to get what *you* want, with nobody and nothing to answer to—as opposed to existing as part of something larger that you have to learn to harmonize with."

—James P. Hogan, *Echoes of an Alien Sky*

One
Unus

Kāmla had heard about the death of twenty-four of Ävidä's offspring at Glimmerwick. The necromancer had joined her at her home in Columbia, the capital of Demurria.

"That was a dismal failure," she told him. "I can't believe the vampires survived that– you assured me the Dawntime spells were unstoppable!"

Ävidä scowled at her from across the living room, where he paced restlessly. His anger was palpable.

"They are," he snarled. "Those spells come down from the fucking Nephilim, so shut the fuck up already, and let me think!"

She fumed at his tone and words but said nothing. She didn't know how the vampires overcame his demilīc; they were young in their undeath, but he'd sent two dozen. She knew he'd shown them the most potent destructive spell he knew because he'd taught it to them after they failed to destroy Glimmerwick the first time.

I guess even the magic of Darhavilon can't eradicate the bloodsuckers.

He turned away from her; his robes swirled about his legs as he paced. Ävidä muttered to himself, trying to figure out how his offspring could fail so miserably—several of them had even died the second death, their phylacteria destroyed in the battle. After several minutes of pacing in her living room, he stopped, and his eyes widened. Kāmla studied him and wondered what he'd just realized—she knew him well enough to know that thoughtful look.

"There's no way the bloodsuckers defeated my līc," he said slowly.

His green eyes narrowed as he turned his intense gaze on Kāmla. Despite the rage inside, she schooled her face to an expression of attentive interest.

"They had help," he breathed.

Kāmla blinked and felt her rage cool. *That changes everything*, she thought consideringly.

"Yes, of course, and there aren't many wizards who could defeat two dozen linked magic users—" she began.

"...other than the Three." Ävidä's words ended with a wrathful hiss. His lips thinned, and he shook his head. "Are they back? We must find out immediately!"

Kāmla was irritated at the idea and grimaced. *If that's the case, we'll have to adjust all our plans—especially mine. I'm not ready to move up my timetable, but I need to do something. The Three will ruin everything if they've returned to Gaea.*

She knew Ävidä was observing her, but he'd assume her expression was related to thoughts of the Three rather than her actual machinations. He had no idea what she was planning; she'd never seen so much as an inkling in his eyes or behavior that indicated he knew the truth. Besides, if he did, she'd already have died horribly. Her continued existence meant he was unaware, and she intended to keep him that way.

Plus, I already know his plans.

She smoothed her expression as they settled down to figure out how to deal with the Three. They spent the next two hours discussing their options but got nowhere.

"We're talking in circles," Kāmla finally said. "Unless we use the Epiphany of Light to look back at events, we've missed any opportunity to uncover the identity of the magicians. We know someone used powerful magic at Glimmerwick because they defeated your offspring. We have nothing beyond that."

"Did the Registry detect anything?" the necromancer asked her.

The original purpose of the Registry Office of the Unified

Government was twofold. First, members administered the Auditum Peritiae Arcanae to children. This served to assess their magical aptitude and direct them into schooling that fit their natural affinities—combat, clerical, technical, and so on. It also determined their Grade, from one at the weakest to seven at the strongest. The second purpose was to track the usage of higher-Grade spells, though this was never meant to be used for nefarious purposes.

When Kāmla took over for her deceased predecessor, Hans Matteo, she subverted the Registry office and turned it into a hub of magical spying. She stopped the Auditum and used the Registry to track down magicians of power through their spell usage.

Kāmla had already called the Registry's main office. "Not when I checked earlier today, but the network doesn't work as efficiently as it used to," she reminded him.

Ävidä's lips thinned at her implied rebuke. It was his fault the Registry had too few employees; he hadn't wanted them tracking his spells, so he'd urged her to reduce the number of people working for that part of the Unified Government.

The robed magician stalked into the dining room and paced back into the living room like a caged tiger. After several minutes he stopped and stared at her. Kāmla kept her face carefully neutral.

"The Three never linked aurae, correct?" he asked.

"That's correct—according to the transcripts Hans Matteo left behind, anyway."

Her predecessor in the Ministry had conducted extensive debriefs after the Sogma debacle. She'd studied them exhaustively, and one of the many interesting things Hans noted was that the Three didn't link aurae, but she didn't know why.

"Call the Registry," Ävidä suggested. "See if the monitors recorded anything around Londinium."

Kāmla's first instinct was to call Patrice, her former aide, but she was dead.

It's a pity. The girl was the best aide I've ever had.

She called the Ministry and waited while the main switchboard transferred her to the head Registry office in Columbia.

"Minister Vicchāya! How can I help you?" a crisp voice said into her ear.

"Have you recorded unusually strong magic use in the last twenty-four hours?" she asked.

There was silence. Then, after a couple of minutes, the voice returned. "Uh, yes, I checked the logs. There are several spikes recorded by the Londinium Ministry. I'm not sure why you weren't already notified about this." More silence. "Oh, it seems that the aide on duty when the surges happened took ill. I'm sorry about that, Minister. You should have been notified. The spikes appeared in a six-hour window."

"From individuals or linked units?" she clarified.

"I don't have that information, Minister," the speaker said apologetically.

"Thank you," she replied crisply.

She hung up the phone and relayed the short conversation to Ävidä.

He nodded thoughtfully at her words even as a sneer crawled over his visage. "Perhaps the old fucks came out of the closet and defended their offspring? If so, that's more than I expected," he seethed.

"Would Imogene and Proventus link aurae if they needed to fight off twenty-four līc?" she wondered aloud.

He scowled. "You told me when we planned the extermination of the bloodsuckers that Imogene and Proventus were never registered," he reminded her. "They could be Grade Seven sorcerers, for all we know."

"I did tell you that, yes. They preexist Unification, and no one's seen them in centuries. Perhaps they are as powerful as the Three. It's been about twelve thousand years since they emigrated from Stygius after the Eternal Night ended."

She only knew because that was public knowledge. One of the Council's requirements of the bloodsuckers was that they share their history and allow scholars to record it in the Bibliotheca Columbia. She'd read the official account that four vampires came to Gaea from Stygius, another planet in the Ring of Worlds. They settled in the land that would become Demurria thousands of years later. At least two of those vampires originally hailed from Atülän, a great island nation on Gaea that was destroyed in a cometary bombardment. Almost all extant knowledge of the Dawntime disappeared with the landmass.

Several hundred thousand people evacuated from Atülän before its obliteration. The survivors were magically gifted, and they believed this gave them the right to rule wherever they settled. They marshaled armies, conquered many lands, and eventually waged war on each other over territory and resources.

The rest of the world called the survivors Lantins after their homeland, and they hated them. Lantins were arrogant and heavy-handed, and their warmongering disrupted the lives of everyone around. After several thousand years, the thirteen strongest wizards in the world made themselves known. They called themselves the Concilium—the Council—and claimed descent from the mages of the Synod, the ruling body of Atülän. They ordered their people to settle and be at peace.

The Lantins rejected the directions of the Council to their peril: the Consiliarii traveled to each nation that rejected their orders and summarily executed the rulers. They didn't kill anyone that complied with their will, but the Councilmembers were brutal and remorseless.

After the purge, the thirteen mages cast a spell calling to all the descendants of Atülän; millions gathered in a great tract of unoccupied land. The Council decreed this was the new homeland of the Lantins, and so it was. In time, Lantin changed to Latin, and their descendants became the people of Rome.

The Roman Empire unified the world via negotiation and war. The great nation thrived until the Council decreed the Empire's time was over. The blood of Atülän was so diminished that no one had the right to that name any longer, and the Empire disappeared with barely a sigh.

Kāmla considered what she knew. *Is it possible Imogene and Proventus are on the Council?*

If they were, it meant the vampire elders were strong enough to fight off twenty-four līc easily, but there was no way to know unless they revealed their membership. It secretly amused her that neither

Ävidä nor the Three numbered among that august body, despite their power.

How powerful did someone need to be to receive a spot in those exclusive, privileged ranks?

She doubted she would ever know.

Kāmla blinked when Ävidä spoke. She'd been so lost in thought she'd forgotten he was there.

"That must be it," he said. "After so long, losing so many bloodsuckers brought them out of their stupor." He paused and thought for a moment. "Fine. We leave Glimmerwick and Āiláo Quán alone and let the corruption take care of the thirstbags. They're not immune to the spell. Nothing is, not even the Three."

"Good," she purred. "Now that we've settled that…"

Ävidä grinned and held out a hand. She took it and let him lead her into the dining room—he loved to fuck her on tables and desks. Like all men, he enjoyed watching the action. Kāmla didn't mind—she liked that, too.

Ävidä looked at Kāmla for an instant after they'd finished having sex. She reclined on the dining table, her heart pounding from her climax, but, already, she was pulling her elbows in and pushing herself upright, always practical. She was a beautiful, passionate woman despite how cold she seemed. Her feelings ranged between extremes of glacial uncaring and molten rage, and that fire came out in her coupling.

She was brilliant, too, which was why he hadn't already killed her. Despite being pristinely nonmagical—her entire family was, as far as he could discern without spending time in Timil Deeps studying them—she had an insight into incantations that was genius. He expected it was because she was a master manipulator, somehow able to twist everyone and everything to serve her needs, even magic itself.

He was teaching her how to become a līc. She would be fearsome when her powers potentiated—if he let her get that far. Ävidä was almost six centuries old. He hadn't survived that long through trust and stupidity but by carefully curating the existence of everyone around him. Kāmla wasn't his first "ally," and he doubted she would be his last.

He turned away from where she now sat on the table, naked and glorious, and used a whispered incantation to cleanse his animate form of the residue of their intercourse. His body was dark-skinned and lean, and his green eyes gleamed with a jewel-like intensity, thanks to his necromantic power.

Ävidä stepped into the living room and then turned around. He caught her subtle change in expression as she crafted a smile for his benefit. She was the best actor he'd ever known, but he was quite good at playing the fool ensnared by her sex and her cunning, cold beauty.

Ävidä wondered which of them would prevail when the time came.

Despite how powerful he was, Ävidä was cautious never to make the mistakes of his creator, Adrienne Vorpahl. The archlīc who'd made him had suffered the true death because of her arrogance.

Ävidä didn't know who accompanied Hayonhwathahonte "Galen" Ohahakehte when the old man tracked Adrienne down in Glacialis and destroyed her. Ävidä knew Adrienne had lost that battle because she'd been alone. If he'd had been with her, they could have defeated the old Kanien'kehá:ka sorcerer and whoever else was there.

No, I will not make that mistake. She lived a thousand years—and I will live until I grow tired of this plane of existence. Then I will ascend and see what awaits in the greater prāṇamaṇḍala, he thought idly.

For now, he had dissembling of his own to do. He smiled at Kāmla, pretending to be blind to her ambitions, and walked back into the dining room. She thought he was a slave to his lusts, and Ävidä was happy to keep her believing that.

After defeating the līc outside Glimmerwick, Imara and Sirenī returned to Eldred Manor in Timil Deeps. They were in the workroom when Imara heard something through the Abyssal Gate that bridged Gaea with their Earthen home.

Alex frowned at Imara's troubled look. "What do you hear?"

"Something's wrong on Earth, but I can't tell what." Imara sounded frustrated by her inability to dial in her magical hearing.

They dashed through the portal to their adopted planet and heard sounds that shouldn't be in their house: a woman screamed, and at least two other voices laughed maliciously.

The Three hurried from the laboratory, through the library, and down the corridor to the main hall. They saw Jordan crab-crawling away from two līc. She bled from multiple gashes on her forearms, which she'd held out to defend herself from a nonmagical attack.

The two undead were skeletal. One was mummified, and the other had tightly drawn, dried-out flesh peeling off old bones stained a dirty brown. Both corpse walkers sported sparse wisps of filthy dark hair that stuck up from their leathery scalps.

Imara identied one of the undead as male. He sported fresh, plump genitals that he'd undoubtedly cut from some man's body while the victim was alive. His stolen equipment jiggled and flopped obscenely with every movement of his otherwise leathery form. The other, she concluded, was female. She had moist red lips on her skull and luscious, bright green eyes set in the bony sockets of her ruined countenance.

The songstress knew gender identity didn't hold much weight for līc—they were spirits stored far away from the bodies they puppeted. They could walk in the corpses of men, women, or children. Imara curled her lips in distaste at the spectacle of the undead and planned her attack.

Jordan crawled away from the līc, her face white, her eyes wide in terror. Imara, Sirenī, and Alex entered the main hall, coronae flaring. Imara saw an impermeable field snap around Jordan with a crackle that drove the līc back; the two creatures spun to face the Three with faces contorted into rictuses of malevolent delight.

Jordan gasped as the shield surrounded her; Imara saw her sag in relief through the sparkling confines of the defensive field. Her autolenses allowed her to perceive movement to her right without shifting her attention from the līc.

Carter lunged through the open door of the house; he stopped short when he saw the Three. "Glad you're here!" he called.

The līc let out bestial shrieks at his words and thrust their hands forward. The male sent a cascade of flames toward Imara and Sirenī, and the women staggered back as the magical fire wrapped around them. The flames elongated and swept from the floor to the plafond twenty feet above their heads. Thankfully, the house was flame-retardant, and the fire didn't damage the walls or ceiling.

Imara took a deep breath, her intrinsic defenses making her impervious to the heat and intense light of the flames. She stepped from the column of fire with Sirenī, who was similarly protected, at her side. The līc released the spell, and the fire swirled into nothingness within a few seconds. The līc looked surprised that neither woman seemed harmed. Without missing a beat, Imara smirked and shouted, letting the power in her voice flash from her lips in an iridescent ring.

The pulse struck the male līc. He screeched and flew backward, smashing into the wall abutting the sitting room so hard that the plaster cracked in annular waves. The ripples of destruction fractured the substrate of the wall before he bounced to the floor.

Sirenī stepped through the shield she'd erected around her friend and knelt. "I'm so sorry," she said as she took a sobbing Jordan in her arms and held her tightly.

The Earthen woman clung to her, shaking with fear and pain. Sirenī began to chant a Level One healing spell, which required less than a minute to complete. The battle raged behind them in the main hall. Lightning and fire passed back and forth in a brutal, close-quarters duel. Thunder boomed deafeningly in the enclosed space.

Sirenī hurried through the chant, eager to get back to the fight. She got thirty seconds into the spell, and the wounds on Jordan's arms closed. By the time she finished, there was no evidence that Jordan had been harmed.

She kissed Jordan's forehead and looked into her eyes. "Do you want me to stay with you?" she asked and then turned to scowl at the two undead as they fought Imara and Alex.

Jordan swiped the tears from her cheeks, took a deep breath, and looked at Sirenī. "Kill those fuckers!" she growled.

Alexander's eyes narrowed in wrath when he realized the līc had violated their home.

I meant it to be a sanctuary, not a battlefield. I never expected there would be Undying on Earth who could pose a threat to us.

His oversight almost cost Jordan her life—just like it had cost Imara her sight years ago, causing forty-eight years of pain and heartache. He chastised himself for his foolishness and refocused on the threat before them.

He nonchalantly caught a lightning bolt in his palm and threw the electricity back at the female līc. He turned his head and saw Carter fidgeting by the entrance to the house; the soldier had no weapons and wasn't strong enough as a magician to duel with the undead as they cackled spells in unfamiliar Earthen languages.

Alexander snapped his fingers and psychically grabbed the gladius he'd made for the soldier. He teleported the sword into the room and set it to hang point down before the soldier. Carter snatched it and made a few test swings. Eldritch golden light sparkled and cracked around his hand and the sword's hilt.

He gasped and looked at Alexander with appreciation. "That tingles in all the right places."

Alexander smirked and turned back to the battle. He called to mind the complex prayer of the Kanien'kehá:ka that could destroy the undead. He'd need time to cast it, though.

"Buy me time!" he shouted into the room.

No one acknowledged his words, but he trusted they'd heard him.

Carter lunged at the female līc. He readied his fancy new gladius while briefly admiring the golden light that still glowed around his hand. His corona was usually a warm, lemony color, but it was much richer and darker around the sword's hilt.

The female sensed or saw him coming. She turned with a shriek and thrust out a skeletal, filthy hand. Flames leaped from her bony fingertips; the heat slapped his face with a sting that instantly made his skin feel tight and dry.

He cringed because his armor was no longer enchanted to absorb spells. Alex had repaired the structure but hadn't had time to restore the magical protections Carter was accustomed to. All he could do was trust Alex as he thrust the gladius forward. The blade entered the stream of flames, and they parted to flow around him. The heat was punishing, but he didn't feel like his skin was crisping up. He burst out a roar of delight as he closed in on her. He drove the blade through her palm, then swiftly yanked it back and flicked it sideways, cutting off three fingers as she snatched her hand away.

She didn't feel pain but keened with rage at his attack. She began to scream in a foreign language—Carter recognized obscenities when he heard them.

Two can play that game.

"Oh yeah, you fucking ugly assrag!" he bellowed. "Why don't you come closer?"

She stopped screaming and stared at him, her moist, green eyes flicking about to take in the field of battle. She curled her arms across her chest, and her body pulsed with a sickly, foul green radiance the color of rot and putrescence. Carter attacked again, but she swept her arms out and stomped her right foot before he could get close to her.

The līc summoned a surge of necromantic force. When she released it, a noxious green wave of power exploded out and smashed into all of them. The few tables in the main hall splintered into shards, and the walls shook as the power blasted out. The blast knocked back Alexander, Imara, Carter, and the other līc.

Sirenī stood unmoving before the attack, her fatal beauty making it almost impossible for her to stumble, trip, or fall.

Jordan remained safe inside her shield.

The male recovered quickly and flung out his hands as he darted sideways and threw bolts of magical energy that shimmered green and ugly. They splattered and burst across Imara and Sirenī's spectral shielding without effect. Simultaneously, the female hit Carter with a psychokinetic punch that threw him out the front door. The soldier bellowed out a curse as he sailed backward, but he held onto his new gladius.

Alexander planted his feet and held out his hands, tuning out everything around him. The sorcerer of Timil Deeps closed his eyes, took a deep breath, and began to speak in the complex language of the Kanien'kehá:ka of Gaea. He began summoning the powerful, slow-building magic his teacher, Galen Ohahakehte, had taught him long ago. The house trembled, and ash and debris rattled across the floor.

The Kanien'kehá:ka prayer took about six minutes to recite, and Alexander couldn't rush it. The People's magic didn't work that way—speaking faster would unravel the spell rather than complete it quicker. It was just the way things worked.

Imara heard Alex's voice raise in a prayer of the Kanien'kehá:ka people. She listened to the growling whine of the power gradient escalate. The floor trembled, the walls shook, and the abstract patterns on the ceiling blurred as the power thickened. She'd been readying herself to destroy the animate forms of the two monsters before her, but she reined herself in. What Alex did would obliterate the bonds of their magic while restoring their souls to the Chains of Mortality.

The songstress caught Sirenī's eye and shook her head minutely. *Alex is casting a Kanien'kehá:ka spell. It will restore the natural order of things and destroy their phylacteria.*

Sirenī let Imara know she understood, turned, and threw herself at the male līc. She got inside his defenses and enjoyed the widening of his shriveled eyes as his leathery face creased in shock at her unexpected maneuver. She felt her lips curl as she smelled rotting meat and something unspeakably foul. She punched him to the floor with psychokinesis, then picked him up and smashed him through the wall into the sitting room.

In a rare demonstration of her athleticism, she somersaulted through the hole he'd made and landed lightly in the other room. She grabbed him with her power, spun about, and hammered him back through the wall, creating another hole.

The līc hit the floor with a screech of rage. He lay there with his flesh, several fingers, and a few toes torn from his body by the traumatic beating.

Sirenī stepped through the new hole and grinned down at the slack-jawed līc.

Imara strode forward with her hands out and let her voice rise to cover Alex's prayer in case the līc recognized the magic, which was inimical to their unnatural existence. Energies flexed around her, and she inhaled, then exhaled a word of power. She hit the female līc with so much force that the līc was punched backward, and one of her stolen, moist eyeballs burst from her head and rolled across the filthy floor.

The līc shrieked in rage, her voice hideous and unnaturally loud. The screeching made Imara flinch as the undead clutched at her face and writhed on the floor, shouting, "You fucking cunt!" in her native language.

Imara's aural magic allowed her to understand every language she encountered. After a few minutes in the presence of anyone, she automatically assimilated their natal tongue.

The līc on the floor scrabbled to her hands and knees, glaring at Imara. "I'll rip your eyes out and wear them next, you bitch," she vowed.

She rose to her feet and began to cast in a different Earthen language, shouting words to a spell Imara didn't recognize.

The līc slammed her hands together, and power burst outward in a bright aura before it flashed across the short distance between them. The sickly green beam sizzled as it ionized the atmosphere and slammed into Imara. The beam struck her full-on, knocked her back, and made her spectral shielding flare into view in iridescent ripples. Imara grimaced as her intrinsic defenses absorbed and diffused the energy.

This līc was powerful, and her sustained attack began to bleed through Imara's embedded wards. Her smile withered as she felt the beam's heat against her skin, she hissed a curse, and then something clicked. She blinked and saw a strange, twining effect travel back along the energy pathway. The līc shrieked as she tried to pull her hands apart, but whatever was happening prevented it.

Imara wasn't sure what to do next.

Carter charged fearlessly back into the main hall. He raced around the right side of the līc, and his gladius flashed like liquid silver as it sliced clean through the corpse walker's arm and sent it spinning away across the floor. The sickly green beam flicked off, and Imara staggered, released from whatever was happening.

Bohuslava shrieked again and spun to face the soldier, whose ferocious glare matched hers perfectly.

"Fucking punch me again, you rotted bitch!" he hollered.

She knew enough Latin to translate his words. She howled and danced back as the soldier thrust his sword at her head, whipped it around, and stabbed at her repeatedly. She screeched and dodged away from the weapon as the soldier swung it about with lethal expertise. The līc backpedaled, but Carter kept advancing.

This wasn't how it was supposed to go. Up to now, the people of Earth had spoiled her and Adam. Since they were always so afraid of the terrors that stalked the night, she'd assumed everyone would be terrified. She and Adam were accustomed to their hideous appearance and aura of evil overwhelming those they hunted, tortured, and killed.

She expected her moist, fresh lips and bright, satiny eyes ripped from her screaming victims to terrify and traumatize any who beheld her. Adam's grotesque new genitals, which he cut from mortal men with great care and stitched to his rotted crotch, offended and upset everyone who saw them.

Their fresh body parts were garish embellishments; grotesqueries meant to confuse and distract. It had always worked before, but these people were like nothing the offspring of Dilşad had ever encountered.

They were unafraid and powerful. It was a bad combination.

Bohuslava had already lost fingers on her left hand and now her right arm above the elbow; she began to see this battle would not go in their favor.

Adam was kneeling with his back to Sirenī. His head was craned up so hard the witch had almost ripped it from his body as she held him with apparently inexhaustible telekinetic force.

Bohuslava saw what was happening and decided to flee. She couldn't save Adam's current skin, but she could escape and help him mount a new animate form. Bohuslava waved her left arm, the stumps of her fingers wriggling obscenely, and a cloud of darkness and flame burst into form around her.

The showy but harmless blast drove the soldier and his thrashing sword away; she spun on her heel and broke for the door. She'd just begun to chant the teleportation spell when something happened, freezing her instantly in place.

The last words of the Kanien'kehá:ka prayer fell from Alexander's lips. The air fragmented into drifting, crystalline shards that spun and glittered in the clear, bright light of the main hall. The sorcerer and everything else froze as the power blossomed; a deep, distant beat echoed into the discontinuity, throbbing with portent.

The frozen moment passed. Alexander had his eyes closed and was floating a foot above the floor. A subtle white light surrounded him. It gleamed over his dark skin and radiated into the chamber as he used one of the greatest spells of the Kanien'kehá:ka people. It was the first time he'd cast it, but he'd been there with Galen when they fought and defeated the archlīc Adrienne Vorpahl, ending her long reign of terror.

Alexander's mentor had sworn the Śāśvatavrata, the Eternal Vow. He would hunt Adrienne down and restore her to the Chains of Mortality if it killed him. Casting the Śāśvatavrata meant Galen was bound to the undertaking for as long as it took in this life or the next —or the one after that—but he had fulfilled his vow before his death.

After Alexander and Galen returned to Galen's home in Kanehsatà:ke, his mentor suggested that they hide Alexander's part in Adrienne's defeat. It seemed like a sensible precaution to Alexander at the time, since it would help him avoid any more notoriety than being an Eldred already produced.

Now it was Alexander's turn to cast the great spell and destroy the loathsome undead violating his home. The light surrounding him winked out, and his feet drifted to the floor. Time glided forward as the energies discharged. Consecrated power irradiated the undead, soaking into them, and propagated along the tethers from their animate forms to their phylacteria. The magic surged so powerfully down those immaterial cords that their soul repositories overloaded with devastating results.

At Sparta Safe in Vienna and Sentinel Vaults in Waterloo, massive explosions rocked the structures as one vault in each location erupted with an unholy storm of dreadfire. The conflagration of necromantic flames, a poisonous green shading to blue as the power expanded with incomprehensible force, billowed out as the buildings trembled and shook.

The walls and foundations fractured as the dreadfire erupted from the vaults; those nearest the blasts were incinerated instantly. Those farther away suffered flash burns and penetrating trauma from the force of the explosions, and those still farther back suffered radiation burns from the unnatural flames. Between the two locations, dozens were killed and hundreds injured.

Two
Duo

Alexander opened his eyes. Sirenī stood before a burned husk that crumbled into ash as he watched—the female had already disintegrated. Carter walked over to the sorcerer. He held his sword loosely with the blade angled toward the floor.

Imara marched straight over to Jordan while she hummed a soothing melody. The songstress smiled and helped her Earthen friend to her feet as Sirenī dismissed the impermeable field.

Richard ran into the house about ten seconds later, breathing hard, his face flushed. He skidded to a halt on the ash and debris-strewn marble floor, his eyes widening in shock at the chaos. Then he caught sight of Jordan and raced over to her, taking her into his arms as she trembled. Alexander noted she didn't cry.

"What the fuck happened?" Richard gasped, furious.

He surveyed the room, then turned back to her and searched her face.

Jordan smiled tremulously at him. "I'm fine," she reassured him "Shaken up and scared, but fine." She gestured to the others, "They took care of the…" She frowned, searching for a suitable word, "…creatures that attacked me."

"Creatures? What do you mean, 'creatures?'" Richard asked, his voice rising with concern.

He glared at all of them. His eyes fixed on Carter in his armor, holding a sword. He felt shocked and betrayed.

Richard took a step toward the soldier, glaring. "You knew something was happening?"

"No," Carter protested sharply. "I felt someone watching me—us—at the job site, but I didn't see anything until after we got home. I had no idea Jordan was anywhere near this shit."

Richard heard the honesty in his voice, but it did little to mollify him.

He rounded on Jordan. Her expression became pinched, and she held up a hand to forestall his words as she stepped back. "Do not look at me like that, Richard Bryson!" she exclaimed. She sounded just like her deceased grandmother, Maria McInerney, in her response. "I was in the garden to double-check the winterizing I'd done. Since I didn't see our friends at breakfast this morning, I walked to the manor to visit with them. I didn't know those things would sneak in behind me and attack or that no one was here." She glared at him with her jaw jutting forward. "This was no one's fault."

Richard's expression softened. He hadn't really been angry, but he was terrified when he thought something had happened to Jordan. Her shirt sleeves were torn and bloody, but her skin was smooth and unblemished, with nary a drop to be seen. For the first time, he realized that the creature's attack must have been unsuccessful.

"Imara, Sirenī, Alex, and Carter showed up just after I got inside. The creatures attacked me, but they didn't hurt me," Jordan reassured him. "And Sirenī put me inside a magic bubble to keep me safe." Her eyes gleamed with wonder as she recounted her experience. "You should have seen it, Richard. They dueled like the wizards in the movies and books! It was fucking incredible!"

She let out a laugh. "They sent lightning and fire back and forth, and Carter fought with his sword. Alex cast some crazy spell that filled the air with white light and burned them to ash."

Richard wasn't happy with whatever it was that had gone on at the manor, but he decided to shelve it for now. He'd speak with Jordan later and ask what else happened—he kept glancing at her torn sleeves, expecting to see wounds. It occurred to him that her unblemished skin didn't mean she hadn't been injured; it just meant one of the magicians had probably healed her.

I can't do this if she's going to be in danger, but I'll deal with that later.

"I'm just glad you're safe," he told her.

He stepped forward, hugged her, and kissed her lightly. She kissed him back and leaned into his side. They turned to face the others.

"Uh, all of you are okay?" Richard asked.

"We are," Imara assured him. She rested a hand on his forearm and hummed softly to help him calm down. "But now it looks like we have some clean-up to do. If you two wouldn't mind waiting in the library for a few minutes? We have some news for you, and since we're all together now, it seems prudent to share it, given that we need to spend the night erecting protective enchantments over this place so nothing like this can happen again."

Jordan and Richard agreed and left the main hall. They ducked into the library, leaving the four people from Gaea alone for a few minutes.

Sirenī looked around the room and said, "Let's fix this fast and then get to the library." She smiled at Carter. "We have something to discuss with you separately from Jordan and Richard, but I'm going to suggest they either spend the night here or that we all spend the night at their place." She glanced around. "I don't think anyone should be alone."

Everyone nodded in agreement, and the Three swiftly set to work. It took Imara, Sirenī, and Alex about twenty minutes to fix everything while Carter watched. He couldn't help them, so he stood out of the way and deftly twirled his sword.

Alexander, Imara, Sirenī, Jordan, and Richard sat in the comfortable chairs in the library. Carter stood with his thick arms crossed loosely over his armored chest and leaned against a desk adjacent to where they arranged the chairs.

"We have to leave," Alexander said. He held up a hand to forestall their saying anything. "It is only for a short time. It is necessary; otherwise, we would never do this. Things are coming that we can address only with resources from several other worlds in the Ring." That wasn't strictly accurate, but he, Imara, and Sirenī had agreed on what to say without mentioning time travel. "We will not leave immediately—we have preparations to make and tasks to take care of."

Jordan looked at Imara and Sirenī, then at Richard, before turning her gaze back to Alexander. "Will we be safe after you leave?"

"Absolutely," Imara interjected. "We'll be casting so many defensive spells that this place will be a fortress, and we now have an anchor stone connected to the Tanager Grid System on Gaea to provide unlimited power and resources while we're gone. We'll fabricate another one and set it up at your house, Jordan, to provide power, heat, water, and whatever else you need to be comfortable, but we're hoping everyone will stay at the manor."

"Back the fuck up," Carter barked. "How do you have an anchor stone? I spent years securing locations around Gaea to force locals to adopt the Grid so they'd Unify. The system only works if the anchor stones are within a certain proximity." He held his right hand with his thumb and index fingertip an inch apart. "I think the distance between two worlds is a little too fucking far."

Alexander grimaced and looked at Imara and Sirenī. The women looked amused—he hadn't even considered Carter's experience with the Grid when they agreed upon their explanation. He stood and beckoned everyone to follow him as he approached the laboratory doors.

They'd rushed out of the library when they heard Jordan scream without hiding the doors behind the bookshelves, so the secret entrance was now out in the open. His partners and friends followed him into the enormous chamber and observed it, amazed.

Carter whistled appreciatively when he saw the small Abyssal Gate. He shook his head and grinned crookedly. "You certainly don't fuck around, do you?" he asked in Demurrian. He stepped over to the portal and looked through. "Gaea?" He gestured to the massive room on the other side of the portal.

Alexander nodded and spoke in their natal tongue. "Yes, I established a permanent portal. It leads to my—"

He stopped, and his blue eyes widened. What he saw made no sense, but at Sirenī's squeal of happiness, he surrendered to the impossible and watched her fat orange tabby waddle up to the Abyssal Gate in Eldred Manor. Marquis had a white house mouse sitting contentedly on his back, which the sorcerer recognized was Charlotte.

He'd given her amṛta—the nectar of immortality—decades ago to test it out. He'd always suspected she was still around, but he'd never seen her after he let her go. The big cat stepped daintily through the portal to Earth like he understood exactly what he was doing.

"He should not have been able to enter the laboratory," Alexander declared in English. He glared at the cat. "This is incomprehensible," he huffed.

Carter burst out laughing at the sorcerer's expense.

"Marquis!" Sirenī cried happily and knelt.

Alexander glowered as the furry beast trotted over to her. Marquis purred loudly as she snatched him up and held him in her arms like a child. Charlotte darted up Sirenī's left arm and leaned against her neck.

Sirenī grinned at Alexander's look and rocked the purring cat. "Who cares how he got in? He's here where I wanted him."

The sorcerer heaved a martyred sigh and muttered, "I'll be right back."

He stepped through the portal.

Carter shared a look with everyone before he stepped through the Abyssal Gate after Alex. Imara caught Sirenī's eye; they laughed while Richard and Jordan stared in fascination. The Earthen couple looked at the anchor stone for the Tanager Grid where it sat on the floor of the laboratory. It was a squat pillar of silvery stone, about two feet tall and half that around, covered in a complex mesh of symbols, words, and geometric patterns.

Alex and Carter were only gone for a few minutes. The sorcerer shook his head as he came through the portal and turned a death glare on Marquis, who ignored him in the way cats have.

"I have no idea how they got in. The doors are sealed just like they should be," he complained. "There is something not right about your cat, Sirenī."

She smirked at him. "He's perfect," she cooed. She turned and carried Marquis and the mouse from the laboratory. "Carry on," she called breezily over her shoulder as she departed.

Alex sighed and looked to Imara, who shook her head.

"You're on your own with that one, Alex," she told him gently. She turned to the others. "This is the anchor stone we'll place elsewhere in the house. We'll put a fabricator in a room off the kitchen. You can create anything you want with it—well, anything from Gaea. We'll show you how to use it before we leave."

She turned in a circle and gestured broadly to take in the room. "This is a workroom for magical experimentation. It's heavily shielded, so nothing can get in or out."

"Except Sirenī's cat!" Alex interjected grumpily.

Imara ignored his grousing. "And it connects to Alex's laboratory on Gaea, which is similarly protected. Eldred Manor is shielded and warded to keep it safe, too. Once we erect the defenses over this property, covering the entire fifty acres, you'll be completely safe. We need the anchor stone to provide the power to sustain the shields and wards." She grimaced. "In hindsight, we should have set up preliminary defenses already. I'm sorry, Jordan."

"It's not like we knew creatures like that even existed on Earth," Jordan said.

Imara nodded with a strained smile. She was still angry about the attack on Jordan, the violation of their home, and at herself. She should have known there were līc and other magical beings on Earth. According to research, they were on most worlds.

The songstress stepped over to the open gateway. "This is the remnant of the Abyssal Gate, which played a pretty important role in the events on my homeworld decades ago."

Richard looked nervously at the Abyssal Gate, but Jordan stared at it in fascination. She stepped over to it, and Richard trailed her by a step. She reached a hand toward the device's frame and looked to Alex and Imara for permission. They nodded, and she touched the cool, smooth metal while the cherry-sized, blood-red jewel at the top gleamed softly and steadily.

"This is what the sorcerers of the Empire were using to bring that demonic being into Gaea, right?" Jordan asked.

Richard's face paled, and his eyes tensed. "Uh, does that mean Smogma can come through this portal, too?" He swallowed nervously.

Alex chuckled and shook his head. "No, Sogma cannot come through. This only connects my laboratory on Gaea to this chamber on Earth. It is utterly secure."

Richard looked relieved, but Jordan frowned dubiously at the small gate. "It seems…tiny."

Alex and Imara looked at one another and laughed. "Imagine it five hundred feet high by three hundred wide, and you get the idea," Imara said dryly.

"I see," Jordan said.

"This is just one piece of the original gate," Imara continued, "and without all the other parts, Alex assures me it can never get that big again."

The sorcerer pointed to the jewel at the top of the oval frame. "This is the master pyxis, but there were over a dozen subordinate pyxides in the full-sized gate. Without those extra pieces to distribute the gate's power, its capabilities are limited."

Jordan stepped back to Richard's side as Alex reached out and rested a hand on the frame, which sat just a few inches away from the wall. "And now that it's active, it can't be deactivated except by me."

Or with spells from the Dawntime, Imara thought with a shudder as she recalled the final moments of the battle. *Even the nuclear weapons of this world couldn't destroy this thing.*

"It's safe and permanently links both worlds, giving us access to the Tanager Grid System," the songstress finished, turning her attention to Jordan and Richard. "Come back into the house, and we'll show you where the fabricator will be set up."

When the Earthen couple departed with his partner, Alexander stepped over to a long table against the same wall as the Abyssal Gate. A single object was resting on it now that Alex had given Carter his new gladius: a large, clear jar containing a hypnotically swirling amber fluid. He gestured for Carter to join him. The two men stood side by side and looked at the jar and its undulating contents.

Carter turned an expectant gaze on the sorcerer. "I assume there's a reason you're showing me the swirly goo?"

Alexander chuckled and spoke in Demurrian. "This is amṛta. Have you ever heard of it?" Carter shook his head. "It is a potent magical material. Imara, Sirenī, you, and I have much to discuss before we leave, but let us follow the others."

They left the laboratory, and Carter grabbed his gladius off the desk in the library where he'd left it. "Thanks for the sword, Alex." The golden glow wrapped over his hand as he gripped the hilt. "Can you recharge my astral displacement sheath so I can store it?"

He turned around and pointed a thick finger to the small artifact situated horizontally on his belt. Alexander ignored the sheath, which he'd already examined, and stared instead at the outline of Carter's well-formed ass through his armor.

"Well?" the soldier prompted.

The sorcerer blinked and flicked his gaze to the sheath. He stepped forward and put his hand on Carter's back, pushing him slightly forward at the waist to better examine it.

Two

Carter put his sword back on the desk and let Alex push him forward; he took his weight onto his knuckles. He trembled slightly as Alex stood close to him and examined the inert astral displacement sheath. The older sorcerer was handsome and powerful, and his magic radiated from his body in waves even when he wasn't using it.

It was an unexpected turn-on.

The soldier looked over his shoulder and saw Alex staring at the sheath resting in the dimple of his lower back. He had a focused look on his handsome, bearded face as he did whatever it was that powerful sorcerers did with dead artifacts.

"I can recharge this," the sorcerer announced. "It appears Wú Xiāng etched the spellforms into the sheath as she constructed it. She is quite gifted."

Coming from Alex, that was a big compliment.

"She seemed extremely talented," Carter agreed. "Many soldiers trade a fortune in MECs for her help with their gear."

Alex nodded and rested his hand on the sheath. Carter hissed in surprise as heat radiated into his lower back; it bordered on painful but remained just shy of that point. He fidgeted in discomfort for several minutes while Alex worked his magic and sighed in relief when Alex removed his hand.

"There. I tightened up the spellforms in several areas and added discharge wards to prevent the sheath from ever losing power again."

"Fuck, man, that's great. Thank you," Carter said enthusiastically as he straightened and turned.

They stood very close for a moment, staring into each other's eyes. Carter swallowed nervously. His palms began to sweat. Alex smiled easily and stepped back.

"Of course, Jack. You are quite welcome," he said breezily.

Carter nodded and flashed a cheerful grin, but his heart was pounding. He snatched his sword off the desk and deftly flipped the blade toward the ground. With the ease of long practice, he reached back, slipped the blade's tip into the displacement sheath, and shoved it home.

Alexander planned to embed the anchor stone in the house foundation under the main entrance and obscurate it that evening when they erected the wards around the property. He glanced at the spot where he planned to put it as he and Carter passed through the main hall on their way toward the kitchen.

It was a large, airy room with a massive table, beautifully crafted appliances, and plenty of counter space along the walls and on an island in the center. The next room down the hall held the silver fabricator. He saw Imara standing there with Jordan and Richard; they came out and joined him and Carter. The group returned to the main hall.

"I can't believe how easily you repaired all the damage," Richard remarked. "That would have taken weeks or months for us to do."

"Well, the magic that made this place allows us to reset the interior to its default state in the event of damage, so it was easy," Alexander explained. "We need only instantiate the repairs and add any finishing touches."

Their Earthen friends marveled at that for a moment before Imara spoke.

"We'd like you to spend the night here, but we'll erect the shields after we finish chatting. You'll still be safe if you stay at your place."

Jordan took Richard's hand and smiled. "I trust you," she assured them, "and I'd rather stay in my own bed."

She led Richard from the house, and Alexander, Imara, and Carter followed them outside and stopped. They watched the Earthen couple head toward the path to the Lower Forty, across which lay another trail leading to Jordan's place.

Alexander looked at Imara, then Carter. "Would you stay with them until we get the defenses established?"

The soldier nodded and snapped a pithy salute before jogging from the house.

Alexander and Imara returned to the main hall. The songstress waved a hand to close the front door. "Shall we get this show on the road?" she asked.

Sirenī rejoined them as they were making their preparations.

Alexander moved the anchor stone to the middle of the main hall. He pressed his hand to the top of the pillar and summoned his magic. His corona flared brightly around his hand as he sent a thread of magic into the device to empower it.

Seconds later, arcane geometries propagated through the air, lancing upward to form a thousand-foot-high pillar of light that passed through the manor and gleamed brightly in the sky. He hoped no one noticed, but nothing could be done about it even if they did.

The sorcerer studied the shimmering column full of rotating geometric patterns and sophisticated spellforms. He waited fifteen minutes for the column of light to withdraw into the short pillar, which glowed with patterns of vibrant mint-colored light all over its top, sides, and bottom. After a couple of minutes, the stone punched down through the main hall floor until it settled fifty feet underground.

It connected to the Grid via the Abyssal Gate, briefly causing the ground to tremble. It would take a few days for the anchor stone to integrate fully with the rest of the system on Gaea; at that point, Alexander could tether the manor enchantments to the Grid.

He smiled and repaired the floor, then turned to find his partners: they were making a fuss over Marquis and Charlotte. Imara was laughing at something one of them had said—she was the only one who could speak Cat—and he smiled, his heart lifting to see them all together.

Practicality reasserted itself a moment later, and he prised the women away from the animals. They went down to the Lower Forty in the growing darkness of the crisp fall evening and stopped at the Gatehouse. Thanks to the thermal regulation spells embedded in their aurae, they were comfortable in the cool air.

They weren't at the center of the property, but they were close. They planned to lay down a perimeter of concentric spherical shields and defensive wards to prevent anyone from entering without their permission. They agreed to grant Carter administrative privileges, allowing him to extend or rescind invitations to others.

They'd insert glyphs into Jordan and Richard's aurae to permit them to come and go freely, but the couple wouldn't be able to grant access to the property. It was a compromise between safety and ease of use and matched Eldred Manor's setup.

It took six hours of sustained casting to set everything up. Imara handled the shields, Sirenī established the active and passive wards, and Alexander set up the credentialing system to enable or revoke access. The individual enchantments were more straightforward, but the spells' interactions were complicated.

They eventually got everything squared away, and the spectral glow of the new shields shimmered in the night air. The external world was visible through the faint haze with a slight distortion as the defenses settled. In a few hours, the shields would be utterly transparent unless they were under attack or, for some reason, someone decided to make them visible.

Three
Tres

After Alexander, Imara, and Sirenī finished setting up the defensive enchantments, they retired to the manor and collapsed. Despite the bolstering effect of the amṛta, they were fatigued by the sustained use of their magic. They usually spent the night fooling around and talking, but sex wasn't on their minds. They settled on the giant bed in their suite and slipped into a twilight doze until just after dawn.

Alexander came out of the light sleep and rolled away from Sirenī's firm rear end. He stretched and lay comfortably on his back, pleasantly relaxed as his mind drifted to thoughts of sex. He couldn't ever get enough of either woman. He wanted them all the time, sometimes as soon as he'd ejaculated.

Sirenī shifted and rolled over. He turned his head and smiled tenderly at her; she wriggled about and kissed him on the cheek, then turned away and stroked Imara's shoulder. The songstress emerged from her doze, and the women slipped from the bed and disappeared into the titanic bathroom.

Alexander stepped up to the mirrored dresser while they were in the bathroom and looked at his reflection. His hair was darker than it had been a few weeks ago, the black color returning through the iron gray strands as the amṛta continued working its way through him. His skin was firmer and his face more youthful; he estimated he looked about forty years old.

Not bad for a man of 223, he thought smugly.

The sorcerer shook his head and ran a hand across his chin. He decided the beard no longer served him.

Alexander snapped his fingers to garb himself in his usual black slacks, black shoes, and white button-down shirt. It was open at the collar with the sleeves rolled neatly to his elbows. He brought to mind the spellforms for a hygiene enchantment for body hair and saw a flicker of red around his fingers. He reached up and swiped his hands down his face and across his neck.

In the mirror, his beard disappeared.

He almost gasped, seeing himself for the first time in over 150 years. Without the facial hair, he appeared to be in his early thirties, like his partners. He had a strong jaw and assertive chin, though the lines were softer than Carter's lethally-planed submaxilla.

He reached up and stroked his smooth jaw, grinning at the crisp feel of air moving over his skin. The sorcerer turned away from the mirror when the women came out of the bathroom; they were murmuring, laughing about something until they looked at him.

Then they screamed.

"What the…" Imara gasped. She stared at him, her eyes wide, heedless of her nudity.

Sirenī clapped her hands with a squeal and shouted, "You shaved!"

Alexander shrugged like it was no big deal as they walked up to him, studying his face. They'd never seen him without a beard, so this was even newer to them than it was to him.

"It seems at least half the men of Earth have facial hair of some kind—most of it is poorly managed—so I decided to remove mine."

Imara examined his face a moment longer, then leaned in and kissed him somewhat tentatively. She broke off and nodded excitedly to Sirenī. Apparently, his smooth skin met with her approval. Sirenī stepped up and kissed him next, and then the daughter of Medusa pulled back with a pleased smile. Their lips felt silky smooth on his hypersensitive skin, and the sensation went straight to his groin.

"That is so much better!" she crowed. She kissed him again with more zest. "I never realized how irritating your beard was."

Alexander laughed and went to take both women in his arms, eager to fuck after experiencing the tingling sensation of their kisses. They squirmed away.

Imara put a hand on his chest with a smile. "Down, boy. We have too much to do today."

He groaned in frustration.

The women shook their heads and remained ruthlessly unsympathetic to his plight. They waved their hands over their bodies, magically styling their hair and drawing perfectly fitted clothes about themselves.

Imara created a simple charcoal blouse, matching slacks, low-heeled black boots, and a slim silver cestus. Her hair twisted into a neat chignon at the nape of her neck, highlighting her lean, lovely features.

Sirenī magicked up a knee-length, asymmetric brown skirt with a snug-fitting tan blouse that revealed some of her cleavage. Her hair wound into several braids hanging slightly off-center to highlight her stunning features. She grinned as cream-colored high-heeled shoes rolled over her feet, adding four inches to her five feet, five inches of height. They were matched by an identically-colored cestus that drew attention to her curvy figure.

Thanks to her intrinsic fatal beauty, she'd be stunning in a burlap bag.

"Ready?" Imara asked.

Alexander reluctantly nodded, his thoughts lingering in the vicinity of his groin, but he gestured for them to precede him from the bedroom. As they strolled out, Sirenī winked a promise at him as she sashayed by. His eyes were on their perfect asses as they walked ahead, and he followed them with a wistful sigh.

Carter, Jordan, and Richard sat in the dining room at the McInerney place, drinking coffee in loose, comfortable clothes.

The Three sat down at the dining table replete with donuts, pastries, breakfast sandwiches, and additional drinks from the Indigent Mug. Jordan's ancient black cat, Emily, slept in her bed at the far end. They served themselves and thanked their friends for picking up the food.

Imara explained the situation as they ate, recounted their defenses, and told them that no one could come onto the property without permission. They'd tell Carter about his administrative privileges later.

"What about Brent and Drëndi?" Jordan asked when Imara finished.

"We'll add them to the list the next time they come around," Sirenī assured her. "They're our friends now, too, and honestly, they may be here a lot more often, or longer, than they expect. I wonder where they've been, now that you mention it."

Jordan held up her phone and said, "Drëndi messaged me, actually, but I forgot about it with everything that happened. They went back to Boston, but someone at Grace Manor gave them a message for," she made air quotes, "Him."

Everyone looked at Alex; he looked blandly back. Before anyone could say anything, Jordan shrieked and clapped a hand to her mouth. "You shaved!" Her tone bordered on accusatory.

Imara and Sirenī burst into laughter. Carter and Richard, still bearded, stared in surprised bemusement at the women but took due note of Alex's smooth face.

"I did, just this morning," the sorcerer affirmed.

"I feel so silly that it took me so long to notice!" Jordan exclaimed.

Carter scoffed good-naturedly. "I didn't notice, so you're well ahead of me. I've never had facial hair before now. I wouldn't have dared."

Seeing Jordan and Richard's curious looks, Imara explained about beards on Gaea. "Since the time of Zeus, powerful male sorcerers have grown beards to set themselves apart."

"The pictures in our art galleries do portray the Greek god with an impressive beard," Jordan said slowly.

"Well," Sirenī temporized, "he wasn't a god. He was a powerful magic user, one of many. I think legends about the ancient Greeks and their magical prowess crossed with travelers between the worlds, eventually inspiring legends about them as gods here on Earth."

"So…not immortal, then?" Jordan clarified.

"Probably not," Imara agreed. "Certainly, we've never met any of them, and if they were immortal, it would be pretty hard to hide on Gaea since magic usage creates vibrations other sorcerers can feel. They couldn't hide and still practice magic, so what would be the point? Besides, immortality is hard to attain."

"Fascinating. So, Athena, Aphrodite, Apollo…" Richard rattled off the first names that came to mind after Zeus. "All magic users on your world?"

"Yes, but so were many other people in ancient Greece and elsewhere on Gaea," Alex explained. "Magic is common in our world because of our species stock, so every country had high-level magic users who probably inspired legends on other worlds." He held up a hand and ticked off several names on his fingers, "Amaterasu, Guānyīn, Śiva, Cernunnos, Mary of Nazrat—"

Jordan held up a hand. "Hold on, Mary of Nazrat? As in Mary of Nazareth—the Virgin Mary?"

"How'd you go from Mary of Nazzit to the Virgin Mary?" Richard asked her.

Jordan laughed. "Nazrat. I minored in Near Eastern studies in college, so I recognize the Aramaic for Nazareth."

"Ah," he replied.

Alex frowned. "I am unfamiliar with the virginal assumption, which seems implausible since she had several children. She was, however, a mighty and benevolent sorcerer who helped many during her centuries on Gaea. She was particularly revered through much of Persia for her beneficence."

"Well, that's just fucking amazing," Richard declared. He sat back in his chair and looked around cheerfully.

Jordan wanted to know more but knew they needed to refocus.

"So, about your leaving… What does that mean, and what does it look like?" she asked.

"We need time to get some things done," Alex answered. "We cannot do them on Earth. However, we have a few more things to wrap up before we leave."

"You do need to visit Grace Manor and deal with whatever mayhem you've created there," Imara pointed out sternly.

Jordan's phone buzzed with an incoming text message. She picked it up, unlocked it, read the long message on her screen, and went pale. "This is a heads up from Drëndi and Brent," she began. "They said the government has moved on intel collected by the Psionic Investigative Division about you, and they're sending agents and marines to escort you to Washington, D.C., for questioning."

Her phone buzzed again, and she read the new message and gasped. "Drëndi says you've been classified as terrorists and foreign nationals by the Department of Homeland Security and the FBI, and they're planning to arrest you if you resist."

"Whoever's involved doesn't know what they're doing," Carter growled. "They can't arrest you. For fuck's sake, each of you is a weapon of mass destruction if you want to be."

Imara smiled at his vigorous support and remained unconcerned. "Reply to Drëndi, please, and thank her for the information she so kindly risked her career to provide. Tell her that she and Brent are welcome anytime, and say we advise they come here as soon as possible if anything happens because of their association with us."

"Assure them we're perfectly safe here," added Sirenī. "Richard, you won't be able to go to work for a while. You'll have to let your customers and employees know you'll be unavailable for the foreseeable future. We'll stay as long as possible but still need to leave."

Richard stared at Sirenī, stunned. "But Paul and Kyle, my work…"

"Richard, we can't leave right now. We could be arrested if we step foot off this property. We're known collaborators," Jordan hissed as if the three sorcerers at the dining table couldn't hear her words. "You are not putting yourself at risk!"

"What about Paul and Kyle?" he grumbled back. "They worked with Carter. They could be arrested, too!"

"Yeah, but it's not like he was on the payroll with fucking records and a 1099," Jordan snapped. "Tell Paul and Kyle to lie and say they have no idea about Carter—they'll do it in a heartbeat. They hate the government even more than you do."

"If it's going to be a problem, they can come to the manor, too. I'm sure you'd vouchsafe them?" Sirenī suggested.

Richard frowned in thought. Finally, his frown softened but didn't subside. "I'll call them and give them a choice." He shook his head and added, "But I can't even remotely tell you how they'll react to magic and, to be honest, some of the other things here...." He looked apologetically at the guests. "Not everyone is like Jordan and me."

He stood up and then went onto the porch to make the calls.

As soon as he stepped out of the room, the people from Gaea looked at Jordan with puzzled expressions, and Alex asked, "What was all that about?"

Jordan sighed. "Well, you're familiar with racism, right?" They all nodded but still looked puzzled. "And you might have noticed everyone you've seen so far is…well, White?"

Sirenī shook her head. "I saw people at Walmart who looked like they were from the Tèng Empire," she pointed out.

Jordan chuckled. "Yes, you saw like two Asian-Americans out of hundreds of Caucasians. We—America—had a considerable movement in the early 2020s around systemic racism, gender advantagism, and sexism that created huge inroads into the problem. Still, there's a lot of inertia behind the systems, and it takes time for real change.

"Richard worries that Paul and Kyle might find it hard to handle being here. It's about more than just the magical stuff, and your ethnicity isn't the problem for them." She searched for words and finally waved a hand to encompass the four of them. "It's more your casual polyamory, shall we say?"

"So, skin color may be part of the issue, but the real problem is how sexually free we are?" Imara rolled her eyes. "We don't have religious indoctrination into shame and guilt or this Puritanical horse shit you have here in New England, where life is misery, and then you die. Still, I can be sympathetic to what they have been conditioned to believe."

Jordan and Richard had discussed the mores underpinning New England culture with the four travelers. They wanted to caution them against expecting easy acceptance from the wider population. Richard had told them that not everyone was as blasé as he and Jordan were with such disparate beliefs.

"Well, it is what it is," Alex said firmly.

"I'm sorry this happened to you," Imara added. "It's not what we wanted. The military at your doorstep was never our intention."

"No need to apologize," Jordan replied. "I've had the best time of my life since you came. Richard and I are so glad to have met you and helped out in our small ways. Grandma M would have been pleased as pickles if she were still here to see all this."

"Thank you," Sirenī said, speaking for the four visitors. She reached out and put a hand over Jordan's. "That means more than you can know to all of us!"

"Now, that's settled," Jordan declared. "What's the next step?"

Before any of them could answer, Richard barged in. "Shit, there are cops at the driveway trying to get in. They've smashed into an invisible barrier, and they're shitting bricks trying to figure it out." He shook his head. "Persephone had Clear message me about it."

"What about Paul and Kyle?" Carter asked, concerned. "What did they decide?"

"Kyle's single and fancy-free. He's bugging out to his grandfather's hunting cabin near Umbagog. He says he'll stay there for a while and wait it out. Paul has a wife and two young kids, and they're open to the idea of coming here, but of course, it feels weird to them since Carter is the only one Paul has met." Richard's voice trailed off. "Can they leave if they want?"

Alex nodded. "They can, but I would caution against that. As you saw yesterday, other forces in this world pose a problem besides the government." He frowned. "An association with us seems rather hazardous at present. To that end, if you trust and care for them, encourage them to come and stay here. I think the government of this world will set up a perimeter around the property, so they had best come soon if they plan to. You and I can meet them at the driveway to the manor."

Three

Richard nodded and called Paul back. "Hey, listen, man, Persephone from the Mug messaged and said cops are already trying to get onto the property, and there was a…uh, car accident in the process. For now, the manor's driveway is still accessible." He listened. "Yes, I said manor. You have to see it to believe it. No, I'm not shitting you. Christ, Paul, get Sue and the kids and get your asses over here!"

Everyone watched, but only Imara could hear Sue shouting in the background on Paul's end of the call, informing him that she was not risking her children becoming test subjects for the "Goddamn United States feebs!"

Richard listened for a moment longer, then ended the call. "They'll be here ASAP."

Alex nodded and stood. He smiled at Imara, Sirenī, Jordan, and Carter, then stepped past them to stand beside Richard. He snapped his fingers, and they disappeared from the room. Jordan was nearest to the teleportation effect, and her ponytail ruffled as air rushed to fill the vacuum.

Anar Iskariótés stared at the message on his encrypted cell phone. His rich brown eyes burned with rage as he reread the message to confirm he understood. He carefully set the device down—a one-of-a-kind prototype fit for the CEO of Zalcent International—and spoke to his empty office.

"Get me the president," he demanded.

"Yes, Mr. Iskariótés," a somber voice replied from speakers embedded around the room.

"And Rudine Ellswyth," he growled. "And whoever the fuck is in charge of the DHS response team."

"Of course," the voice replied. A second later, it added, "I have the President of the United States."

Anar waved a hand to have his assistant patch POTUS through.

"Mr. Iscariot," the man himself said in clipped tones. Anar knew the man hated him, but powerful men always hated those with more power. "What do you want?"

"Bob." Anar could picture Robert Campbell sitting at his desk, fuming. "I want to know what the fuck you think you're doing with the situation in Maine? I've had my people watching them since their arrival in the area."

Anar listened to the silence on the line and seethed. He fantasized about wringing the man's neck.

"I received reliable intel that the foreigners are escalating and pose a risk to the people of the United States," the commander-in-chief said.

Anar laughed sardonically. "You stupid shit! They're the most powerful sorcerers to ever cross between Gaea and Earth. People like them dueled thousands of years ago and created the fucking Sahara. Do you know what they could do to the United States if you threatened them? You're such an ignorant twat!"

The speaker system had such high fidelity that Anar could hear Bob grinding his teeth. "Listen to me, you fucking asshole!" the man spat. "You run a corporation, but I run the fucking United States! I don't care how much money you contribute; you can't speak to me that way."

Anar laughed mirthlessly. "Bob, you're starting to irritate me. One more word out of you, and I'll pull the plug." He waited for a beat. "Was that too subtle? If you don't make this right, there will be consequences for you."

He made a gesture, and his assistant disconnected the line before the president howled at him.

The fool doesn't understand how unimportant he is, Anar thought with a sneer.

The corporations controlled the world, and Zalcent controlled all of them. Anar ran the United States and every other country, and no one even knew it. He'd spent centuries gaining power, one step at a time, until he ruled it all.

Anar drummed his fingers on his desk. "When will Rudine be here?"

"She's en route to the airport in São Paulo now. I estimate she'll be in Austin, Texas, in about fourteen hours," his assistant replied. "The

Department of Homeland Security tasked Special Agent in Charge Jennifer Kelly to oversee the situation in Maine. She is…unlikely to be effective. She doesn't appear to be familiar with magic users."

Anar cocked his head and narrowed his eyes. "Why the fuck send her then? Jesus Christ, I have to fucking do everything for these assholes. They should have sent Beatrice Lambert of the PID. At least she knows her ass from her elbow," he grudgingly acknowledged. "How are we coming with the purchase of Grace Manor?"

"We had to buy the management company running the facility to secure access, but it's all in hand. I've expedited the paperwork through our banks."

Anar smiled at that. "You're the only one I can rely on," he told his assistant.

"Thank you, Sir."

Anar waved a hand over his desktop to bring up a holographic display. He had plenty of work to do while he waited for Rudine. By the time she walked into his office, he'd have put the finishing touches on a proposal for the Panamanian government. It would help the country's economy and make Zalcent over a trillion dollars in three years—and the corporation would only spend a few million in startup costs.

He grinned. That was the kind of thing that made him happy.

Richard staggered slightly when they appeared at the end of the manor's driveway just shy of the barrier. He felt like he was falling even though his feet had never left the ground.

He turned to Alex and said, "Cut the shit and tell me what's going on. You three leaving in a rush, with mysterious things to do on other worlds… What's happening to trigger this flurry of activity? You told me you planned to settle here for the long haul, but now you're departing in a mad rush."

Alex stared at him with his luminous blue eyes. "I knew you would realize there was something else going on. Earth has been infected with a powerful corruption, a magical disease that could render the world uninhabitable."

Richard felt the blood drain from his face as the sorcerer spoke.

"It will take a long time, but there will be sickness, objects breaking down, and worldwide chaos. We have a lead to a possible cure, but Imara and Sirenī need training in the mystical force, which is different from magic. We need time, so we are creating it," Alex said.

"Fuck me," Richard breathed. He looked toward the road for a moment, then back at his friend. "Are we going to be safe here?"

"Oh, yes. You have my word. The field effects will sanitize anything entering the property. Only those authorized will be able to pass through the barrier. That includes you and Jordan, obviously, but permanent residents will need to be credentialed separately to allow unrestricted access to the property.

"There will also be places in the manor where they cannot go, like the workroom and primary bedroom, and while we did not add additional protections around the Gatehouse, it is safe to say that no one knows how to activate it from this world. However, someone could come from other planets in the Ring of Worlds. It is unlikely but possible."

Richard nodded. "Well, no one came through in the fifty years between your first and second visits, so it stands to reason the Gatehouse won't become a hotbed of activity."

At that moment, a ragged red pickup truck pulled up to the driveway. It stopped well away from the invisible barrier; Richard had sent Paul a text message cautioning him not to pull into the driveway proper. His friend honked urgently as police sirens whooped nearby.

The back of the beater had a tarp over some belongings lashed down with nylon straps. Paul's wife, Sue, sat in the passenger seat; she looked stressed, afraid, and angry. Eric and Cassie sat on the bench seat in the back. Paul honked again; Alex held up a hand and waved them in.

No sooner had the pickup crossed the barrier threshold than two cop cars pulled up and turned into the driveway. The barrier began about ten feet from the road, just deep enough that the cars could pull in and accelerate slightly to try and catch up with the truck.

Three

The car in front smashed into the invisible barrier just like the other vehicle had at Jordan's place. The hood accordioned, and the windshield spiderwebbed with cracks. The second vehicle plowed into the rear of the first and crumpled the trunk. The two officers in the first car bounced around like balls as the airbags deployed.

Four
Quattuor

Alexander gestured for Richard to attend to Paul and Sue. He stepped through the barrier and walked over to the driver's side door of the police vehicle. He focused, made a swiping gesture, and ripped the door off the car. It fell to the driveway's Demurrian pavement abutting the street with a loud bang. The driver fell out, nearly unconscious; Alexander caught her in his arms so she wouldn't hit the ground.

"Let me help you." He sat her on the pavement with her back against the twisted front wheel. "Stay still. I will check on your companion."

He passed in and out of the barrier around the front of the vehicle and ripped off the passenger door. The sorcerer also helped that cop to the ground. This one had a bleeding gash on his forehead. Alexander considered healing the man but decided against it. Instead, he snapped his fingers to manifest a handkerchief and pressed it to the man's wound.

"Hold this and remain still," he instructed.

The young man complied with a mumbled thanks.

Alexander straightened and walked toward the second car, but the two officers in that one pushed out of the front seat and fumbled their sidearms free. He pursed his lips and snapped the fingers of his left hand. Before either man could raise his gun, both weapons fell to pieces; the sorcerer had triggered an expansion of the internal shear lines in the metal. The bullets tumbled from the splintered clips to sprinkle and bounce along the pavement at the road's edge.

The cops stared at their hands in shock.

"There is no need for guns," Alexander admonished. He turned and strode back through the barrier.

"Hey!" one of the men hollered as he came around the passenger door and chased after Alexander.

The sorcerer stepped through the shield, spun, and saw the officer go for his taser. Before he could unholster the device, the cop ran face-first into the barrier. Blood sprayed from his busted nose as he bellowed in pain and fell on his ass, clutching his face.

"Whud da fug!" he cried. Blood ran through his fingers and spilled onto his shirt.

"You cannot cross the barrier protecting this property. The military cannot cross the barrier. Your government cannot cross the barrier. Leave. Us. Alone," Alexander said sternly.

With that, the sorcerer turned and walked over to Richard, Paul, and Sue with a relaxed smile. Paul extended a hand, and Alexander shook it and repeated the action with his wife. Richard introduced the Arsenault family, pointing out Eric and Cassie in the truck. Alexander smiled at the children but stayed focused on their parents.

After the introductions, Paul rubbed his right hand nervously over the back of his neck. He looked uncomfortable and ragged. "Thank you for letting us come here," he finally said. He glanced at the cops, their cars, and the tree-lined driveway. "Rich assures us you've got the space, but we don't want to be an imposition. I mean, with the kids and me and Sue and all...."

Alexander waved his hand dismissively. "We have more than enough room, and you are all quite welcome. I would not have offered if I was in any doubt. I will say that while I have authorized the four of you to come and go at will, leaving the property may prove difficult, as you can surmise. We have it on good authority that the military and government are en route."

Paul nodded. He seemed overwhelmed by the speed at which everything was moving.

"And your," Sue waved her hands as she fished for words, "*Star Trek* force field thingy can keep them out? It won't drain or deplete or whatever force fields do?"

Alexander raised an eyebrow and looked at Richard, unfamiliar with the reference.

"*Star Trek* is a collection of American TV shows and movies. Their force fields always failed," Richard explained. "I told Sue that wouldn't happen here, that it was like a force field on steroids."

"Ah, yes." Alexander got the gist of the idea. "The impermeable fields will not fail. They are tied into an anchor stone that provides unlimited power. I am certain the *Star Trek* people used an inferior power supply," he said.

Paul and Sue blinked at his serious tone.

The sorcerer turned and gestured up the driveway. "Feel free to bring your vehicle to the house. I will assist you in unloading your things." He turned his attention to Richard. "Would you prefer to stay with your friends?"

Richard nodded. Alexander smiled, snapped his fingers, and disappeared.

Richard grinned at Paul and Sue and their slack-jawed expressions. "I'm telling you, this is like nothing you've ever seen, but these people are incredible. They've been nothing but kind to Jordan and me, and they knew her grandmother fifty years ago. Maria trusted them, too."

"What the fuck did I just see?" Paul muttered in reply. "Did he… Was that… What the fuck, man?"

"'Magic,' I believe, was the word you were looking for," Richard said. He wanted to laugh because it was awesome, but that could easily have been misinterpreted. "Yes, it was, and it's the real fucking deal. I mean hardcore shit. Wizard duels and undead and fucking force fields."

Sue shushed both men; she looked over her shoulder at her children. They were pressed against the narrow rear window of the driver's side of the truck, peering out at the adults.

"They can hear you cursing." She was always after them to stop swearing in front of the kids.

Paul looked at his wife and blinked. "He fucking teleported, Sue!" He gestured toward the cops and the cars, with one smashed against the invisible field their truck had breezed through. "There's a fucking force field protecting the man's house, for Christ's sake!"

"Dude," Richard said, putting a hand on Paul's shoulder as he saw Eric and Cassie shifting uncomfortably in the back seat of the truck as their dad half-yelled at their mom. "Calm down. You're upsetting Eric and Cassie."

He looked at Sue, but she waved it away since she was barely holding it together herself. "Come on, let's head up to the house. Trust me when Alex says there's room. There really is. You won't believe it," Richard told them.

Still looking a little wild-eyed, Paul got in the driver's seat. Sue went to the passenger side and waited while Richard squeezed onto the bench seat behind her. She got in as her eleven-year-old son, Eric, pushed over to sit next to his seven-year-old sister, Cassie.

Kāmla left the town of her birth at seventeen and never went back. She wasn't prone to nostalgia or sentiment and didn't mythologize the past to improve it. The flip side of that tendency in her mind was to negativize the past more than warranted since she'd had a good childhood, but she ignored that tendency.

Despite that, she considered the whole place nothing more than a sordid homage to the obnoxious Eldred family: a lineage of powerful sorcerers who lorded arrogantly over the rest of the populace—not just in Timil Deeps, but everywhere. Demurria had been at the forefront of the Unified Government, which was intended to replace the past empires, monarchies, and social classes. The fact that everyone still treated the Eldreds with such deference and respect defeated the whole purpose of the great homogenization.

Because of Unification, people felt free to learn how to be productive in their own ways, on their own merits, without needing to fulfill archetypal roles or for son and daughter to follow father and mother in trades and lifestyle choices. Because of this, someone like Kāmla Vicchāya could escape the quaint misery of Timil Deeps and become an influential and respected upper-echelon minister in the Unified Government.

Kāmla pulled her car into the parking lot of the town hall of Timil Deeps—she hadn't even turned off the engine, and she already couldn't wait to leave. She looked to her right and saw the sprawl of the elegant estate at the edge of town, not far from the cliff that formed after the great quake.

The Eldreds were royalty in the old days, with a litany of famous names attached to critical historical events. They dabbled in whatever magics interested them, disregarded the law, and took it upon themselves to maintain a controversial grip on the flow of wealth and power that others now eschewed.

Alexander Eldred wasn't even on Gaea right now, but she felt his presence in the town, loathsome and foul. The citizens she saw were relaxed in the sunny autumn chill. People walked alone or in groups—side by side or arm in arm—through the quaint downtown area with its shops, galleries, cafés, bistros, and artisanal autotech boutiques.

The lively coastal town had a bustling, festive air that grated on Kāmla's nerves and reaffirmed her decision to leave. It was always like this; everyone in Timil Deeps was content to live in the shadows of Eldred Manor and its sprawling estate—except for outliers like Kāmla.

The corruption will take care of that convivial air. They will understand when it all falls apart.

Her thoughts were dark and hateful, like her goals in life and the formative feelings of her childhood in Timil Deeps.

Kāmla's family had pleaded against her departure, but she'd left anyway. Later, they'd rejected all of her invitations to come and live with her in Columbia. It was only a two-day drive on the perfect roads of Demurria, but her ancestors had lived in this town for six generations. They venerated the Eldred family. They thought Alexander was kind, generous, and admirable.

It made her nauseous if she thought too much about it.

Kāmla hadn't told her parents or siblings she was visiting Timil

Deeps. She hadn't spoken to anyone in her family in years and was better off for it. She cringed in disgust, her reddened lips curling into a sneer as she thought of her family, especially her loathsome and pathetic parents.

With a deep breath to calm her pounding heart, she released the steering wheel and focused on her mission. She smoothed her face, stepped from her car, and straightened her chèuhngsāam. She ran her fingers through her hair to smooth it back from her face and mentally composed herself before she marched into the town hall.

Alexander settled Paul and his family into the spacious manor, with its two upper floors of guest bedrooms in the east wing. The house was without a television or a computer, which Eric noticed immediately and despaired.

Imara and Sirenī, curious about the developments on State Route 26, walked the property. They planned to circle both driveways in a way that prevented them from being apparent to those on the other side of the barrier. They started on the edge of the unpaved driveway by Jordan's house. As they walked down the street, Imara hummed a level three Obscuratus, making them invisible to anyone on the road.

"We need to pave this driveway," Sirenī remarked.

Imara nodded as they approached the barrier at the intersection of the driveway and the road. The first federal agents had arrived, and the police car that crashed into the shield was already gone. There were black SUVs with tinted windows blocking Route 26.

Imara and Sirenī watched people scurrying around. Instructions seemed to be coming from a central figure who they heard referred to as the SAC—or the Special Agent in Charge. The woman was lean and striking, with a short dark bob, olive complexion, and a thunderous expression. She clearly didn't like whatever the agents around her were saying.

Imara studied the technicians in blue jackets with FBI and DHS logos and initials. They stood before the barrier and passed a variety of instruments over it. She assumed they were trying to detect the energy emissions of the field effects.

They watched the hustle and bustle for several minutes before the SAC held up her hand. Everything slowed to a halt as people turned to face her. "Enough," she called out. "When are the technicians from Zalcent arriving?" she demanded.

Several agents scrambled with their phones; each seemed desperate to please her and provide the answer she wanted. Finally, one held up a finger, indicating they had information. "Their private jet is landing at the Oxford County Regional Airport now, ma'am. They should be here in thirty minutes."

The SAC nodded, turned away from everybody clamoring for her attention, and whipped open the door to an SUV. Just before she disappeared inside, she announced, "Get me when they arrive!" She slammed the door in the faces of the agents staring after her.

Imara and Sirenī saw the SUV leave and continued their walk to the manor driveway. On the road beyond, they saw a tow truck with a purple and gold logo drawing the ruins of the crumpled police cruiser onto a flatbed. The other cruiser had been pushed fifteen feet away from the car caught between the front end of that one and the barrier, which gave the hooker room to move the ruined vehicle.

Four police officers were standing around, one with a bandage over his nose and smears of blood on his dark uniform. The oldest was a woman talking into her shoulder mic, arguing with someone at the other end who kept telling her to pack it up and head back.

Imara and Sirenī listened for a few minutes before they turned and walked up the driveway to the house. The air was crisp, but the thermal regulation spells embedded in their aurae kept them comfortable as they walked.

"Even with everything going on, can you believe how well we've settled in on this world?" Imara broke the silence. She dismissed the Obscuratus enchantment. "Despite how primitive it is, we're mostly safe, comfortable, and together again."

Sirenī's expression was pensive. "Even though we're leaving. Now we have this new house, and we're all together, and Carter is...interesting and fits in with us surprisingly well. I have this foreboding, though," she said and stopped to face her partner. "I'm worried about traveling through time and trying to master the mystical forces. I haven't even gained full control over my intrinsic powers. What if Medusa reacts? I can't control her. I feel like things are going to spiral out of control."

Sirenī inherited her fatal beauty from the ancient sorcerer Medusa. Aphrodite's bloodline also carried the power, which manifested sporadically in each lineage. Sirenī had both aspects of Medusa's power but couldn't control the monstrous side.

"I understand," Imara said sympathetically. "Being blind felt like the worst thing that could ever happen, but it wasn't. Being separated from you and Alex was horrible, and then losing Layton…that was the worst. I became resigned to my blindness and aloneness, but both have been healed now that we've reunited. I never wanted to master the mystical forces; I never cared about them. But Alex thinks we need that power, and a large part of me agrees."

Imara took Sirenī's hands. "Don't worry, my love. We'll figure out Medusa. Maybe you can integrate her somehow? I've thought of it off and on over the years we were apart, and I feel like she's got a different master harmonic than you. If that's the case, maybe I can blend them? You didn't need me to synchronize the amṛta to your master vibration, but maybe hers is out of sync with yours."

Sirenī nodded slowly, comforted by Imara's words. "That makes sense. I try not to think about her because I'm afraid I'll lose control. If I can somehow integrate Medusa, that could change everything." Her eyes gleamed with excitement. "Maybe we can work on that when we go back in time."

"Absolutely. We need to harness everything we can to handle what's coming. You know, we're already more powerful than we realize."

"We don't know our limits," Sirenī agreed.

"We need to find out what we can do with the amṛta," Imara said. She paused and frowned. "And then…there's that word I spoke.…"

"I know. I can't believe we haven't talked about it since giving Alex the executive summary that night," Sirenī remarked. "That was different."

Imara nodded. "It wasn't my vocal power. It was something else. I can't feel it now, but it was intense when it happened."

"So long as we're together, we'll figure things out," Sirenī promised. She took a deep breath. "I've been thinking about something else: when do you think we should look to get pregnant?"

Imara put her hands on her slim hips. "This may be irrational, but I'm ready now. I've waited forty-eight years to have a family with you and Alex!"

Sirenī cupped Imara's cheek. "And…Layton? How are you doing with his memory?"

Imara took a deep breath as her heart spasmed painfully. "It's been eighteen years. I still grieve for him—the pain goes to sleep, then wakes up again. It comes in waves. I don't want more children to replace him, but I'm alive and have another chance."

"Layton could reincarnate to you, you know. Have you ever sensed his presence?"

"No, but that doesn't mean much. When I was blind, I couldn't see magical aurae or the spirit world unless I astral projected, and I've never been able to leave my body like you and Alex, so that was rare. I could look for his spirit or perform a summoning to find out if he has crossed over or remains in the astral realms, but…"

Sirenī squeezed Imara's hand. She then tucked it around the crook of her arm, and they resumed walking. "I'm happy to help in any way I can, and I'm ready for kids if you are. Alex hardly needs to do anything more than what he's already happy to do morning, noon, and night."

The two women burst out laughing and shook with amusement, readily conceding that Alex's lustfulness made for an easy start to the process of pregnancy.

"Do you think we can control our pregnancies? Not their duration, but the timing? I haven't had a cycle in twenty years, but I expected one to begin at some point post-amṛta."

Sirenī frowned. "I've never stopped menstruating. I'm surprised you did, actually—we'd easily live three centuries without amṛta, so we'd be fertile for almost two hundred years." They approached the manor. "Why did your cycles stop? Was it the grief?"

"I don't know for certain, but I think it's from the spell. My cycles became irregular before Layton died. Since I blended my master harmony with that of the amṛta, I figured things would start back up again, but maybe I need some deeper healing."

"Well, I can perform a delving and see if there are blocks in your subtle body obstructing things, and then we can go from there?" Sirenī suggested.

Imara smiled at her. "Let's do that—sooner rather than later if we can find the time."

They stepped into the manor just as a young girl raced out of the sitting room. Her face was screwed up like she'd eaten something sour. She ran into Imara and bounced off her thighs with a squeal of surprise. She landed on her rump on the floor, and her eyes widened as she stared at them.

She focused on Sirenī after a moment. "You're glowing." Her voice rang with innocent wonder. "How come you glow?"

Sirenī crouched down and helped the girl up. "Well, I have a very special power that makes me glow, but you know what?"

"What?" the girl asked.

"You have a special power, too, because not everyone can see my glow when I don't want them to," Sirenī said.

The girl's eyes widened, and she glanced at Imara for confirmation.

The songstress nodded. The girl grinned gleefully and ran off, shouting for her mother. The two women watched her go and burst into laughter.

"I'd be delighted if our children were like her," Imara said.

Brent and Drëndi sat in their Boston office. They were on a conference call with Assistant Director Beatrice Lambert.

Their boss spoke in a hurried, clipped voice that was unlike her usual tone, "You absolutely must get back up there," she commanded. "I'm telling you, what's happening in the Middle East is the start of bigger problems. I have the strongest presentiment that something terrible is happening. It's going to spread around the world, and it's going to make the SARS-CoV-2 mess, and its fallout, look like a joke."

The agents shifted uncomfortably and looked at one another.

"But why send us back to Maine?" Drëndi asked. "Can't we do more to help you?"

Beatrice held up a hand, glanced out of the camera frame, nodded, and faced the camera again. "Trust me on this. You need to be there. I can't emphasize how strongly I feel that—" She stopped speaking and glanced aside again, her eyes widening in exasperation. "I saw you the first two times, MacKenzie," she snapped.

Beatrice turned back to the camera once again. "Look, I have to go. I'm briefing the president in three hours and need to get to the airport. I'll be in touch when I can, but you need to get there ASAP. I'll clear you for an indefinite stay en route to D.C." She paused, licked her lips, and leaned toward the camera. "You're the only people I trust. Something is going on. Good luck."

With that cryptic, whispered warning, she closed the videoconferencing app.

Brent and Drëndi stared at each other, stunned by the unexpected interaction and their orders. After a few minutes of thoughtful silence, Drëndi shut down her computer. She stood and grabbed her go-bag, then turned and looked at Brent. He did the same, and they left.

Alexander showed a flabbergasted Paul, Sue, and their older child, Eric, around the sprawling, opulent manor. Cassie joined them at some point, dashing to catch up to the adults and sidling next to her mother. The dumbstruck couple seemed to be barely holding it together. It was a lot for anyone to take, and they didn't have the luxury of time before getting thrown right into the thick of things.

Jordan and Richard hadn't had that luxury, either, after four strangers appeared in their garden on the night Richard proposed. Still, they'd adapted remarkably well, partly because Grandma M had raised Jordan in the sure but secret knowledge of the existence of magical visitors from another world. When Maria told Jordan the tale of the Three on her deathbed, Jordan hadn't believed her. Still, a part of her had been preconditioned to accept the reality of the situation by her grandmother's subtle coaching over the years.

Richard was a pragmatic, practical man with a love of science fiction and fantasy stories, which allowed him to be open to the fabulous and magical. He was a dedicated nerd beneath his tough exterior.

Paul and Sue were practical folks, too, but they lived in a more hardscrabble world where the wondrousness of things didn't exist for "normal" people who had no room in their lives for magic. They worked, cared for their kids and their small, tidy home, and worked some more, just as their parents did.

The Arsenaults could barely comprehend being welcomed into a home that would've cost more than twenty million bucks to build and appoint. Alexander's blasé attitude and unconcern were so contrary to their expectation of the ultra-rich that it boggled their minds as much as the magic.

The sorcerer and Richard escorted the Arsenaults to the second floor with its twelve massive bedrooms, en suite baths, and enormous walk-in closets—possibly more extensive than the square footage of Paul and Sue's home. They picked a room on that floor at Alexander's urging.

Then everyone trooped upstairs so the kids could pick their rooms from the twenty-four smaller suites on the third floor. Each room had a compact attached bathroom and generous closet space.

"This is bigger than my apartment in college," Richard joked.

Paul grinned. "It's a lot nicer, too, and no shared bath!"

The two men laughed while Alexander watched, pleased that he was able to help his friends.

Five
Quinque

Imara and Sirenī relaxed on a settee in one of the many groups of comfortable chairs and couches arrayed around the sitting room. Marquis spontaneously manifested out of thin air, waddled over, and jumped up next to Sirenī. He fell over onto his side against her thigh and purred loudly.

The two women enjoyed each other's company, just as they had five decades earlier, and now focused on what was ahead of them instead of their past.

"Does it ever feel strange that we're not on Gaea anymore?" Sirenī asked.

Imara grimaced. "Definitely! I never expected to leave Gaea, never mind returning to Earth after fifty years. I'm enjoying being here, though. And once we get past this corruption business, however long that takes, I'd like to visit other worlds in the Ring. Have you ever wondered about the first world, where the Nephilim lived?"

Sirenī absently patted Marquis, who alternated between starting to fall asleep and attacking her hand. "I have. What would it be like? Would their homeworld be amazing, or would it be like ours? They were an advanced civilization, as far as we know. What does high technology look like on that scale?" she wondered.

They lapsed into a brief, thoughtful silence. After a bit, Imara shifted to get more comfortable.

"Do you think Alex aged much while we were apart?" she asked. "I recall him looking much the same, but time dulls the particulars of memory."

Sirenī considered the question. "No, I don't think so. It's hard to say. We still don't know how old he was when we met him."

"Older than us," Imara remarked dryly.

Her partner laughed. "Yes, definitely that! I would have said he was in his forties back in the day, even though I knew he was much older. I think he looked about the same when we reunited." Sirenī pursed her lips. "He'd probably stopped aging by the time we met him. I read somewhere that the Eldreds live six to seven centuries."

Imara bit her lip. "Alex started his training with Galen at fourteen, and Galen was quite aged by then. Did we ever find out when Galen was born? We could estimate Alex's age that way."

"We could just ask him," Sirenī suggested.

The songstress shook her head with bemused exasperation. "I asked him once, but he refused to tell me. I believe it bothers him that he's much older than you and I. I was never bothered by the age gap."

"Neither was I. Speaking of that era of our lives, did it upset you when he said he loved me, too? I was so jealous when I met you two; you were already in love. You were this goddess. I really admired you. You became my role model when we first came together.

"Because of my fatal beauty, I'd never removed Aphrodite's Veil, gone out with anyone, or attended public schools. The risk was always too great that the Veil might slip or get pulled off by someone else, so I had to be tutored at home. Everyone was captivated by me, but they were also afraid.

"I wanted to hate you initially because you could love and touch someone without compelling them into slavery. It made me so bitter and envious."

Sirenī's raw confession surprised Imara.

"Why didn't you ever say anything about all this during those ten years? I thought we shared everything."

Sirenī looked mildly embarrassed. "I didn't say anything because it was stupid and childish of me, and anyway, it didn't take long for Alex to tell me to take off the Veil. I was terrified of what would happen, but you were supportive and encouraging. Then when I did take it off, you were both fine. Somehow, you were immune. I don't even pretend to understand it."

"You were immune to my voice, too. There's some strange thing between us, maybe karma of some kind, but it's something profound and real."

Sirenī took a juddery breath, "I've never told anyone any of that. At first, I didn't want you to be mad at me, and then I felt foolish. After our first true night together, all that pettiness fell away, and I understood what it was to be loved in a way that I never had."

Imara reached out and took her partner's hand. "I'm only two years older than you, but when I started sleeping with Alex…I felt incredible—mature and worldly. I'm sure you picked up on some of that when we first met. I hope I wasn't too obnoxious because no matter how I felt, I was still young. My time in Louden, and Layton's death, taught me just how naïve and foolish I was back then." The songstress snorted. "Besides, you're the most beautiful woman in many worlds. I just kept waiting for him to leave me for you for a while there."

Sirenī barked a laugh and held up a finger. "First, you really were mature! Everything about you was—and still is—mature and elegant, with poise and grace. Second: your voice. Every word you speak is like music, even when you're irritated. Back then, I just knew he'd never look at me like he looks at you.

"I could see how in love he was with you, which was part of why I was so jealous. I never thought anyone would look at me like that because I couldn't ever be my true self while wearing Aphrodite's Veil.

"I never thought you and I would have a relationship independent of Alex. He takes up so much space, but I can't even find the words to tell you how much I value our connection."

"I didn't think we'd fall in love the way we did, but I'm so glad it happened," Imara said. "I can't imagine my life without you, dear heart."

Their threesome was initially complicated, but Alex carefully navigated their disagreements. He supported them by helping them figure out solutions to their frictions so that Imara and Sirenī maintained their agency and sovereignty. He'd once told them he didn't want to interfere in the natural development of their relationship by placing arbitrary limits upon it. At first, it angered them, but they came to understand it was actually unconditional love.

Imara sighed. "I can't believe how long ago that was. It feels like another lifetime."

"That it was," Sirenī concurred.

She smiled down at Marquis as she continued to stroke his fur. He'd fallen asleep against her leg, and his mouth was partially open while he snored.

Imara smiled fondly at Sirenī as she recalled their youth. Her partner always looked perfect in a way only her unique magic could achieve. When she sobbed uncontrollably, she was lovely. When she screamed and raged, she was beautiful. When the rain soaked her to the bone, she was stunning. At first, it drove Imara to distraction to be around another female who never looked messy, disheveled, or frumpy.

Imara heard tiny footsteps and leaned around Sirenī. She saw Sue and Paul's little girl buzzing into the sitting room. Her eyes lit up when she saw the two women on the couch with Marquis, who woke up in the way cats have and spied the tiny human immediately. He rolled agilely to his feet and hopped lightly to the floor. He walked a few steps, laid down, and fixed his golden eyes on the little girl.

She shyly crept into the room and smiled nervously at the two women.

"Can I pet your kitty?" she asked.

"Of course," Sirenī replied, smiling. "His name is Marquis."

"I know," she replied with childlike honesty.

She hurried over, fell to the floor beside the cat, and happily began petting him. Imara met Sirenī's eyes and raised her eyebrows. Sirenī looked at the girl.

"I'm Sirenī, and this is my friend, Imara. Can I ask your name, honey?"

The girl nodded agreeably. "I'm Cassie. Mommy said I could talk to you, that you aren't strangers because we're living at your house. Is this your house? It's huge."

"It is our house, yes," Sirenī agreed. "Does it seem big to you? I suppose it must be, but it's hard to tell. It's nice to meet you, Cassie. Can you tell me how you knew Marquis' name?"

Cassie didn't reply for so long that the two women began to wonder if she was going to, but she finally looked up at them through the veil of her long hair. "I dunno. I sometimes pick up things, like names and stuff, but I don't try to. Mommy said it makes people uncomfortable, so I don't talk about it much, but you said I had a special power, so I figured it wouldn't bother you."

Sirenī glanced at Imara again, and the songstress nodded, indicating Sirenī should keep talking. It was interesting to meet someone on Earth with clearly developed psychic abilities besides Brent and Drëndi. The special agents were more sensitive than psychic, but Cassie clearly saw aurae and other things, implying a robust latent power.

Imara looked at her aura and decided she would rate at a middling Grade One with formal training—perhaps she and Sirenī could teach the girl to use her power. It would be helpful for her and good practice for them when their children were old enough.

"That's right; you do have a special power, Cassie. We aren't bothered by you knowing things. Do you pick up anything more from us?" Sirenī asked.

Cassie pushed herself up and sat with crossed legs. She scrunched up her face, staring at them for about a minute before she shook her head.

"Just your glow," she said to Sirenī, then shifted her gaze to Imara. "I can maybe hear something from you, but that's it. My mother and father are loud right now. I was with them, but it got uncomfortable, so I left."

"That's understandable," Sirenī said. She looked at Imara and spoke in their particular way. *She's interesting for an Earthen person. A bit of magical ability. How unexpected.*

Absolutely. She's one to keep an eye on. I bet she causes no end of trouble for her parents when she's a teenager.

The two women shared a bemused smile and then felt more than heard Alex's arrival. He peeked around the door frame to the sitting room and smiled briefly at Cassie and then the two women. They smiled back at him. He strolled over and joined them on the couch.

They shifted to make room between them, as was their custom, Imara to his left, Sirenī to his right. He said nothing, merely sat with them with their bodies touching. They enjoyed the quiet moment of togetherness before getting back to business.

Kāmla recalled Ävidä Saclendra's words while searching the Timil Deeps' birth registry. *"Either way, once everything progresses enough, we will return to the position that would have been ours by right of birth before all this folderol with the Doctrine of Unity."*

Powerful wizarding families were the royalty of the ancient world. They weren't monarchs, but they were monarchic. They didn't rule over the land, but their whims and will were law. Those with weaker magical power had less ability to influence social circumstances, while those with the most were a fearsome bunch, accustomed to getting everything they wanted whenever they wanted.

Sorcerous duels were common in those days, often ending with a winner while the loser remained alive, crippled, and ignominious. Some fights ended with the deaths of one or both participants. No matter the outcome, there were no consequences for those who won as that was the nature of duels, which were entered into by consent of all parties.

The Doctrine of Unity halted casual dueling, and now only the most egregious offenses were likely to result in magical combat. It was still legal, but there were appropriate restrictions that valued the safety of others above the egos of the participants.

Kāmla knew Gaea's people had Unification to thank for peace and freedom. Homogenization initially moved slowly, but it gained speed as the Grid expanded. It was incredibly time-consuming in the beginning when the technicians had to place an anchor stone every eight miles across the seabed of the oceans because the system only functioned if they were close enough to eliminate latency in the network. Installing the stones across the seafloor took specialized magic and autotech diving equipment, but Kāmla firmly believed the horrendous expense in time and lives was worthwhile.

She devoutly believed that the Council of Wizards knew what was best for Gaea, and Unification ended the millennia of sorcerers ruling their little fiefdoms. It stopped the commonplace and deadly duels that affected innocent lives. Furthermore, it eliminated corruption and secrecy by establishing a worldwide government that operated completely transparently.

Kāmla never experienced cognitive dissonance at managing covert operations for the Unified Government. She kept secrets from the public and her fellow ministers, but she did it for virtuous reasons and was quite confident of her righteousness. She honestly believed her actions were the best for everyone—although she never questioned whether anyone else believed that.

She scowled as she thought of wizard duels and the accursed Three as she leafed through another drawer filled with records. She felt frustrated by her slow progress. She'd already been looking for a few hours but needed to confirm her suspicions before her presence was missed in Columbia. She had a knack for ferreting out secrets once she knew to look for them, and she was positive she'd find what she was looking for.

Ävidä's words had triggered an alarm in her head. She'd only just put the pieces together about what his words might mean and what they meant for the world. Kāmla was devoted to Unification with a ferociousness she never let anyone else see—it was her purpose. She would crush anyone who stood in her way as she strode forward to fulfill Gaea's destiny.

Ävidä had a radically different vision from hers, and she was comfortable with that. What bothered her was how he saw himself in the endgame: he wanted to rule.

Those days are done. We can never, ever go back.

Her jaw was tense with the urgency of her mission and desperation to escape Timil Deeps. She rolled her head and felt her neck crack and pop, which brought her slight relief. Only escaping from the town of her birth would allow her to relax, but she had to find what she sought.

It happened as her fourth hour drew to a close. She stood among the neatly maintained records while her head ached and her jaw throbbed. The next paper she pulled was the one she needed. She almost cackled in triumph but resisted the undignified expression.

She looked at the old certification that logged the birth of a male child, the third and youngest in the family. The mother, Marissa Eldred-Almas, died unexpectedly in childbirth despite attempts by a medician to save her. His father was devastated but had two older children to raise, so the infant's maternal grandparents collected him and raised him at their home in Timil Deeps. Kāmla looked at their names, and her lips curled with distaste because they were Eldreds. Well, one of them was, anyway—Idris Eldred. The other was Tatiana Romanova, a sorcerer born to another powerful lineage that was thankfully extinct.

Her lips curved in a satisfied smile as she read the scrawl of the signatories on the document and admired the newborn's tiny handprint. The child's father was listed as Lorenzo Almas. He'd died three years after the birth of his progeny, and then his two older children, Madeline and Andrew, went to live with their grandparents, too.

Kāmla stared at the document, reading and rereading everything on it so that she committed it to memory. She wasn't willing to risk forgetting a single detail of the crucial information and brought the magically preserved document to the nearest replicator. She placed the paper flat on the monatomic crystal plate, face up. The plate glowed brightly for one-fifteenth of a second and went dark.

She removed the original and waited for one-thirtieth of a second as a second flash produced an identical copy. The only difference from the original was the tag inserted into documents by every legal replicator. Kāmla's unregistered device produced exact copies without tags since paper trails were dangerous even in magical polities with a plethora of transparency. She removed the replicated document, folded it neatly, and put it in a hidden pocket of her chèuhngsāam.

She returned the original to its proper place in the catalog, closed the drawer, and let out a relieved sigh. Then she spun on her heel and hurried back to her car. She got in with a grunt and sat there for a moment, grateful that no one had recognized her. When she backed out, she cut across the parking lot and swerved onto the road so quickly that several other vehicles had to shift to avoid her; irate drivers honked their horns and shouted at her recklessness.

Kāmla ignored them.

They're meaningless—most will die in the next couple of years, anyway.

Patrice was just one of an endless number of victims who'd feed the prāṇa of their suffering and death into the reliquaries that would furnish power for those in charge.

There will be only one person left in charge…me.

Kāmla drove swiftly along the road out of Timil Deeps. Speed limits were effectively nonexistent on Gaea: magical safeguards built into the streets and vehicles prevented accidents. That was why it only took two days to drive to Columbia, which was just a hair west of the continent's midline.

The minister's thoughts churned as she blew past the site of the disastrous roadblock.

That bitch Sirenī Adamma turned into her Medusa form, and the tramp ravaged the entire countryside before Imara Inanna, prim cunt that she is, summoned the arrogant fuck to cause even more havoc and destruction before they fled the scene of their many crimes. How could they, and Alexander Eldred's obnoxiously arrogant family, be so gifted while some people hardly have any magic at all?

She knew that everyone sensed magic to some degree, thanks to the genetics of the World One species stock, but feeling power was different from wielding it. Most people rated below Grade Four, but a dangerous few could cast spells that affected the entire planet.

Kāmla grimaced and ground her teeth as she roared away from Timil Deeps. Her hatred of the Three burned so hotly that her pleasure at finding the damning document withered. She had dossiers on them, but Alexander's only went back sixty years to May 27, 1923, when he sought out Imara Inanna and recruited her to his world-altering cause.

Kāmla could acknowledge that Gaea's people owed the Three a small debt because neither she nor anyone else wanted to grow up in a world controlled by the demon overlord Sogma. She just wished they'd had the decency to die while annihilating the Abyssal Gate and a legion of the Empire's greatest sorcerers. They waged war on foreign soil, cast spells that disrupted the magical utility system worldwide, and recruited rebellious sorcerers to their cause against the admonishment of the Unified Government.

And they had the fucking audacity to survive!

The minister clenched her fists on the steering wheel and accelerated, swerving around traffic ahead of her at three hundred miles an hour. She passed countless cars and drove for over a hundred miles before her rage and sense of injustice and unfairness began to cool inside her. It finally fell back to smoldering embers instead of the inferno it became as she left her hometown.

She took deep breaths to relax and soothe her bitter heart, but it was difficult. Kāmla was in her mid-seventies, the same as Imara and Sirenī. Without biweekly rejuvenation and prolongation spells, Kāmla would look three decades older than her contemporaries. She had no intrinsic magic; she was one of those who could feel it but couldn't wield it.

She smiled as she slowed her vehicle and held up her right hand. She kept one eye on the road as faint, poisonous green flames flickered across her fingers. She had years to go before she could cast powerful spells like dreadfire, but she was well on her way.

She was just in time, too, considering the impact its passage was having. The collagen in her skin was thinning, and she'd found fine lines around her mouth and eyes even with the enchantments she used to prolong her youth. She could feel the softening of her muscles, noticed less elasticity in her breasts, and felt that her shapely lines were blurring. Aging was inevitable. She was keenly aware that it was happening every minute of every day—while Alexander remained unchanged from the first time she'd met him.

They'd run into him in the central commons of Timil Deeps, a luxurious and expansive park with benches and pavilions for the arts. It was dotted with small eatery carts, performers, and activities for children and adults alike. The commons were lovely, and flowers bloomed even in the depths of winter. Snow never dared do more than romantically dust the boughs of the trees and the lawns or rime the flowers with lovely, crystalline frost.

Kāmla despised it because everyone who went there was blinded by the simple pleasures imposed on them by the ogrish thug who kept them all complacent as they whiled away their lives, achieving nothing. Alexander was attending a performance at the pavilion his family had built centuries before when they established the commons. It was some sappy play about unrequited love and tragic loss, and it bored Kāmla to tears.

She smiled bitterly as she recalled that humiliating moment of her parents and siblings bowing to him and how her mother reached over and tugged at her sleeve, hissing at her to show him respect. While the rest of her family groveled like slugs, she refused to bow—she'd never bowed to anyone in her life and never would. The scion of the Eldred family had just smiled at her family and wished them a good evening, then turned away.

Just like that, the most powerful man in the world dismissed her existence—and that upset her most of all.

Tricia Welter nervously straightened her suit jacket and smoothed her slacks. She took a deep breath and knocked on the door, reminding herself to relax her death grip on the bouquet she'd picked up for her date.

When Wú Xiāng opened the door to her home, Tricia's heart tripped. The Tèng woman wore a skintight, black chèuhngsāam with red dragons twined around phoinikes picked out in thread-of-gold. Her long her was piled on her head with a few pieces artfully curled around her temples. She'd highlighted her lovely almond eyes with subtle ochre and deep crimson eyeshadow and had dusted her lips with a fancy, glittering polish that made them sparkle and shimmer when she spoke.

Tricia proffered the flowers, and Xiāng took them with a grin. "They're beautiful, Trish. Thank you," the sorcerer said.

She never tired of hearing Xiāng's accent. "You're welcome, Xiāng," she replied.

Her date's eyes lit up. "You've been practicing! Your accent is much better," she complimented. She backed into her home long enough to levitate a glass vase from elsewhere and placed the flowers in it. "This will keep them until we return, and I can attend to them properly."

She set the vase on a table by the door and stepped out. Tricia made space for the petite magician while Xiāng closed the door and activated a powerful wizard's lock to seal it.

Tricia offered her arm, and Xiāng took it, allowing the taller soldier to lead her down the walkway to the street. She'd taken a vehicle from a car park and held the door for the other woman, then closed it when Xiāng was seated. Tricia hurried to the other side, slipped into the driver's seat, and hit the button to start the engine.

"You look lovely, Trish," Wú Xiāng told her.

Tricia looked at her. "And you're fucking mind-blowing, Xiāng," she replied.

The sorcerer smiled at her, and Tricia pulled away from the curb, thrilled and nervous about their first date.

Six
Sex

The scene at the property's periphery grew more chaotic as the military set up blockades on the roads adjacent to Jordan's sprawling acreage. Locals detoured along back roads to circumnavigate the property and travel to or from Bethel and the other towns up State Route 26. People couldn't reach West Paris—the sister town to South Paris—via 26 or High Street because of the roadblocks.

This meant the small town of Steadfield was essentially locked down since it sat snug against the side of South Paris. The military and federal authorities took over the Pendleton Rest. They set up tents on the roads around the property and in the parking lots of the Rest, the Indigent Mug across the street, and Grace Manor's primary and side lots, too.

At Grace Manor, the feds scared away the people waiting to go inside, leading to some grumbling and unrest. DHS agents investigated recent events at the nursing facility because they seemed connected to the other unexplained phenomena that had happened in the area—the Oxford Hills were too small to have multiple perpetrators for such paranormal shenanigans.

The townspeople were upset about the disruptions to their lives, but the government and the military didn't care. DHS put a terrorist spin on the news they released to the media, making it sound like a serious threat to everyone's safety.

The Feebs, as Sue called them, used that narrative to justify an overwhelming presence by implying Jordan's property was now a cult compound. Supposedly, said cultists had infiltrated Grace Manor first and were rumored to have the components to build a compact fusion weapon. Many locals were conservative and scoffed at this obvious spin job, but enough people bought into the story to cause drama.

Conservatives said, "They're putting together a nuke at the nursing home, but they're not storming Jordan's place." Everyone knew the McInerneys; Maria and her granddaughter were well-liked. "Why isn't the government evacuating Steadfield, South Paris, and everywhere else if that's the case?"

Liberals had a different take on things. "They're putting together a nuke at the nursing home, so why hasn't the government stormed the place? They're a threat to the greater good!"

The roadblocks inconvenienced everyone, but the special agents and military on site said nothing to the reporters who swarmed the scene. Most people thought the story was such a patent absurdity that they laughed it off. After all, how likely was a facility full of the aging, sick, and dying to be a hotbed of sedition and recruitment for terrorist philosophies and radicalization? Still, almost everyone obeyed the government's instructions and stayed indoors except to run necessary errands. It was a well-worn pattern for Americans, accustomed to oppression and the loss of civil liberties over the last twenty years.

The Indigent Mug stayed open for two reasons. First, Persephone Plunkett was unmoved by the propaganda, and second, she privately thought the government people could fuck the hell off. She did a booming business serving the feds and the soldiers because money was money, whether paid out by government-sponsored assholes or her regulars. She missed her regulars but philosophized that the people entering her establishment were just doing their jobs. She did hers; they did theirs just like cops, nurses, doctors, politicians, and trash collectors.

After Paul and Sue Arsenault and their children were "kidnapped" by the cultists, people professed concern while rubbernecking and gossiping. The situation couldn't remain equilibrious for long because the government and Zalcent International were interested in people like the foreigners from Gaea, and they were surprisingly confident that they would prevail.

Paul, Sue, Eric, and Cassie ended up sleeping in the big bedroom on the second floor. Paul thought the kids could sleep in their own rooms. Eric agreed, but Sue and Cassie were too nervous about being apart the first night. When Eric looked mutinous, his mother gave him a gimlet stare, and he sulked into compliance. Paul and Sue couldn't quite process or believe everything they encountered that evening and needed some time.

The Arsenaults took to their room and collapsed in total exhaustion. Sue enjoyed the massive bathroom, unlimited hot water, and the fact that the towels somehow returned to the warming rack in the bathroom, dry, plump, and incredibly soft and absorbent after they were used. She kept taking them and tossing them in different places around the room, but as soon as no one was watching, they disappeared and reappeared in the bathroom, clean and ready for use.

Sue's last thought before sleep was, *Screw force fields and wizard duels; this is the kind of magic I can get behind. Perpetually clean homes and towels that somehow wash, dry, and fold themselves? Hell, yeah!*

Alexander, Imara, and Sirenī let the Arsenaults have their space on the second floor.

The Three went to the library to deliberate. Their discussion regarding their departure included how they could best protect their Earthen friends in their absence. They kept going around and around on the subject.

Finally, the songstress held up a hand. "I told you both that our harmony was incomplete. You cannot tell me it hasn't occurred to you that he might be the fourth?"

Alex scoffed. "I admit that I like him. He is a respectable, trustworthy man. I would even say he is a true friend. I cannot see him filling any role greater than that."

Imara sighed. He'd always disagreed with her about their harmony, but she heard the gaps in the song formed by her, Sirenī, and Alex. There was a fourth member; their triad was a tetrad. She knew it as unambiguously as she knew she loved them both. She turned her gaze to Sirenī for help.

"I like him, but you both know I never think about the whole triad-tetrad shit that you two obsess about," she said. "I'm happy to be with you, here and now." She shifted her gaze to Imara and smiled. "You've said since we were young that you feel our harmony is incomplete; you won't get any arguments from me. I don't understand how you hear and see the world, my love, but I trust it will all work out in due time."

Imara nodded in acceptance at Sirenī's reasonable words but was slightly disappointed in the lack of support. Alex had that feeling of mulish obstinacy about him; she knew he wouldn't budge on the idea.

"Time itself will tell us if I'm right or wrong, and maybe it isn't Jack," she conceded, though she didn't believe that even for a second. "Either way, he can't protect everyone without an advantage…and the amṛta will give him that."

Alex agreed on that point. "I concur. Giving him the last portion of amṛta makes sense with both the time we have and what we know of his character," he acknowledged.

Imara knew there was more to it than that, but she let it go. She'd be proven right soon enough.

Alexander sent his avatar to find his friend. It was the same mystical method by which he'd visited with Imara and made love to her in Louden. It wasn't teleportation; the sorcerer remained where he was, but it was more substantial than a spectral projection. Those looked substantial but were intangible—a specter couldn't interact with material objects, and most people didn't have the psychic ability to hear them speak, either.

His mystical avatar was a superior version of that—a full manifestation of the self that could interact, have sex, and eat or drink. Such an avatar didn't last beyond laying down to sleep, however. At that time, it would disappear as if it had never been. As far as the sorcerer could tell, it was faster than teleporting and didn't generate any magical resonance detectable by others. It was the perfect solution.

Alexander mentally located Carter by thinking in his direction and connecting to his presence. Everyone had a particular vibration that a talented sorcerer learned to recognize as a matter of course. It made magical interaction over a distance possible. He located Carter in his bedroom in Jordan's house and sent his avatar there.

Carter was startled when Alexander appeared soundlessly and suddenly in his bedroom. The soldier was lounging in his sweatpants on the bed, thinking. He propped himself on his elbows and frowned at the intrusion.

"Really, man? What if I'd been jerking off?" he demanded in Demurrian.

Alexander laughed. "I have seen other men jerk off," he said dryly. "Besides, you usually do that in the morning before showering."

Carter's frown turned into a scowl.

"Would you join us at the house?" the sorcerer continued.

Carter growled. "I'll be there in a few minutes."

"Thank you. We are in the library," the sorcerer replied and disappeared.

Carter arrived fifteen minutes later. The Three sat in a cluster of four chairs, the last remaining unoccupied. He sat and raised his eyebrows, looking from one to the other. They all seemed unusually serious, and he began to feel nervous.

"Okay. This feels fucking weird," the soldier declared.

Sirenī burst out laughing and clapped a hand to her mouth. "I'm sorry. I know we intended to be serious, but come on, it's Carter! Just spit it out and let him decide."

Carter looked from Sirenī to Imara, who rolled her eyes and gestured to Alex, to whom the soldier directed his attention. The sorcerer sighed and nodded.

"We must leave, as you already know. We need to travel through time so that I can train Imara and Sirenī in the union of the mystical and magical forces."

"Wait," Carter interrupted. "Time travel? You've got to be shitting me. Besides, I didn't think the two forces were unifiable. No one ever has." He cocked his head at Alex's smug expression. "But you did, of course."

Imara chuckled, and Sirenī giggled.

The sorcerer of Timil Deeps looked rather grumpy at their reaction. "Yes, I have," he declared. "And it was no simple thing. I hope to teach the technique to Imara and Sirenī. It took me decades to understand. I expect it to take them weeks, months, or years, so we will travel back in time and return as close to our departure point as possible."

Carter shook his head. "Okay, fine, time travel and the two forces. And why the fuck are you doing this?"

"Alex pushed the issue of getting us all together again because he had a vision of a great corruption sweeping over many worlds," Imara explained. "It's already begun on Earth and other planets in the Ring. He feels Sirenī and I need as much power as we can muster to prevent his visions from coming to pass."

The soldier digested her words in silence before nodding slowly. "I can see that. What do you want me to do while you're gone? That's why you wanted to talk to me alone, right?"

The others looked at one another.

"Well," Sirenī drawled, "we do want you to take care of things while we're gone, but before we go, we wanted to offer you something. It's not a thing you should accept lightly, but we don't have a lot of time for you to think about it, either."

"You're killing me with all this circling around. Just spit it out."

"We want to offer you amṛta, which will make you immortal and give you more magical power, though we cannot know how much," Alex said bluntly.

Carter's jaw dropped open, and he stared at the sorcerer, speechless. *Is this a joke?* He took a good thirty seconds to recover from Alex's blunt words.

Then he looked at the others and realized they were serious. He blew out a breath and shook his head, though more in surprise than anything else.

"I'm not sure why you're offering me this. I'm just a grunt. Isn't that stuff scarce? I always thought it was just a legend, like ambrosia and all that other shit," Carter said.

"Well," Sirenī explained, "the various legends of divine foods are all based in fact. The philosopher's stone and ambrosia are reddish, gelatinous substances. They grant immortality to those who consume them but not youth and health. You can still experience the infirmities of age and suffer from maladies."

"So you can get the flu?" Carter scoffed. "You just won't die from it. Sounds janky."

Sirenī laughed. "Exactly. The golden apples are a fruit that conveys eternal youth and health but not immortality. Someone can still cut off your head."

Carter smirked. "I can see how that might be problematic."

She grinned back. "Amṛta comes to us from the Nephilim. It's semi-liquid, amber-colored, and offers the best of all worlds: immortality, youth, and health."

Carter nodded thoughtfully, leaned forward in his chair, and rested his elbows on his knees, his hands dangling. "Okay…" He held up a hand to tick off points on his fingers. "So, virtually indestructible." Tick. "Eternal youth." Tick. "Magical power I've never had." Tick. "Sounds great, but that doesn't answer the other part of my question. Why me?"

Alex glanced at Imara; she took over the thread of the conversation. "Well, you've proven yourself a capable warrior and a good friend over these last few weeks. I don't believe you have any thought of going back to Gaea and resuming a normal life there after what happened at the Nephilim Temple?"

"Fuck no," he grunted. "I've got a target on my back on Gaea. Maybe I'll visit at some point, but nothing's tying me there. Here's as good a place as any to hang my sword."

"Then the question could just as easily be, why not you?" Imara asked reasonably.

Carter shook his head and held up his hands. He looked at each of them in turn, his expression slightly puzzled but serious, his shaggy beard hiding the tension in his jaw. He had a nervous tingle in his hands and feet and felt a little dizzy like he'd been hyperventilating. This conversation wasn't what he'd expected when Alex appeared in his bedroom.

He worked through his conflicting feelings and started with the simplest element. "It's not that simple. You can't offer me something like this and say, why not you? That means some fuck down the road is equally worthy of consideration. This is big. It'll change my life forever. I'll never die, not until I ascend or something like that. This changes the trajectory of my entire fucking existence."

Alex's expression was grave. "The truth is, we offer this to you because we trust you, Jack Carter." He paused, glanced at Imara, and added, "You are our friend."

Carter caught the quick look between them and frowned.

What do they know that I don't?

He felt a flurry of emotions in his head, which swept over his face. It was a mixture of pleasure, surprise, delight, uncertainty, and anxiety. He shifted in his seat as he tried to process it and come up with a coherent reply. He defaulted to his usual humor.

"Well, I guess if you're going to get all intense about it, then I have to say yes," he said with a crooked grin.

Alex smiled and looked pleased. "We are all agreed, then?"

Everyone nodded.

"We must administer the amṛta immediately. We were unconscious for approximately three days, but I do not know how it will affect you."

Carter nodded and stood. His palms were sweaty. "Fine by me."

The others followed suit as Alex went over to the bookshelves that hid the entrance to the workroom. The sorcerer waved his hand; the shelves obligingly disappeared to reveal a set of double doors. They opened soundlessly into the Earthen laboratory.

Alex stepped through and returned seconds later with the vessel of amṛta in his hands. The single portion of matter shimmered and swirled hypnotically in the covered jar. Carter stared at it, his mouth dry, feeling as nervous as he had as a teenager the first time he got lucky.

Alex gestured with his head toward the main hall as the doors to the laboratory closed, and the bookshelves promptly reappeared. They left the room and went up the stairs.

The house was quiet, and their steps were, too. They walked silently on plush crimson carpeting with an abstract golden pattern threaded sinuously throughout. The lights in the house were bright enough to see but gentle on the eyes, and the walls were all done in light colors with dark wood accents and polished metal fixtures.

They angled toward the bedrooms on the second floor. Alex turned into the first door on the left, which was directly across the hall from the Arsenaults. Imara entered last and closed the door, then sat on one of the two couches set to either side of a low coffee table. There was an easy chair at either end, forming a neat little sitting area.

Carter surveyed the room to distract himself from his nervous anticipation of what was coming.

Will I be like the Three when all is said and done, or will I just be an amped-up version of myself?

He shrugged off those thoughts because he didn't have a fucking clue, and speculating drove him crazy.

There was a beige and gray brick fireplace to the right of the door sandwiched between two large windows with gauzy curtains drawn across them. There were also two more windows on the right-hand wall set to either side of a door that led to a large walk-in closet. During the day, they'd let in lots of natural light despite both walls being interior.

On the left-hand wall sat a long, low dresser with a mirror. Straight across from the entrance was the door to the bathroom; Carter recalled thinking the bathroom was as large as his apartment in Columbia. He shook his head and admired the sizable bed against the far wall. It was a sprawling affair covered in pillows, fine sheets, and luxuriant heavy spreads, all done in crimson and gold to complement the tastefully subdued luxury of the room.

The sorcerer instructed the soldier to lie down on the bed.

Carter stepped on the heel of his left shoe with his right to pop his foot free; he reversed that for the other foot and kicked his sneakers out of the way. Imara wiggled a finger, and his shoes whisked up against the wall by the closet. He grinned at her and swaggered over to the bed, determined not to show his nervousness.

Alex walked ahead and set the jar on the left-hand bedside table. The sorcerer nodded toward the bed. Before Carter could lie down, Sirenī held up a hand.

"Wait!" she commanded.

Everyone looked at her in surprise.

She grinned and stepped up to Carter. He thought it was amusing how his thickly muscled figure dwarfed her petite curves, even though he wasn't overly tall. She looked at him, her eyes nearly level with his because of her chunky, high-heeled shoes.

"I can't take it anymore," she declared.

She reached out to cup his face. He started to lean back slightly, but she seized his head firmly for one so tiny. She narrowed her eyes in concentration. He felt a pleasant tingle buzz through his body. The vibrations traveled straight down his chest and belly to his cock and balls.

He was grateful he didn't get fully erect since he was wearing sweatpants without underwear, but his semi was apparent even at half-mast. Sirenī felt him squirm slightly and flicked her eyes down; she lifted them and winked.

"It'll be our secret," she mouthed.

She tugged his head lower to continue doing whatever she was up to.

Clearly, getting me hard isn't her goal, he thought with a crooked smile. He was nervous enough about the amṛta that his dick went flaccid without anyone but Sirenī noticing it.

She slid her hands up his face to his head. She gently raked them through his bushy curls; it felt nice, and he relaxed. She pulled her hands back and surveyed him critically. He felt an airy sensation around his jaw and scalp and frowned. He reached up and gasped. He'd been given a shave and a haircut! Carter ran his fingers over the neatly trimmed, reasonably lengthened hair on his head and his smooth jawline.

He dropped his gaze to Sirenī. "What gives?" he demanded.

He'd been rather fond of his shag after decades of military neatness.

She flashed an adorable smile and shrugged. "I couldn't take it anymore. Just because you came to another world and aren't sleeping with anyone doesn't mean you need to let yourself turn into a wild man." Her smile transformed into a saucy grin. "Besides, didn't that fellow from the gym, José, 'give you his digits,' as Richard described it?"

Carter let out a guffaw at her words and nodded. "He did, and this will make a nicer impression; I'll give you that."

She fluttered her lashes and sauntered over to sit next to Imara on the couch. Imara put an arm around her as they sat at an angle to watch the two men.

Alex smiled at Sirenī's antics and tipped his chin toward the bed. Carter lay down with a smile, but his nervousness reasserted itself as he waited.

Alex sensed his anxiety and tried to reassure him. "Relax. You will not feel anything." The sorcerer removed the vessel's cover and then focused. He levitated the remaining portion of the amṛta from the jar and held it above Carter's face. "Close your eyes."

The soldier obeyed and took a deep breath as Alex lowered the amber matter onto his forehead. In a moment, it spread out and disappeared into his body; the subtle glow faded swiftly as if it had never been. Carter twitched and sank into deep, dreamless unconsciousness.

Alexander consulted his internal chronometer and discovered it was sometime after midnight on Sunday morning. He turned to face his partners. "That was easy. Now we wait."

Six

The Three left Carter's room and headed up to their bedroom. The sorcerer set the empty monatomic vessel on the large dresser. He then snapped his fingers and retrieved from his aura the journal he'd found with the amṛta. He ran his thumb over the simple, unadorned cover, set it beside the jar, and patted it once before turning away.

The women sat on the end of the bed. He raised his eyebrows in anticipation as Imara and Sirenī began to remove their clothes; a sultry smile curved Sirenī's lips while Imara grinned at him. He sauntered over, his dick already stiffening as he became excited just from anticipating what was coming.

Sirenī shifted to her knees at the end of the bed as she stripped, and he stepped over and kissed her. At the same time, he fumbled with the button and zipper on his trousers, eager to get his pants off and feel his skin against theirs.

Imara helped, sliding her finger over the buttons on his shirt, which caused them to self-undo and released the fine fabric from his lean, muscular form. He wasn't bulky with thick slabs of muscle like Carter, but he was still well-built.

Alexander kissed Imara hungrily and crawled onto the bed with her and Sirenī as they invited him to lay between them. Sirenī shoved him onto his back, and he grinned at her rough handling, but Imara leaned down and caught his mouth again before he could react. She kissed him aggressively as Sirenī straddled his hips and sat slowly on his cock, not bothering with any other foreplay; he groaned into Imara's mouth as Sirenī's tight heat slipped over him.

Part of his mind noted that the behavior was unusual. They loved foreplay and enjoyed a slow buildup to their pleasure. Alexander liked to delay his climax for as long as he could, but he wasn't averse to a shorter fuck by any stretch.

It was just unusual for Sirenī to mount him so quickly. He didn't spare too much thought for it, though, distracted by the pleasurable sensations accompanying her actions.

The songstress broke off the kiss and stroked Sirenī's full breasts as she slid up and down his aching erection. He tugged Imara's breast to his mouth to kiss and lick her nipple. Then he reached over and pulled at her waist; she knew what he wanted and threw a leg over his head to straddle his face with her back to Sirenī.

Alexander gave himself entirely to the pleasure of sex with his partners, his mind blanking from worries about the future and how long Carter would be out of commission while the amṛta worked its way through his being.

Seven
Septem

Two days after they gave Carter the amṛta, Imara and Sirenī went into the workroom and shut the doors. There they experimented with their magic, practicing using gestures to cast spells. Imara was proficient at combat magic with gestures and had a knack for casting lightning bolts, and throwing fireballs, blades of ice, and gales of flesh-stripping frost.

Sirenī could teleport with a snap of the fingers, but her combat spells tended to form less coherently with gestures than words. It turned out she had even greater psychokinetic power: Imara conjured heavy objects that weighed up to fifteen tons, and Sirenī moved them with her mind and a graceful twiddle of her fingers. She could create impermeable fields that were denser and stronger and tune and adjust them with ease.

Overall, they were pleased with the improvement and decided to keep practicing their gestural spellcasting over the next few days—or until Carter woke up.

It never hurt to be prepared.

Three days came and went without Carter waking from his amṛta-induced coma. During that time, the government blockade around the property expanded to a tent city populated by federal agents, military, and Zalcent technicians sent to study the situation in the Western Foothills.

October 29 dawned cold and overcast. Twenty years ago, there'd already be snow on the ground, but the planet was warmer, and winters were milder. Still, people's breath fogged in the cold air, and the gray light felt heavy and oppressive. The soldiers and special agents staffed rotating watches. They froze their asses off at night but were often too warm during the height of the day.

Portable heaters that ran on solar batteries kept the tents on Route 26, other roads, and parking lots warm, but they could only do so much with the wind snapping at the canvas. It was still nippy when people stripped down and changed. Thankfully, DHS opened several rooms at the Pendleton Rest so the soldiers and agents could take showers regularly. They kept them short even though there was endless hot water, and the Rest made a killing on the service fees.

Life remained fairly routine inside the barrier once it became evident that the Three were correct, and no one could pass unless they'd been authorized. Jordan and Richard half-expected their cellphones and internet access to get suspended, their bank accounts frozen, and their Amazon deliveries to stop. None of that happened, though. Mail piled up on the ground outside the barrier, but no one felt safe getting it.

After a couple of days, Jordan brought the issue to Sirenī, who levitated the mail through the barrier. Then Alex solved the problem by creating a five-foot-high wooden cabinet. It was three feet wide and deep and sat on the ground to the right of Jordan's driveway. He put a plaque with her street number and requested that all deliveries be placed inside. Once the cabinet doors closed, the deliveries relocated to Jordan's porch in neat stacks.

Several special agents from DHS tucked themselves into the cabinet but didn't relocate to the porch; they merely got squished into the wooden armoire and had to get back out when nothing happened. One of them had the clever idea of getting in with a package; the parcel ended up on the porch, and the agent got out of the cabinet, swearing.

Those on the property didn't need deliveries, anyway. They could get whatever they wanted from the fabricator. Jordan and Richard weren't accustomed to the magical device and didn't feel comfortable using it yet, but it was the easiest way to have fresh food. They could get takeout from the Redbriar Bistro; the delivery driver merely placed the bags of food in the mail cabinet to send them to the porch.

Paul, Sue, and the kids settled into a routine over the first few days. They arrived on Sunday, and Sue enrolled her kids in online classes on Monday. They started Tuesday morning; Eric complained until Sue rounded on him with a glare that would have stopped a charging bull. He closed his mouth so quickly that he bit his tongue.

Sue, Eric, and Cassie walked across the Lower Forty to Jordan's and did about five hours of classes that first day, including an assessment. Eric scored ahead in math and science and slightly behind in language arts, so his classes were structured accordingly. Cassie did well across the board and seemed to enjoy her coursework.

She'd always been more biddable than her brother regarding schooling, but she was only in second grade while he was in sixth, so his classes were more demanding. Sue knew that school was still fun for her.

Imara and Sirenī came out of their twilight sleep Wednesday morning, and they knew. Alex watched them, bemused, as they leaped from the bed and hurried into the bathroom. The room was soundproofed, so they felt safe discussing a strange feeling they both had: a gentle fluttering sensation in their abdomens. It was unlike anything they'd felt before, even though Imara had already been pregnant.

The daughter of Medusa deftly delved Imara; the songstress turned her magical sight on Sirenī, and thus they confirmed their expectations. After some discussion, they decided to keep the news from Alex. With everything going on, they believed it was best for the sorcerer to focus on what he had in front of him without adding anything extra that might prove distracting. Their situation would continue for months, and they needed to ensure everyone was settled before they departed. They could tell their partner about his impending fatherhood soon enough.

Imara and Sirenī acted normal around their lover and friends. They exchanged secret smiles and held hands more than usual, but a lot was going on, so it didn't seem odd to anyone for the women to be more affectionate toward one another.

As Richard expected, Paul and Sue couldn't help but stare at the threesome. Everyone stared at Sirenī when they first met her because she was invariably the most beautiful person they'd ever seen. That was her magic, though; once people spent time with her, they tended to relax and act more naturally. Paul frequently scratched his head those first few days and tried to imagine how one man managed two women; he had all he could do to keep his marriage working well. Being from Earth, it never occurred to Paul that the Three supported each other, so Alex didn't have to "manage" anything.

Richard shrugged when Paul brought it up and explained that the travelers came from another world where that stuff was an everyday thing. Paul only half-believed Alex, Imara, Sirenī, and Carter were from another planet, but Sue never doubted it for a minute. She liked the strangers, but there was something about them; they didn't seem like they entirely belonged on Earth.

The situation at Grace Manor grew more complicated when half a dozen soldiers and federal agents charged into the facility. Special Agent in Charge Jennifer Kelly had planned ahead and sent in single, unattached females and males, people without partners or dependents who wouldn't be missed if they fell under the sway of the cult.

The soldiers and feds came out an hour later and threw all their gear on the pavement in the side lot, including their phones, smartwatches, and other electronic devices. Meanwhile, the people inside the facility had unplugged or deactivated every computer or other device and were cut off from the news and the web. Such sensible precautions meant no one outside could hack the Internet of Things and spy on the residents via connected devices.

The tree in the courtyard remained in full glory as if it were high summer instead of nearly winter. The rainbow-hued, apple-like fruits fell daily, and everyone there ate them regularly. The apples sustained their health despite lacking other foodstuffs, and no one went hungry.

Alexander knew those in the facility had asked for his assistance. On Wednesday, after he, Imara, Sirenī, Jordan, Richard, Paul, Sue, and the kids ate breakfast, he went to the library in the manor and projected his avatar to Grace Manor.

He appeared in the courtyard amid a small gathering of people sitting around the tree. They seemed to be meditating. The square was a comfortable temperature, and the people looked at ease despite the lateness of the season and the briskness of the weather. In this place the great tree thrived, and in its presence the people flourished, too.

Alexander studied the occupants of the courtyard but turned when someone spoke.

"Please, come this way," a young man said serenely.

The fellow was dressed all in white, his head was shaved, and his bottom lip, nose, eyebrows, and ears were pierced. Body adornments were typical on Gaea, though seeing this many on one person was unusual. Alexander scanned the young man's aura and found several other piercings, at which he cocked his head and raised an eyebrow.

He couldn't stop himself from asking a personal question. "Did the nipple and penis rings hurt?"

His tone was so mild the young man just smiled and shrugged philosophically. "Having holes punched through your body is always gonna be a little uncomfortable, right?"

Alexander nodded and followed his guide into the facility through one of the four doorways off the square. Inside, people were everywhere. The building was full to bursting with the original occupants, their families, and pets. People had heard of the Miraculous Event and came seeking help, enlightenment, or whatever they needed. Alexander didn't think there was enough space left to stuff even a single additional person, but the facility was peaceful.

The sorcerer heard their destination before he saw it. A woman cried out in pain, punctuated by Hélène Castonguay's steady voice telling the woman she was doing great. Based on what he heard, he knew immediately that the woman was giving birth.

The young man stopped outside the room and gestured Alexander past him. The sorcerer nodded his thanks and went inside. He discreetly studied the laboring woman squatting near the side of the smallish room while a tall man, on his knees, held her forearms in his strong hands, and two other women supported her from the sides. There was barely any room for him to stand unobtrusively out of the way.

Hélène was behind the expectant mother, down low, facilitating the delivery. Alexander grimaced, appalled at the woman's pain. Without hesitation or forethought, he cast a healing spell. Such practices were standard fare on his homeworld, and the woman instantly relaxed as the magic washed over her. Her reddened face softened, her body eased, and her breathing evened out. He knew the pain was still there—she was giving birth, and nothing could change that—but it was distant now.

Hélène looked over her shoulder at him and smiled but never stopped talking to the woman. The man—he assumed it was the baby's father—and the other two women gaped at him, their mouths open in wonder. He smiled at them but raised his eyebrows and nodded toward the woman giving birth; they looked chagrined and focused their attention where it belonged.

Alexander stood still and tall for twenty minutes while the woman birthed her child. The baby howled within moments of emergence from the birth canal, red-faced and with a good set of lungs.

"It's a girl," Hélène told the mother and father.

They cried from the intensity of the experience.

Hélène cleaned the baby and delayed cutting the umbilical cord for about a minute; then, she tied it off while one of the other women severed it. The mother had been assisted into the bed by then, and they placed her baby in her waiting arms. She looked across the room at Alexander.

"Thank you," she said softly. "I feel great."

She laughed giddily while her partner grinned sappily at her and his daughter.

"You are quite welcome," Alexander said kindly.

The father looked at Alexander and nodded in appreciation.

The sorcerer smiled and waved away his expression of gratitude—he'd hardly done anything. It only seemed incredible to Earthen people because they lived without the gift of magic. He waited while Hélène wrapped up with the parents and newborn.

She joined him by the door and smiled. "Please follow me," she said.

Alexander considered her as they walked down the hall. Hélène was changed from the bitter, burned-out woman he'd first met when he stepped through the doors of Grace Manor with Carter. She'd been on edge, her body and mind exhausted by her job and the pain and suffering in which she immersed herself every shift she worked. Now, she looked healthy. She seemed serene and glowed with a radiance that shone through her aura with pure, bright colors that moved in liquid swirls.

He blinked to open his third eye and looked at the people of Grace Manor with his psychic sight. Their aurae shimmered with the luminous qualities of tranquility, peacefulness, and hope. The facility glowed with soft pastel colors, and the miasma of pain and despair was gone, washed away by the spell he'd cast just over a week ago.

It was hard to believe how much had happened since.

Hélène walked past the door leading to the courtyard and down a corridor to another room. He followed her into the room and raised his eyebrows at the broom-closet-sized space. A chair and desk sat against the left-hand wall; there was nothing else because there wasn't room for more.

Hélène smiled at his expression. "We work with what we have. Space is at a premium, even with every room except the bathrooms given over to housing people now that we've run out of food in the kitchens."

Alexander frowned. "I will speak with my Earthen friends about arranging food deliveries. I am certain we can come up with something. If not, I will figure out something else."

She nodded appreciatively, her eyes lighting with gratitude. He spoke quickly to fend off further thanks—he was arrogant and smug, but he didn't like an excess of praise.

"I was told by mutual friends that you wanted to see me?"

His hurried change of topic amused her.

"We need your help. Molly and I had several dreams in which members of our movement, or whatever you want to call this," she waved a hand in a circle to include the entirety of Grace Manor, "move to other locations. In the dreams, they bring a single apple from the Mother Tree with them and place it in the ground. It grows a Daughter Tree and creates a place of hope and healing for others."

She paused and added, "And Lord knows, we need that right now."

"How many times have you had this dream?"

"Every night since the fourth day after you came and saved us."

"I did not save anyone. Eliminating suffering is not saving—all I did was cure the diseases affecting the people here," he corrected gently.

Hélène looked skeptical. "Alex—may I call you that? You healed people of diseases that kill them. Everyone here was dying, including all the other staff and me. You didn't just cure diseases; you opened our hearts and gave us hope." She smiled. "You can squirm all you want, big boy, but you saved us."

"Ugh," he grunted. He felt uncomfortable, which was an unfamiliar and unpleasant experience for him. "Very well," he acknowledged grudgingly. "If we must call it that…"

"We must," she said crisply.

He glowered for a moment. "Okay," he conceded, surrendering to the inevitable. "While humility is an infrequent experience for me, I feel humbled by your words and appreciation."

"You're welcome," she replied sincerely.

Alexander gratefully switched topics. "Regarding your dreams, it seems a greater force is calling you. I have worked with an ascended being called Valas Amris. Sometimes celestial beings work through conduits at this density of the prāṇamaṇḍala to facilitate transformation. I believe this is what is happening with you."

"First, I don't completely understand anything you just said,"

Hélène laughed, "but I get the gist. That said, how do we do this? We can't leave because we'd be arrested and detained by the government in a heartbeat. The only reason we're safe is that everyone who comes in becomes so hopeful and content that they never leave. But we don't have any space left, and things are reaching a tipping point."

"The solution is simple," he assured her. "It will take me a day or so, but I will create a device to allow you to send two people at a time to other locations. You will need to know the name of the place and its general location for the device to work."

Hélène's eyes gleamed; she clasped her hands with happiness. "Thank you so much, Alex!" she cried joyously.

He smiled, then reared back as she dove in for a hug. She gave him a quick, firm squeeze and darted from the tiny space. He blinked, let his avatar dissipate, and opened his eyes. He was in the library, surrounded by the books, treatises, and grimoires he loved so much.

He inhaled deeply and pushed himself to his feet. He waved a hand to reveal the doors to his laboratory and walked through. He stepped through the Abyssal Gate to his workroom on Gaea. He smiled fondly at the familiar chamber with its Spaera Mystica and tables full of parts, pieces, and artifacts half-built or half-disassembled.

He opened his psychic sight and examined the far corner of the workroom. A complex wizard's web of shields, Obscurati, and other enchantments protected his greatest treasure: the Dawntime Grimoire.

The Pāskendiñoldor was an ancient book, though he didn't know its actual age. The author was a being named Therendik. Alexander didn't know the wizard's gender, place of origin or anything else about them. The book was written in Darhavil and contained powerful spells and rituals that most mages could never memorize or hope to cast.

Even Alexander wasn't sure just how much he understood about the enchantments. He thought he grasped them, but who knew? There weren't any other people from Darhavilon alive for him to compare notes with.

It was a priceless treasure, and other wizards and even the Unified Government would kill to have it. Thankfully, most people believed it was a myth, though he didn't understand why: he'd used a spell from the book to save the world from Sogma and destroy the Abyssal Gate.

Where did the people of his homeworld think he learned such a powerful enchantment?

He shook his head, blinked to close his psychic sight, and turned toward the tables arrayed against the wall. On one of the tables, he had a chunk of polished, sparklingly clear locrunite, a gleaming jewel the size of a grapefruit.

"You will do nicely," he told the gem.

He sliced it in half with a beam of magic and held the faceted gem in his hands. This form of locrunite was easy enough to create with magic, but it took a lot of power, and he was glad he already had this one at hand. It was a byproduct of his experiments that created the monatomic vessel for the amṛta and Imara's autolenses.

He took a deep breath and called to mind the spellforms of the Et Alas Mercurii, a spell of rapid transit. The sorcerer brought the spellforms to mind and went over them carefully. He wanted to ensure the enchantment would do what he wanted so long as Hélène and Molly supplied it with the correct targeting information. He knew the magic inside out but took his time evaluating it anyway.

It never hurt to be cautious.

After several minutes, he decided the spell would be perfect with a few adjustments. He manifested the spellform in the air before him and made the requisite changes, then recited the words to anchor the enchantment in the locrunite hemisphere.

The arcane geometries flexed and warped, forming a cage around the chunk of crystal and slowly contracting until they sank into the gem. From the right angle, he could see the spellforms glimmering within the stone. He finished the incantation and smiled, pleased.

He estimated the project took him about fifteen minutes. The ease with which he'd embedded the spell into the locrunite was pleasantly surprising. He revised his estimate of the effect of the amṛta on his powers with this new piece of data. Before taking the nectar, he expected a working like this would take him two hours. It took him months to etch each of Imara's autolenses with the Epiphany of Light, and it was brutal, painstaking work.

Even though embedding the traveling spell into the gem was more straightforward than etching the Epiphany of Light, it still went faster than he'd expected. He grinned and snapped a white cloth into existence; he wrapped the hemisphere neatly in the fabric, took one last look around his arcane workroom, and stepped back through the Abyssal Gate to Earth.

He placed the wrapped crystal on an empty table in his laboratory and exited the room. The door swung shut behind him, and the bookcases reappeared. He left the library and went to check on Carter.

Imara decided to take a bath while Alex was occupied at Grace Manor. She filled the colossal tub in the bathroom of the primary suite with hot water and conjured a fragrant tea mixture. She scattered the herbs and leaves in the swirling water filling the big basin and smiled as her favorite blend filled the air with its luxuriant fragrance. The songstress let her clothes dissipate.

She slipped into the tub and let her mind wander through the phases of her life, which she divided into segments based on notable events that bookended each period. She leaned back in the perfectly contoured tub lazily waving her hand to stop the water's flow as she relaxed.

She thought about her first sexual encounter with Alex. She'd shown him she was ready and wanted it to happen. He'd been his usual self—disciplined, restrained, reserved. She'd lost patience with him and demanded that he submit to her. Her vehemence had astonished him, but her desire for him was like physical pain in her body. She'd known that only being with him sexually would relieve the ache.

Then there was their time together before they went to find Sirenī in Glendale, and after she left home to be with them. That was a challenge to Imara because she felt so insecure about Sirenī's unbelievable beauty. Now her beauty was so familiar that Imara forgot how astonishing it was, but she was reminded of it now and again. Sirenī was always stunning and looked great, no matter what happened.

Imara felt dumpy, frumpy, and inescapably plain next to Sirenī, but they'd gotten over that after they fell in love. That was another watershed moment. She and Sirenī loved Alex, and he loved them with such unreserved devotion it was difficult to be jealous. Of course, there had been some ups and downs, but they'd pulled together and gotten past it.

Imara and Sirenī developed a love that existed independently of their male partner. Their love felt miraculous and wonderful, and it was pivotal, for without that bond, they wouldn't have been able to help Alex save the world. They would have fallen apart under the tremendous strain of what they endured if they hadn't been able to lean into one another unconditionally.

When Alex came to her in Louden after their forced separation, the birth and loss of Layton, and her blindness, they'd made passionate love. The smoldering coals of her passion burst into bright, cleansing flames. The fire disintegrated all her worries into a pile of ash that blew away.

That fire left only unyielding determination behind. She mentally flitted over recent events: taking the amṛta, fleeing Gaea, forgiving Carter, meeting Jordan and Richard, and settling on Earth. It had all happened so fast.

Now she was going to travel through time—but even though she'd heard the spell's words, she had no fucking clue how to cast it. Spells were more than just incantations: they were formulae applying programs to reality for those who could use them. She trusted everything would reveal itself but was still afraid despite her confidence.

When Imara returned to the bedroom, she spied the monatomic crystal vessel centered atop the dresser. Beside it sat Alex's journal, the one he'd found with the amṛta. She decided to peruse the journal and settled herself in one of the chairs in the sitting area.

When she'd held the book in the Nephilim Temple, she'd hummed a melody to reveal any magical power in the book but found none. Now, as she looked at it through her autolenses, she saw an oblique, diffuse glow around the pages. She narrowed her eyes, then closed them, but she saw things the same with her eyes opened or closed—the Epiphany of Light granted her the ability to see anything, anywhere, from any point in time.

Eyelids can't prevent that.

She smiled wryly at that thought and opened the cover of the book. She recalled the first page was blank and was about to flip to the next page, but her eyes fell on the sheet of parchment, and she gasped. Shimmering lines of text slithered across the surface and formed into a fine script. Each letter was incredibly tiny, but she could read it easily with her enhanced sight. She studied the iridescent ink since she'd never seen anything like it, but she couldn't identify it if her life depended on it.

 She frowned and focused on the words. Her eyebrows almost crossed her forehead and merged with her hair as she read, so great was her amazement. She stiffened in her seat and hurriedly flipped pages.

Eight
Octo

Sirenī sat with Jordan at the dining table, chatting quietly, while Sue monitored her children in the living room. She could hear the woman instructing her children, her tone even and patient. Sue had a background in primary education, even though she'd gotten pregnant with Eric young enough that she hadn't done much with it. Jordan had explained to Sirenī that Sue was more than up to the task of schooling her kids when she'd asked.

Sirenī developed a sudden craving for donuts and lattes while chatting with her Earthen companion. She hesitated, then grew irritated that yet another government was trying to control her and her partners. She felt the anger burn in her breast. It was mainly targeted at the Ministry but overflowed toward the people in this world doing the same thing.

What is it about governments and their operatives that make them such overbearing assholes? she thought irritably.

"Are you wearing the pendant I conjured for you?"

Jordan blinked in surprise. "Uh… No, I'm not, but I usually do."

Blushing, she told Sirenī she had to take it off when she and Richard fooled around. She liked to be on top, and the heavy pendant often swung into his face when she leaned over to kiss him. Sirenī laughed, and Jordan relaxed, then finished her tale: after bopping him on the teeth and nearly taking out his left eye, she took it off because she just wanted to have sex and not cause her partner grievous bodily harm.

When she'd recovered, Sirenī offered a helpful suggestion. "Might I suggest you flip it around when you're on top so it's on your back?"

Jordan laughed and nodded. "That would be simpler!"

"Would you mind getting your pendant? I want to get a latte and donut, and you're more than welcome to come with me, but I'd like you to be prepared. I'm sure we'll be fine."

Her friend stood and hurried upstairs, returning moments later with the heavy locrunite pendant hanging between her breasts. Sirenī stood and smiled when she saw the golden chain around Jordan's neck.

"It has powerful enchantments to protect you from pretty much everything." Sirenī reminded her.

She leaned over and rested her left hand on Jordan's shoulder. A magician didn't need to touch passengers to take them when they teleported—but she'd only practiced the teleportation spell with a snap a few times in the workroom. She didn't want to appear in the Mug and realize she'd left Jordan in the dining room. She snapped her fingers, and the infinite darkness of the spell embraced them for just a moment.

They appeared in the Indigent Mug with a pop of displaced atmosphere. Sirenī turned a dazzling smile on the crowded café, instantly captivating the agents and soldiers sitting at the tables or standing around talking. They stared at her, mouths slack, unable to tear their focus off her.

If one of them had a sufficiently developed will, they could break such a low-level enchantment. She waited for ten seconds, but no one moved. She spun around with a regular smile for the proprietor. Persephone grinned at the two of them.

"Nice to see you, ladies!" she called.

She beckoned them to the counter past the people standing in line staring at Sirenī. They all turned and kept the daughter of Medusa in their sights as she and Jordan strolled to the counter. Jordan felt self-conscious with everyone tracking them.

"This is a clusterfuck, isn't it?" Persephone groused as they reached the register.

She irritably gestured to include the contents of her shop and the tent city in the parking lot outside.

Sirenī looked around the room before turning her attention to the sturdy redhead behind the counter. "Persephone," she began, pronouncing her name as the ancient Greeks would, "why are you so relaxed after I just teleported us in here?"

The Mug's owner laughed and glanced at Clear. They stood at the espresso bar and continued making beverages as if magic happened around them daily.

"My dear woman," Persephone began after she got her laughter under control, "I'm relaxed because I'm comfortable with magic. I'm not from Earth, either."

Jordan gasped, wide-eyed at the revelation. Sirenī knew the two women had known each other for years.

"I should have known. You've always been so calm and even about all this." She gestured gracefully to the customers and tents outside the store to include the blockages, cordons, and investigators. "All this shit hasn't got you ruffled. We're from Gaea, World One. Where are you from?"

A calculating glint came into Persephone's eyes, and she stared at Sirenī for a moment. "World Seventeen," she replied with a slight challenge.

Sirenī nodded. "Ah. Anïj Vor."

Persephone nodded, impressed.

"Beautiful world," Sirenī continued. "They integrated vampires about two thousand years ago, didn't they? I recall reading about it once. Unfortunately, that's all I remember about it."

"Good memory," Persephone complimented. "I was born there and raised by my uncle after my parents were killed."

There was a clatter from the end of the counter. The women turned and saw Clear staring at their mother, almost accusingly.

"You've never told me all of that, but you tell Sirenī and Jordan in the middle of the coffee shop like we're all chatting over dinner?" they scowled.

Persephone glanced at them apologetically. "I'm sorry, baby. I didn't mean to share it this way. I always meant to tell you, but…the time never seemed right. You're from Earth. So why should it matter how my parents died? It was such a long time ago, and you never even met them. Let's keep the past in the past. Besides, you've been to Anïj Vor several times to visit with Uncle Berannon and Uncle Vic," she reminded them.

Clear didn't look mollified—they just grunted and turned back to the espresso machine. Sirenī heard them muttering about their mother. It was clear Persephone would have some explaining to do with her child later on.

It struck Sirenī when the Mug's owner said, *"A long time ago."* Persephone's tone made it clear she meant decades or centuries, not years. Sirenī opened her psychic sight and nodded when she confirmed her suspicions. Persephone Plunkett was a semilamia—a half-human, half-vampire hybrid that only a queen- or kingmaker could create by using the vampiric essence to save a life without turning the individual into an Undying.

A regular vampire could turn a human, but there was a greater risk of failure during the transition, and generally, such fledglings were weaker than those turned by a maker. The stronger and older the vampire, the more powerful the gift they conveyed and the more likely their bite was to be successful.

Semilamiae were exceedingly rare; Sirenī had only read of two others. Most vampire makers turned people entirely, but whoever bit Persephone hadn't wanted to make her a vampire for some unknown reason.

"Fascinating," the daughter of Medusa murmured. She shook off her distraction with a toss of her curly hair. "We've been dying for donuts and a latte."

Persephone looked relieved when Sirenī changed the subject. "Two dozen vegan donuts, coming right up. I'll throw some other goodies in, too."

"None of this lot," she added with a curl of her lips as she glanced around the shop, "deserve the fancy options I keep for all of you."

Sirenī and Jordan laughed and looked around at the federal agents and men and women in military fatigues. Everyone was armed and looked dangerous, but they stared at Sirenī and watched her every move with their mouths slack.

Hmm. I'll have to remember this the next time I think of my fatal beauty as a curse instead of a blessing, Sirenī thought.

For the first time in a long time, she felt proud to be descended from Medusa.

Sirenī and Jordan chatted idly with Persephone and Clear until their order was ready. Persephone remarked that none of her employees would come to work as things stood. She hoped that after a week or so, her employees would feel safer and be willing to show up for their shifts. Even with just the Plunketts running the place, it only took about eight minutes to get everything together. Clear and their mother had to fill a long list of orders after they left, though.

Jordan grabbed the two lattes, and Sirenī picked up the box of donuts. They said goodbye to Persephone and Clear. Sirenī stretched with her free hand, rested her knuckles on Jordan's shoulder, and awkwardly snapped her fingers. The Mug sluiced away from them, and the dining room tumbled crazily into place. The enchantment pushed matter out of their way as they manifested, air whooshing away from the volume they occupied.

Sue must have been coming back from the downstairs bathroom. She caught them teleporting in and fell into the easy chair in the living room as her legs gave out. Eric and Cassie craned their heads to look at the women when their mom toppled into the chair as if her strings had been cut.

Sirenī glanced casually at Sue to make sure she was breathing normally and was satisfied when Sue started to sit up. Jordan looked relieved, then grinned sheepishly.

The daughter of Medusa set the box of baked goods on the table and took one of the lattes from her friend. "Persephone was unexpected," she remarked in an aside to Jordan.

"I was shocked by her blasé attitude," Jordan said quietly, keeping an eye on Sue. "What's up with her being from another world? I've known her for years, and I never suspected!"

Sirenī nodded as she retrieved a glazed chocolate donut with toasted coconut sprinkled on top. She took a bite and savored it for a moment. "She obviously puts effort into fitting in here, but she isn't aging at a normal rate. She must move around a bit to keep people from picking up on her unique nature. Humans would notice that someone isn't aging after ten years or so, so she can't have been here any longer than that."

Jordan shook her head. "Persephone's owned the Mug for twenty years." She sipped her latte and nibbled on a strawberry-frosted cake donut. "I'm not sure how she's managed that. I've known her since I was in my teens, but I never noticed that she doesn't seem to age."

"Ah. She probably has confoundation wards in her aura, or in some piece of jewelry she wears, something like that. It would keep people from noticing if she targeted the spellforms to her age or appearance," Sirenī explained.

"I get it; she's trying to be inconspicuous, which makes sense…but you four aren't trying to fit in." Jordan raised an eyebrow. "You hornswoggled those people in the Mug without lifting a finger. It's inspiring, Sirenī."

Sirenī laughed and looked embarrassed. "Thanks, love." She flashed a smile. "Can you even imagine Alex trying to act like an Earthen person? He cast a healing spell in the middle of an eldercare facility without considering the consequences for the people or us."

Jordan swallowed her first bite and laughed heartily.

Eric and Cassie entered the dining room, and their eyes lit up when they saw the donuts. Sirenī gestured for them to take one apiece and to take one to their mother. Sue would benefit from a boost to her blood sugar. The kids gleefully took the donuts and darted back to the living room, giggling.

On Wednesday evening, Carter remained unchanged, and Imara and Sirenī were doing their own things. At loose ends, Alexander returned to Grace Manor earlier than he'd expected.

The sorcerer teleported into the main foyer with the cloth-wrapped gem. A white-clad occupant hurried off to fetch Molly and Hélène.

They came and greeted him warmly. Then they turned on their heels, and Molly beckoned for him to follow.

Alexander followed the women into a spacious common room. He surmised the residents tried to keep this space open so everyone could gather there. A sizable portion of the population currently filled the space while leaving a clear area near the entrance.

Alexander idly scanned the crowd and saw the ramrod-straight postures of men and women who clearly had military experience. He also saw the young man with the piercings and nodded politely while considering the backgrounds of the people called to stay at Grace Manor and what purpose they might serve in the future.

Just what did I create when I helped the original occupants of this place? he wondered.

He thought about whether what he'd done was a good thing and decided it was. He flashed back to the pain and hopelessness he'd felt; the haze of suffering was so strong even Carter felt it with his limited psychic abilities.

Alexander realized everyone was waiting and returned his attention to the crowd with a smile. He flipped away the fabric that covered the locrunite hemisphere and held it up so everyone could see the softly glowing gem.

People craned their necks to look at it while he explained how to operate it. The device was certainly simple enough: the person using it needed to visualize the destination they had in mind while resting one hand on the gem and touching the traveler with the other. Two people could be dispatched in a twelve-hour window, after which the device needed about that long to recharge.

After Alex explained its operation, Molly and Hélène repeated his words back to him to ensure they'd understood what he'd said. He confirmed they were correct, and they turned to beckon two people forward from the crowd. A young man in his twenties and a woman in her forties, both in white, stepped forward. He had stubble and short hair while the female's hair touched her ears on the sides and was longer on top. They had the same quiet serenity as everyone at Grace Manor.

Eight

Molly held the crystal hemisphere in her left hand and looked at the woman. "Are you ready, Sister?"

The woman nodded fearlessly. She carried a small shoulder bag with a few essentials, and her traveling companion had the same. The most important items were the two apples they were bringing to their destination: one to eat and one to plant if everything went according to plan.

"Be safe," Molly said softly and touched her shoulder.

The woman nodded again, and the crystal flickered with shimmering, orange-red light. The woman disappeared with a whoosh of air. After a few seconds, the crystal hemisphere regained its naturally lucent transparency. The young man stepped forward; Alexander saw his eyes shine with fervor. Molly repeated herself almost verbatim with him, only substituting Brother for Sister, and then sent him on his way. After the second translocation, the locrunite hemisphere turned a cloudy, iridescent white.

Molly looked at Alexander questioningly.

"The artifact needs to recharge, at which time it will regain a clear appearance," he explained.

She thanked him and turned to her flock. The remaining people cheered and applauded as she showed them the cloudy crystal. They came forward and crowded around Alexander, Molly, and Hélène. They shook his hand, touched his arms and shoulders, and peppered him with compliments. Some asked questions about who he was or where he came from. He told them the truth without elaboration, though he didn't bother explaining how he did "those crazy, cool things," as one resident put it. After a few minutes, the people dispersed in pairs or small groups.

"They took that rather well," Alexander murmured when he was alone with the two women.

"They trust and believe in miracles," Molly said simply.

Alexander nodded while Molly wrapped the crystal hemisphere in its white cloth and clutched it tightly. Despite being nearly one hundred—Alexander knew that was ancient on Earth—she looked vibrant and lively. Her hair had a glossy dark shine that made her look fifty years younger than she was, if not more.

"Where did you send them?" he asked.

Hélène answered that the first location from their dreams was a small hospital in North Carolina. "The facility houses several hundred people and has a wing dedicated to terminal childhood conditions."

"Do you hear words in your dreams, or do you have an internal knowing?" he asked.

Molly frowned in thought. "I get an internal knowing."

They looked at Hélène. "I also have the feeling, but I hear the place's name. I see it written out somewhere in the dreams, too, like on a slip of paper, a sign, or a brochure." She frowned. "That's how I remember it, anyway."

Alexander said, "Either way, you are doing what your dreams urge. Now you must see if the messages change." He took a deep breath. "My partners and I must leave soon. I do not know when we will return, but I hope quickly. I will speak with my Earthen friend about getting you food weekly. It may not be much."

Molly reached out a hand and rested it on his biceps. She smiled luminously. "Thank you for everything you've done. Any food you send our way will be helpful. We're so grateful to you, Alexander Eldred. Our lives have a purpose now, and we can share hope with the entire world. The Miraculous Event will live on and keep growing." Tears welled in her eyes. "May I hug you before you leave?"

He smiled, nodded, and embraced the tiny woman gently. He felt the strength burning in her body and spirit. Then he shook Hélène's hand when Molly stepped back.

Sirenī returned to the house that evening and found Imara curled up in the sitting room in sweatpants and a loose, comfortable shirt that covered her from neck to wrists and waist.

Imara looked up from a small, familiar-looking book when Sirenī entered the room. The songstress smiled and scooted her legs back on the couch to make room, and the daughter of Medusa sat down at an angle to her partner. Sirenī crossed her thighs and smoothed her embroidered skirt as she nodded toward the book.

"A little light reading?" she asked in Demurrian.

Imara nodded and replied in the same tongue. "Alex put it on the dresser beside the amṛta vessel, so I thought I'd take a look. It turns out to be fascinating reading...." She hesitated, then added, "And it turns out to have another layer of text, written by…well, me."

Sirenī's eyes widened, and she snapped her fingers, her chic cream blouse loosening into a shirt that matched Imara's style. At the same time, her skirt billowed down her legs and shifted to form comfortable, loose-fitting pants. Now dressed comfortably, the daughter of Medusa turned to face her partner and crossed her ankles under her thighs. Imara mirrored her pose, and they leaned toward one another.

"Tell me everything," Sirenī demanded.

Imara held up a hand. "There are passages here that I warned myself not to share, but I'll tell you what I can. There's some exciting stuff in here. But first, let me start with some news I discovered. We're pregnant—for eight years."

Sirenī's jaw dropped. "Fuck that! I can't waddle around for eight years!" she protested.

Imara laughed and hushed her. "We'll be in the first trimester that whole time. Everything will be fine, but it is the way it is."

Sirenī frowned. "Well, I suppose if it's the first trimester the entire time, I can manage it."

Imara held out the book. Sirenī snatched it from her hands and flipped through the pages. She saw only the same faded text, abstract diagrams, and passages written in Darhavil and Saṃskṛta that she'd seen when she glanced through it previously.

Dejected, she returned it and said, "It's the same as when I first looked."

Imara flipped to a page she'd dogeared in the first third of the journal. She flipped it around, and Sirenī looked at the content. She saw the Saṃskṛta abjad written in an eye-strainingly tiny hand and the neat, well-formed shapes of Darhavil script. She looked from the pages back to Imara's face, eyebrows raised.

"On these two pages, I wrote the time travel spell I heard myself casting, which I mentioned to you and Alex a few days ago."

"Go on," Sirenī urged.

"The spell is particular; it requires proximity to an Infernal Gate to work. I have to cast it within a quarter mile of a Temple or Gatehouse to travel back or forward in time. The constancy of the Nephilim structures provides a stable element so the time travel spell can anchor as we go."

The songstress paused and licked her lips. "We're not allowed to tell Alex anything."

Sirenī leaned back, frowned, and drummed her fingers on the back of the settee. "I guess I can understand that. I'm dying to know everything you've written, of course, but I can't even imagine the burden of knowing what's coming, written by yourself at some unknown point in your life, but left for Alex to find at some point in his...."

Imara sighed and dropped the small book into her lap. The tight binding caused it to flip shut. "It's strange. I feel dislocated, having a map for some future portion of our lives but knowing I must keep most of it to myself. The time travel period isn't that long from start to finish, though, so it's not like I read about the next fifty years of our lives or anything."

"That's good," Sirenī said. "So, is there anything else you can tell me?"

"Yes. You'll need to defeat a spell called the Kathreftis tou Narkissou."

Sirenī thought about the spell name and quickly placed it: the Mirror of Narcissus.

It was a Grade Seven enchantment. It could reflect anything—light, magic, electromagnetism, or solid objects—at a target, a point of origin, or wherever the caster designated. It was complicated to cast because it created an impermeable, localized field effect that functioned as both a lens and a mirror. From one side, a person could look straight through and enhance or magnify any objects or even cast spells; from the other side, the viewer saw only a solid, silvery screen, just like a mirror, that perfectly reflected anything before it.

"How can I counter it? Standard cancellation?" the daughter of Medusa asked, then shook her head before Imara could reply. "No, that won't work; the Mirror reflects everything, even cancellation spells. A standing wave can't be introduced into the spell because it can't reach the spell due to the distortion ahead of it."

Sirenī frowned, eyes narrowing as she wracked her brain.

Imara revealed, "I didn't write what you did in the journal, but I know you successfully dealt with the Mirror."

The daughter of Medusa gave a Carter-like half-shrug, a gesture all of them found themselves doing more often these days. "Oh, well. The situation will take care of itself one way or the other. We know I succeeded since you wrote about it, so I'll worry when the time comes. I know I'll figure it out because I did…do…will." She blew air between her lips as she tried to keep the concepts of time travel straight in her head. "Whatever!"

Imara laughed as Sirenī sat forward and grinned.

"I have some news of my own, as it happens."

Imara turned her focus from the journal to her partner. "What is it?"

"It turns out the erstwhile Persephone Plunkett is from World Seventeen!"

Imara gasped, and her autolenses glinted in the sitting room's warm light. "Are you certain? How did you find out!" she demanded.

"Yes, I'm certain. She told me. Jordan was with me at the time—we teleported to the Mug to get some donuts and beverages. When we got there, I charmed everyone in the café, and Persephone didn't bat an eye at either bit of magic. That's when Persephone told me about it."

Imara listened to Sirenī's paraphrase of the conversation with Jordan, Persephone, and Clear earlier in the day. The songstress was happy to have something else to focus her mind on—and the news that they were not the only people in the area from another world was somehow heartening.

Sirenī added, "She sent us home with two dozen donuts and a few other goodies. I left them on the table in the main hall, minus one each for Sue, Eric, Cassie, Jordan, and me."

"Excellent," Imara grinned. She leaned forward and kissed Sirenī lightly.

They stood up and walked out of the sitting room arm in arm into the main hall.

Paul was crossing through; he stopped nervously when he saw them and shifted from foot to foot as if uncertain how to address them. The songstress smiled and said hello to him, and he nervously mumbled a reply, staring at Sirenī as he darted past them and out the front door. The two women watched him go with some bemusement, then turned to the box of donuts, from which Imara gleefully took one and began to eat.

On her way to the kitchen, Jordan walked downstairs and saw Marquis sleeping on the couch with a couple of her black cats. She had no idea how he got out of the manor, but she knew how he got into her house: the pet doors she'd installed for her cats. Her all-black clowder seemed content to have the orange tabby wandering about. Even Emily, the crabby old lady, just ignored him from her lofty pinnacle atop the dining table.

Her felines had always wandered freely in and out of the house through the pet doors. Most of them were older and only went onto the farmer's porch once the weather turned cold, eschewing the chilly exterior.

Marquis barely fit through the pet doors. Jordan caught him squeezing through later that night, presumably on his way back to the manor. She watched him heave his stolid body and hefty belly over the lip of the egress points. She swore he looked exasperated as he struggled onto the porch. Once there, he turned, put his ears back, and sat down to glare at the offending portal.

It took him a few minutes to muster the energy to breach the second pet door, and it went about the same as the first. Jordan smothered her laughter with her hand as she watched him go.

Nine
Novem

Friday dawned sunny and clear; it was unseasonably warm, with temperatures hitting the mid-sixties. Usually, everyone in town would be celebrating Halloween, but because of the federal and military presence in the Oxford Hills, people were hesitant to do anything. They were also stressed because a vicious illness was spreading across the Middle East and had just reached Asia and Europe. No cases had been reported in the U. S., but everyone was still worried.

Sirenī popped into the Indigent Mug every morning to collect drinks and donuts for everybody at home. Since she knew Persephone and Clear were familiar with magic, she left Jordan at the house and levitated the pastry boxes and drink trays. She let enough of her fatal beauty off the leash to charm the other customers into unthinking immobility. Persephone told her people suspected something had happened, but the government wasn't letting on that magic was afoot.

Persephone didn't charge her for the food and drinks. When Sirenī held out Jordan's debit card, the semilamia waved it away. "This is the highlight of my day," she grinned. She gestured to her other customers. "These people aren't exactly the life of the party."

Sirenī laughed and glanced around the café. Everyone stared at her in slack-jawed wonder, but she could imagine they were usually pretty dour. "I can see that," she agreed. She nodded toward one of Persephone's employees. "I see some of your staff is back?"

Persephone grinned over at the girl, whose name tag read *Alyssa*. "Yes, she braved the insanity to come to work."

"I was sick of staying home with my boyfriend!" Alyssa exclaimed. She stood at her station making a pile of breakfast sandwiches. "God, he follows me around all the time and constantly asks for—" she stopped, blushing pink.

"Ha!" Sirenī barked. "Sex?"

Alyssa laughed and nodded.

"You're not alone. My partner is always after that, too."

Alyssa scoffed. "Well, that's a no-brainer—you're stunning." She smiled and tossed her long dark hair over her shoulder.

"Thank you, Alyssa. That's very kind of you!" Sirenī smiled and said goodbye to everyone before teleporting away.

It occurred to her when she got home that Alyssa had been calm about her using magic—perhaps Persephone had warned her ahead of time about Sirenī's abilities. She smiled and spread the food and drinks on the dining table. Alex and Imara teleported into the kitchen and walked through. She kissed them both, then turned and grinned at Jordan and Richard as they came downstairs.

Paul, Sue, and the kids came through the back door a few minutes later. She said hello to them, and they greeted her with more warmth than they had previously. She thought Eric and Cassie were adjusting better than their parents, but kids were always more adaptable.

Eric followed Alex around a couple of times, hoping to see something extraordinary. Sirenī knew that Alex cast simple illusions on both occasions to reward the boy's patience. One time, he created a pair of two-foot-tall knights in fancy, impractical armor riding pegasi. The warriors charged about on their winged steeds and fought demons, monsters, and dark knights in short but violent interactions in which the sorcerer never showed any blood or gore.

Eric loved every minute of it. He stared at the incredibly lifelike fabrications in awe. Sirenī thought he also exhibited some hero worship for Alex, which the sorcerer ran away from emotionally, if not physically. She figured Eric was trying to work up the courage to ask to see things like fireballs and lightning bolts but suspected he'd have to be satisfied by the phantasmic knights.

Sirenī and Imara caught Cassie watching them with a serious expression and trying to emulate their movements. She attempted to roll her hips when she walked, curl up on the couch and tuck her feet like Sirenī, or put her hands on her hips and raise an eyebrow in expectant admonishment like Imara when something—usually her brother—irked her. Sirenī confirmed with Sue that it was okay for Cassie to do that because she didn't want to tread on the other woman's toes and cause problems. Sue said she didn't mind and thanked Sirenī for checking in.

Jordan and Richard mentioned in passing that they enjoyed having Paul and Sue on the property. The foursome ate dinner every night since their arrival, hanging out at Jordan's house rather than the manor. Jordan told her that Paul and Sue were worried about dirtying the opulent estate or ruining the elegant furniture or appointments.

Sirenī shook her head, puzzled. "Don't they know they can't do that? Everything in the house has hysteresis patterns built in, so it's fully self-maintaining. They couldn't get the place dirty if they worked at it."

Jordan laughed. "I know, I tried to tell them. I think only time will help them become comfortable with it. You have to understand that building your home would cost millions of dollars here on Earth, so we worry about ruining nice things."

Sirenī raised an eyebrow. "What's the point of having something if you don't use it?"

"So everyone can see you have it," Jordan replied wryly.

"Ah, 'status symbols,'" Sirenī said, bemused. "How peculiar."

"Well, we've told them to relax and enjoy living there, but it's difficult for them to handle. Give them time," Jordan replied. "You know Richard and I aren't your typical Mainers, but Paul and Sue grew up with a lot of puritanical stoicism. They're more traditional."

"I'll keep that in mind," Sirenī told her friend.

Jordan and Richard had told Sirenī, Imara, Alex, and Carter about Puritanism. They'd explained that everyone growing up in Maine absorbed those mores along with the warm summers and cold winters.

They informed every aspect of the culture and lifestyle of Maine. While the postcards and calendars showed picturesque villages and beautiful scenery, the people embodied a vague cynicism and believed that life would always be hard.

Sirenī trusted the Arsenaults would relax in time.

Everyone collected their drinks and donuts and sat around Jordan's table while Eric and Cassie disappeared into the living room before they started their schooling. The adults had taken to leaving their phones off and in drawers because the cameras and microphones could be activated remotely. They also felt better having the devices out of sight in case the government attempted to hack them.

Living without cell phones wasn't an easy adjustment. The Earthen crew was addicted to their electronics and had never done without technology because it was so ubiquitous. People lived on social media, and Zalcent's Presence platform was particularly engaging. Everyone who used it loved how the algorithms worked. It was social media the way people wanted it to be. Even though Zalcent generated obscene amounts of revenue from the platform, they monetized the system without alienating their users. It was a delicate balancing act, but they somehow managed it.

The kids were miserable without their tablets, especially since Eric was an avid gamer. For him, the manor house felt like a prison even with all its attributes.

At least at Jordan's place, they could access the internet on their tablets and watch television. Sue had a laptop that she used to stay on top of her social media accounts when she was at Jordan's, and she allowed the kids to play on their devices during their lunch break and after school until dinner. She kept her cell phone off and in a drawer in Jordan's living room with all the others.

Jordan turned her phone on as they sat at the table and chatted. As soon as it powered on, it dinged to indicate an incoming message. The redhead smiled when she saw the sender but frowned when she read the news. She looked up from her phone and met her friends' curious and expectant gazes. They sat around the dining table in their usual places, with Sirenī, Alex, and Imara to her left and Richard, Paul, and Sue to the right. She keenly felt Carter's absence from his customary spot beside her fiancé.

"What is it?" Sirenī asked.

"It's a message from Drëndi."

Rather than explain, Jordan handed the phone to her. Sirenī quickly scanned the message, pursed her lips, and returned the phone to Jordan.

"Drëndi and Brent are in town and trying to get to us. They've driven along every road they can find on the map and can't reach the property. The government has it completely cordoned off, and their credentials can no longer get them through—the president officially took PID off the case and told them to have no further involvement," the redhead explained.

Everyone shifted at this news, some thoughtfully, others nervously, except for Alex. "The solution is simple." He stood up, pushed his chair back from the table, and stepped over to Jordan. "Tell them to come to the cordon near the Mug."

Jordan nodded and swiftly typed out a message, then looked up. "Drëndi read it." Her phone dinged an instant later, and Jordan read the message. "Give them ten minutes," she told the sorcerer.

Alex nodded and strode out the door. Everyone jumped up to follow as Jordan sent a thumbs-up emoji. She powered off her phone and stuffed it in the drawer with all the others as she zipped through the living room. The group blew past the slightly startled kids. Sue told Eric and Cassie to watch TV—no hardship there—and followed along, curious to see the foreigners in action.

Alexander marched down the driveway toward the road. As he approached the barrier with Imara and Sirenī close behind and the Earthen adults trailing, one of the people on the street saw him and began to shout, drawing the immediate attention of those nearby.

Soldiers came hustling up, rifles held in the low-ready position. They weren't aiming at the sorcerer, but the threat was clear.

Federal agents with an alphabet soup of acronyms on their jackets scurried among the soldiers. Special Agent in Charge Kelly marched through the group, drawing everyone's attention thanks to her olive skin, striking looks, and short, chic hair. She stopped before the barrier, marked on her side by traffic cones set across the roadway about a foot from the shield. Alexander strode to the end of the driveway and stopped. He planted his hands on his hips and stared across the invisible field effects, assessing the situation while the SAC stared back.

Her attention shifted to the people behind him, then returned to Alex. She spoke clearly and loudly. "Are you the foreign national in charge? I'm Special Agent in Charge Jennifer Kelly of the Department of Homeland Security. I'm authorized to negotiate a peaceful surrender for you and, I've been given to understand, three others who are," she coughed, "not of this world?"

"I am not in charge." The sorcerer gestured to Imara and Sirenī, who stepped up on either side of him. Agent Kelly's attention riveted to Sirenī for a moment, as was typical. "We are equivalent." He raised an eyebrow. "We require you to bring Brent Eton and Drëndi Sørensen to the barrier. If you do not, I will come out and…retrieve them."

His tone was mild, but his threat was also unambiguous.

Jennifer Kelly was having none of it. "I'm not sure you understand how this works. You're intruding on United States soil without the permission of the government. You don't make demands," she said aggressively.

Alexander stared skeptically at her. "You do not own the world, Special Agent Kelly, nor does the government that employs you. Furthermore, I do not require permission from you, your government, or anyone else."

He saw Imara lean back from the corner of his eye.

"This is going to end poorly," she muttered to Sirenī from behind him.

He kept his expression stern even though he wanted to smile.

"And you cannot stop me."

Agent Kelly reared back at his words and scoffed. "Are you shitting me with this?" she barked. She held out a hand and waved the military behind her forward as she stepped back. "You do not want to start a war with the United States, Mister!"

Alexander sighed, tired of oppressive governments and irrational fears. He extended a hand and snapped his fingers. Every firearm in a six-hundred-foot arc shattered along its internal shear lines and burst into so much useless metal, plastic, and scrap. He'd used this same spell to stop the cops from drawing on him when all this chaos began.

The military men and women jerked back as their firearms fell apart and bullets spilled to the ground unfired from the ruined clips and magazines. The ammunition tinkled and bounced across the asphalt. The soldiers and federal agents instinctively went for their sidearms, but those were broken, too, shattered in their gun belts and shoulder holsters.

Alexander started to step forward, but Imara put a cautionary hand on his upper arm. He looked at her, and she shook her head.

"Don't hurt them, Alex. They're doing their jobs, and we are foreigners here," she reminded him.

He nodded, and she let him go.

Kāmla looked up as her new administrative aide, Malcolm Edwards, knocked at the door and peeked his head inside. She nodded, and the young man slipped in. He stood straight and tall, like a soldier—he'd served in the Unified Military—and she saw him stop himself from saluting.

"Minister Vicchāya, illness has spread throughout Columbia. Twenty-four people have succumbed so far, and there are several reports of…altered individuals who are behaving erratically, but so far not dangerously." Malcolm hesitated, then added, "Several others have reported issues with buildings, cars, and other contrivances. You asked me to keep you apprised of matters like this."

"Yes, I did. Thank you, Malcolm," she said and waved him off.

He stood to attention, almost saluting again, then pivoted and marched out of the room without ever glancing at the robed figure in the corner.

When Malcolm closed the door, Kāmla turned to Ävidä, smiled, and said, "Well?"

Ävidä grinned as he strode from his customary place in the corner of her spacious office. "Everything is working exactly as the new spells were calibrated to do. The corruption destroyed Byrne faster than I could siphon off the power of the dying population, plus it annihilated the entire ecosystem and atmosphere. Somehow it even affected the sun, perhaps through the electromagnetic flux lines between the planet and the star…"

His voice trailed off, and he shook himself.

"Regardless, this version of the spell is superior in every way, and so far, it's working exactly as I desire." He stepped over to her and took her hands. "Soon, you and I will rule together, revered as the superior beings that we are."

He grinned at Kāmla and tugged her to her feet. She smiled predatorily and twined her arms around his neck. She pressed into him and felt his quickening erection through his robes as she tilted her face to receive his greedy kiss. She kissed him back, passionate and hungry for her own reasons, ones Ävidä Saclendra would never understand—not that he needed to, of course.

Alexander was sorely tempted to make an example of the men and women blockading the property, but Imara's cautionary words stayed his temper.

Yes, they are doing their jobs, and none of them are responsible for the decisions of their government. I see how we could be considered foreign nationals, but we just want to be left alone. We will be living on Earth for the foreseeable future. There is no point in making a total cockup of everything.

Everyone backed up as he stepped through the invisible barrier. The feds and soldiers struggled to process what had happened to all their firearms. A dozen enterprising soldiers drew their combat knives and assumed ready stances. The remainder of the soldiers and federal agents stared menacingly, most with their fists clenched and their faces tense.

Alexander raised his eyebrows and looked at Special Agent in Charge Kelly. Her hands rested on her hips since her gun lay in pieces at her feet. She slowly raised her left hand with the fingers splayed wide, presumably to keep everybody still. She stared at Alexander with a stern, fearless expression.

"I'm prepared to do whatever it takes to complete my mission," she said firmly.

Alexander nodded, swept his gaze across the scene before him, and then turned back to the SAC. "I understand, but I am also determined to do what I must to complete mine. If I fail, not only will this world be destroyed, but so will many others. My mission requires me to disregard yours. Once again, I ask you to allow Brent Eton and Drëndi Sørensen to come through your blockade."

Kelly shook her head. "I'm afraid I can't do that."

She turned, looked over her shoulder, and gestured with a chopping motion that immediately had ten soldiers moving forward, hands and knives ready; they closed swiftly and smoothly on Alexander. He watched them for a moment, then looked back at Kelly and shook his head as the nearest soldier shouted, "Get on your knees and put your hands behind your head!"

Sirenī looked at Imara. "Did that soldier just tell Alex to get on his knees?"

Imara had an anxious look on her face. "Yes, unfortunately. I hope he responds reasonably; these people aren't dangerous to us and are entirely within their rights to make a fuss about our presence."

Sirenī shivered with concern. "Yes, but Alex will never bow to anyone."

"I know." Imara sighed and shook her head as they watched the situation unfold.

Alexander extended his hands. The oncoming soldiers saw they were empty and assumed he would comply with SAC Kelly's demands. They were wrong.

Alexander summoned his magic and felt the pleasure of it flow through him, tingling deep in his chest and pelvis. Orange-red light gleamed around his hands, and he swirled his fingers in a graceful gesture. Whips of power flared from his hands and slapped into the soldiers approaching him and the semicircle of people behind them. Soldiers tumbled away from him and into their compatriots, clearing a space before him.

Kelly ducked and rolled under the chest-height energy bands with a gymnast's grace. She came to one knee and drew a knife from her right boot, but he snapped his fingers, and every blade within a hundred yards crumbled into shrapnel just as the firearms had. Kelly fell back with a cry of surprise, though the crumbling of her knife hadn't injured her. Soldiers and federal agents hollered and shouted as their combat blades and pocketknives burst apart in sheaths and pockets.

Alexander smiled and turned his palms out, then pressed them down. His magic radiated outward and targeted every vehicle within a few hundred yards. All but one were empty, so he pulled his magic back from it. He exerted his will on the SUVs, sedans, and Hummers and smashed their rooves into the interiors with a cacophony of twisting metal, shattering glass, and splintering plastic.

Vehicle alarms blared, and horns wailed in frantic, distorted warbles until he slammed every chassis into the ground so hard that some vehicles bounced up off the road. They spun in the air, their wheels splintering off their busted axles as the frames crumpled like paper and smashed back to the pavement.

Glass and plastic ricocheted from the hulks. The alarms cut out while the horns made a final deflating *bleeeeeeeep* as the ruined machines lay crumpled on the tarmac. Wheels rolled away from the shattered vehicles in graceless arcs and fell over with dull thuds as they ran out of steam.

The sorcerer put his hands on his hips, still glowing with his corona, and took a deep breath. He glanced around and cocked his head as people backed away, faces writ with fear.

Yes, you should be frightened.

He raised his voice. "Do not threaten us. Do not continue this absurd farce. I have not harmed any of you, and today, I will not." He glanced over his shoulder at Imara. She smiled appreciatively. "But I have limited patience and much to do." He smiled coldly. "In case you think this," he gestured at the ruin before him, with one SUV sitting pristine amongst the ruins, "is all I can do…"

He raised his arms over his head and spread his fingers toward the sky. His corona flared bright red around him, and wind whipped across the gathering. He didn't say a word as crimson lightning flashed from his fingertips. The thunder was deafening, and people reeled away from him, terrified, as a dozen bolts screeched into the sky. The lightning strobed and faded away, and he dropped his hands and surveyed the scene before him.

Everyone stared expectantly at Jennifer Kelly. She wasn't afraid of Alexander; she was angry and had a murderous expression. Her beautiful olive complexion was mottled and her jaw was clenched. Before she could open her mouth, two figures raced into sight, Brent huffing while Drëndi looked like she was out for a gentle stroll. They slowed as they came upon the scene; Alexander saw their eyes slide over everything, but he'd harmed no one. He could have destroyed everything with less effort than he'd employed while showing restraint.

Brent looked across the gap and met Alexander's eyes with an appreciative nod. He and Drëndi wound their way through the feds and soldiers and crossed the wide gap surrounding Alexander. All of Route 26 was bare before him except for a few crushed vehicles; the people had backed off to give him plenty of room. The two special agents reached him and walked past him through the barrier. He turned and followed without a word.

Imara and Sirenī fell into his arms and hugged him tightly. He squeezed them, and they exchanged kisses, then he shook hands with Brent and Drëndi.

The group retreated to Jordan's house.

As soon as the adults left, Eric ignored his sister's questions and ran upstairs to the spacious attic of the old farmhouse. There was a window at the front of the building, and he hoped he'd be able to see the street from there. He wanted to see magic beyond the excellent knights and monsters Alex had made for him a couple of times.

He could see the street from the attic, and he grinned as he watched the spectacle. When the blood-red lightning flashed into the sky, Eric fell back from the window with a squawk. He hurriedly picked himself up and sheepishly looked about, grateful that his sister wasn't around to snark at him. He licked his lips and returned to his vantage point, but the show was over.

Short as it was, it had been the most incredible thing he'd ever seen.

Alex is a badass.

Ten
Decem

Nine hours after the stranger returned to his home, Sergeant Carlos Ramírez straightened and pressed his knuckles into his lower back. In high-handed fed fashion, SAC Kelly tasked the military servicemembers with cleaning up the debris from the "terrorist attack."

Carlos had difficulty seeing the terrorism in the assault since the only person injured was a soldier who cut his fingers on his shattered knife blade when he reached into his pocket. Sure, the weirdo with the lightning fingers had crushed their cars and ruined their guns and knives, but he hadn't hurt anyone.

Carlos figured anyone with half a brain could see that the tall, stern Black man could have killed everyone there. The hair on his neck had stood on end when the man sent those bolts into the sky, but it was all just one more weird thing happening in the Oxford Hills that they weren't supposed to talk about.

They'd all heard rumors about the events at Grace Manor. It was just down the street from the McInerney property, which was protected by an invisible shield that no one could explain.

Everyone gossiped in low tones to keep Her Highness from overhearing them. No one wanted to get on her bad side: she had a tongue like a wood rasp and a temper to match.

After the debacle and before she told the soldiers to clean up everything, Special Agent in Charge Kelly blathered on for ten minutes about terrorism, cults, and fancy experimental weapons. Ramírez didn't buy the party line after watching the stranger fire lightning from his fingers. He only had six years left to get his twenty-five, and then he was out. He'd dealt with shit all around the world and was ready to put his guns down.

Carlos wanted to spend time with his wife and kid, Martina and Raúl. His son was nine years old and fighting leukemia with every bit of strength he had. Even thinking about his kid made him well up, so he shut the emotions away. Carlos was terrified that he'd never stop crying if he set them free. That wasn't something a man, a soldier, had the right or freedom to do. He'd been raised to believe men should die up on their white horses rather than show any weakness at all.

He squared himself and his gear and took a deep breath. He'd stayed in the military for the insurance. It was the only way for him and Martina to cover Raúl's devastatingly expensive medical bills at Dana Farber Boston Children's Hospital. The hospital was a great place; everyone there was amazing and kind, and they really seemed to love the kids…but Raúl was still fading. Carlos could barely think about the last time he'd seen his son: Raúl was thin and drawn, his skin translucent, his eyes haunted.

But maybe there's hope, he thought desperately. *They say a miracle cured everyone at Grace Manor. Maybe I can borrow some of that for Raúl.*

Carlos glanced around. No one was paying him any attention, so he slipped away.

After watching Alex disable the soldiers and feds, crush their cars, and shoot red lightning from his fingers, Paul and Sue took the kids back to the manor. The couple wanted to discuss the situation, so they sent their kids to the rooms they'd picked. They hadn't eaten dinner, so Eric and Cassie reluctantly obeyed, albeit complaining about being hungry as they went upstairs to the third floor.

Sue ignored their entreaties and slammed the bedroom door, then began to pace. She felt stressed by everything that had happened. At the same time, she felt strangely reassured by Alex's self-restraint. He'd been confronted by the Feebs, The Man, and their guns, and he'd shut them down, but he hadn't hurt anyone.

She spun to a halt and glared at her husband. "I feel safe," she blurted as if he'd spoken.

Paul held up his hands. "I didn't say anything," he protested.

She glared a moment longer, covered her face with her hands, and laughed. She'd been tempted every day to leave the property despite the risk to her family, but now she wanted to stay. She felt a weight ease off her shoulders and dropped her hands, her laughter subsiding.

Her husband stared at her warily as if she might attack him at any moment, then said, "I feel safer, too, especially after watching Alex bust guns and crush cars without breaking a sweat. I've never seen anything like it. I always knew there was something off about Carter, but finding out he's from another fucking planet...Jesus Christ." He shook his head. "He's so funny, though."

"He's human, Paul," Sue said tartly. "Why wouldn't he have a sense of humor?"

"Alex doesn't," he pointed out.

"Yes, he's earnest, but I'm sure he's got a sense of humor," she countered.

"Really? Why? Has he been flirting with you?" Paul got a mulish expression.

"For heaven's sake, Paul," she scolded. "He's not flirting with me. He's already sleeping with two women."

"What if he wants a third?" he demanded.

Sue stared at her husband. Paul's jealousy always surprised her because it came up at the damnedest moments. "Paul Arsenault, do not make me take you over my knee," she threatened.

His eyes lit up. "What can I do to make that happen?" he leered.

"Keep talking nonsense, Mister," she threatened.

They laughed, and he swept her into his arms and kissed her passionately. A knock at the door caused Sue to pull away. She smoothed her shirt and went to see who it was.

"We're hungry," Cassie whined.

Eric stood behind her and nodded.

"Don't you know how to use the machine thingy in the room by the kitchen?" Sue asked.

Her children nodded.

"Good. Go get food for yourselves." She started to close the door but opened it back up. "And sleep in your rooms tonight, okay?"

"Yippee!" Eric cried.

He turned and sprinted down the hall before she could change her mind. Cassie laughed and hurried after him. Sue watched them disappear, slammed the door, and swiped her finger up the narrow metal panel that locked it.

She looked at her husband. "Where were we?"

He waggled his eyebrows. "You were going to spank me," he reminded her.

Carlos walked past the Indigent Mug and hoofed it to South Paris. He approached the Market Square intersection and turned left down a dead-end side street. There were houses on the lefthand side of the road, a cemetery at the end, and Grace Manor on the right. The military and federal agents patrolled both entrances to the facility on Monday and Tuesday.

Carlos heard that on Wednesday, a call came down from Kelly's boss—or someone even higher up the food chain. When the call ended, she stormed into the command tent and pulled everyone back from Grace Manor.

Hopeful entrants immediately flocked back to the side lot. Carlos surveyed them from the edge of the lot beneath the setting sun with his heart pounding, though he didn't know why. He stared at the crowd in the parking lot and studied the building, looking for anything weird and cultish.

He finally shook his head with a sigh of disgust. Despite the upbeat atmosphere of the people waiting to go inside, it looked like a nursing home. He started to turn away when a branch cracked nearby.

He spun, hand going to his hip where his belt holster usually sat, but he wasn't carrying, and besides, his sidearm was in pieces in a trashcan at the blockade.

Carlos clenched his fists, but it was only an older man in a white outfit who looked like he'd come out of the graveyard. The man smiled at Carlos and angled toward him. The stranger stopped a couple of feet away.

"Good evening, brother," the man said politely.

He looked seventy, but his voice was a mellow baritone. He gestured behind him at the graveyard.

"I visit my wife's grave a few times a week," he said. His expression turned wistful. "She died ten years ago, and I thought I'd be with her soon, but now…" The man shrugged and made a gesture indicating himself. "I'm healthier than I was when I was twenty. I was healed by the Miraculous Event, you see."

He spoke as if his words explained everything. Carlos began to cry. The stranger stepped toward him and awkwardly patted his shoulder, one man to another. Most men never learn how to comfort another man when he cries—it isn't the accepted thing. Instead, men tell each other to suck it up and put their big boy pants on even when their hearts break. The sergeant wasn't sobbing, but his tears were serious business.

"You've got a lot of pain, son," the old man said kindly. "I'll stand here, and you just let it out. We'll talk when you're ready. Take your time."

Carlos and the stranger stood near one another and looked at the side lot as the sky finished darkening. The people in the parking lot ignored the two men and gathered around their little communal fires. After about ten minutes, Carlos cleared his throat.

"I'm Carlos Ramírez."

"Nice to meet you, son," the older fellow said. "I'm Donald Atkins, but everyone here calls me Donnie."

"Nice to meet you, Donnie," Carlos said. He turned and offered his hand. Donald had a firm grip. "What do you mean when you say, 'the Miraculous Event?'"

He was grateful Donnie hadn't said anything about his lapse.

"Well, that's a bit of a tale," Donnie said thoughtfully.

The older man paused to collect his thoughts, then launched into a quick recounting of the healing of everyone in the facility. When he finished, Donnie turned to Carlos and cocked his head, his expression striking a perfect balance between grave and compassionate.

"Who are you losing?" the older man asked.

His tone was gentle but pragmatic. He spoke as one man to another who understood the pain, shame, and difficulty of feeling. Carlos froze, unable to speak.

He cleared his throat and almost whispered, "My son. Raúl. He's nine. Leukemia."

His shoulders trembled as he wrestled to control himself. Donnie gave him a moment before speaking.

"Well, son, I can't guarantee they'll let me help you, but I think they just might. Wait here."

Before Carlos could reply, the older man strolled through the impromptu campground, talking cheerfully to people before disappearing into the facility. Carlos hunched his shoulders, stuck his hands in his pockets, and watched the door with a desperation that felt unbecoming and insane. He shuffled his feet to try to stay warm and keep his toes from freezing.

The soldier had almost talked himself out of his nascent plan when the inner door opened. Donnie came outside with a petite woman whose luxurious mane of curly dark hair was visible from this distance. The woman remained in the vestibule while she talked to Donnie. He listened attentively and nodded, his face grave, before he turned and exited the outer door. The woman looked through the glass straight at Carlos even though he stood beyond the campfires. She appeared to study him for a few seconds, then nodded and disappeared back into the facility.

Carlos felt a prickle of a different kind as Donnie ambled across the side lot, talking and smiling. Like anyone who's been in battle, the soldier had excellent situational awareness. He knew someone was watching him. The military man kept his eyes relaxed and slowly turned his head; out of his peripheral vision, he caught sight of someone in the window of a house across the dead-end street from the side lot.

Whoever it was backed away when Carlos turned and looked at the second floor. Part of him wanted to walk over to the house and pound on the door, but Donnie reached him before he did anything rash.

The older man shook his head as Carlos turned to face him. "Zalcent International bought the place," he offered. "They've sent their lackeys up to 'study' the Miraculous Event. I'm sure their goons are also stationed at the blockade with you soldiers."

"Uh, yes, they've got technicians stationed with us and the feds."

He spied a small parcel in Donnie's right hand.

Donnie nodded sagely. Then he asked, almost reverently, "Did you see him? Alexander Eldred?"

Carlos frowned as he shifted his train of thought from the watcher in the window and Zalcent International to the unfamiliar name. Zalcent's products were everywhere, online and off, and the multinational conglomerate had interests in every industry. It also had a reputation for bottomless corruption and was a true juggernaut.

Zalcent existed in its present form because of the COVID pandemic and the transfer of wealth that happened when a handful of companies made tremendous amounts of money while the world's people sheltered in place and waited out the virus. Many of those people still struggled financially and emotionally to recover, and it had been ten years.

Carlos cleared his throat. "Dark skin, about this tall?" He held his hand about even with his skull to indicate the same height, a tidy six feet. "Well-dressed? With some kind of—I dunno—abilities?"

Donnie's face broke into a delighted smile. "That's him!" he whispered. He cleared his throat and spoke more normally, his deep voice vibrating with excitement. "He performed the Miracle, you know. We were all dying of old age, dementia, or diseases of some kind. He used some magic to save us. I saw him recently but didn't get a chance to thank him." His tone grew wistful at the end.

Carlos nodded slowly, not sure how he felt about all this. Didn't the Bible condemn sorcerers and witches? He struggled to recall the passages but wasn't as devout as his wife. Martina could quote chapter and verse, but Carlos was a half-assed Catholic at best.

All the sergeant knew was that Alexander could have killed people at the blockade, but he didn't. He just collected those two feds who'd been kicked out of the cordon earlier that day and returned to his property…inside the forcefield.

What the fuck am I doing here?

He opened his mouth to tell Donnie he was all set, that this was a mistake, that he was sorry for the bother. As if sensing his indecision, the old buck grinned and offered him the parcel in his right hand with a flourish. Carlos stared at it, palms sweating. He reached out, carefully took the bundle, and folded back the white cloth to reveal the damnedest-looking apple he'd ever seen: shiny and vibrant, with a subtly rainbow-colored skin that looked natural but like nothing the trees on Earth produced.

The Army sergeant stared at it, then looked up at Donnie with a question in his eyes. The older man nodded.

"Give it to your son. I promise this will heal him, but he has to eat it all." He looked grave. "Every bite, but not the core and seeds."

Carlos felt hope surge. He ruthlessly quashed it. If he let it blossom, and this crazy scheme in his head failed, he might not be able to come back from that. "Thank you!" he said huskily.

Donnie raised his gray eyebrows. "What are you waiting for, son? Go save Raúl!" he instructed.

He made a shooing motion.

The sergeant spun on his heel and ran easily back to the cordon. He asked his buddy to cover for him and took an Army Jeep that he promised to have back before sunrise. His buddy waved him off and said he'd take care of it. Carlos took State Route 26 toward Gray and the Maine Turnpike; he wanted to speed but kept it reasonable.

Carlos called his wife when he reached Gray, and it was too late to turn around. Martina answered immediately, her voice joyful at hearing from him despite the hour. He exchanged text messages with her daily but couldn't talk to her as often as he'd like.

He told her he was coming to Boston and had a few hours to visit her and Raúl. She was surprised because he never did things like that. He'd told her he was being posted in Maine at the "cultist's" property, which was only a couple of hours from their home in Worcester. They'd always lived on base until Raúl's condition worsened. Then, they'd checked him into Dana Farber and bought the house.

He told Martina to meet him at the hospital at the usual entrance and insisted they needed to see Raúl that evening, no matter what. Martina sounded uncertain about that, but she agreed.

He got choked up and had to take a moment. He pretended he'd fumbled his phone to cover the fact he almost burst into tears again. Carlos tried his best never to cry around her when he was home; he wanted her to believe he was solid and dependable. Martina had told him more than once that she wanted to know she wasn't alone in her sadness and fear and that her husband's manly stoicism made her feel like she was the only one struggling. Carlos wanted to tell her how he felt but couldn't bring himself to do it. He worried she'd think he was less of a man.

They ended the call. He turned on the radio and drummed his fingers on the wheel while listening to hard rock. He sang loudly and off-key to keep himself distracted. The drive was busy through some areas: around the exits to Portland and Westbrook, in Maine; around Portsmouth in New Hampshire; and again at the junction of 95 heading into Boston. It took him about two hours and forty minutes to get to the hospital and another ten to park in the on-site garage.

He sat in the Jeep for a minute, then grabbed the apple and jumped from the vehicle. He marched determinedly to the entrance where Martina waited, pacing. She stopped and stared at him with worry as he approached. He knew he was acting a little crazy, and he squeezed her desperately when they embraced.

He pulled back and kissed her gently, careful of the fragile-feeling apple in his left hand. He took her hand in his and almost dragged her into the hospital. She yanked on his hand to stop him just after they entered, a frustrated expression coming over her face.

"What is happening?" she asked him in Spanish, her voice sharp.

"You're behaving like a madman, my love! Why do we have to do this?"

Carlos shook his head, his expression pleading. "I only have a few hours, Martina. I…this could save Raúl!"

Her hands flew to her mouth, and she gasped, looking at the white-wrapped fruit in his hands as he held it up to show her.

"Don't ask me how. Just trust me."

She nodded, turned, and led the way.

Carlos and his wife told the nurse on duty that he was being deployed last minute and wouldn't be able to see his son for months. Because Raúl was so sick and likely wouldn't survive that long, the nurse compassionately granted them fifteen minutes to visit him despite it being after hours.

When they went into the comfortably appointed room, they did their best not to wake the other kids, many of whom were light sleepers. The place was decorated in bright colors and cartoony themes, and Raúl shared the area with five other children.

They tiptoed to his bed, and their son came awake when Carlos touched his shoulder and whispered his name. Raúl smiled broadly when he saw his parents, especially his father. They smiled at him with the pained rictus parents get when their kids are dying.

Raúl put his thin, stick-like arms around his dad's neck. "Don't cry, Daddy!" he whispered.

He said it in English. He only spoke Spanish with his mom and a couple of the nurses.

"I can't help it," Carlos said, "but it's only because I love you so much."

He held out the wrapped fruit. "Take this. I want you to eat it."

Raúl frowned but unwrapped the apple. His eyes lit up at the rainbow-hued skin, which shone a soft light across the boy's face in the dimly lit room. Carlos hadn't noticed the glow when Donnie handed it to him, but he saw it now.

Martina gasped. "What is this?"

"I swear to God, it's a miracle."

She searched his face, nodded at whatever she saw, and looked at Raúl. "Eat the apple, *mijo*," she whispered. "It will make you feel better."

Raúl shrugged and bit into the fruit. His eyes widened at the astonishing flavor and the sudden rush of sweet juices. He took a larger bite and began to eat with a verve he hadn't shown for longer than his parents could recall. They watched him consume the whole thing, leaving only the core. Carlos took that from him, wrapped it carefully in the white fabric, and started to tuck it in his pocket. Martina stopped him with a hand on his forearm. Carlos looked at her questioningly. She took the bundle from his hand and placed it in her purse.

"I'll take care of this," she said softly.

Carlos hesitated then nodded. Raúl was what mattered, not wherever Martina disposed of the core.

They stayed with Raúl until the nurse peeked her head in, having given them almost half an hour with their son. At seeing her compassionate but stern look, the couple nodded and stood. Carlos leaned down to tuck his son in and kiss his forehead.

"I'll see you soon, champ," he whispered, giving him a knuckle bump.

Martina kissed Raúl and promised she would be by in the morning as usual. The little boy nodded. "I love you," he whispered sleepily.

If the lights had been on, they would have seen the effects of the magical fruit already at work as the blush of health began to radiate over his frail body.

They thanked the nurse profusely for letting them see their son and left the hospital. Once outside, Martina grabbed her husband's muscular arm and spun him to face her with a force that her compact frame hid well.

"Tell me what just happened!" she commanded. She spoke English, so he'd know how serious she was.

Carlos nodded as the tense energy fueling him drained in a rush. They took Martina's car to an all-night diner near the hospital. Over coffee, pancakes, and bacon, he told her everything.

Carlos returned to Maine an hour before the sun rose. He thanked his friend for covering for him while he performed what was, he decided, his life's most crucial singular event.

Martina and Carlos had finished their impromptu breakfast after midnight. She had driven back to the hospital parking garage so he could pick up his Jeep and then did something she'd never done before: she told him to make love to her in the back seat of her car.

He'd been shocked, but no more than she was.

She'd grown up in a strict Catholic household, but she didn't stay in the faith because of that: she stayed because she believed. She dated Carlos for two years before they got engaged, which lasted for a year before they married. Martina didn't have sex with him until their wedding night. He had a high sex drive, and their long courtship was hard on him; she knew he masturbated while they dated and when he was deployed, but she turned a blind eye to the sin because she loved him.

She didn't want him to be unhappy when she wasn't there to care for his needs. She'd gotten curious and asked him once who he thought about when he did that. She feared he would name some beautiful celebrity or model.

Instead, he smiled and said, "You, my beloved."

She'd never forget the warmth in his eyes and voice when he said that.

Carlos didn't believe in God and the church like she did. He grew up Catholic, but he'd never taken comfort from the faith and didn't put his trust as freely in things he couldn't touch, see, or talk to. Martina felt sad they couldn't share that, but he went to church with her when he was home and prayed with her when she needed extra strength to deal with their son's illness.

After they'd married, she'd hoped she and Carlos would have at least four children. She'd always wanted to be a mother, but no matter how hard she tried, she only brought one child into the world. Martina had given up on having more kids, but when she watched her son eat the strange, blessed fruit that God had put in Carlos's hands, something inside her shifted.

She felt a quickening in her body and knew God was giving her another chance, but she also knew she couldn't wait. She'd never imagined doing it in a car, but she saw her husband so infrequently when he was deployed that his presence now was a miracle.

It was her only chance, and Martina seized it, even though she wasn't a woman who had sex in cars, on couches, or after a picnic in the woods. She didn't consider herself "adventurous" enough to do the things her girlfriends bragged about, but she wanted another baby with Carlos as much as she wanted Raúl to live a long, full life.

Carlos had gotten out of the car's passenger side, reached down, and jerked the seat forward. He undid his belt, button, and zipper and got in the back seat on the same side. He'd pushed his pants and briefs down around his ankles.

It had been a while since they'd been together; Martina wasn't surprised when she saw he was already rock hard. He smiled at her and waited patiently as she shyly slipped into the backseat and closed the door. She grinned nervously as she fumbled with her pants and eased them down. She'd slipped her right leg out of her jeans but kept her panties on, too embarrassed by her wanton behavior to remove them.

Carlos didn't care; he took her in his arms and pulled her across his lap. He reached down and deftly slid her panties aside like they had sex in the backseat all the time. Martina reached down and stroked his stiff cock while they kissed. He moaned low in his throat as she handled him. She broke off kissing him and looked into his eyes as she mounted him. He groaned deep in his chest as her heat and wetness engulfed him.

Martina moved slowly while he wrapped his arms around her. She felt something wet on her face and reached up to gently wipe away her husband's tears. They didn't speak about it as he stared into her eyes. His love, desperate desire, and hope lay bare for her to see. It was the closest she'd felt to him since Raúl's diagnosis.

Carlos apologized after ejaculating because it happened faster than he wanted. She didn't orgasm but hadn't expected to under such awkward circumstances. She shushed him and held him close.

"It's okay, my love," she whispered.

Martina got up before dawn and dressed with her usual care. She went to church, which was a benison for her soul even before her son was diagnosed with leukemia. She knelt to pray the rosary, offering to take any burden upon herself if only her son were saved. She stayed for about an hour, stood, made the sign of the cross, and departed the church.

On her way out, she circled to the side of the rectory and took the core of the strange apple from her purse where it had sat overnight. She stared at the remains, still pearly white and unblemished despite being eaten many hours ago. Martina felt something as she held it: she wasn't sure what it was, but it was soothing and gave her a strange feeling of hopefulness.

Martina smiled and pressed a hand to her stomach through her coat thinking back to her time with Carlos just a few hours before. Then she knelt on the cold ground, arranged her dress around her knees, and removed a spade from her purse.

She'd dreamed of burying the apple's core in the rectory yard. Her dream had felt so real and urgent that she'd decided to follow through. She did her best to smooth the soil in the center of the yard and make it look like it was before.

Martina left the church and arrived at the hospital in time to join the kids for breakfast. Most of the food went uneaten since they were often nauseous from their treatments. When she entered the small cafeteria, Raúl wasn't there.

With her heart in her throat, Martina hurried to the nurse on duty, who happened to go to the same church. Angela took Martina's hands with a look of joy on her face and spoke rapidly.

"It's a miracle, Martina. I don't know any other way to say it except that your prayers have been answered!" Angela cried. "He woke up this morning glowing with health. I've never seen or heard of anything like it."

Martina collapsed into Angela's arms and sobbed in relief. Between blubs, she managed to ask Angela where Raúl was. The nurse told her he was having blood drawn and would come to the cafeteria at any moment. She guided Martina to a chair and told her to wait there.

Martina half-fell, half-sat, and mumbled, "I must call my husband."

"Of course," Angela agreed.

The nurse smiled joyfully as she went over to help the orderlies with the children's breakfast. Martina fumbled her phone from her purse. She could barely see through her grateful tears, but she managed to message her husband.

Deep in her heart, she knew God worked through Maine's people —nothing evil could save a child's life.

Carlos barely slept after he got back to Maine on Saturday morning. He lay down, but his mind was racing. He got up, took a ten-minute shower at the Rest, and dressed. When he took his phone out of his pocket and read the message from his wife, he thrust his arms in the air and hollered in joy.

The other men changing in the room set aside for their use looked at him askance. Carlos told them the good news, and they gathered around, pumping his hand and slapping him on the back.

He dashed from the Rest without his coat and ran to Grace Manor's side lot, past the hopefuls waiting to go inside. He pounded on the outside door until a woman in her fifties came outside.

"Can I help you?" She glanced at his fatigues, "Sergeant Ramírez?"

Her eyes were penetrating and vaguely suspicious. The winded soldier held up a finger while he panted for air. "Can you get Donnie for me?"

The woman gave him a skeptical once-over, nodded tersely, and disappeared. She reappeared five minutes later with the wily older man, who smiled when he saw Carlos. He raised his eyebrows in a silent question; Carlos nodded and burst into tears and ugly, wracking sobs. He couldn't stop; his wife's message had ripped off the lid of the box he'd been stuffing his feelings into for the last few years.

"There, there," Donnie said compassionately.

He took Carlos's shoulders and turned him toward the back of the facility, where he could release his pent-up feelings privately.

"I'll be back, Sharon," Donnie told the woman who'd answered the door.

Eleven
Undecim

November 4 dawned bright and sunny. Jack Carter blinked and saw the light shining through his bedroom windows. He felt excellent. He stretched lazily and slowly pushed upright. He looked around, smacked his lips, swung his legs over the side of the bed, and sat there for a moment. He rolled his head, but nothing popped or creaked. He stood and swung his arms, then held up his hands and studied them.

"Huh," he grunted.

Imara had healed him the evening of their arrival on Earth. Her magic was strong enough that she ended up repairing all of his old injuries and scars, but as good as he'd felt after that, he felt even better now. His hands felt stiff a few days after Imara's healing, but even that residual effect of his life as a soldier was gone.

Not anymore, he thought, pleased.

Carter wore the same clothes as when he received the amṛta. He expected he'd need to shower and change before leaving his room, but he sniffed his pits and smelled nothing. He went to the mirrored dresser and saw that his hair was still neatly trimmed, and he had no beard growth. He also didn't have to piss after lying in bed overnight, which surprised him.

He assumed he'd slept for a day, more or less, and wondered if the treatment had failed. The soldier scowled at the thought and marched from his bedroom. He ran into Paul as soon as he stepped into the hallway. The man flashed a grin at him, and they shook hands.

"How's it goin', man?" Paul seemed much more relaxed than when Carter clapped eyes on him last. "All trimmed up, eh?" his friend added with a grin.

Carter grinned back, flashing his even, white teeth. "Yep," he replied, rubbing his smooth jawline and cheeks. "Sirenī gave me a shave and a cut before I—" he caught himself before he mentioned the amṛta. "Passed out," he finished lamely.

"That must have been a hell of a bender, man," Paul said and clapped Carter on the back, "because you've been out for nine fucking days!"

"What!" Carter exclaimed.

The two men laughed, and Carter put an arm around Paul's shoulders in a comradely way. "It really was a hell of a bender," he concurred.

Well, the amṛta definitely worked because I feel great, he thought excitedly as they went downstairs.

When he saw Sue and the kids, she and Eric said hello to the soldier while Cassie stared at him with narrowed eyes.

"You have a funny aura, Mr. Carter," Cassie announced. "It's gold."

Sue looked vaguely horrified by her daughter's words.

He waved away Sue's concerns and smiled. "I'll bet I do, Miss Cassie," he replied then looked at Sue. "In this house, seeing aurae is the least of what you'll encounter."

Sue smiled at his comment. He could tell something had shifted for her over the last nine days.

"Let's get some breakfast," she suggested.

Paul and their kids followed her to the kitchen.

Carter went to the sitting room. He strolled casually in and waved. The Three stood up. Alex shook his hand, and Imara and Sirenī gave him quick hugs.

"Come have tea with us," Imara said.

They sat around a circular table with Imara's tea service on it. Sirenī poured him a cup of tea and levitated it from her spot beside Imara. The songstress looked at him with her brow minutely furrowed; when she caught him watching her, she broke into a smile.

"It's good to see you up and about," she said lightly in Demurrian.

"Thanks," he replied in the same language. He grinned. "I can't believe I was out of it for nine days. I thought it was overnight, and it failed somehow."

Imara's autolenses allowed her to see the changes in his energy field. He'd assimilated the amṛta without resistance from his natal harmonics, like Sirenī. That was the opposite of her and Alex. She wondered what the difference was between them.

Perhaps someday, I'll be able to figure it out.

"What happens now? Shit, what happened while I was under?" Carter wanted to know.

Imara laughed, Sirenī giggled, and Alex smirked. They took turns filling him in on what had occurred with the soldiers and feds outside the barrier when the sorcerer went out to retrieve Brent and Drëndi. Alex explained that the two special agents were at Jordan's house in the guest bedroom, and everything of Carter's had been moved to his room in the manor.

Now it was Carter's turn to smirk. "So, he finally made a move, did he?" referring to Brent's infatuation with his partner.

Sirenī looked at Carter and shook her head with a grin. "Technically, Drëndi made the first move, but let's call it mutual. They seem to be doing well with the change, but things in the government are a mess."

"In what way?" Carter asked.

Alex took a deep breath. "There are reports of illness in the Middle East, Africa, and parts of Asia, India, and Europe. Brent and Drëndi said they heard unconfirmed reports of infrastructure failures. Their boss, Beatrice Lambert, ordered them to come here for safety. I assume she wants to maintain a connection with us, too. Surely, she senses the corruption afflicting this world."

Carter grunted. "Where's their stuff?"

Alex explained, "I teleported their necessaries to one of the guest rooms on the second floor. They will come here to sort things out soon."

"Well, aren't we fiendishly efficient," Carter said with a crooked smile. "Paul and Sue seem to be getting on well."

Imara nodded. "We embedded vitality and rejuvenation spells in the barriers around the property. Everyone will experience improved health, and with that comes an increased sex drive. Paul and Sue have disappeared several times over the last few days and returned looking rather relaxed."

Carter guffawed. "These people don't know what they've been missing all their lives. You know, the marvels of magic and all that."

"Oh, yes. They're in for a pleasant surprise," Sireṇī said mischievously.

"Joking aside, we know there's a kṛtyā bīja—a magic seed created by the sorcerer behind the corruption—somewhere on Earth," Imara said soberly. "We're assuming the Middle East because of the plague starting there. Unfortunately, we don't know anything else."

Sireṇī rested her hand on Imara's. "That's why we're leaving."

Alex told Carter, "You'll be in charge of everything while we're gone, and we've given you administrative privileges with the barrier. You can authorize or deauthorize anyone you want, permanently or temporarily.

"We've also connected with Persephone and Clear Plunkett to let them know they're welcome should the need arise. I authorized them both two days ago. If all goes to plan, though, we'll be back before you have a chance to miss us."

Carter nodded. "Well, Alex, you sure know how to show a man a good time—nine days unconscious, trapped inside a barrier for my safety, and now saddled with responsibilities. I feel like I'm back in the military!"

Alex mimicked his levity with a mock salute and said, "Welcome to life with us, Lieutenant Colonel Jack Carter."

The sorcerer sobered after that and looked at his partners. "I believe we should leave without delay."

Imara and Sireṇī nodded and stood.

Carter felt some anxiety at the suddenness of it all. "Wait! How…how do I know what the amṛta has done to me?" he asked nervously.

Alex gestured for the four of them to stand in a square, and they joined him in the center of the room. The sorcerer of Timil Deeps smiled and extended his left hand.

"We are still discovering what has changed within us. I believe the process takes time to propagate fully and that these changes will continue to occur. You will find it easier to cast spells once you have learned them, and your magic will be powerful." He paused. "*Very* powerful."

Sirenī arched a perfect brow. "Like Grace Manor?" she asked tartly as he snapped his fingers.

The sitting room sluiced away from them. Carter blinked, and the Lower Forty fell into place around him with a flickering stutter.

"Exactly like that," Alex answered blandly. "We will leave via the Gatehouse to go to Byrne first. We must retrieve something that survived the planet's destruction. From there, we can determine our next destination."

Carter spotted an odd look on Imara's face when Alex said this, but it was gone before he could bring his total awareness to it, making him wonder if he'd even seen it. The sorcerer appeared not to notice the songstress' fleeting expression and continued to speak.

"We must let the others know we will be leaving. Jordan, Richard, Brent, Drëndi, and you will be welcome to see us off." He frowned slightly. "But I do not feel Paul and Sue would benefit from observing the Gatehouse in action now."

Carter agreed. Paul and Sue were settling in, but they didn't need to watch the Three use the ancient Infernal Gate system just yet. They'd already been emotionally overwrought by force fields, limitless food and water, and who knew what else. Transportation between planets, dimensions, and universes might be too much.

The four of them walked in silence to Jordan's place. Carter contemplated the changes in his life since he left Gaea. They were myriad, but only the amṛta was difficult for him to wrap his head around.

The nectar of immortality and high-level esoteric shit are way above my pay grade, he thought with a crooked smile.

He flexed his fingers as they walked and enjoyed the feeling of freedom in the motion. He couldn't remember the last time his hands felt so good.

When they reached the house, Sirenī gently tugged her hand free of Alex's and begged off, mentioning that she wanted to say goodbye to Marquis, who might be at either house at this time of day. She snapped her fingers and disappeared while the others went inside to give everyone the news. The rest of the morning and afternoon passed in a blur as Alex and Imara prepared Jordan, Richard, Brent, Drëndi, Paul, and Sue for their departure without sharing too many details. Sirenī returned about forty minutes later, and by mid-afternoon, they had everything as fleshed out as they could.

At one point, Sue asked about her family. "My parents live here in Topsham, and my older sister lives in Binghamton, New York. Can they come here for a while if it becomes necessary?"

Alex nodded without hesitation. "The manor can house dozens of people."

He looked at Paul, silently extending the same invitation. The other man waved it away.

"It's just my dad and me, and he's a fuckhead," Paul said bluntly.
"Ouch!"

Carter laughed at Sue's sneaky elbow jab after Paul swore in front of the kids. They were in the living room watching TV and would undoubtedly perk up when they heard swearing. It usually heralded that the adults were talking about things unsuited for little ears.

Carter grinned inwardly.

"Well, he is," Paul told his wife somewhat defensively.

She sighed.

There was nothing more to be said besides goodbye, which would occur at the Gatehouse. They exited Jordan's place to head back to the Lower Forty. They didn't need to take anything with them since they could create whatever they needed with magic or make purchases on other worlds in a pinch. Paul, Sue, Eric, and Cassie exchanged goodbyes with the Three, and Carter followed them from the house.

He could tell Alex, Imara, and Sirenī were eager to get going. He knew waiting for him to wake had delayed them by over a week. There wasn't anything he could do about it, but he still felt oddly at fault.

As they walked along the path to the garden, the Three reiterated to Carter, Jordan, Richard, Brent, and Drëndi the possible dangers of leaving the manor. Sirenī had done so every day because her fatal beauty could freeze people in their tracks, but the others didn't have that ability. If they left, they could get attacked or arrested. Everyone agreed it was best to stay on the property for now.

At the Gatehouse, Richard and Brent shook hands with the Three. Jordan and Drëndi walked behind them and distributed hugs. Carter saw tears in Jordan's eyes.

"I'm going to miss you," Drëndi said after she stepped away.

"We'll miss you, too," Imara said. She smiled warmly at everyone.

Carter stepped up, and Alex held out his hand. They shook, then he gently hugged Imara and Sirenī.

The daughter of Medusa kissed his cheek and whispered, "You stay safe. I'll kick your ass if you get hurt while we're away."

He grinned and stepped back. "You bet," he said quietly, his voice husky.

His emotions were more potent than he'd expected, which was surprising. He cleared his throat and joined his Earthen friends. Jordan and Richard had seen the Gatehouse activate, but Brent and Drëndi were in for a treat.

Alex faced the stone cube and extended his left hand. A holographic screen appeared, glimmering crimson in the fall afternoon light. Jordan and Richard watched eagerly while Brent and Drëndi's eyes widened in anticipation.

Carter blinked; he'd never seen the holographic interface before. On Gaea, people put a hand on the side of the Gatehouse and focused firmly on their intent to travel to a specific planet in the Ring, only a few dozen of which were known. He wondered how the interface worked and saw Alex tap a finger on the floating panel the way their Earthen friends used touchscreen devices.

Whatever the sorcerer tapped caused the system to activate. The pyramid sank into the cube, and the sides folded outward and somehow twisted inward when they hit forty-five degrees. They dropped out of sight, leaving behind the cube's floor with a circular dais raised incrementally above it. A shimmering red curtain drifted twenty feet into the air and faded toward the top. The Three stepped through the crimson haze onto the transportation platform and blurred out of focus.

Suddenly, the curtain flashed and became brittle and plastic-looking. Carter had seen the system used before, so he kept his attention on his companions. They flinched back when the light solidified and snapped one hundred feet into the sky. It sluiced down into the dais, which was empty. The walls immediately extruded from the base, untwisting and unfolding as the cube reformed. The pyramidal top rose into place.

Carter sighed and glanced around. "Well, that's that." He felt sad and strangely alone despite being with his Earthen friends. "Shall we?" He gestured at the pathway.

The group turned to head back to Jordan's house. Along the edge of the trees, Carter paused and looked back to the hibernating plants in the garden and the quiescent structure at its heart. He stared wistfully at the Gatehouse and felt oddly adrift.

I miss the Three already.

Carter knew their friendship was strange. He met them because he was ordered to track them to the Dark Continent and kill them. He knew now that was something no one could have done—especially since they'd already taken the amṛta by then. They forgave him without batting an eye and accepted him without reservation. They were the most authentic people he'd ever met.

He sighed and shook off his maudlin thoughts since they wouldn't help. He hurried to catch up with the two Earthen couples, who'd paused about ten feet along the path when they realized he wasn't with them. Richard and Brent nodded as he caught up; Jordan and Drëndi smiled, and he realized they understood he was sad. Together, they walked back to Jordan's place.

That evening, Richard took Carter aside. He handed the burly soldier his phone and pointed to the message he'd gotten from José, the young man Carter flirted with at the gym.

"Shit," Carter muttered. He reread the message and grimaced. "What does he mean I 'ghosted' him? I was unconscious for nine days, not that he knew that. Why would he say I must have died?"

"Ghosting is when you blow someone off after seeing them a couple of times," Richard explained.

"Or fucking them, if that's all you wanted," Brent remarked as he joined them.

Carter blinked.

"I heard you say someone thought you died?" the special agent added with a raised eyebrow.

Richard gave Brent a look, but Carter waved it away.

"I'd rather know what it means. I didn't ghost him—we didn't make any plans. He just gave me his phone number, and I told him I didn't have a cell phone."

Richard looked a little guilty. "I didn't want him to think you'd lost interest while you were out of it. Alex said you were in a magical trance of some kind and talked about Prada and handlebars or something like that."

Carter stared at him blankly, then burst out laughing. "The prāṇa-maṇḍala?" he guessed.

"That's it!" Richard snapped his fingers and pointed at him. "Yeah, that. Anyway, I sent him a couple of messages pretending to be you. I thought you'd only be out of it for a day or two, but it went on way longer, and I forgot to respond to José's last message and…well…"

"*Richard,*" Jordan hissed. She got up from the dining table and joined them. "I sent the flirty messages," she explained. "Richard wanted to send shit no gay man would say."

Richard laughed. His messages had been rather crude, he acknowledged. "I'm sorry, man," he told Carter. "He thinks you flirted with him and blew him off."

"Ah, yes. Thus 'ghosting' him," Carter rumbled. He sighed and handed Richard's phone back. "Well, it's not like I'd be able to bring him onto the property right now, anyhow."

He made a grand gesture to encompass the whole thing and mimicked giving a tour: "And on your left is our magic fucking mansion, where there is plenty of magic but where I do no fucking."

Everyone laughed. Sue gave him the death eye from the dining room even though she had a grin on her face. Carter mimed being wounded, and they returned to the dining room to enjoy an early dinner. The kids ate in the living room and watched TV.

Richard looked happily around as the conversation ebbed and flowed, thinking, *My life is pretty damn good.*

Twelve
Duodecim

Byrne was a blasted landscape of utter ruin. The Gatehouse sat near the heart of a once-great city that was nothing more than mounds of debris smothered under sulphuric mud and ash. The slurry steamed in the frigid air. The city was still except when pustulous bubbles burst and released toxic gases or slabs of stone peeled from the sides of buildings in leprous chunks.

When the Gatehouse activated, the pyramid sank into the top of the cubical base, and the accumulated sludge poured off the sides. The subsentient automation controlling the Infernal Gate system detected the toxic environment and activated defensive measures to protect those arriving at the terminus.

The system paused the arrival of the travelers while the automation analyzed their biology. Protective field effects formed around the Gatehouse, pushed the debris back, and created a biocompatible atmosphere.

The sharp, opaque curtain of red light formed within the defensive perimeter, and the travelers arrived. The Three looked at the devastation with expressions of horror. World Two had been like Gaea and Earth—a green planet with massive oceans, many rivers and lakes, blue skies, and billions of people. Now, only one being lived in the entire world, and the sky was a black ceiling that seemed to hover oppressively just over their heads.

When the calamity destroyed Byrne, survivors escaped through the Gatehouse to Gaea and Omejis. They raved about people going insane, turning into monstrous creatures, and rotting alive. They told outrageous stories about planes crashing, cars exploding, and ships sinking. They spoke of buildings, bridges, and dams collapsing without warning. People talked of their loved ones and animals dying from a sweating plague that struck fast and killed within a handful of hours while the seas boiled.

Researchers and magicians from Gaea traveled to the planet to look at the catastrophe firsthand. They returned swiftly, stricken and unable to describe the horror as everyone who remained on Byrne died. The records were public knowledge, and Alexander read everything he could get his hands on after he had the vision of a new corruption. He realized now that nothing could prepare anyone for this. The dark magic had seeped into everything except the Gatehouse.

And a single celerity moth, he reminded himself.

Alexander knew they didn't have any time to waste. He looked over the city's ruins and saw variously heighted mounds of slurry. They comprised vague shapes with the remnants of a civilization disintegrating beneath them.

He turned to Sirenī. "Can you create an impermeable field to protect us once we leave the Gatehouse?"

He felt genuinely concerned now that he'd seen the destruction firsthand. Sirenī took a few seconds to continue studying Byrne before she nodded slowly.

"Yes, but the corruption is still active. I don't think I can create a shield that will last more than a few hours, so we've got a time limit. Where is the celerity moth?" She grimaced and added, "And how the fuck did she survive this?"

"I do not know," he replied.

Imara held up a hand. "I've got this," she assured her partners.

Alexander looked at Imara and saw her staring at the surrounding landscape. She turned her head slowly and allowed her body to track along with her gaze as she searched. He knew she used the Epiphany of

Light inscribed on her autolenses to look around the planet but also knew there was no guarantee she'd be able to find the moth that way. He started to say something when she stabbed a finger toward the wasteland.

Imara had barely turned beyond one hundred eighty degrees when she found their target.

She didn't exactly see the moth; instead, she perceived her. That was the thing about her autolenses: the Epiphany of Light permitted her to perceive anything in the universe. A wandering thought could have her looking up close at distant stars or down to the molecular level in her bloodstream.

Her years of discipline in modulating her voice so she didn't accidentally enchant people when she spoke served her in good stead. Working with her eyes was slightly different, but she felt she'd done well so far.

She saw the giant moth fluttering around a shrunken depression. There was a withered tree with a few flowers growing underneath the feeble shelter of its stunted boughs, a carpet of anemic grass, and what looked like the partial remains of several flowering shrubs. Imara watched the moth flutter from the tree branches to the blossoms beneath.

She looks weak, the songstress thought. *There's no time to waste.*

"That way," the songstress said firmly. She looked at Sirenī. "We have to hurry. She's dying."

Sirenī closed her eyes. She created an impermeable field around them that was thick and tinted a rich golden color dense enough to blur the landscape beyond. The sphere had a flat plane transecting it. The Three stood on that as Sirenī lifted them into the air and sent the globe hurtling in the direction Imara pointed. They flew over the blasted landscape and passed steaming sinkholes ten miles across, the remains of countless cities and towns, and the wreckage of a dead world.

The toxic atmosphere and the spell of corruption tried to destroy the shield. Sirenī continually maintained it, reinforcing and adapting it as they flew above the wasteland, but it was taxing work even with the amṛta. It took two hours to cross the continent and a narrow, sulphuric sea to reach the next landmass. At a slight elevation a few hundred feet above sea level, Sirenī brought them to a hover twenty feet above a small depression, which was slowly but inexorably shrinking.

Imara studied the queen celerity moth. She had a wingspan of fifteen inches across at the widest point. Her wings were covered in fractal patterns that glowed with subtle iridescent highlights as energy appeared to radiate across them. The few flowers that cowered beneath the crumbling tree wilted steadily as they watched.

The songstress looked from the depression to her partners. She shook her head as a startlingly intense fury bubbled up inside her. A trembling wave washed through her; Imara clenched her fists and took a deep breath. Harmonics pulsed in the air, and her corona flared.

"Imara," Alex cautioned.

Sirenī looked at her and shook her head. Imara saw the strain on her partner's face and wished they could link aurae. The Three together would be unstoppable. Instead, she stepped off the edge of the platform transecting the impermeable field and felt the instant bite of the corruption like a thousand stinging insects. She grimaced and fell to the floor of the depression. The pain subsided within moments now that she stood within whatever protected it.

She took a breath and began to hum. She brought the words to a life-giving enchantment to mind and began to sing the spellsong. Her voice rose and fell in rolling, ethereal waves as she sang in the ancient language of the Dawntime. Energy swelled out from her and pushed against the corruption. Power sizzled; arc discharges blasted out and machined furrows in the wasteland that surrounded the depression.

Multicolored radiation flared around her, and the tree in the center of the bowl of rock burst with life. Its dull, brownish-gray bark flushed with the vibrant hues of new growth while needle-like leaves erupted across the branches. The grass that carpeted the depression grew lush and thick, and flowers bloomed in lemony flares of petals and bright green leaves. They gave off a delectable fragrance.

Imara continued to sing, pitting her magic against the corruption that destroyed the world. The horizon where her magic met the necromancer's spell flickered and flashed as the growth in the depression expanded. She put more will and energy into the spellsong and forced herself to channel more power. She drank deeply from the natural currents of energy that flowed through the universe, the bubbling spring of prāṇa that powered everything.

Her corona glowed brighter until it became a tempest around her in Byrne's still and silent atmosphere. She felt an unreasoning hatred for the destructive magic. It was a violation like nothing she'd ever experienced—it was worse than being apart from those she'd loved for so many decades. Her anger began to overwhelm the words of her spellsong, and she trembled as the power flowing smoothly through her became erratic.

Then her partners were beside her. They dropped into the depression and put their hands on her shoulders. She felt the invitation from Alex and gratefully accepted it. She reached out and connected to his aura and felt power flow in a torrent from him to her. His magic was a flood that sizzled through her nāḍī, bright and burning.

Her voice evened out, and the darkness receded.

"We cannot save Byrne like this," Alex told her. "We must collect the moth and leave."

She knew he was right, but it filled her with despair. She let her spellsong trail off and stood in the echoes of the magic. She trembled with the intensity of her feelings but finally nodded.

"You're right. Let's go."

Alex studied her for a moment, but she avoided his gaze. She was too upset, but she'd get over it.

Someday, I will return. I'll take the dark magic from this world and destroy it!

Imara inhaled deeply and looked around. The corruption pressed inward on the depression, and the tiny bastion of life began to shrink at an accelerated rate as if the dark magic was eager to prove that nothing could stop it. She looked at Alex and felt his power mixing with hers. He gave her a reassuring smile, and she turned to Sirenī.

"Give me a moment to convince her to come with us."

Imara stepped over to the celerity moth. She'd sat on a tree branch the entire time, slowly fanning her iridescent wings. Imara extended a hand and listened for the insect's master harmonic. The corruption's noise blanketed everything, but after a few seconds, she tuned that out. She cocked her head, turned her right ear toward the insect queen, and heard the faintest glimmer of a vibration.

"She's close to dying. I have to heal her," Imara told Sirenī and Alex.

"Allow me," Alex said.

The sorcerer extended his left hand and snapped his fingers. Energy flared, and the moth stilled. Colors washed over her wings in fluidic swirls as the fractal patterns began to glow brightly. The light continued to grow, and the queen celerity moth lifted from the branch, her wings a colored blur. Imara held out her hand, and the moth flew over and alighted on her palm. The insect was surprisingly heavy.

Imara had already absorbed the moth's language. She used it to introduce herself. \I'm Imara. These are my companions, Sirenī and Alex. We're here to help.\

\I am Thīaterīka,\ the queen replied. \The sickness is deep. Leave now, or it will take you.\

Imara shook her head as she held the beautiful being in her hand. "Oh, no," she countered. She let her voice ring with two tones—Demurrian for her partners and Thīaterīka's language for the queen. "I am not giving up. You're coming with us, and someday we'll return here and save this world."

\Admirable. I will not live to see it. I am old, and my time is done.\

"No!" Imara's voice rang out. "I am not giving up."

The songstress turned to Sirenī. "Let's go."

Then Imara looked at the moth and spoke aloud for their benefit. "We're taking you with us."

The insect fluttered her wings but said nothing.

Imara turned to face her partners, her expression triumphant. "We're ready."

Sirenī snapped an impermeable field around them, identical to the one earlier. She watched the depression shrink beneath them as they sailed into the sky. With a sudden, violent convulsion, the corruption swept into the tiny depression and consumed the last vegetation on Byrne. The tree, grass, and flowers disintegrated, deliquescing into the leaden ooze.

Sirenī spun the sphere and accelerated toward the Gatehouse. The corruption gouged at her impermeable field with greater force. She could only assume it was because the moth was no longer resisting the dark spell. She glanced at the moth sitting perfectly still on Imara's hand. She was beautiful, but she needed time to regenerate; she'd thrive on Earth, Gaca, or some other world in the Ring, and someday they'd bring her back to Byrne.

Sirenī could tell Imara felt a visceral hatred of the corruption. She felt it through their connection and knew her partner well enough to understand Imara's thought processes. The songstress would never settle until she'd eradicated the enchantment.

The corruption constantly sought to penetrate her shield. She had to continually regenerate the outermost layer of the orb to prevent the potent magic from burrowing into the interior.

Halfway back to the Gatehouse, she ground out a question for Alex. "Why couldn't we teleport?"

"When people were trying to escape the corruption, teleportation failed—or produced erratic results. Those results included people teleporting inside objects, which the modern form of the spell was designed to prevent. The researchers theorized the dark magic bleeds into the paratroposphere."

The paratroposphere was the closest astral realm adjacent to the material plane. Teleportation perforated the astral interface, but the enchantment had safeguards to prevent materializing inside objects at the destination.

Sirenī was impressed and horrified that the corruption interfered with things enough to negate those safeguards. She took a deep breath and pressed her palms toward the boundary of her impermeable field, using the motion to focus her magical energies and willpower. Even with the amṛta, resisting the corrosive effects of the corruption grew more problematic with every passing mile.

Imara and Alex could link aurae and increase their power, but they couldn't do that with her because of Medusa. She'd transformed into the rampaging monster when they'd tried in the past; Sirenī had no reason to assume it would be any different today.

She began to sweat from the strain. They were almost to the Gatehouse when her impermeable field began to lose altitude and drift toward the seething mire below. She saw Alex notice their decline. He cleared his throat to catch Imara's attention. She looked where he pointed and turned to Sirenī without a word.

Sirenī tried to smile, to reassure Imara that she was okay, but she could only grimace.

Imara kept her palm open so the moth could rest on it and began to sing. Her voice filled the impermeable field, and she hung first one melody, then another, and a third in vibrational rings in the air. The three parts of the spellsong oscillated and pulsed, and Sirenī felt the magic brace against the inside of the orb and reinforce the internal space.

"We are only a few miles away," Alex told her. "I will attempt to activate the Gatehouse remotely so we can land inside the protective field effects."

He closed his eyes.

Sirenī grunted and focused on keeping them moving. She could reinforce the exterior or fly faster. She trusted Imara's magic would keep them safe and put all her dwindling energy into flight. They picked up speed, and she saw their destination come across the horizon as they raced above the sludge.

Just a little farther…

Twelve

Alexander reached out with his will and felt the response of the Nephilim structure. The machinery sent a wordless query, and he returned a feeling of urgency and a need for safety. He felt the reaction of the Gatehouse as the pyramid sank into the cube and the walls unfolded and retracted; they were still a mile away, but a shimmering red bubble took shape around the superancient artifact.

Sirenī saw the red bubble and nodded to Alex, her face lovely despite the evident strain. Her impermeable field arced toward the ground and collided with the defensive measures around the open Gatehouse. Alexander thrust his left hand forward and counteracted their inertia while Sirenī dropped them to the dais. They landed with a thud but stayed upright, while the moth fluttered her wings in agitation but didn't lift off Imara's palm.

Sirenī dropped to her knees, gasping, and Alexander squatted down and took her in his arms. He held her until her trembling eased, and she told him she could stand. He helped her to her feet, and she wrapped her arms around him.

"That was the hardest thing I've ever done. If the corruption afflicting the Ring of Worlds is this bad, we're fucked," she said tiredly.

"The spell affecting Earth feels nothing like this," Imara said. "This harmonic is unmistakable, and I haven't picked up anything like it on Earth. It could be there, but I think the necromancer changed the spell to mitigate its effects to avoid destruction on this scale."

Alexander nodded. "I concur. I do not think the new attack uses the same enchantment. This one destroyed everything, which is counterproductive to harvesting power." He let Sirenī go, still concerned by her weakness. When he saw she was okay, he asked, "Where to now?"

"How about Omejis?" Imara replied. "I've always wanted to see it."

He looked at Sirenī, and she shrugged tiredly. "I'm game. I've heard it's beautiful."

Alexander nodded and focused on World One Eighty-Four.

Omejis was Gaea-like. The world had two massive oceans and one supercontinent that spanned the equatorial region. The supercontinent zig-zagged north and south of the tropics as it circumscribed the globe, so the mainland was tropical. There was no ice at either the north or south poles, and it had no axial tilt, so the weather was temperate year-round. Four massive canals transected the supercontinental landmass from the North Ocean to the South Ocean. This allowed merchant vessels and pleasure craft to travel unrestricted between the two bodies of water.

The Gatehouse sat atop a broad, flat-topped hill. People reached it by climbing forty steps from the street to the hilltop. A city surrounded the Gatehouse. It was built between and on the sides and tops of many other hills. Guards stood at attention on all four sides of the plaza surrounding the building. Travelers came through the Infernal Gate system to Omejis often enough that the guards were familiar with the experience.

When the pyramid sank smoothly into the cubical base, one of the armor-clad men tilted his chin to his shoulder and spoke into a radio. The guards casually prepped their compact, handheld railguns in case the newcomers were violent. When the walls collapsed and twisted away to reveal the three travelers, the guards didn't relax, as the people of Omejis knew many beings in the Ring of Worlds were weapons.

Imara led the way off the dais while holding the queen celerity moth. Her arm hadn't tired, for which she was grateful. The Three stepped away from the Gatehouse, and it returned to its idle state. She listened to the local harmonics, uncovered the strains of a pretty language that appeared to be spoken worldwide, and assimilated it.

They knew enough about Omejis to expect a city official from the Gatehouse Transit Authority would come to the plaza. They didn't know who it would be or the name of the city they'd come to and bided their time without moving much.

About fifteen minutes after they arrived, a chubby man huffed his way up the forty stairs. He paused to speak to the commander of the guards, then approached the newcomers with a sweaty smile and a quick bob of his head.

"Greetings, my friends! Welcome back to Omejis. It's been some time," he said to all of them. He spoke with a slightly nasal fluidity that reminded Imara of a combination of Tèngyīn and a dead language once spoken near Londinium. "It's good to see you again, Imara, Sirenī, Alex."

The official extended his hands and took Imara's free hand while she watched, bemused. He held her hand for a moment, then moved to Sirenī. He held her hand briefly before moving on to Alex to do the same. He spoke to each of them as he went.

Sirenī and Alex nodded and smiled at him. Imara knew they had no idea what he'd said; thankfully, he didn't ask anything that needed a reply. It was apparent that he recognized them, though, and no wonder with time travel involved. Imara wished she'd written more details about situations like this so she would know how best to handle them.

Shit, I wish I had written his damn name down!

The bureaucrat glanced over his shoulder and waved at the guards; they stood down, and he turned back to the Three with a beatific expectation. Taking that as her cue, Imara spoke up.

"Thank you. It's so good of you to welcome us back. Could you refresh my memory about how long it's been since our last visit?"

The stranger smiled broadly. "I forgot how good your accent was, Imara. Just like a native," he complimented. He turned and gestured for them to precede him to the stairs. As they went, the official tapped his chin in thought. "It's been about eight years since you departed to the Bitter Islands. Aeronwen and Sulwyn have been keeping me updated, you know. It sounds like you've been doing well in Temple City."

Imara bobbed her head in a nod and glanced at Sirenī. *He knows who we are and says we're in Temple City on the Bitter Islands. He mentioned people talking to him about us.*

What the fuck? Sirenī sent back.

Imara gave a minute shrug that the official didn't see.

"I suppose you must have left through the Temple there to come back here? I'm sure Sulwyn or Aeronwen would have flown you had you asked," he chatted merrily as they began descending the broad stone steps toward the beautiful city artfully sprawled across the hills. "You know they'd do anything for you, as would we all."

Imara smiled with what she hoped looked like grateful appreciation since she had no idea what was happening. Unfortunately, she'd neglected to mention details like this in her writings in Alex's journal —her future self outlined the broad strokes but not the particulars. That was already proving annoying.

Sirenī caught her eye again. *Do you know who this man is?* she asked.

No, and that's really irksome, the songstress replied.

Imara jerked her attention back to the mysterious official and tried to make sense of his words.

"…stay in the same place as before?"

"That would be lovely," Imara confirmed.

She wondered how to get some answers without seeming weird, but the bureaucrat merely smiled at her warm reply and continued chatting with her.

They walked along a wide boulevard between brightly colored buildings. Most were two to four stories high and sprawled organically around and up the hills. Many of the hills had immense structures on top that looked official rather than residential. Thousands of people walked around in the hot air beneath the blazing sun.

There were thin strips of greenery lining most roads that separated the boulevards from the sidewalks. Most of those were covered in dense cushions of green grass fringed with low bushes. There were no trees to be seen, and Imara didn't recall seeing them around the Gatehouse plaza or other hills. She heard and saw skimmers flying above but saw only foot traffic at ground level.

They reached a four-story building ten minutes from what Imara considered Gatehouse Hill. They followed the bureaucrat inside; he chatted all the while, pointing out the tastiest local eateries and the best shops in the area. He claimed some were the same as eight years ago, while others had changed.

Inside the well-appointed hotel, the Gatehouse Transit official spoke to the clerk and arranged for them to stay in the penthouse apartment. He turned to face the Three. "It's the one on the left this time, but it's a mirror of the righthand suite. You'll feel right at home!"

Imara thanked him and the clerk.

They followed the bureaucrat up four flights of stairs to the top floor of the building. There were only two doors off the long hall, which ran from one end to the other. The bureaucrat led them to their room. He touched his finger to a pad on the door, which unlocked with a mechanical whir and click. He opened the door and gestured for them to precede him.

They did so with smiles. Sirenī and Alex took their cue from Imara.

"All your biometrics are still on file," the official remarked. "The governor of Rilladwen will continue to cover your stay after everything you did for us eight years ago. So many lives would have been lost if you hadn't used your extensive…ah, capabilities to help the evacuation." He shivered; his smile faltered briefly. "Thankfully, though, you were there! We could never repay you."

Imara smiled and said, "I'm so glad we were able to help."

His smile returned full force, and he bowed to them. As he departed, he spoke over his shoulder. "Let me know if you need anything!"

"Thank you," Imara called.

When the door locked, she turned to her companions and laughed giddily. "What the fuck just happened!" she exclaimed in Demurrian.

Alex shook his head with a bemused expression and shrugged. "That was unexpected."

Sirenī burst into laughter. "How does this work? Did we come here and time-travel into the past? This only makes sense if it was our future but his history. Otherwise, he couldn't know us since we've never been here."

Thirteen
Tredecim

Alexander surveyed the penthouse apartment. He stepped across the broad, open interior and looked out a glass door that led to a long, narrow balcony paralleling the hallway and running from one end to the other.

He looked over the attractive city, admiring the disposition and layout of the buildings, the way they seemed to flow naturally up and down the many hills and across the verdant tropical landscape. Despite seeing rooftop gardens on many of the two and three-story buildings, he didn't see any trees.

The sorcerer turned from the view and saw the celerity moth flitting about the spacious room. She angled toward a couch slightly wider than the norm for either Gaea or Earth but otherwise the same. It had plush rectangular seats and rear cushions, with a low back and throw pillows artlessly arranged along its length.

Pretty flowering bushes rested in elegant clay pots on either side of the couch. The bushes were round and covered in dark, shiny leaves interspersed with lovely pink blossoms. The moth fluttered over to settle on the left-hand bush and fanned her wings. Alex assumed she was considering whether the foliage was edible. It was reasonable to believe she was ravenous, given the environment in which the moth had lived.

"That was interesting," he said finally. "Clearly, time travel is at work, as Sirenī suggests. I know there is a Nephilim Temple on this world; we should spend the night here, then teleport to these Bitter Islands and cast the time travel spell. We can use the Temple to come back to the Gatehouse, thus meeting," he paused, then waved a hand dismissively, "whoever that was for his first time and our second."

Imara yawned. Alexander knew she'd expended a lot of energy on Byrne singing the Dawntime spellsong, and Sirenī had used everything she had to fly them to and from the depression where the moth lived.

Of course, they're tired.

Imara stretched her arms over her head. "Well, whatever we do, it will have to come after I rest."

"Byrne took it out of me, too," Sirenī grumbled. She surveyed the room and said, "Not that there's much room for the three of us to sleep,"

"I am not fatigued," Alexander said. "I expended no energy on Byrne. You two did all the amazing work."

"I always knew you were a lazy shit," Imara gibed, which caused him to laugh heartily.

When he sobered, he asked Imara, "Will you gift me the language you spoke with the official? It will help with my exploration. I want to find out exactly where these Bitter Islands are and see what the locals know of the Nephilim Temple."

Imara beckoned him over to her. She put her hand on his chest, smiled, and began to sing, She collected the language of Omejis and passed it over to Alex.

He'd always loved listening to her sing and was grateful he could enjoy it without becoming enchanted.

"Thank you, my love," he murmured.

He kissed Imara lightly on the lips. Then he went to Sirenī and did the same.

As he slipped from the room, he heard Imara say, "Bath or bed?"

He paused, the door open just a whisker, and listened for Sirenī's reply.

"We can take a bath after we nap. I haven't felt tired in weeks. I didn't miss it, as it turns out."

"Me neither," Imara agreed.

He smiled, closed the door silently, and then headed downstairs to the lobby. He was surprised that a technological society with aircars didn't use elevators, but every culture had its quirks.

He approached the clerk on duty. "Good day. I came through the Gatehouse earlier today with my companions."

The clerk appraised the sorcerer with a curious glint in his eyes. "Ah, yes, I heard it activated. It hasn't done so for a few years."

"The gentleman who met us on the hilltop, could you refresh my memory of his name?" Alexander asked.

"That was the chief of the Gatehouse Transit Authority, Amlodd," said the clerk with a dubious gaze.

Alexander ignored the look that told him he shouldn't need to ask such an obvious question. "Yes, that was it, thank you." He knocked his knuckles on the counter and turned away.

Once outside in the tropical climate, Alexander was thankful for the magic that regulated his personal environment and kept him perpetually comfortable in the unrelenting equatorial heat. As he passed a building, the sorcerer touched his bare hand to one of its bricks—the stone was scorching.

He wandered the streets for about an hour; no one he passed seemed overcome by the sun's intensity, which was interesting. The locals favored loose-fitting garments made of breathable fabrics and hats with wide brims. They moved about at a slower pace than the people of Gaea and appeared well-adapted to the temperature.

Alexander looked for a bookstore and finally found one. The proprietor sat on a stool behind the counter. She was an older woman he estimated to be in her seventies, with frizzy gray hair. She had a book resting on a stand on the counter before her.

"May I help you?" she asked cheerfully.

Alexander smiled as he looked around the tidy shop full of shelves of books and a few artifacts. He'd always loved books, ever since he was a child.

He turned his attention back to the proprietor and said, "I certainly hope so. I need maps of the Bitter Islands if you have any."

She nodded at that request and gestured toward the right side of the store. "Maps are over there, organized alphabetically. You'll find what you're looking for under Islands-slash-Bitter. Anything else?"

"Actually," the sorcerer said, "there is. I need information on an event about eight years ago, where three people helped an evacuation?"

She flashed a mischievous smile and chuckled. "Really? You need information on the biggest event on Omejis in…oh, I don't even know how long?"

Alexander played it up, giving her a sheepish smile and an abashed shrug.

"Well, you don't need a book for that," she said. "It's common knowledge. Eight years ago, there was an unexpected eruption by the second biggest volcano of the Bitter Islands, Mount Lauremanda. No one was prepared; there were no foreshocks, no warnings that she was going to blow her top off. And let me tell you, that's exactly what Lauremanda did—blew the top third of the mountain right off!"

She shivered. "It was horrible. There was no chance of rescuing most of the people in the city lower down the mountain." She looked past Alexander, her gaze abstracted by the memory,

"What happened next?" Alexander prompted.

She came out of her reverie and smiled. "Three strangers from Gaea who'd come through the Gatehouse right here in Rilladwen a few days before the event went through the Gatehouse again to the Temple at the Bitter Islands.

"They flew over to Lauremanda, where they held back the pyroclastic cloud, magma, and rocky debris so boats and shuttles could arrive to help everyone evacuate. One of the three of them, the man, opened some kind of mystical gateway on the beach to Temple Mount and ushered people through to safety. He and one of the women even rescued all the wildlife and pets on the island, too. Not a single life was lost. It was truly a miracle."

She looked at him cagily and raised an eyebrow. "Come to think of it, you look astonishingly like one of those three travelers."

"Me?"

She nodded. "Who did you say you were again?"

Alexander doubted much sneaked by her. *She probably suspects who I am.* "No one of any import, I assure you. Thank you for the information."

She smirked, laid her finger alongside her nose with a conspiratorial wink, and said, "Sure thing, hon. You let me know if you need anything else."

He nodded and thanked her again as he turned away. She went back to reading, but he felt her gaze flick to him from time to time as he browsed the maps.

He found what he wanted and looked over the high-resolution imagery. He studied the unusual zigzag of the supercontinental landmass. The locals called it *Ednyfed.* He located the Bitter Islands, about twelve hundred miles north of Rilladwen, the city with the Gatehouse. He found additional maps that showed the terrain.

He saw the details of the cluster of ten volcanic landmasses. They reminded him of Colonia Constantinum, a volcanic island group off the western coast of Demurria, but those islands were much smaller than these. The largest volcano on the Bitter Islands had a Nephilim Temple nestled in the caldera, aptly titled *Temple Mount.* Less than five miles away lay Mount Lauremanda, which the imagery showed in its current condition, with the top third missing and the city on its flanks crumbling and unoccupied. Next, the sorcerer found a map showing Lauremanda's original appearance. Before the eruption, the two volcanoes on their separate islands were almost the same size.

Did Imara, Sireni, and I somehow cause this? Alexander wondered. His usual pragmatism quickly reasserted itself. *It would have happened at some point, anyway. Volcanoes erupt all the time.*

He turned his thoughts to the task at hand. The maps were of good enough quality that he could see the golden shimmer of the superancient shield surrounding the Temple. He squinted, picking up something unexpected: instead of the double doors he was familiar with, there was a sizable wheel-shaped disk engraved with a pattern where those would be. He couldn't see any further details, but the circular entrance was discernible.

Alexander committed the maps to memory and replaced them on

the rack. He thanked the proprietor once again and left the bookstore. He walked around the side of the building unhurriedly until he came to a narrower street that was unoccupied. He darted down the road and snapped his fingers to return to the hotel room.

Nothing happened.

Alexander frowned, held out his hands, spoke the teleportation spell, and clapped them together. He startled several tiny birds roosting in the shade of the small bushes that lined the narrow street but remained right where he was.

He scowled as he considered the few obstacles he knew that could prevent teleportation. To his admittedly limited knowledge of the local species line, no one on Omejis had magical capabilities. They certainly didn't have the technical capacity—aircars were impressive compared to elevators, but stopping displacement through time and space was a whole other level.

What is stopping me? The corruption? We could not teleport on Byrne, either.

He'd gone to that world knowing that was the case, thanks to the researchers from Gaea. They'd proved that the dark magic bled into the astral planes and disrupted the horizon between the material world and the paratroposphere. The only logical conclusion he could draw from his current circumstances was that the corruption was active on Omejis. He'd hoped to land on a planet unaffected by the necromantic attack, but that wasn't the case.

Alexander swore and retraced his steps to the hotel. As he ran through the streets, people stared at him in shock. No one scurried in the tropical heat unless they had no choice. He pounded on the penthouse door until a sleepy Sirenī whipped it open with a scowl that looked pretty instead of exasperated. In his agitation, he forgot that his biometrics were on file from eight years ago.

"Alex!" she exclaimed exasperatedly.

He grinned sheepishly as he darted into the room. "I discovered the corruption is active on this world. I think we must get to the Temple and travel back in time immediately before we become caught up in the events of the present."

"How do you know?" Imara asked a bit grumpily.

"I could not teleport back to this room."

The urgency in his voice galvanized his partners. Imara hurriedly got off the bed and dashed over to collect the queen celerity moth, who'd eaten her way through half the blossoms on the bush she'd selected earlier. Since they had nothing with them, they hurried from the room and found a locked door that Imara said would lead to the roof.

Their biometrics didn't unlock this door, so Alexander snapped his fingers to use his magic on it. The mechanical whir of the locking mechanism sounded, then the door swung open. They hurried through and climbed a flight of stairs to the roof. They stood there for a moment, their attention caught by the lovely view of the city.

It will not be like this for long if we do not find a way to stop my vision from becoming a reality, Alexander thought somberly.

"I've got this," Sirenī declared. "At least there's no magic to fight against."

"I've got the Obscuratus," Imara said.

She sang quietly, and the air pulsed around them with shimmering, iridescent colors. She nodded at Sirenī, who swept her hands out and surrounded them with an impermeable field transected by a flat plane like the one she'd created on Byrne. They lifted into the sky with a whoosh of air blowing past.

The daughter of Medusa looked expectantly at Alexander. He recalled the maps he'd studied and pointed toward the Bitter Islands. Sirenī waved her hand gracefully and sent the sphere hurtling through the air.

It took about three hours to cover approximately twelve hundred miles. Without the interference of the corruption, Sirenī had them cruising above the great ocean with ease. The water, caught between the pull of two moons—one of which orbited almost twice as fast as the other—was turbulent. That smaller body was much closer to Omejis and zoomed through the sky. Most planets had more than one natural satellite; Gaea and Earth were slightly unusual in their singular state.

Omejis was a panthalassic, so the oceans spanned the entire globe, unhindered by land except for a few islands north and south of the supercontinent. The moons of Omejis tugged at the hemispherical seas, yanking titanic waves from the wide bands of landless water that spanned the planet.

Most worlds in the Ring with human stock on them had similar gravity, which made it easy for travelers to go between them without experiencing sudden shocks caused by rapid gravitational increases or decreases. Omejis was no different. The waves below the Three rose twenty to thirty feet before smashing back down. They flowed in a broad east-to-west direction. As they got closer to their destination, the waves in the calmer waters surrounding the Bitter Islands settled down to six- to ten-foot swells.

Eventually, the islands appeared in the distance. The cones of ten volcanoes rose above the sea's surface. They were covered in lush vegetation and teeming with life. Small cities sat about a third of the way up the volcanoes on the four biggest islands. Each city organically followed the landscape rather than changing nature's preestablished architecture. The Bitter Islands were warm but not tropical and covered in dense greenery and exotic flowers. Nothing taller than a three-foot-high bush was visible as they approached.

Nestled in the partially collapsed cone of the tallest volcano, set roughly in the center of the cluster of islands, the arc of the superancient shield glimmered brightly in the evening light. They'd reached their journey's end, and Sirenī slowed their bubble to a stop just shy of the golden field effects that protected the Temple. She looked at Imara, then Alexander. He nodded and gestured her to move forward; she willed it so, and their bubble collided with the shield and passed through.

Sirenī grinned in triumph and set their impermeable sphere down ten feet from the massive circular portal of the Nephilim Temple. She dismissed the field effect with a wave of her hand so that the Three stood on the lush grass carpeting the caldera.

Alexander studied the interior of the barrier and frowned.

Why does this place feel so familiar? he wondered. He couldn't put his finger on it, but it was there.

The high walls rose a hundred feet above the level bottom of the shattered cone. Part of the wall had collapsed in some distant antiquity when the volcano erupted. It had created a breach in the circular perimeter about a quarter mile across, which was undoubtedly how most people accessed the caldera if they wanted to come to the Temple —or, more accurately, to look at it through the shield.

The Temple sat dead center in the filled-in cone of the extinct volcano. Alexander assumed that if the ancients had put a Temple atop a volcano, then they'd also stoppered that mountain for good.

It was probably easy for them. After all, they'd built an intra- and inter-universal transit system that has worked flawlessly for over one hundred million years.

The Three took a long look at the beautiful setting. It was easy to admire the Nephilim. They were legendary beings. They had created thousands of genetic variations of humans and seeded them on alien worlds to see how they evolved. There was a dark side to all greatness, however, and the legends and theories couldn't hide that unpalatable truth.

On Earth, the Nephilim were fearsome, Hellish, cannibalistic giants. The legends about the ancient ones were like that on many worlds. Alexander reserved judgment—he'd never met a Nephilim, so he didn't know what they were really like.

Surely, they had the same ratio of assholes that every planet seems to have, he thought wryly.

Imara dispelled the Obscuratus and looked at her companions. "What now?" She gestured to encompass the environment inside and outside the ancient shield. "I can cast the time travel spell here; it's as good a place as any. We already know we go eight years into the past."

Alexander nodded without hesitation.

Sirenī just grinned. "Let's do it."

Imara shifted Thīaterīka to her shoulder and ensured the insect was settled before she focused on her magic. She still felt a little logy from her expenditure on Byrne, but she knew she could cast the spell—she'd already done it since Present Amlodd thought he knew them from eight years before. Future Three went back in time and met Past Amlodd, but he didn't know about that.

She began to hum until she felt her magic rise in a scintillating corona that swirled around her body. She'd written the enchantment in the journal along with instructions for its use, so she knew what to do. She began to sway as she let the power build and brought the words to mind.

Sirenī and Alex stood at her shoulders, near but not touching. She'd explained to Sirenī about the time travel spell and what she'd written about it, but she hadn't told Alex. He trusted her implicitly, though, and waited patiently while she worked.

Imara inhaled deeply and began to sing in Demurrian. The words of the time-traveling incantation fell from her lips, and she felt echoes roll away and come crashing back as time began to buckle. Future Imara had written the spell in the journal, and Present Imara had the book stashed in her aura even now, in case she wanted to refer to its contents again.

She raised her arms over her head and let her voice go. As it rose and belled outward, the spellsong's melody filled the caldera with cascading ripples, ethereal and pure. The wave of sound rolled down the volcano like the magma that once flowed from the crust of Omejis through the vent provided by the mountain. It washed over Temple City one-third of the way up the peak, and citizens stopped in their tracks. In the buildings, everyone froze, enraptured as her magical power flowed over them and held them enthralled.

She finished the spellsong and went immediately into a second rendition of the chant to continue building strength. The energy gradient throbbed in the air in rhythmic counterpoint to her voice, becoming a deep pulse that echoed the pauses and phrases of her spellsong. The air around them began to blur as her power spun out, swirling in a multicolored tornado that whipped at their hair and clothes as the currents of energy billowed and shimmered.

The energy gradient became an overwhelming, pounding force that radiated up from the floor of the caldera and crashed through their bones and teeth—a visceral thunder created by Imara's escalating power. Sirenī raised her hands to catch her hair as her clothing fluttered and flapped. Alex didn't have to worry about his hair, but the dust and grasses the spell tore into the air stung his face, and he held up a hand to shield his eyes.

Imara ignored the wind and debris. Her dark hair whipped over her face and blew about her mouth, nose, and eyes with abandon, but she was lost in her spellsong. The celerity moth on her shoulder trembled slightly in the chaotic winds that whipped Imara's hair and clothes about and spun dust and grass through the air. Beyond that, the insect remained unaffected by the magical storm and continued to sit contentedly on the songstress's shoulder.

Imara's spellsong rose to greater heights, and the air vibrated with a dozen radiant echoes of her voice. The power she'd raised snapped into orderly, luminous field lines. They spiraled and looped outward from her body before curving back on themselves in multicolored flux patterns as they propagated through hyperlocal spacetime.

The air around them stilled. Sirenī and Alex dropped their hands and looked around, fascinated to see the spell at work. Imara continued to sing; the caldera began to blur beyond the cage of flux lines radiating around the three of them. The Temple seemed to fall away, and the crater's walls became distant as the Three traveled through time. Energy cycled around them like a hurricane's vortex. Simultaneously, they stood still in its eye, illuminated by hypnotic pulsations of every hue of the rainbow and more variations of color than they could count.

The cage of flux lines remained stable, oscillating around them, sustaining them in safety as the hyperlocal universe rewound itself by eight years. Imara sensed they'd reached the proper time when an echo of her song fluttered in her acute hearing. She let the melody fade, and the flux lines contracted as the echoes of the magic dwindled.

Imara's corona faded. She looked at her companions and collapsed. The celerity moth instantly took flight as she folded to the ground. She didn't lose consciousness, but she felt depleted and weak. Sirenī and

Alex knelt beside her. He drew her head into his lap while Sirenī held her hands above Imara's body. The songstress smiled up at them as they stared at her in concern.

"I'm just tired," she protested. Her voice sounded feeble, but she could feel her vitality returning. "It was exhausting to summon that much power after what I did on Byrne, but I'm already feeling better."

She smiled reassuringly at her partners. They weren't convinced, and Alex held her gently in his lap while Sirenī looked sternly at her.

"Let me delve you to make sure everything's okay," Sirenī said.

Imara reached up and caressed Alex's forearm. He smiled lovingly at her as Sirenī used her psychic sight to scan through Imara's body. She sighed when she finished, and Imara reached out to her partner with her free hand.

The baby? Imara conveyed to her partner.

"Everything is fine. It worked," Sirenī said, pleased.

Imara almost burst into tears but managed to keep from over-reacting.

Alex studied the women with a skeptical expression, and Imara knew they'd let the cat out of the bag. He looked from one to the other, his eyebrows slowly climbing his forehead.

"What is going on? What do you mean 'it worked?'"

Imara caught Sirenī's gaze and smiled; then she looked at Alex and said, "Help me up. We're not having this conversation with me lying on the ground."

They shifted positions and helped her to her feet. The songstress unnecessarily dusted herself off and extended a hand to Thīaterīka. The moth landed with a flutter of her wings. They shimmered brightly with glorious iridescent patterns that moved hypnotically across the fragile-looking appendages.

Alex gasped and pointed at the substantial insect's thorax. "She has offspring."

The observation distracted him for the moment, which Imara capitalized on. She and Sirenī looked at the moth's underside and eagerly peeked at three softly glowing eggs.

"That's incredible. I can't believe she survived on Byrne by herself with these eggs all that time!" Sirenī exclaimed. "Now that's a great example of motherhood."

"That's amazing," Imara concurred. "I don't know how she did it, but she protected them while her world disintegrated and everything died. It must have been awful to be alone at the end, knowing she might die. Still, she did everything in her power to keep her children safe."

She looked at Sirenī and held out her hand. Sirenī reached out and held fast, her eyes welling with unshed tears. Alex looked from one woman to the other. Imara knew he sensed what was happening, but here and now wasn't the place to tell him they were pregnant.

Fourteen
Quattuordecim

Ävidä Saclendra sat on a throne before an assemblage of hundreds. His green eyes glittered in his rugged, granite-like visage. He always had the same hard, cold, and demanding look. He was a necromancer, and a powerful one, offspring of the greatest līc ever to live, the dark terror Adrienne Vorpahl.

He held his stern demeanor for his dark children. They needed a firm hand to rule them and focus their dark desires. Without him, they wouldn't work together for ten minutes, never mind the years his great plan required.

Some of those in the assemblage wore heavily embroidered robes of all different colors with wards and sigils woven into the fine artisanal garments. Some wore finely woven metals, garments from exotic materials he didn't recognize, and others just their animate forms. Most of them were grotesque, desiccated, suppurating, oozing, skeletal, or some combination thereof, but a few of the naked ones were rosy, life-like, and beautiful.

Others wore supple human leather pants and vests, richly colored and finely stitched by hand. It wasn't easy to skin people without ruining the material—Ävidä knew a few talented harvesters, but they were rare.

Making human leather is an art form, he thought.

All but two of those before him—his second-in-command, Lucullus, and the Persian—had one thing in common. All were his dark offspring, carefully cultivated from the plebeian masses, each given the promise of immortality and great power so long as they served him. Lucullus considered Ävidä his dark father in undeath despite the fact that he'd become a līc on his own.

Though he sat by himself on his cathedra, a hefty throne made of luminously white, softly glowing soulstone, he was not alone. He shared his right eye with Kāmla Vicchāya. She was in her office on Gaea and privy to this secret meeting through a powerful enchantment that was difficult for many to cast. It only took him thirty hours to recite the complex phrases of the Epiphany of Light and bind the spell to his eye. Fortunately, he had a stockpile of thefted energy to draw on to maintain the power-sucking enchantment.

The risk of miscasting—and thus the consequences—scaled in geometric proportion to the spell. If someone miscast a cantrip or a charm, they might burn the skin of their fingers. Miscast a fireball or lightning bolt, and spellburns could flicker across their torso and legs. If someone miscast the Epiphany of Light or Sound, they'd likely make a crater two hundred feet in diameter, and the interior would glow cherry red for weeks.

Casting any of the three Epiphanies was a risk that demanded an excellent reason. Ävidä believed the risk was worth the reward. He showed Kāmla Vicchāya what it meant to be a līc, to be Undying, and to live by the pain and death of others. It wasn't a path for the faint of heart or those who couldn't commit their heart and soul to the practice. Anything less than absolutism was a failure. To be a līc was to take life and torture, rape, murder, and feast on the flesh of the living. He ate people while they screamed and begged for mercy. Every depraved act gave power to a līc, feeding them with the energies of pain, suffering, and death.

If Kāmla couldn't commit to this—and Ävidä had his doubts—then she couldn't participate in his grand scheme. She was naïve but powerful, so he wanted her on board, but he'd need to see if she would go the distance. Ävidä expected her to fail, but he was amenable to being surprised, too.

Kāmla wasn't one of his dark offspring. She'd come to the darkest necromancy on her own. She grew up in the shadow of the world's most gifted magic user, Alexander Eldred, and her hatred of the sorcerer drove her to gain the power to rival him. Ävidä knew she'd be unable to stand toe to toe with Eldred, but he also knew her unreasoning hatred might drive her to try.

I certainly wouldn't risk fighting him. She may be powerful and dangerous, but she's no Eldred.

He smirked, knowing she could see from his eye but not hear or sense his mind.

But what would she think if she could read my mind or see the foul, vile things crawling through my head?

His depravity and willingness to do anything to survive were bottomless. His smile broadened at his thoughts. His children assumed it was intended for them, but they were no more aware of his actual goals than Kāmla. He let the smile linger a moment and smoothed his expression, becoming stone-faced and impassive once more.

Groups shifted and merged as his offspring moved among one another with varying degrees of cunning and intent. Most were unfriendly, but many were allied with the understanding that such alliances could shift as quickly as circumstances warranted.

He felt pleased by the mob before him; he sat forward on his cathedra, lifted his hands, and threw back his hood. The gleam of magic flashed like liquid metal in his right eye as he swept his gaze across the multitude. The gathering stilled as his dread offspring quieted, turned to look at him, and listened to his words.

"My children." His voice rolled easily through the spacious hall of his citadel. The room was in shadow, but the undead could see clearly, thanks to their magical nature. "The time has come. You've all been told which worlds are yours to oversee. Most of you will transit the Nephilim gates to your new homes in the coming weeks. You may do as you see fit with the local populations, provided you share most of the energy you acquire with me."

He grinned slyly. "I know you will take some power for yourselves; it's only right." His offspring tittered and laughed, looking at each other sideways as they acknowledged this truth. "I hope you play, indulge, and discover new and creative ways of draining vital prāṇa from your toys."

His children and guest from Earth, Dilṣad, began to murmur excitedly. They shifted in anticipation. His children's myriad faces and raiments undulated as they moved and chattered quietly. He waited a few moments to let the tension build, then thrust up a hand, palm toward the group, fingers spread. Necromantic energies sparkled and danced around his fingers.

"As I am not one for self-indulgent bloviating, let the celebrations begin!" he called.

The group cheered, three hundred roaring voices of all kinds—high-pitched, deep, rumbling, rough, silky, childish, and cultured. The various tonalities and ranges rumbled together into a swelling clamor. Ävidä let it go for a few moments, then swept his fingers in a graceful gesture. Virulent green light washed over the enormous double doors at the entrance to the hall, and they swung open.

Living and reanimated servants pushed six large, wheeled cages into the room. They were filled with hundreds of playthings captured from twenty different worlds. There were men, women, and children of all shapes, sizes, and ages. The living servants directed the zombies to push the cages and place them in predetermined locations around the vast room, three to each side. The handlers then ushered the zombies from the space and followed behind, swiftly closing the doors with a loud thud.

Ävidä watched indulgently as the terrified people began to scream, struggle, cry, or faint when they saw the motley throng in the chamber. They were all beautiful, nubile, young, and full of vitality. Vaporous green traceries already floated in the air in faint, sparkling threads that began forming clots of tortured, pain-filled psychic energy.

The archlīc laughed in delight and watched his children split into groups around the wheeled pens. They studied the tastiness within as anticipation and terror built between the two groups…and the gates opened. His offspring began to feed and play, the magical currents condensing into solid energy streams as the party began.

Fourteen

Kāmla shivered as she watched the madness begin. Ävidä's demilīc and līc offspring tore into people as they screamed, thrashed, and tried to fight or escape. Wailing children of all ages were ripped from their parents' arms and peeled like apples while they howled and tore their vocal cords. Their parents screamed just as loudly as they tried to stop the insanity.

But you can't stop it, she thought.

She became so turned on by the spectacle that she had a mini-orgasm without even touching herself.

She watched the power-mad undead rip intestines out of people's stomachs, coiling the hot, greasy organs around their wrists as their victims squealed and writhed. Flickering, sulfurous green energy crackled around the loops of their guts as the heaving coils throbbed with a surge of blood and shit as adrenaline dumped into their systems. She could imagine the fetid stench that filled the air as people lost control of their bowels and bladders. Some of the līc assaulted their victims more conventionally with gang rapes for those who maintained functional genitalia. Those people couldn't scream since they were being fucked in every hole.

The līc in the great hall glowed with the noxious green energies they stole from their victims. Several of them cackled in crazed delight and reveled in the orgiastic violence.

Kāmla watched with an avid leer; her cold exterior washed away in the heat of the moment. She began to get lost in the haze of sexual excitement and ruthlessly reined herself in. She needed to stay focused and keep her eyes on the goal. Ävidä thought he had everything under control, including her, but she had plans that didn't include a man dominating her.

She felt resistance to her right and scowled. She looked at her hand and tightened her fist to draw more energy from the girl beside her. Her administrative aide was an exceedingly annoying girl who constantly made mistakes. Kāmla couldn't abide that and had found a better use for the stupid bitch. Now the foolish young woman lay on the floor, surrounded by a spreading pool of blood as Kāmla stole her life force.

She'd called the girl into her office at the end of the day and hit her with Lethargum Cantatio, which stunned her and knocked her to the floor. The Grade One spell only took two words to cast, but anyone with even a modicum of magic could resist the charm. The idiotic girl couldn't even withstand a basic charm—thus proving she'd serve better as food than help.

Kāmla got up and dragged the girl around her desk beside her chair. She was a pretty thing, full-figured and curvaceous. Kāmla stroked her cheek while she lay there, head lolling, then tore her blouse open. She looked at the globes of her breasts and licked her lips, tempted to ravage the girl, but she exerted iron self-control and plunged her nails into the girl's abdomen. She carved the girl's flesh with a word of power and peeled back the hot, slippery tissues of her belly. She reached in, looped the girl's guts around her right wrist, and sat in her chair.

Now, Kāmla looked down at the dying girl's body and admired the quiver and pulse of her guts. She could see the movement of blood through her aorta and hoped the fool would last long enough for Kāmla to achieve her goals. She tugged on her intestines and squeezed, feeling the ropes of muscle quiver and squirm in her fist.

The minister focused on the rich pump of blood and shit through the quivering small intestines as she sucked the vital energies into herself. The virulent green sparkles of light flickered and flared over her arm as she took a deep breath and began to chant. She quietly cast a complex spell, her gaze abstracted as she held the words of the magic in her mind. She made sure to do it perfectly—there would be no coming back from a miscasting.

She turned her focus on Ävidä.

She held a talisman engraved with magical symbols and arcane geometries in her left hand. As she recited the incantation, the device began to glow with a dull, leaden radiance. The medallion was a one-time-use device, a repository of a complicated spell that Kāmla had researched extensively but didn't have the wherewithal to cast. She'd used several intermediaries until she reached someone with that skill.

She purchased the device through a series of favors and the costly exchange of mass and energy credits. It bankrupted her to acquire this talisman, but it was worth every drop of blood, sweat, and scheming.

She finished the activation spell and went rigid in her chair. Her back lengthened and painfully arched as the connection she'd manipulated Ävidä into making between them allowed her to entangle this spell with the one he'd cast. The medallion in her hand burst into eldritch golden flames that seared her hand with a bright flash. The sickly-sweet sizzle of human flesh assailed her nostrils. Kāmla inhaled deeply, and the pain and stench of cooked meat thrilled her as her body relaxed.

She'd succeeded.

She glanced carefully at her left palm and saw a ropey mess of scar tissue. The shiny ridges blurred and faded away even though the pain of the burn lingered dully. She took a breath and tumbled sideways as the room oscillated around her. She heard the distant echo of words as the flicker and flash of Ävidä's thoughts burst across the field of her mind in strobing flares.

A triumphant grin curved her reddened lips as she breached every one of Ävidä's defenses and gained access to his deepest secrets. She'd manipulated him into casting the Epiphany of Light by fucking his brains out, as well as wistfully wishing to see the orgiastic theater he'd planned to celebrate the planting of the kṛtyā bījā. He'd capitulated quickly, eager to show off his prowess like all men. She'd made a big deal of it and fucked him some more, and he'd willingly connected their minds to let her see through his right eye.

Now, she'd connected to his thoughts without his awareness. Indeed, his thoughts didn't indicate he knew she was listening as she carefully plucked every filthy secret from his deliciously vile mind. He'd always dismissed the Epiphany of Sound, but she'd figured out how to use it to listen to his thoughts without his knowledge.

Kāmla had worried he'd be able to see through her right eye as she could through his, but she discovered that he couldn't. He was irritated at himself for overlooking that. She cackled in delight and wove through his mind, looking, probing, evaluating.

And the great fucking archlic doesn't even know!

She saw memories of his master, Adrienne Vorpahl. She watched the monstrous archlīc rape and maul Ävidä while he was alive, battering and breaking his body and mind until she could mold him into her perfect servant. Kāmla admired the horrifying depths of depravity Adrienne reached in her murderous rampage of more than a thousand years of terror.

It was awe-inspiring.

Kāmla shook her head and continued to study Ävidä's mind. She saw spells and incantations she didn't even know existed. She also discovered protected memories, magically sealed and warded to prevent spying like hers. She stayed well away from the glimmering wizard's web of defensive enchantments and studied the warded memories from a safe distance.

Every protection a wizard erected around their thoughts was imperfect. Thoughts inside the barrier resonated with similar or adjacent but related thoughts outside, causing seepage. The glimpses were small, momentary flickers, intuitive urges, and sudden insights. Kāmla watched them for several minutes and was rewarded by the ghostly impression of a book. The name came to her, written in Darhavil: Pāskendiñoldor.

She made a mental note of the name and moved on, careful to remain wide of the dangerous wizard's web. She had no doubt it would incapacitate her if she triggered the wards, and Ävidä would know she was in his mind if that happened. She shivered, terrified at what he would do to her if he uncovered her betrayal.

Someday, I'll confront him, but not yet.

Ävidä watched the festivities until his appetite increased beyond all reason, and his lust made him rabid. He raised a hand and beckoned imperiously from his luminous soulstone cathedra. Within seconds, a tall, skeletal figure emerged from the orgiastic horror in the main hall. Lucullus's smoldering eyes fixed on Ävidä as he approached with a tasty treat for his dark father.

The archlīc grinned maliciously as his second-in-command—who would soon become an archlīc if things continued apace—trudged stolidly up the steps of the dais upon which Ävidä's throne rested. He held a squirming six or seven-year-old child in his arms; the morsel dug at the skeletal form of the tall, fiery-eyed līc and wailed in terror. Ävidä studied the līc as he approached. Lucullus was covered in blood; strings of meat hung from his jaw and teeth. The gristly evidence of his feasting displayed hanks of muscle marbled with ribbons of glistening fatty tissue and the delicate tracery of veins.

The little boy was covered in blood, too, but none of it was his own; he was wriggling and howling, trying to escape while Lucullus held him with just enough force to bruise but not unduly damage him. The skeleton knelt before Ävidä and extended his arms, offering the squirming child to his dark father. The archlīc smiled, revealing his even, white teeth in a monstrous expression that made the boy howl in terror. His shrieks escalated in a fevered frenzy as the archlīc began to eat him alive.

Through his right eye, Ävidä knew Kāmla saw everything going on as blood fountained onto his face and stained his robes. He had no doubt the minister was thrilled with the violence—she was a monster inside a beautiful body, as depraved as anyone he'd ever met.

With the meat and blood of his plaything came the hot surge of vital energy. It was the same power vampires fed on, but the suckers only drank the liquid; they didn't eat the flesh it pulsed through. The līc consumed everything. They broke bones to get the marrow; sucked eyeballs from their sockets and popped them between their teeth; and ripped out the tongues of screaming victims to savor the spongy, slippery morsels.

Līc would gleefully yank the testicles from a howling man or dig out the ovaries and uterus of a screaming woman. Those tender, life-generating nuggets carried a lot of vital energy. There was magical power in every piece of the human body, in all its fluids and components. The only exceptions were shit and piss, as those contained no vital energies because they were what was left over from the things that brought life, not a source of such themselves.

Ävidä knew there was a myth that children had more vital force than adults because they had many years ahead of them to live. That was a lie; everything about them was smaller, so they had less mass to eat and enjoy. On the other hand, they were more sincere in their terror and more intense in their trauma. That made the power they gave sweeter, if not more potent or voluble.

The skinny form in his arms twitched and tried weakly to escape, but the thin arms only beat harmlessly against Ävidä's head as he leaned in for each bite. He was careful not to perforate anything vital and kill the child too quickly. That just wasted the remaining energy.

He paused in his feast and looked over the writhing, shrieking madhouse on the floor. No one līc had ever fathered so many dark children, and Ävidä prided himself on bringing so many undead into the world. The glut of energy he'd gained from his experiment with Byrne gave him the ability to seek out and shepherd desperate, impressionable would-be necromancers along the dark path. His hundreds of offspring allowed him to send six of them to fifty different worlds, along with dark seeds that would take five to ten years to reach full maturity. The amended corruption spell would bring power into the magical phylacteria secreted in his keep when that happened.

He'd told Kāmla Vicchāya they could rule together, but that was a lie. He would reign alone, superior above all, just as his family had for ages before the travesty of Unification cut off their balls and rendered them weak and pathetic… He heard a wet crunching sound and glanced down; his blood-covered face creased into a scowl as he saw stark, jagged white rib bones sticking through the skin of the boy's chest. He'd squeezed his hands too hard on the brat's torso while thinking of his family's fall from grace before the inanity of the Unified Government.

"Fuck," he grunted.

He tossed the tiny corpse aside, angry that he'd killed his plaything before milking him of every drop of power he had to give. He growled and stood suddenly, forcing Lucullus to step back as Ävidä ripped off his robes to reveal his lean, muscular animate form and proud erection. His appetites were thoroughly inflamed by the feast before him as he strode naked into the crowd below. He bellowed in pleasure and primal power as he sank his teeth into the flank of a screaming man while snatching a writhing woman out of the mass before him, jerking her to his side to use next.

At the same time, one of his children, deceptively dainty and petite, grabbed and ripped off the man's left arm with an insane giggle. Her blond pigtails were soaked with blood and bounced playfully as she ate. Ävidä grinned at her as he laughed; he shoved the maimed man away and turned his attention to the shrieking woman he'd grabbed.

Before Ävidä raped her, his eyes fell on the only figure in the room he didn't control and couldn't be sure of—a monstrously obese figure whose skin was stretched taut and filled with a syrupy, glisteningly noxious fluid. It circulated slowly beneath the flesh of the līc while his pendulous genitals swung between his thighs, as bloated—and flaccid—as the rest of him. He had shiny yellowy fingers jammed in a woman's mouth and was ripping out her teeth with a crazy, high-pitched titter of delight.

Ävidä turned his burning hot gaze on the face of his current victim while two feet away, the little blond girl used her lips and teeth to suck an eyeball from the screaming man, who had fallen to the floor and was thrashing in terrible pain as blood hemorrhaged from his awful wounds. All around him, madness reigned, and it would until every last plaything in the room was dead.

Kāmla now understood everything, and in discovering what she needed, she severed her illicit magical connection to her Undying partner. She tugged on the ropes of the intestine coiled around her right wrist and forearm as they rubbed squishily across her palm; it elicited a weak moan from the dying girl on the floor. The minister straightened and glared down at the girl, scowling as the enormous blood pool spread around her.

She couldn't even bleed right. Cunt.

She now knew the fifty different worlds receiving the kṛtyā bījā, which Ävidä always kept secret. Most of his offspring would depart to those worlds, but he planned to keep Lucullus and two dozen others behind.

She also knew the location of his citadel, which he'd also kept hidden—World Two, where he'd tested the first-generation corruption spell. His fortress was encapsulated in a vacuolation of spacetime, separate from Byrne's desolated existence. She'd discovered that even before he tested the corruption spell on Byrne, he'd isolated an island within a vacuole because he'd thought it was beautiful. He'd lived in his castle there for over a century while he undertook his great work. He had a Gatehouse on the island, which was how he came and went from it.

Ävidä planned to rule absolutely over the fifty worlds he'd selected, intending to keep breeding populations of humans alive on each. They'd constantly regenerate and provide an endless, highly renewable energy source. He could maintain his power indefinitely; he was immortal, and time no longer kept its tight grip on him.

Undying experienced the passage of time, but they adjusted to a new definition of it with their undead immortality. It wouldn't matter to Ävidä when those fifty worlds fell because he and his offspring would rule over playgrounds of endless billions. Energy would constantly feed into the phylacteria on Byrne and provide limitless power for the archlīc and those he deigned to grant it to.

Kāmla smiled and extricated her hand and forearm from the loops of her aide's intestines. She had the roadmap of her partner's plans.

Now, I just have to figure out the weak points and exploit them.

Finding things was her particular strength. She did not doubt that her instincts would lead her to every vulnerability Ävidä had, and she would carefully exploit them, one by one, until she destroyed him. His plans for her were the same. It only remained to see who killed whom first.

Fifteen
Quindecim

Imara's eyes widened as she looked at and into the queen celerity moth's eggs. "You have offspring. Did I put them at risk by taking you through time with us?" she asked the elegant creature. She spoke aloud for the benefit of Sirenī and Alex.

\You did not. The eggs are safe, protected by my life force. We were dying on our world. Here we are safe and strong. Your mate's energies restored my failing vitality,\ the moth replied.

The songstress smiled and glanced at each of her companions. "Her name is Thīaterīka. I've already given her your names. She says her offspring are safe, and your healing spell revitalized her, Alex."

Sirenī smiled at the news, although Alex looked unconvinced. Imara knew he wasn't off his previous question—he knew something was happening outside the norm.

"It's a pleasure to meet you," Sirenī told the moth.

Thīaterīka fluttered her wings, though Imara didn't know what it signified. She could speak and understand the moth's language, but her nonverbals were as opaque to Imara as to anyone else.

"Will your offspring be able to restore your species?" Sirenī asked.

\Yes,\ Thīaterīka replied via Imara's translation. \I bear three queens. One is my own. The others are from the last queens who died after we failed to stop the corruption. We determine the number and type of offspring we need to control our species so we always live in balance with the world.\

Imara's partner smiled and clapped her hands. "That's wonderful, Thīaterīka. I'm so delighted for you." Imara frowned at her. "I mean, the death of your homeworld sucks, but at least you can save the celerity moths."

\What do you mean?\

Imara translated for the moth. \That's what humans call your species. Do you have a name for yourselves?\

Thīaterīka fluttered her wings. \We do not.\

As Imara relayed the message, she was keenly aware of Alex's steady gaze but kept her focus on the moth. They couldn't take Thīaterīka with them through the following stages of their journey. Of course, Imara was the only one that knew what to expect from the forthcoming future history of their lives. Sirenī had some foreknowledge of what was coming, but Alex was unaware and needed to remain such. She'd hinted about it in the journal but never came right out and said why he needed to stay ignorant.

Poor Alex. He has no idea what to expect...

Imara smoothed her expression and faced her companions. She directed her words to Thīaterīka. "If you're amenable to it, I'd like to send you through the Nephilim Temple to Earth. You'll be safe there, and we can reconnect once we return to our previous time."

Thīaterīka fluttered her wings in acceptance. She remained silent and sat comfortably on Imara's left hand. Sensing Thīaterīka's contentment, the songstress looked at Alex for approval.

In response, he gestured toward the massive circular door that led to the Temple. Abstract patterns were etched into the gigantic bronze-colored disc. It protruded from the walls of the Temple about six inches. As the Three approached with Thīaterīka, lines of red light shimmered subtly along the relief carved into the metallic material. Then, the wheel smoothly rose along the outer façade of the building.

They went inside the Temple. A light glimmered slowly to dazzling brilliance and cast a shadowless glow from the air. The dais in the back of the Temple was identical to the one on Gaea. As they approached it, a subtle crimson gleam emanated from the periphery of the circular platform, forming a hazy curtain that rose to the ceiling.

Alex stopped three feet from the platform and summoned a holographic display. He studied it briefly, tapped several times, and looked over his shoulder at Imara. "You can place her on the dais."

Imara stepped forward and extended her hand through the curtain of light. Thīaterīka fluttered off her hand onto the center of the dais.

\You'll be safe in the garden at Jordan's place. Please stay in the woods there until we come back to find you.\

Thīaterīka fluttered her wings in agreement.

Imara felt a moment of fear but reminded herself that she already knew Thīaterīka had lived on the property all this time. Since they were eight years in the past, that meant the celerity moth had been near them during their stay on Earth. She clarified that with the moth before she left.

\Thīaterīka, we're sending you to Earth at an earlier time. We'll arrive in your future at some point, but we won't yet know you because of how things play out. Please avoid us until we reach out to you.\

\Very well.\

The queen celerity moth's whispery vibrations of understanding reassured the songstress. Imara smiled and backed away from the dais. She nodded at Alex, and he tapped the display. When he did, the shimmering curtain hardened to a bright synthetic red and flickered out, revealing the empty platform. Alex waved a hand to dismiss the holographic display and faced the women. He studied them for a moment; Imara knew what was coming.

He cocked his head. "Back to my question: what worked?"

Imara and Sirenī smiled and held hands. The women placed their free hands on their lower abdomens.

"We're pregnant," the songstress told him.

Alexander's knees weakened, but he managed to stay upright. His ears rang as he processed what Imara said.

Both of them. When?

He knew how frequently they'd had sex since they reunited—pretty much every night, often more than once. He had forty-eight years of separation to make up for.

After a moment, the shock wore off, and he took a deep breath. He felt something tingle through him and felt an unbridled happiness well up. The emotion was so strong it blew past his usual staid reserve. Orange-red electricity crackled around him, and his eyes began to glow a strident crimson as his feet drifted off the floor. He held out his hands, and his partners came to him and took hold, with Imara on his left and Sirenī on his right.

They laughed as his magic slipped around them and embraced them and his unborn children. They lifted into the air and hovered, rotating slowly.

"I…am overjoyed," he told them.

Imara saw tears well in Alex's eyes. They refracted the crimson light into prismatic sparks. She felt him pull her and Sirenī against his chest; he buried his face in the gap between their heads. Imara felt so comfortable in their embrace that she closed her eyes and floated in their shared joy. After about ten minutes, they dropped gently to the ground, and Alex's magical corona subsided. He released his partners to arm's length with a happy smile.

"Will the babes be safe with everything we must do?" he asked. "Magic can be risky.

He looked from Imara to Sirenī, face to belly, and back again.

"I believe so," Imara hedged. "I'm confident the amṛta will keep them safe," she said, her voice modulated to project certainty.

She couldn't enchant Alex into believing her, but she could seem confident enough to overcome his worries. Alex studied her for a moment, then looked at Sirenī, who gazed blandly back. He went and rested a hand on each of their bellies and gave them a soft look. Imara and Sirenī grinned at his happiness.

After a few moments, Alex dropped his hands and cleared his throat. "I spoke with the proprietor of a bookstore in Rilladwen. I learned about some events from our journey to Omejis. Three days after our arrival, the next mountain over from this one erupted without warning. We traveled from the Gatehouse in Rilladwen to the Temple, flew to Mount Lauremanda, and held back the lava and pyroclastic debris. This gave the citizens time to evacuate.

"Apparently, we saved everyone with our actions, even the pets. Remember the Gatehouse Transit Authority official we met, Amlodd? He indicated that the governor is happy to cover our stay—all because of our actions with this event."

Imara blinked and said, "Did you follow all of that, Sirenī? I feel like it's awfully convoluted."

Sirenī laughed. "It certainly is."

Alex chuckled. "Well, we know what we must do because Amlodd also said he figured we must have left via the Temple. He inadvertently provided a map for the next steps in our journey."

"Well, let's go, then," Sirenī said excitedly. "But first, can you gift me their language?"

Imara transferred her understanding of the local dialect to her partner. Then Alex gestured for them to step over to the dais. She and Sirenī stood side by side as the shimmering red field surrounded the platform.

"Try activating the holographic interface. You should have an intuitive understanding of the system, like me—I believe it comes from the amṛta," he explained.

The two women nodded, and Imara held out her hand, willing the display to form before her as she'd seen it do for Alex. When nothing happened, she frowned, dropped her hand, and looked at Sirenī. She repeated Imara's gesture, but nothing happened for her, either. She glowered at the dais as if it were at fault. The women slanted glances at Alex.

He raised an eyebrow and looked at the dais; a holographic pane formed immediately in front of him. His eyes narrowed, and he studied the panel. The icons and text on the hovering display altered to a densely packed script, and Alex looked at it for several moments.

"I see," he murmured. "Amṛta provides higher-level access to the

Infernal Gate system, but you need to gesture to summon an interface panel."

"You don't need to gesture," Sirenī pointed out.

Alex shrugged. "I have no idea why the system seems more responsive to me. That is a topic for later consideration. Try again with a gesture."

Imara took a breath and reached out a hand, fingers spread. She directed her mental attention to the dais—nothing happened. She frowned and focused. It should have been easy.

I can sing people to death, but I can't activate a holographic display? she fumed.

Imara narrowed her eyes slightly and "pushed" her thoughts at the machinery. She felt a click as if something inside her had connected to something in the superancient artifact. A crimson display flared under her hand, and she dropped it to her side. She studied the floating panel with fascination and was relieved to see everything written in Demurrian. Alex's displays were all in Darhavil, and she'd dreaded having to wade through the language. She understood it, could read it fluently, and could speak it enough to cast spells, but it didn't come easily to her.

The songstress mentally thanked the control system and dismissed the display. She turned to Alex. "How did you get that textual content to show up?"

"I asked the system how you could access it. I believe the automation or whatever runs these systems is either intelligent or semi-sentient. The display always shows the correct entry when I want to go to a specific planet. I assumed it could handle requests of different kinds."

"Huh." She looked at Sirenī and summarized her experience. "Your turn, love."

Sirenī listened and nodded, then extended a hand. She pursed her full lips. Another holographic pane appeared with a list of planet names written in Demurrian, except for one notated in Darhavil.

Imara could see it easily from beside her partner, and she pointed at the entry. "What's that planet? I'm not sure of my translation of the Darhavil."

Alex looked at it. "It says Ôrëńen. It has a numeric designator of four zeros." He looked at them excitedly. "It could be the homeworld of the Nephilim."

"Well, someday we'll have to go there," she said, tempering his enthusiasm. "For now, we have a task to complete here."

Alex studied the display for a moment longer and sighed. "Yes. Someday."

Imara touched his shoulder gently and looked at Sirenī. "Why don't you do the honors since you've got the display up?"

Her partner nodded and read the names below entry zero-zero-zero-zero. They saw that Gaea was the second world on the list under entry zero-zero-zero-one, with Byrne after that and Earth under zero-zero-zero-three. Imara was fascinated reading the other planet names, many of which no one on Gaea knew. People from her homeworld had gone on numerous expeditions to other worlds in the Ring over the last several thousand years. Not all planets had living civilizations or ruins near the Gatehouses, so travelers and scholars didn't always uncover names. They scrolled the list and stared, shocked, by thousands of worlds.

"What's that one? Pritanea?" Imara pointed to World Fourteen-Fourteen.

Alex narrowed his eyes. "I believe it is a panthalassic, like Omejis. It has islands and a few microcontinents. No land animals exist, and the abundant ocean life is non-carnivorous."

Imara frowned and asked, "How do you know that? I've never even heard of this planet."

He shrugged. "I must have read about it somewhere."

Sirenī smirked. "Well, you read a lot and remember everything, annoyingly enough."

The women chuckled at the fact. Alex had always been a voracious reader. Even before the amṛta, he'd only slept for an hour or so a day. That left him plenty of time to practice magic, study spells, and fulfill his appetite for reading.

And for sex, Imara thought.

She recalled their early years together—making love anywhere and everywhere. She felt a quickening in her nethers and grabbed Alex's shoulder and Sirenī's wrist. They looked at her, surprised.

"Before we go anywhere…" she said with a sultry, suggestive smile.

Alex's eyes lit up, practically glowing as he immediately surmised her meaning. Sirenī laughed at his reaction and leaned close, kissing him lightly.

"What better way to pass an hour or two?" the daughter of Medusa agreed.

She waved a hand negligently to dismiss the holographic pane.

Two hours later, they lay together on a half-assed mattress Alexander had conjured. They enjoyed the afterglow of their lovemaking and stirred languidly. Imara and Sirenī got up first. Alexander watched them, marveling at their beauty and willingness to be with him.

"Thank you," he said as he pushed upright.

His partners looked at him quizzically. "For what?" Imara asked.

"The gift of your love," he said.

Sirenī stepped up to him and hugged him tightly. "You're welcome."

Imara took his hand and smiled warmly.

They cast hygiene spells to freshen up. They didn't get oily or have body odor after taking the amṛta, but sex was a sticky business. Cleaning up afterward was refreshing.

Hygiene spells couldn't be used in place of regular washing. They could disrupt the body's microbiomes and throw things out of balance with overuse, but they were otherwise safe. They were also more effective than a shower at refreshing the body because they cleaned inside and out, depending on how one used the spell.

Sirenī summoned the interface for the Infernal Gate and selected the Gatehouse in Rilladwen. They stepped onto the dais to fulfill the circle of events that began eight years in the future.

Fifteen

It was evening when they appeared in the Gatehouse. The guards stationed at each of the four sides of the plaza could have been the same, for all their appearance was uniform in their combat gear and posture. The commander leaned toward his shoulder mic, communicated with someone in the Gatehouse Transit Authority, and then resumed his position watching the newcomers.

"Isn't it strange that the guards don't communicate with us, even to tell us to stay where we are?" Sirenī observed as they stepped off the dais. They stood side by side, far enough away from it that the walls unfolded and twisted back into position, and the pyramidal cap rose out of the cube. "I mean, I would, in their place."

Imara grinned. "They don't expect anyone coming through the Gatehouse can speak their language. I assume the Transit Authority chief speaks several local languages passably enough to talk to newcomers. I'm sure the guards only speak the local dialect."

"Ah. That makes sense," Sirenī said. "It should be Amlodd, though, right? I mean, if we understand things like we think we do…"

They didn't have long to wait—it was indeed the same gentleman. He wasn't any fitter than when they'd first met him eight years in the future, and he huffed and puffed to the top of the stairs that climbed the hill out of the city. He wiped his forehead in the evening heat before speaking with the guard commander. They talked for a moment, then he hurried over to the three sorcerers and smiled.

"Greetings, greetings," he called cheerfully in his native tongue. "Welcome to Omejis!"

"Thank you," Imara said flawlessly. "It's very nice to be here. We've heard your world is lovely."

The official's eyes widened; he was obviously impressed. "You speak like a native," he declared in his nasal version of the liquid syllables of the language. "I'm quite impressed! Most travelers through the Gatehouse don't speak Cymraeg or even make an effort to learn." He rubbed his hands together, pleased. "I'm Amlodd, chief of the Gatehouse Transit Authority. May I have your names, please?"

"I'm Imara Inanna. This is Sirenī Adamma," she said with a smooth gesture toward her companion. She moved her hand. "That is Alex Eldred."

"Charmed," Sirenī said, smiling.

She spoke Cymraeg with a heavy accent, the same as English, but her dazzling smile made up for that. Amlodd's jaw dropped open. Imara thought he probably didn't even hear her speak, never mind notice her enunciation. Sirenī giggled and leaned into Imara, reining it in. Amlodd shook his head and snapped his mouth closed. He smoothed his loose-fitting shirt, suitable to the tropical atmosphere, and acknowledged Alex.

"Pleasure, pleasure," he chirped. "Let us go into Rilladwen. I'm happy to help you find lodging after registering your biometrics with the city. We do that with all travelers."

He gestured toward the same set of stairs he'd come up—the same ones they'd take years from now. "Do you know how long you'll be staying? We have a currency exchange and can handle monetary units from half a dozen worlds, but I'm sure travelers like yourselves understand how complex that is." He smiled apologetically. "Still, as indelicate as it is, we'll need to determine how you can pay for things while you're here."

Imara walked by Amlodd's side while Alex and Sirenī followed. Imara perceived him glance at Sirenī's belly. She assumed he was contemplating his impending fatherhood.

He doesn't realize we'll be in the first trimester for eight fucking years. But I'm not going to say anything about that since that would mean explaining how I could know that. She hated withholding information from her partners. *What a pain.*

"We have gold," she lied smoothly to Amlodd, "but is there something else you need? We also have skills that may prove useful."

Amlodd frowned thoughtfully as they walked down the stairs, considering her words. Imara already knew their near-future actions would serve them in excellent stead as far as their stay on Omejis was concerned, so it was just a matter of delaying until the eruption. She also knew how long syncretizing the magical and mystical forces would take. It was why she'd sent them eight years into the past.

She admired the soft lights that began to shine in subtle hues all over Rilladwen as the sun sank into the sea in the distance. Unfamiliar stars started to twinkle in the sky, which she resolutely ignored. Imara's autolenses provided enough visual distraction just looking at things around her; looking at the sky brought on a dizzying slew of additional phenomena for her brain to sort through, and she was already tired enough.

"What do you mean by services?" Amlodd asked. "Naturally, we have laws...." His voice trailed off as he tried to intuit her meaning.

Imara stifled a laugh as she realized he'd misinterpreted her words. She held out a hand and wiggled her fingers to cast a simple cantrip. A tiny silver-white unicorn appeared on her palm, lifelike and perfect in every detail. It galloped in place, jumped some imaginary obstacle, and reared, its mane and tail billowing in a magical breeze. Lightning flickered around its horn, and it dropped back on all fours. The unicorn extended its right front leg and bowed to Amlodd, then disappeared with a shimmering sparkle.

The official laughed in delight and clapped his hands at her simple display.

"Ah, you are from Gaea, then?" he beamed. "We have hosted travelers from your world several times over the centuries. They were always accommodating with local issues, but none spoke Cymraeg when they arrived. They had to use some kind of enchantment to learn the tongue, and none ever sounded like you. Let us get you checked into your accommodations, and I will speak with the governor on your behalf to determine compensation if that works?"

"That would be delightful," Imara agreed.

She had an overwhelming urge to lie down and sleep. She'd been tired after her expenditure on Byrne but recovered enough to cast the time travel spell. Now, though, she was beat. It was the first time she'd wanted to sleep since taking the amṛta. Maybe this time, she'd nod off and dream. She missed that.

Amlodd pointed things out to them during the short walk to a building they'd passed when they arrived in the future. The plaque on the front undoubtedly stated the name and purpose of the building, but Imara couldn't read Cymraeg despite being able to speak it.

"Registration of your biometrics will only take about ten minutes," Amlodd explained. "This is the Gatehouse Transit Authority's central office. Well, our only office since there's just one Gatehouse. We have a

Temple in the Bitter Islands, though—no one can reach it, of course, but it's a popular tourist destination."

They smiled and nodded, pretending to be surprised. He led them to a desk and told a clerk to register them as guests from Gaea. They stated their names, and the clerk's eyes bulged when they spoke Cymraeg. He almost fell out of his chair when Imara spoke with such a perfect accent that she could easily have been a local.

"You speak beautifully," he complimented. He smiled charmingly and leaned forward to get closer to her.

She sensed Alex tense beside her at the flirtatious tone and grin. The young man was handsome, with lovely dark skin and a beautiful smile. He looked fit under his uniform; she immediately thought of Carter with his mischievous grin and quick, snarky wit. She smiled back at the clerk and sensed Alex bristle.

Really? After forty-eight years, now you're jealous?

"Thank you," she said to the clerk.

The clerk maintained his easy charm while he took their names and had them press their hands to a glass scanning plate. It registered their fingerprints and palmar vascularity.

"You'll be able to use this everywhere on Omejis," the clerk explained. "I'll set up an account for you, and Chief Amlodd will register it with the banking system. You can pay for all commercial transactions with a fingerprint or vascular biometry."

He grinned at Imara the whole time he spoke, never paying attention to Sirenī. The songstress found that odd, but perhaps he was somehow immune to her fatal beauty. She filed it away for future contemplation, thanked him, and signed her name to complete her registration. Sirenī and Alex did the same, and the clerk gave each a folio of information that explicated local customs and laws to help them navigate their visit to Omejis.

Amlodd thanked the clerk and ushered them from the Transit Authority building. He led them to the hotel from eight years in the future and had them press their palms to the reader embedded in the reception desk. Amlodd told the clerk to put them in the penthouse suite, and the clerk confirmed, appending the bill to the Transit

Authority's account pending the establishment of finances for the travelers.

The Three had a day or two before the expected eruption of the volcano and planned to wander around Rilladwen. Imara thought it would be nice to play tourists on a world where no one knew who they were.

Amlodd led them up the stairs to their suite—the one on the right, this time, as he'd mentioned. He told them they could call any restaurants in the area to deliver food, then said he would return in the morning to speak with them at around ten local time.

He bowed his way out of the room with a broad smile and a cheerful good evening.

Alexander stripped, stepped into the shower, and enjoyed the hot water rinsing his skin despite being clean already, thanks to the amṛta and hygiene spell he'd cast. After a couple of centuries of bathing regularly, he just enjoyed the ritual.

He dried himself with a wave and walked into the bedroom naked. His partners were in bed. They wore loose-fitting, comfortable shirts and pants suitable for sleep. He stopped and contemplated them, feeling overwhelming love and happiness that they were pregnant. He'd always wanted children with them and felt delighted that it was happening. He wasn't usually so emotional, but he accepted his feelings and sat with them.

Sixteen
Sedecim

The day after the Three left, Carter went into the closet in his titanic suite. The combined bedroom, bathroom, and wardrobe were more extensive than his apartment in Columbia. Carter grinned as he looked around the walk-in closet. Hundreds of garments could fit inside, and he was surprised to see how many clothes were in there.

He saw those he'd gotten from Walmart when Jordan took him shopping, and he assumed the rest—all cut in the style of Gaea—came courtesy of Imara, Sirenī, and the fabricator. The styles of Gaea were looser than those of Earth but similar in cut and color. He smiled, pleased by the thoughtful touch.

His combat armor stood in a unique niche designed expressly for it. A piece of paper was folded in half, tucked into the collar, which he plucked out and opened. Sirenī's elegant script filled the page:

Imara and I thought it would be nice to upgrade your armor. We hope you like the new features.

Sirenī & Imara.

P.S. Check the top drawer of your dresser. Alex left you a little something, too.

After the postscript, the letter also contained command words he'd need to memorize to activate the various enchantments. He was impressed by their list of enhancements and considered what they could do for him in battle.

Carter went to the long, low, mirrored dresser against the wall opposite the closet. He opened the top drawer and raised an eyebrow as he took out a package. It wasn't large but had some weight to it. He opened the lid and whistled in appreciation at the heavy handgun tucked into the black velvet lining.

A note from Alex explained that the sidearm was made in the Earthen style and was based on the Desert Eagle 50, with a self-perpetuating clip that never ran out of bullets. The projectiles were magically charged like miniature grenades to provide extra punch and explosivity. The sorcerer ended his message on a wry note:

Do not shoot anything you do not want to destroy.

The soldier slipped the handgun into his combat armor's belt holster, which magically shifted to accommodate the oversized sidearm. He admired the gear for several minutes with a happy smile. He closed the closet door behind him and put the notes from his friends into the handgun box, which he returned to its drawer.

He glanced around the room before leaving. When the heavy wooden slab swung closed behind him, he locked it by swiping his finger down the metal panel set a few inches above the doorknob. All the doors in the house had locks; he wondered if the Three had explained their usage to everyone.

As Carter descended the stairs, Richard ran through the front door, breathing hard. Carter took the last steps three at a time and hurried over to his friend. They almost collided as they skidded to a halt together.

"What's wrong?" the soldier asked.

Richard bent over slightly, put his hands on his knees, and took several deep breaths. "I haven't…sprinted like this…since high school! Give me…a sec." He finally straightened. His color and respiration were returning to normal, thanks to his excellent physical conditioning. "The government perimeter is gone!"

"What the fuck?" Carter nearly yelled. He reined himself in and shook his head. "When? Why?"

Richard shrugged. "Jordan and I have been walking down to the end of the driveway every morning. We cut back across the Lower Forty and down your driveway." He waved his hands in the air to mark out the route they walked. "When we got there this morning, the perimeter was gone. We saw cars driving on 26."

Carter frowned, his forehead creasing in thought. He doubted the United States government had given up; he knew it was unlikely from the limited research he'd done on Jordan's computer. Still, something must have changed. He wondered if it had to do with the corruption? The dark magic's influence may have escalated as Alex had predicted, but his intuition told him it wasn't that simple.

"Something else is going on here. I'm going to reconnoiter and see what I can find out."

He raced upstairs without waiting for Richard's response. He went straight to his closet and stared at his armor in consternation.

Now, how do I get into the fucking thing?

It was always a pain in the ass to get the tight-fitting gear on, but it never stood on its own before. He frowned and touched the left shoulder with his right hand then squawked in surprise as the suit lurched into motion. He started to step back, but the armor reached out and grabbed him with its empty gloves. It leaned forward and sprang open into a multitude of pieces that flipped and spun their way about his person.

The soldier yelped when the crotch piece snapped over his equipment; it was tighter than he usually wore his groin protector. The breastplate swarmed over him and slammed shut, squeezing the air out of his chest. He grunted as the armor settled fully into place—the process took only three or four seconds.

The suit felt too tight, and Carter reached down to tug at the crotch protector and pull it away from his genitals before his nuts burst. Before he could, the suit flexed and expanded to settle perfectly around his body. He groaned in delight as the unpleasant pressure disappeared from every part of his body, then held up his hands and looked at them. They were coated in matte black material, and the stiff protective panels on the backs of his fingers and hands were feather-light and flexible.

Carter jogged and moved in place, lifting his knees high and shifting his arms around. He twisted to test his range of motion. It felt natural, even better than the original. He expected the women had used the original underlayment for his armor that Alex repaired as the base for this suit.

He stood there and grinned like a kid at a birthday party. He reached back and felt for the hilt of the gladius Alex had given him, pleased to feel it resting comfortably in the astral displacement sheath on his belt. He touched the grip of his new sidearm—it was solid and hefty, just the way he liked.

He left his bedroom, swiped a gloved finger to lock the door, and hurried downstairs. Richard's eyes widened as he saw Carter's spiffy new combat gear.

"Dude, badass!" he congratulated.

Carter smirked and flexed, showing off his armored suit. "Imara and Sirenī gave it to me," he explained. He pointed his thumb at his chest to indicate the light-eating black armor, then switched to his index finger to point to the hefty handgun at his hip, "And Alex gave me this."

Richard held out a hand excitedly. He was familiar with firearms, and Carter drew the gun and handed it over to him by the barrel. The redheaded man took the grip and admired the heavy, chrome-plated gun, etched around the barrel and clip with faint, abstract designs. He hefted it, turned it this way and that, and then snapped it up and sighted down the barrel. He drew the slide to check if a round was chambered—there was—and expertly aimed it away from the soldier, then flipped it and handed it back.

"Fucking awesome," Richard enthused. "No maker's mark or safety. This is a hand cannon, man."

Carter laughed. He liked that term. "Keep everyone inside."

Richard nodded, turned, and stumbled. He had almost tripped over Marquis, who had stealthily approached the two men and lay on the floor behind Richard's feet. He looked innocently up at them with wide golden eyes as Richard grumbled under his breath at the plump orange figure.

Marquis lay where he was, unconcerned that Richard almost stepped on him. He watched Carter laugh and stride away, followed by the redheaded fellow. As soon as they were gone, Charlotte appeared. She ran tidily from the sitting room and halted on her haunches near the cat. They glanced at each other, then out the open door, then back at one another.

Marquis rolled lithely to his feet. Charlotte climbed his back leg and scuttled across his back to sit between his shoulders. He trotted from the house with surprising agility but didn't follow Carter and Richard. Instead, he headed into the woods surrounding the manor.

He and Charlotte liked to coordinate with their property mate.

Carter turned left out the door and jogged down the driveway to Route 26. Richard went to the path that led to the Lower Forty. Carter realized no one had closed the front door but didn't bother backtracking since no one could enter the property.

He angled off the driveway when he got close to the road and slipped into the chilly woods. The trees were leafless, and the ground was littered with crunchy, dried detritus. He took a deep breath of the sharp, biting air as he chanted the Obscuratus incantation and moved smoothly but silently to the street.

Richard was correct—the DHS and military presence was gone. Cars traveled in both directions, and the drivers were undoubtedly relieved to take the usual routes to their destinations around Steadfield, South Paris, West Paris, and Norway.

Carter studied the road. His gut told him someone was out there, so he squatted against a tree. He draped his thick arms over his knees and relaxed his eyes. After about ten minutes, he spotted it across the street, tucked back in a woody area—a covert surveillance shack. He saw soldiers in fall/winter digital camo with scopes, cameras, and other devices. They moved smoothly and as little as possible so as not to break the vertical lines of the trees. He spotted people wearing a civilian variant of the digital camo fatigues and assumed they were Zalcent employees.

After about twenty-five minutes, he saw nothing else of note. He pushed slowly to his feet and was pleased not to have any pain or numbness in his hips and knees after squatting for so long. He felt limber and easy in his body as he slipped away from the road and circumnavigated the property anticlockwise.

Carter found more surveillance shacks located about every quarter mile around the property. He never got a good look at anyone until he circled back to Jordan's house, where the Pendleton Rest abutted along her land's periphery. He saw an individual wearing a black coat with the Zalcent International logo on the left breast.

He waited patiently, invisible thanks to his obscuration, and stared to the side of the man so as not to trigger his prey instinct. All humans could perceive someone—or something—watching them. Carter learned long ago to avoid looking directly at targets to avoid triggering their psychic alarms.

The man stood outside the surveillance post. He wasn't wearing clothing that kept him inconspicuous among the trees and wasn't careful of his steps. He bit his lip, glanced over his shoulder at the shack, and then sauntered up to the barrier. He must have known where it was because he stopped just a few steps away and squinted.

Carter quietly backed away from the barrier and the unknown technician. He spun about and hurried to Jordan's house. The adults had gathered in the living room—Richard, Jordan, Sue, Paul, Brent, and Drëndi. At the dining table, Eric and Cassie watched a movie on Sue's laptop. Black cats wandered about, mostly ignoring the humans or stopping for an occasional pet.

Everyone looked at the soldier when he entered the room. He stood there, feet shoulder width apart in his combat armor, with his right hand resting on the butt of his sidearm.

"What do we know about Zalcent International?"

"A lot," Jordan replied. "About their public stuff, anyway."

Brent stepped away from the easy chair and nodded at Carter's getup. "Nice armor."

"Nice handgun," Drëndi said simultaneously.

Carter chuckled as she unfolded from the chair. He realized he wasn't going to get an answer immediately as the blonde special agent approached. Drëndi held out a hand, and he handed his gun over.

He watched Drëndi handle the gun. She was clearly a professional, and she offered it back to him after a few seconds.

"Awesome," she enthused. "Where'd you get it?"

"Alex made it for me."

"Can you make me one?"

Carter grinned ruefully and shook his head. "No, unfortunately. That's way above my skill level."

Well, it used to be. I don't know any spells to do something like that, but I can figure it out. He considered his skill with magic and revised his answer. "Maybe."

Brent laughed. "She's a gun nut, though you'd never know it. She's also an expert marksman with more weapons than I can count."

He sounded proud as he said that—as if he had something to do with it.

She grinned and returned to her chair. "I'd love a gun like that."

"The bullets are magically charged to explode. Like mini-grenades," Carter told them expansively.

"Now I really want one!" she cried.

Brent scoffed. "Who would you shoot with it?"

She looked at him with a mock-wounded expression. "Bad people and magical monsters."

"I can see that," Brent said thoughtfully.

Carter brought it back to his question. "So—Zalcent International?"

Brent began, "Well, they're a multinational conglomerate with fingers in a lot of pies, including aerospace, weapons, telecommunications, internet service, pharmaceuticals, biotech, future tech, military contracts, artificial intelligence, machine learning, you name it. They even make devices, such as smart appliances, virtual assistants, cell phones, and neural networks for household use. They've got a robust social media platform called Presence. It's trendy.

"They've been sniffing around this property for a while, since before the blockade. Assistant Director Lambert said they were involved in one of our recent message exchanges, but that was all. She reiterated that Drëndi and I should remain here and that circumstances in the Middle East are getting worse. There are power and communications blackouts and unconfirmed rumors that the Karkheh Dam in Iran is failing—or has failed. I'm not sure which."

Everyone sat silently, digesting that information.

"Why do you want to know about Zalcent?" Jordan asked.

"The military and the federal agents left, as you and Richard saw, but people continue to watch from covert surveillance shacks around the property. Most of them seem like soldiers. They're wearing digital camo, but I saw someone wearing a Zalcent International jacket," Carter said.

"Ah." Jordan glanced about to see everyone else's reactions. "Do you think we can leave the property?" she asked after a few moments of awkward silence.

Carter had been thinking about that. He nodded slowly and stroked his smooth chin. "I think so, but until we're certain, I want to accompany anyone who leaves. Whoever remains behind will be safe inside the barrier. I don't want people going off alone." He looked at Sue. "The kids won't be able to go to school just yet, I'm afraid, not until we know what's going on."

She nodded. "I went to college to be a teacher but never worked in the school system. I'm enjoying supervising their schooling, to be honest." She glanced at her husband, and he smiled lovingly at her. She returned her gaze to Carter. "I've corrected several glaring gaps in their education," she added crisply.

Carter chuckled, then glanced around the group. "Donuts and lattes may not be off the docket if things go well."

Jordan and Richard high-fived. They missed their daily dose of the Indigent Mug.

Paul cleared his throat. He seemed uncomfortable, and Carter wondered what he planned to say.

"I know you came here with the other three from wherever—" he began.

"Gaea," Jordan interjected tartly.

"But that doesn't mean you can decide stuff like that for everyone.

Something else has gotten the government's attention if the perimeter is gone. Maybe they've lost interest in us."

Before he could continue, Brent and Drëndi laughed. "I don't mean to be rude," Brent began, which always meant someone was going to be just that, "but the situation isn't that binary. The government didn't give up. Zalcent International is the biggest company in the world, and they would kill, literally murder, to get their hands on a magic user's DNA."

He shook his head. Carter could tell he was searching for the words to explain how desirable that genetic material would be. He finally just shrugged and kept speaking.

"The value of that genome would be in the tens of billions, just for the raw code. The ability to sequence the portions of it that give someone magical abilities on par with Alex or Imara or Sirenī? I can't even comprehend it. Every country on this planet would sequence it into people left, right, and center, and we'd have super soldiers fighting magical wars on every front."

Drëndi nodded, her expression and tone sharp. "The genetics would get onto the black market, and criminals would use it, too. It would be a bloodbath, Paul." He looked chagrined. Her tone softened, and she smiled to take the sting out. "Alex, Imara, and Sirenī left Carter in charge. He's the only one of us who would be completely safe outside the perimeter. Do you have any idea what he's capable of? He was an A-tier operator on his world and has mad skills."

Carter stared at her, surprised by their vigorous defense. He didn't need help defending his leadership but appreciated the support. "I am in charge," he confirmed bluntly. He turned his sharp, dark eyes on Paul. "I have administrative privileges regarding the barrier. You can leave alone if you want to, but Zalcent will snatch you up from the sounds of things, and you will disappear."

Paul looked mulishly at them, but Sue put a hand on his arm and shook her head when he looked down at her. He sighed and grumbled his assent, not that Carter gave a fuck. He waited a moment, and when no one else spoke, he jerked his chin toward the front door.

"I'll be back."

He marched out of the living room onto the porch. Brent and

Drëndi moved like there was no tomorrow, grabbing their coats from the rack near the door and hurrying after him.

"Wait! We want to come with you, just to the perimeter," Drëndi said.

Carter waited while they slipped into their boots.

The perimeter was quiet when they reached it, but Brent and Drëndi could see the blind tucked into the trees across the street. It was almost invisible; they might not have noticed it if Carter hadn't pointed it out, whispering in case anyone had parabolic microphones trained on their position.

Carter stepped through the barrier and stood there, hand on his gun, staring straight across the street. Nothing happened, so the soldier glanced over his shoulder and nodded at his friends, then turned right and walked along the side of the road toward the Pendleton Rest.

He felt eyes on him, but he tried to act casually. As he approached the Rest, he moved away from Jordan's property line; the Rest was the last property before the town line of Steadfield-South Paris. Carter saw the bed and breakfast and noted the empty parking lot. Across the street, the Indigent Mug was so full every spot was taken.

He chuckled to himself. No one appeared to be staying at the Rest, but it seemed everyone was gossiping at the Mug now the government was gone. He could appreciate that. There was a well-established grapevine in the Unified Military, which was no different for civilians in a small town.

Gossiping might not be our most admirable trait as humans, but it's definitely common to all of us, he thought amusedly.

He turned to his right and headed toward the back of the property, stalking along, ready to fight…but nothing happened, and his adrenaline rush was for nothing. He walked about a mile around the perimeter of Jordan's property and cut back into the woods. He stopped inside the tree line, relaxed, and waited to see if he noticed anything beyond what he'd already sensed.

After a few minutes, he felt a tingle along the nape of his neck. He looked left and felt nothing. He looked right and sensed a presence farther along the property line. He turned and moved swiftly but silently through the woods, gliding over the leaf litter and fallen branches, barely disturbing them with his passage. Carter was a stocky man, but he moved silently across the carpet of dried leaves and small branches strewn across the ground.

As he approached the source of the mental tingle, the sensation in his body grew into an irritating itch. Something felt gritty and annoying behind his eyeballs and breastbone. It subsided when he saw what was causing the problem.

Carter stopped in his tracks, surprised to see another līc on Earth. For a planet without magic, this was the third necromancer he'd seen. However, with a population over eight billion, it was reasonable to assume plenty of magicians were hiding among Earth's regular people. Some of that number would be necromancers, especially since the Earthen stock didn't have magic by birth. The only people who did have it were travelers from other worlds, people with mutations that gave them some limited abilities, or those who trucked with demons and death to gain power.

Carter didn't know whether this one was from Earth or Gaea. If she was from his homeworld, she could have come to Earth long ago or more recently via a traveling spell. She certainly couldn't have come via the Gatehouse since they'd arrived; there was no way Alex wouldn't have known if the system activated.

He stood still and studied the figure for several minutes. He eventually decided it didn't matter where the undead was from—it was a problem for him to fix either way. She wore skintight, supple black leather and heeled biker boots that gave her a few extra inches of height. She had curves in all the right places, but there was no mistaking it—she was definitely a corpse walker.

From the neck down, the līc looked alive—the skin was firm, youthful, and glowed with apparent health. From the chin up was another matter altogether. She'd mutilated her face, cutting the skin into strips and flaying them back from her bones, muscles, nerves, veins, and connective tissues. She'd folded the ribbons of skin into loops and twists and pinned them in place with metal rings. The tissue jiggled and bobbed grotesquely as she moved.

It made no sense to Carter why līc mutilated themselves. The fuckers wanted to live forever and committed horrible acts to make it happen. Then they ensouled a prepared corpse with leathery skin and obscenely large, deformed breasts and genitals or occupied a child's remains. He shook his head, unable to wrap his mind around the insanity.

Why not just keep your biological body in good shape? he wondered.

He never learned enough about necromancy to know if that was possible. Maybe the magical cost was too great.

He canceled the Obscuratus and stepped up to the barrier. He met her glittering gaze through the invisible shield. Her eyes were round and overly large in her skull in the absence of eyelids. She stared back at him through the barrier that she couldn't see; a grin quirked the musculature of her lips, and she blew him a kiss.

He laughed and shook his head. He'd fought undead several times during his Unified Military service. Most Undying abode by the Doctrine of Unity and treaties with the Council, but some cleaved to the old ways—namely, immortals preying on mortals. He'd killed any he'd come across in his missions. He hadn't fought any līc, but he was confident he could destroy her animate form if not her phylacterium.

Plus, I've taken amṛta. Fuck with me at your peril!

He projected total confidence. The līc saw this, and her mouth curled.

"Is that a smile or a sneer?" he asked in Demurrian. She clenched her fists and hissed at him. He grinned back. "Sneer, then. You're so over the top with all that fucking facial drama."

Her expression became curious. "You're not afraid," she said in English. "You'll be fun to play with."

"I already helped kill two of your ilk," he replied in the same language. He waved a broad hand dismissively. "I'm sure I'll kill you, too, before long. Just for the record, the name's Carter." He smirked. "I'd hate for you not to know who put your sorry carcass down."

"You killed Adam and Bohuslava?" she scoffed. "I don't believe you."

The hoops of skin around her face bobbed and jiggled. They looked wet, and Carter hid his shudder of distaste.

"Also for the record, I am Patrine. Why don't you come out from behind your little barrier and face me, soldier?" she taunted scornfully.

Carter held his arms out. "Show me how powerful you are. Come through the barrier and face me. Wow me with your stolen power, you corpse fucker."

Patrine clenched her leather-clad fists, and a foul green nimbus wrapped her hands. She slammed a fist into the barrier, and spectral defenses crackled into view as the field effects absorbed the blow.

Carter laughed as he heard her knuckles break against the shield. She was dead, so she didn't feel any pain. She shrieked in rage anyway, then used her magic to repair the broken bones. He heard the crackling of her phalanges as she fixed them, which gave him time to snatch his handgun from his belt holster. He sighted and pulled the trigger in one smooth motion.

Seventeen
Septendecim

The bullet passed through the shield and slammed into her animate form; the impact blew her off her feet. She shrieked in inhuman rage and bounced several times before halting.

The bullet's explosion blew a hole in her chest nine inches wide and ripped out a portion of her posterior rib cage and spine twice that size. The detonation sent a spray of gore spattering across the shield in front of Carter; the greasy debris slid to the ground. From her back spewed a combination of atomized blood, bits of meat, and chunks of debris.

She had landed ten feet away from where she'd been standing. She lay on her back for a moment, then rolled over onto her hands and knees. Bits of her innards dripped from the appalling wound in her chest.

Carter admired the explosive force of his gun. "That was nice," he told her conversationally. "I should have aimed for your head. Why don't you come back over here so I can shoot you properly?"

While Undying survived wounds that would kill mortals, he knew that if he destroyed enough of her animated remains, she'd die after a fashion. Vampires and ghūl died for real, but līc just lost their current skin. They had to enter a new meat puppet to interact with the world again, which many undead prepared and stored in stasis fields to keep them "fresh."

The līc pushed herself up on one knee, gore dripping from her body. She finally rose to her feet. She looked down at her wound, then reached up and touched the edges of the enormous hole. Her facial muscles contorted in rage; the hoops of flayed skin looped around her visage quivered gelatinously as she looked at the soldier.

"We'll see how well you do when that shield doesn't protect you, asshole," she sneered. She turned and sprinted toward the nearest covert surveillance shack.

"Fuck," he growled and took off after her.

He ran fast, but he wasn't as supple as she was. He caught up to her as soldiers burst from concealment and drew down on her, flashlight beams crisscrossing as they aimed. The four males and one female soldier yelled at her to halt, but their shouts died in their throats when they got a good look at her.

"What the fuck?" the female soldier yelled.

Patrine bore down on the first soldier and leaped onto him. He fell onto his back, screaming as her flayed face paused inches from his. He clawed at her. She reared back and raised her left hand. Necromantic energies crackled as she plunged her stiffened fingers into his abdomen, punching straight through his combat gear. She yanked her hand back and stood, holding a pulsing loop of his guts, and began to drain his vital energies while he writhed and screamed and grabbed his intestines, desperately holding onto them as he died.

The power she stole from him flared brightly with an angry, sulfurous gleam. She flicked the fingers of her free hand—flames surrounded them, and she pointed at the blind. A firebolt blasted from her fingertips with a roar, and the canvas walls and roof of the flimsy structure burst into flames.

Carter caught up with Patrine just after she threw the firebolt. The other soldiers lined her up in their sights but weren't firing because she had their dying comrade's guts in her hand. They didn't want to do any more damage to him.

Carter fired his gun as he ran. He'd spent years practicing firing while moving and was highly accurate: the bullet penetrated her upper arm and exploded, blowing the limb off below the shoulder. Her hand, still holding the soldier's intestines, fell onto his body as he lay there moaning. Patrine howled in fury, but she'd drawn enough energy from the man at her feet that she began to regenerate the limb and threw a fireball at Carter.

Although fireballs were weaker and slower moving than firebolts, they could still cause damage. Patrine likely expected him to tuck and roll away from the sizzling globe of liquid fire, but Carter just grinned and advanced. The flames hit him, and rainbow-hued spectral defenses crackled into view as the embedded wards absorbed the magic. He lunged through the fire and swung a fist.

Patrine was quick on her feet and danced backward.

He went after her, but she kept dodging, cackling, and swearing at him. Carter maintained his focus and situational awareness. Flames lapped at her fingertips, and she tossed another firebolt. He was safe in his armor but threw himself to the right anyway.

The projectile hit the burning blind and exploded with a thunderous boom. Heat billowed outward, twisting and distorting the air in writhing shimmers. He craned his head and saw another līc. She looked young and pretty. Richard, Paul, and Kyle would have said she was perfect—blonde, well made up, trim figure, big breasts. He blinked at the unexpectedly pure vision and kept his gun trained on Patrine while he reached back and grabbed the hilt of his gladius, ready to draw at a moment's notice.

The shack's explosion had knocked down the stunned, indecisive soldiers. The closest man sailed through the air and smashed into a tree with a crunch. He fell to the ground and lay unmoving; Carter knew immediately that he'd broken his back and ruptured internal organs. Two other soldiers rolled around on the ground, moaning, burns covering their faces and hands. Their gear was smoldering, but they didn't appear to be severely injured.

The female was the only one still on her feet. She finally decided to act, whipped up her rifle, and fired. She sent three-round bursts at Patrine and the co-ed. The flayed woman laughed as the bullets hit kinetic wards; they pancaked and bounced to the ground. The rattle of the gunfire was loud, but no more so than the firebolts and exploding shack.

Carter saw someone stagger out of the woods—the Zalcent technician he'd seen earlier. The man stopped and stared at the burning shack and the līc. His eyes widened. He reached up and adjusted his glasses as if that would make what he saw easier to process.

Then he just stood there, staring at the undead in shock.

"Futuo," Carter growled in Demurrian.

I need to get this over with.

In one smooth motion, Carter drew his gladius and flung it at the beautiful young līc that stood fifteen feet away. Patrine howled as the sword slammed into the Undying creature just below her breastbone. He spoke a command word, and the sword and animated corpse flew toward him. The hilt went right into his hand, and he snarled at the pretty undead.

She looked shocked and frightened, which wasn't what the soldier expected from a corpse walker.

"Please!" she begged. "I'm only doing this because that bitch made me!"

"Necromancy is always a bad choice," he snapped while Patrine screeched out, "You fucking cunt!"

Carter jerked upward and slid the razor-sharp sword straight out the top of the corpse's pretty blonde head. He shoved his gun's muzzle into the horrific wound and fired twice, blowing her body apart and destroying her animate form. Green light flared around the ruins as they splattered to the ground.

Lightning flashed, and he reeled, skidding across the leaf litter as his armor absorbed the electrical discharge. He laughed and faced Patrine, seeing she'd stopped regenerating her arm. He could tell from her stance that she wasn't as confident as when she first saw him. She'd expected an easy battle against an Earthen man, but that wasn't how things turned out.

She screeched and took off at a dead run toward the technician, who still stood there gawking. Carter aimed and fired; Patrine hit the ground and skidded, her left leg amputated mid-thigh by his bullet.

He stalked toward her as the female soldier ran over and grabbed the technician; she dragged him to safety and trained her gun on Patrine.

Carter thought he saw the līc grimace. She reached up with her left hand and grabbed one of the metal rings holding back her loops of skin. She ripped it out and disappeared with a pop as she activated the magical charm. He stopped and stared as air rushed into the vacuum.

"Well, that wasn't what I expected," he muttered.

He sheathed his sword, holstered his gun, and surveyed the scene. He turned to the technician and the soldier.

"You two okay?"

The woman nodded. She'd stayed focused and collected during the short, crazy battle.

Carter nodded back and walked over to the two injured men. He took a knee and hoped that what Alex had said about the amṛta boosting his magical abilities was true. He cast the only healing spell he knew, which he'd failed to complete more often than he'd succeeded in the past. Energy surged around his hands, and the soldier produced the aurora of a powerful sorcerer for the first time in his fifty-plus years. He blinked as a lemony yellow nimbus crackled around his hands and forearms as the magical energies leaped to obey his command. He completed the incantation and let out a whoop of delight as power exploded out of him. He healed both men simultaneously.

He stood and stared at his glowing hands, flabbergasted. He'd never felt such power. It had surged through him, potent and blissful.

Is this what they feel like?

He thought of his friends and marveled at the feeling of his magic as it coiled inside him, begging for release. He reluctantly let it go, and the corona around his hands dissipated.

Carter watched the four survivors for a few seconds as the three remaining soldiers and the Zalcent tech conferred quietly in urgent tones. They reached an agreement; the female soldier and technician stepped cautiously forward. Carter looked at the two men who stayed back and rolled his eyes.

"Nice one, twats," he said in Demurrian.

He focused on the female and the technician.

"Thank you for saving our lives. I'll report this to my superiors, so they know you helped us against those…things," the man said quietly. He sounded sincere and not a little overawed. "Um, what were they? And dude," his eyes widened in geeky wonder, "did you use *magic*? I mean, I heard the rumors, but…damn."

Carter raised his eyebrows and considered his response for about a tenth of a second. *Are these people blind?* He answered sarcastically in English. "No, those were special effects!"

The man reared back, shocked. Carter softened his tone and broke into a charming smile, his swarthy features lit by the last flames burning in the blind. The fire hadn't spread to the dry trees around the shack.

How that hadn't happened was anyone's guess.

"Sorry. I don't mean to be a twat like them," he said, chucking his chin toward the soldiers. They glowered at his disparaging remark. "Yes, I used magic to heal them. Those two charmers were līc. They're nasty, undead monsters—"

"I get it," the other man interrupted. "I played Dungeons & Dragons."

Carter raised his eyebrows. Richard had mentioned the game several times; the soldier assumed it was like *Calamitas*, which was popular on Gaea.

Before he could reply, one of the men hanging back scoffed and said, "Come on, Thurley, you still play!"

Carter was about to tell him to shut the fuck up and let the men talk, but Thurley managed the situation just fine: the technician turned and gave the soldier the finger. All of them laughed easily—though with the shaky edge brought on by adrenaline—and he saw there were no hard feelings.

"I know what a līc is," Thurley went on. "An evil necromancer who animates a corpse and hides its soul somewhere safe. That means you didn't kill the one you cut in half and shot and…whatever."

Carter nodded. He glanced at the remains of the co-ed. "You can take the corpse if you want, to study it or whatever you people at Zalcent are doing, but I assure you that you aren't prepared for what's happening. You've never dealt with magic of any significance on this world. These līc are bad news. I'm not sure about the blonde, but the flayed woman could have killed all of you in all the blinds you've set up around the property. You're in over your head."

Thurley nodded. "I'll tell my bosses that, too." He scuffed a toe, then stuck out a hand. They shook. "Thank you."

"You're welcome," the soldier grunted.

He nodded at the woman, then chucked his chin at the twats again. They nodded respectfully and went up a notch in his estimation. Carter turned and stalked back to the safety of the barrier, formulating his report in his head as he went.

It only took Carter ten minutes to relay what happened at the barrier, but his friends' questions tacked an hour onto that. When he described the effect of the bullets on the līc, Drëndi, Paul, and Richard looked so eager to get their hands on a similar weapon that Carter made a mental note to check on it as soon as possible.

After their discussion, they walked to the manor for dinner. Jordan had plenty of food on hand but didn't feel like cooking or cleaning up. Carter was just as happy to grab some chow that reminded him of home. He enjoyed living on Earth, but he did get pangs of homesickness.

The fabricator responded to intent as well as verbal commands. Carter assumed those needed to be given in Demurrian rather than English, but he wasn't sure. He knew that words were most often indicators of intent, so maybe the language somebody spoke was irrelevant. Either way, all someone had to do was touch the activation glyph on the front of the silvery sphere to trigger the autotech machinery.

Carter selected food and desserts and asked what everyone wanted to drink. People helped him bring the platters into the kitchen and set them on the massive table to the left of the door. Drëndi, Jordan, and

Sue wanted a bottle of wine. The men opted for beer, Eric asked for a soda, and Cassie asked if she could get coconut water.

Carter got Eric's drink, which the boy said tasted like a cross between cola and root beer and discovered that coconut water was available via the Grid.

Who knew? he thought as he handed the bottle to Cassie with solemn ceremony.

Everyone talked and laughed over the meal. The women split a second bottle of wine, and the men drank more beer than they should have. Carter had told everyone that Patrine called the two līc that slipped into the manor and attacked Jordan *Adam* and *Bohuslava*. He saw Jordan shiver when he mentioned the incident. Thankfully the Three took care of her injury, so she only had bad memories instead of scars.

As the night wore on and the conversation started to die, Jordan cleared her throat and looked at Carter. "I want to learn to shoot."

He nodded. "That's smart. Nothing can get through the barrier, but we don't know what's coming. The līc attacked in the open, with people watching. I'm sure they expected to kill me and the nitwits at the surveillance shack, but if they're this bold, then some shit may be coming our way." He looked at everyone, including the kids. "Learning to defend yourselves is smart."

"Too bad we can't do magic like you," Cassie piped up from her place at the table. Everyone looked at her in some surprise, and she blushed and shrugged. "Well, it's true. Magic is wwwaaaaayyyy funner than guns."

Carter laughed and smiled at the precocious little girl. "Well, it can be, but guns are quicker and easier for most people unless you're a magic user like Alex, Sirenī, or Imara."

"Can I learn to shoot, too?" Eric looked at his parents, expression pleading.

Paul nodded while Sue shook her head, then everyone at the table —including the Arsenaults—laughed. Sue amended her negative response with, "Your father and I will talk about it!" in a tone that indicated the topic was shelved for the night.

There was a pause. Sue drank the last of her wine and set the glass down. She looked at the others. "I'm becoming comfortable with this situation. That's something I can't say I ever imagined might happen. The walking dead and magic and *Star Trek* force fields…"

Paul put his hand on her shoulder with a grin that turned into a tender smile at her words. She looked at her husband intently for a moment, then turned to smile sweetly at her kids. "Stay in your rooms again tonight."

Eric scowled. "Mom! Gross."

Cassie looked at her brother. "Why is it gross for us to stay in our rooms?" she asked innocently.

No one made a sound as they watched Eric flounder. He desperately looked around for someone to rescue him from his sister's question, but no one came to his aid. Finally, he flung his hands up.

"Never mind," he muttered. "It's not gross to stay in our rooms."

When they finished, Carter suggested Jordan and Richard should sleep in one of the bedrooms on the second floor rather than return to their place. The couple talked it over quickly and agreed.

They trooped from the kitchen and walked along the corridor to the main hall. The couples walked side-by-side while Carter, Eric, and Cassie trailed along. Everyone said goodnight to the soldier and disappeared upstairs. He went to the front door and opened it to step outside for a minute.

He jumped back in surprise as Marquis sauntered in. The tabby purred and rubbed against Carter's right boot, then tottered past. He blinked as he saw the mouse on the cat's back: the tiny white critter sat between Marquis's shoulders and clung to his thick fur. He shook his head at their antics—strange even for his homeworld—and stepped outside.

He saw light flickering by the anchor stone in the central area at the core of the circular drive and walked over. His eyes widened as he beheld the largest moth he'd ever seen—it had a fifteen-inch wingspan, at least. The moth rested on the anchor stone and slowly fanned its wings. Stunning iridescent fractal patterns radiated over them, and

Carter stared, mesmerized. He didn't know the moth's species but knew it was magical. He was confident that nothing like it existed on Earth.

Where did you come from, little one? he wondered.

It was a mystery he doubted he'd ever solve.

He watched the moth until he started to grow cool. It seemed fine where it rested, and the soldier finally gave it a feeble wave and went back into the house. He closed the door behind him and debated sliding his finger over the locking plate; he decided against it in case someone wanted to leave early in the morning and he wasn't around.

Carter went past the door to the library and the stairs on his left. The entrance to the sitting room was to his right, but he passed that, too. He headed down the hall to the kitchen and glanced at the space: the chairs had resettled at the table, and all the dishes, utensils, and bottles were gone.

The soldier stepped into the fabricator room. He drew his gun from its holster and set it below the autotech sphere, which hovered a few feet above the stone floor. He looked over the options etched into the surface and selected *duplication*. With a smile, he focused on the "hand cannon" on the floor.

The autotech machinery began to shimmer with a subtle golden radiance as the device analyzed the weapon. After several minutes, the golden glow dissipated, and the surface pulsed red. Then the machine became inert. It couldn't replicate the gun.

Alex made it especially for me.

Carter felt a surge of happiness at the thought. His sidearm couldn't be duplicated because Alex had made it that way: the Grid system could replicate anything it scanned unless it was marked with specific sigils to prevent that. He grinned as he picked up the sidearm and holstered it, his belly and balls tingling warmly. He knew those emotions weren't reasonable. Alex was happily involved with Imara and Sirenī, but Carter still felt them.

That was a dangerous road to go down, even in his head, so the soldier ruthlessly trained his thoughts on firearms for his friends. He requested a Unified Military standard-issue handgun and touched the activator. Immediately, the machine fabricated the weapon. He picked it up, confirmed it was suitable, then requested enough for everyone. He added a crate for the handguns and bundled them in niches within the foam interior.

Carter closed the crate and carried it into the sitting room. He turned to the left of the spacious room, with several clusters of chairs and couches artlessly arranged to provide cozy little sitting groups. He placed the box on an empty table against the wall adjacent to the door.

Then he went upstairs to his bedroom and into his closet. Carter reached up and touched the collar of his armor, idly wondering how to get out of it. He need not have worried: all the pieces came apart and flipped or rotated as they flowed off his body and assembled neatly in the niche set aside for it.

He still wore sweats and a T-shirt, soaked with sweat, and he wrinkled his nose at the clammy feel. He stripped, showered, and crawled into bed to let the twilight doze overtake him.

Richard slipped out of bed just after sunrise, right around the time he'd usually hit the Mug and the gym. He was trying to get the fabricator to produce coffee but had no luck. He wasn't sure what he was doing wrong, either. Alex had made it sound so simple to use. Fortunately, Carter breezed in and greeted him.

"Coffee?" the soldier asked.

Richard nodded, and Carter rested a hand on the silvery sphere. It lit up and produced a cup of coffee.

"You try. Remember to keep your intent clear."

Richard tried again, picturing two more cups of coffee. The machine responded immediately, and he grinned.

"Can we get this thing to make a free weight set, a treadmill, shit like that?" Richard asked after his triumph.

"Easily. We've got gymnasiums on Gaea and do resistance training, cardio, the whole deal." Carter flexed, his T-shirt bulging around his massive biceps as if it were sprayed on. "I didn't get these without sweat and hard work, you know."

Richard clapped a hand on his shoulder. "I know, Muscles. It would be nice if you could get that ripped with magic."

"There are spells for health and fitness, hypertrophy, body fat, all that shit. I think manipulating matter is Grade Six or Seven, though—way above my skill levels."

Richard nodded, then tried his hand at one more fabrication: pancakes and syrup. That worked, too, and he grabbed the tray and headed upstairs to the room he and Jordan had picked, which was adjacent to Carter's. He slipped inside and presented the tray of pancakes, syrup, and coffee with a flourish, careful not to jostle anything.

Jordan smirked and climbed out of the massive bed, wearing only a snug T-shirt, her enspelled pendant, and boy-cut underwear. Richard felt his dick stiffen at the sight of her as she sauntered over to him, and his lounge pants tented at the crotch like a teenager.

She took a sip of coffee. "Mm, that's good."

She drank more and then set the cup on the tray. A mischievous expression stole over her face, and she reached down and caressed his cock through his flimsy pants. Richard growled with desire.

"The pancakes can wait."

She turned and sashayed back to the bed. She looked over her shoulder at him with a smile and bent forward to rest her hands on the mattress. She rocked her perfect ass from side to side in invitation, and Richard worried he was going to come in his pants.

"Woman, you are amazing," he said huskily as he set the tray aside.

"Why don't you show me how amazing you think I am?" she purred.

She hooked the thumb of her right hand under the waistband of her underwear and slipped them down to reveal a creamy expanse of flesh. Richard ripped his shirt and lounge pants off, then joined her at the bed.

After their lovemaking, he sprawled on the bed beside her, his heart pounding.

"I love you so much," he told her.

"I know," she breathed back contentedly.

SEVENTEEN

Carter put the exercise equipment on a mental back burner. He took his coffee into the sitting room and set it on the low table in the same seating arrangement where he'd last talked with the Three. He grabbed the box of guns off the table and brought them to the sitting area. He opened the box, took the guns out, and inspected them individually.

Handguns on Gaea didn't have the same moving parts as those on Earth. They didn't clog or use gunpowder as a propellant for the bullets, so there was no residue or debris to accumulate in the barrel. The clips also didn't come out; the grip and magazine were a single unit.

Enchantments produced an unlimited supply of bullets in these particular guns. However, after about ten shots, the magic would require a few seconds to generate another "clip" full of bullets. These bullets didn't have the same explosivity as his, but they still carried plenty of stopping power.

Carter sighted down each barrel and looked over every bit of the sidearms, one each for Jordan, Richard, Paul, Sue, Brent, Drëndi, and Eric. He wondered if he could set up a firing range in the laboratory. It would be safer than firing outdoors since the guns were more dangerous than Earthen firearms of equivalent size. If that didn't work, he'd figure out something in the woods on the property, but that wasn't ideal.

He had complete trust in the defenses the Three established around the property, but it paid to be cautious. It made him feel better to teach his friends basic firearm safety, handling, and marksmanship. Brent and Drëndi were professionals and wouldn't need tutoring, but they could take turns teaching the others.

The soldier smiled as he closed the box and leaned back on the couch, stretching his right arm over the back. He sipped his coffee, enjoying the peace and contentment of the morning hours alone. He was startled when Marquis appeared from nowhere, catching him by surprise for the second time.

The feline jumped onto the couch and stepped up to Carter. Marquis had a purr like a motorcycle's engine. Carter dropped his right arm from the back of the sofa and scratched the cat's blocky head, eliciting louder purring.

"It's up to us, isn't it, big fella?" he said in Demurrian. The cat stared at him intently, golden eyes steady. "We've got to keep everyone safe, no matter what."

The cat turned and half-fell, half-lay down next to him, stretched along his right thigh, and let out a huge, gusty sigh with a little snort at the end. Carter put his arm over the back of the couch again and sat in contemplative silence, enjoying what every nerve in his body told him was the calm before the storm.

Eighteen
Duodeviginti

Amlodd came by the following day and gave the Three a list of simple tasks they could pick from if they wanted to exchange magical services for currency. Surveying the list, Alexander handed the sheet back.

"We would prefer something more substantive," he said.

Amlodd frowned as if he didn't understand the other man's thicker accent. He looked at Imara, puzzled.

"What Alex means," she clarified, "is that we have more capability than most travelers you've met from our world. We can help with bigger projects if you have anything like that."

"Let me check with the governor," he replied. "She'll know of public works on a larger scale that may benefit from your unique abilities." He turned away, took out a phone, and called the governor. They talked briefly, and he turned back to them with his usual broad grin. "I may have just the thing."

He went over to the low table before the couch, which faced a blank wall at the far end of the room opposite the bed. He picked a small, rectangular object from the table and pointed it at the white expanse. The Three had seen it when they surveyed the room eight years in the future but hadn't paid any attention to it then, given the circumstances that forced them to rush away.

Amlodd fiddled with the device he'd picked up and turned on a monitor embedded in the wall. It was enormous, taking up half the surface area. He accessed a settings screen, and a form appeared. Amlodd swiftly entered information on the device that Alexander had learned from his Earthen friends was called a user ID and password.

After entering his credentials, the official asked them to come closer and showed them a video of one of the four great canals transecting Ednyfed. There was an enormous break in the wall of the structure. The footage showed several colossal pieces of whatever building material the locals used to construct the channel crumbling into the ocean. Huge waves raced away, concentrated inside the canal.

"This happened four weeks ago. We have crews in the canal to make repairs, but as you can imagine, it's slow going. Those walls are almost half a mile high, and the waterway is about two miles wide. The crack runs down to the seafloor. We're afraid it may get worse while we wait," Amlodd explained gravely.

"We would be pleased to assist," Alexander said as he continued to study the ultra-high-resolution video. "Is this imagery an accurate representation of the canal?"

Amlodd was surprised by that question but nodded. "It is. A drone filmed this about midway between the Northern and Southern Oceans."

"Excellent. Prepare yourself."

Alexander looked at his partners; they nodded agreeably before he snapped his fingers.

Amlodd opened his mouth, but whatever he'd been about to say became an actual squeak of shock as he saw gusting winds blowing viciously across the top of the canal walls, ripping the sound away. The Gatehouse Transit chief clapped a hand over his mouth to stop any further embarrassing noises from escaping and swallowed nervously, staring fearfully toward the edge of the structure.

The walls appeared to be about 400 feet thick. They were solid and well-made, and the four people appeared about fifteen feet from the edge. The Gatehouse Transit chief seemed to suffer some vertigo as he stood there, weaving slightly despite trying to remain still. Imara grabbed his shoulder and steadied him with a smile.

Eighteen

Teleportation was not an everyday experience for the people of Omejis, despite the technological sophistication of the current civilization. Alexander understood that Amlodd hadn't been prepared for the immediacy of his actions, but he'd done it with an ulterior motive: to determine if teleportation worked at this point in time.

He turned his attention to the far wall a couple of miles away. It was barely visible to Alexander's eyes without binoculars.

"It only makes sense to be efficient. It seems like your people are worried that this could escalate," the sorcerer said.

He walked the fifteen feet to the edge of the canal wall and looked down interestedly. He then looked across the way, barely able to discern the cracks with his unaided eyes. He whistled in appreciation of the sophistication of the great channel, impressed that the people of Omejis built it without magical assistance.

There were structures superior to this on Gaea, such as the trans-Sahara canal. It led from Lake Chad northeast across Al Khem in a straight line, connecting to the Nile River delta near Khere-Ohe, where the sorcerers Seth and Horus dueled in ancient times. That structure was raised straight from the world's bones with the combined magics of hundreds of sorcerers who linked their aurae to increase their power exponentially. This canal, one of four, was made by sheer brute strength and engineering genius. It was an inspiration, an achievement any civilization could be proud of.

Alexander turned from the edge as Imara and Sirenī came to stand beside him, the songstress on his left and the daughter of Medusa on his right. He looked at Imara as she appeared to stare across the canal at the fracture rending the colossal wall of the channel. He waited while she scanned it with her unique sight, which was superior to a magic user's psychic vision—even his. Finally, she nodded and turned to address both of her partners and Amlodd.

"The fracture goes straight down to a subsidence in the seafloor. I can see that whoever built the canals didn't line the base with anything to provide a solid foundation," Imara said. "We can readily fix this and give you devices you can place at the other canals to replicate the spells we'll use here."

Amlodd looked at her, amazed.

Alexander knew that saving the people from the eruption of Lauremanda would earn them the most profound gratitude of Omejis. It was an action that rendered an excess of aid with the four canals superfluous, but fixing them worked in everyone's favor by keeping the people of this world safer in the future.

The supercontinent shifted and breathed with the normal rhythms of a living world. Given the sheer scale of the four canals, the bulwarks must have been under tremendous stress since their installation. Damage to the marvelous structures was inevitable, and he was amazed that this was the only problem that had occurred.

Sirenī smiled at Amlodd and walked over to him. Imara still had her hand on his shoulder but dropped it when Sirenī approached. The daughter of Medusa looped her arm through his and coaxed him toward the canal's edge. He was nervous and sweating but didn't complain or try to move away.

Alexander looked at them. Sirenī smiled at him, then at Amlodd. "You're safe with me."

Amlodd searched her face and smiled back weakly.

Alexander extended his hands, and Amlodd flinched involuntarily as flickering energies crackled with red and orange flares around them. The sorcerer spoke several words, and spellforms propagated into a large sphere that slowly rotated on its axis. Arcane geometric forms, equations, and lines of text were visible as he contemplated the best spells to fix the canals.

Out of the corner of his eye, the sorcerer saw Imara look downward, presumably to study the seabed. After a couple of minutes, she lifted her gaze.

"We should convert the walls to a locrunite-reinforced nanocarbon, keeping the same width for the walls and creating a two-hundred-foot-thick floor connecting the two sides. The bottom portion of the canal should be at least one hundred fifty feet below the seafloor to preserve the marine environment."

Alexander nodded at her words and spoke in Demurrian, adjusting and expanding the spellforms he'd manifested to incorporate Imara's suggestions. Sirenī reached out with her free hand and pivoted the globular form. She tapped twice on one set of geometric patterns. They expanded and flattened before her as if they were displayed on a screen instead of projected by Alexander's magical force.

"This won't do," the daughter of Medusa said. She pointed to the equations and the complex geometries articulated by the math. "This will cause the entire seafloor to convert; we need to add a limiter to the propagational parameters." She frowned. The spellforms shifted as she exerted her will, and she smiled. "There, what do you think?"

Imara scanned the transforms Sirenī had specified and nodded. "Definitely. I'm glad you caught that."

Alexander nodded, pleased, and swiped away the complex structure before him. He held his hands in front of him with his palms six inches apart at solar plexus height. The spellforms that had loomed large a moment ago reappeared between his hands in miniature. They were now too tiny to discern their details but identical in every way.

"You should step back a bit. This will take us several hours," he cautioned Amlodd.

The transit chief nodded weakly, but his smile was sincere as he took several steps away despite his sweaty nervousness. "You're too kind," he said.

It had nothing to do with kindness. The sorcerer didn't want the chief to fall off the canal's edge and plunge to his death. It would strain their relations with the locals. Alexander tactfully kept those thoughts to himself and focused on his magic. Ecstasy flushed through his body.

He brought the first spell to mind and began to chant. Energy swelled around him as his corona surged, billowing upward from his feet and spiraling around the four in a swirling aurora of orange-red light. The sorcerer exerted his will and felt the syncretic surge of magical and mystical forces thunder through his nāḍī as an energy gradient thrummed in the air, growing louder and more intense.

A vigorous magical wind whipped around them and blew at their hair and clothes. Below them, the ocean lashed, and a rippling wave of churning water expanded outward in a fan-like pattern. The surging waves swelled into five-foot white caps as his magic began to influence reality, but this was just the preliminary spell. He finished chanting that one and began to recite the next. The spellforms glowed between his hands and pulsed rhythmically like a heartbeat.

The ground trembled along the canal's length, and Amlodd pulled out his phone. Alexander was aware of him stepping away from the sorcerers and holding the device to his head. He couldn't hear what the other man said, but as the trembling grew stronger, he suspected the official was reassuring people in the government that everything was okay.

Inside Mount Lauremanda, lava bubbled and popped in great bursts of molten rock and superheated gases. There were many lava tubes through the mountain; some self-sealed over the past couple of millennia while others spiraled and twisted in a labyrinthine maze. At the heart of this tortuous grouping was a pack of Undying—the six offspring of Ävidä Saclendra dispatched to Omejis to set the kṛtyā bījā in place and feed it with the blood of as many people as could be acquired.

In this case, they had only a few people they'd caught and maimed while hiking the slopes of the ordinarily quiescent mountain. They placed the wounded people on the coarse basalt floor of their chosen space. It was a few hundred feet across in both directions and about half that high, and the dark seed rested in the center of it.

The Undying, five females and one male, all wore the scalps of their victims. They preferred naturally honey-blonde hair and wore the thefted locks in intricate braids about their heads and down their backs. They acquired the hair by peeling the scalps from their screaming prey using the magically sharpened nails on the tips of their fingers.

Līc tended to congregate in small groups, called curses, and adopt uniforms of sorts. This cluster wore simple leather clothing in neutral brown colors that offset the desiccated skin of their skulls, hands, and feet while contrasting with their stunning golden hair. Some līc adopted animate forms that looked alive, but it took energy to feign life. Many Undying went with a mummified look and stole a piece or three from the living to create a horrific contrast between the two aspects.

These six smiled all the time because their lips were peeled back from their brown, broken teeth. They had no noses, just holes with flaps of dried flesh partially covering the nasal pits, and eye sockets that gaped obscenely below the well-coiffed hair of their victims. The people the līc harvested to feed the kṛtyā bījā on Omejis had dark curly hair in all but one case, and that was a redhead. There was no one to scalp, so they cut their victim's hamstrings and watched the dark flower take them.

They made bets about who'd die first and last, who'd get a root in the cunt or the ass, and which people would tear their vocal cords screaming. After the last of the victims died—a child, quite unexpectedly, so no one won the bet—the līc joked about the awful deaths.

The first root of the dark flower that touched the human mulch climbed over a man's hand. He turned, shrieking as he tried to fling the obscenely pulsating tendril away, but it held on, twining around his limb and puncturing his wrist to burrow beneath the flesh. His scream escalated as the root grew up his arm and caused excruciating pain. His arm bloated and swelled, becoming reddish purple as the fibers wormed through him. The other fertilizer watched in horror while the līc leered in sexual thrall.

In minutes, the people were all impaled on a root or two. They screamed and writhed as the tendrils expanded through their bodies, bursting out, crawling over their flesh, and burrowing back elsewhere until they were consumed. The tendrils dragged the human mulch into a pile atop the seed, where they took a day or two to die. As that happened, their vital essences drained to power the corruption spell of the kṛtyā bījā. The dark seed took root in the rock of the lava tube, sinking the first magical vibrations of corruption into the basalt.

The Conciliar Hall glowed with golden light. The tower spanned high above, focusing the light of the sun, moon, and stars into a prismatic kaleidoscope that washed down the crystal and stone walls to spread like liquid across the polished black floor.

Ten people sat in ornate cathedrae arranged in a perfect circle.

They wore black robes that obscured their bodies and faces and helped keep their identities secret. Every member knew who else sat on the Concilium Magorum, so the concealment was pro forma rather than necessity.

"Why did you summon us?" Her cathedra shimmered with an aura that indicated she was the most powerful mage present. "We all have much to take care of."

The weakest member of the Council stood. "I called this emergency session because of two things—first, several members are absent. Do we know where they are?" Her voice was shrill. "Second, what are we going to do about the līc uprising? You know what Ävidä Saclendra did to the vampires."

The councilmembers looked at each other, their visages obscured by their shrouds. After a couple of minutes, when no one else spoke, the strongest stood. She reached up and lowered her hood, revealing rich dark skin, penetrating amber eyes, and a multitude of crimson braids the color of blood. Her features were stunning, her presence fearsome and intimidating.

"Janessa, I believe I speak for all of us when I tell you it is none of our business where our brethren are. They have a mission that does not concern any of us and will return when they can," she said sternly. "As for the līc uprising, we are already working on that." She narrowed her amber eyes. "How did you not know of this?"

Janessa reached up and yanked off her hood. Her slim, pointed features were a mask of irritation. "Well, forgive me, Thalatte. I hadn't been informed about any of that."

"Consider yourself informed," Thalatte replied coldly. "Is there anything else? I have much to oversee in the Tèng Empire. They are considering Unification at the highest levels now that Liáng Bo is dead."

No one spoke, and the councilmembers left the Conciliar Hall one by one until only Janessa was left. She stood in the tower alone and fumed at the disrespect with which she'd been treated. She'd been a councilmember for almost a century; she knew Thalatte was an ancient demihuman of some kind.

She's also a bitch, Janessa thought. *Someday soon, she—they, the assholes—will regret how they've treated me.*

Omejis had a stable crust with two tectonic plates underlying the supercontinent. Thanks to that geology, quakes were rare. The volcanic islands tended to grumble and shake, and many of the younger ones regularly erupted. They were located far from Ednyfed and largely unoccupied, except by researchers studying volcanology, so no one paid any attention.

The four great canals were cut straight through the main landmass, transecting its features and bedrock, spaced equidistantly around the planet's circumference. Over the two hundred twenty years that the canals existed, the sands of the two oceans gradually followed the tides' push and pull to coat the exposed bedrock and subsurface of the supercontinent.

Sand had traveled the length of each channel to extend the materials of the two oceans—separated by Ednyfed for eons—into one body of water and a global seafloor. There were no foundations beneath the canals as the walls were built before the ocean flooded the trenches and were made well. They'd lasted, with minimal maintenance, for over two centuries of local time. The water flowing through the canals had eaten into the bedrock, softening it in some places and causing more than one subsidence.

This subsidence was beneath one of the walls of the grand canals and stretched about four miles long. The loss of all that supportive rock beneath the wall made it begin to sag; it buckled over the next fifty or sixty years. Now the stone was splintering, with great chunks toppling into the sea to smash to the silty floor of the canal.

The continental bedrock was about fifty feet beneath the young, sandy seabed running through the canals. It could support the weight of the continent above, but it wasn't an evenly distributed blend of igneous, sedimentary, and metamorphic stone. There were places where softer, salt-water soluble rock infiltrated the harder types, and it was there the trouble developed.

Imara, Sirenī, and Alex modified a spell to transform the stone walls of the canal, and some of the seabed, into nanocarbon. The material was made of densely packed fullerenes composed of a hundred molecules of carbon arranged in a roughly spherical shape.

Nanocarbon was the material of choice for construction projects on Gaea. Most building foundations and interior structures were created from the ultradurable material. The canals were too large for the nanocarbon on its own, however. To offset this, the Three incorporated gleaming locrunite threads into the constituents, adding resilience and elasticity to the structure that would last for ages.

Nanocarbon was interminably durable against natural causes and difficult to destroy with magic. Someone could unmake it easily enough with the proper spells, but those were only known by the sorcerer who cast them.

Imara and Sirenī watched Alex chant several different spells. After he completed each one, he had to wait for the magic to empower and allow the effect to manifest. The spells were easy for the sorcerer to cast, and he spent most of the hours the project took standing in place, waiting for his magic to work.

Imara was grateful that her partner was a patient man.

Alex metamorphosed a foundation of solid, locrunite-laced nanocarbon two hundred feet thick from the bedrock. The sandy seafloor of the channel remained intact, the ecosystem unaffected by the spell. Once the flooring stretched the length and width of the canal, it propagated up the walls. Anyone watching saw a shimmering wave of orange-red patterns shine through the waters of the planetary panthalassa, gleaming beneath the sea's surface like fire as it rose from the depths.

The orange-red light erupted from the choppy surface of the global ocean to surge up the walls in a scintillating wave. As it passed, the magical corona metamorphosed the light gray stone of the original construction into dark gray nanocarbon laced with shimmering, iridescent strands of locrunite.

While Alex set the enchantments to fix the canal, Imara and Sirenī walked from the edge to stand near Amlodd, who had found a spot where he could tolerate the vertiginous location. The women waited until they saw what Alex was doing and then worked on their part of the process, creating three pyxides to transform the other canals.

Imara raised her voice in ethereal song and collected the enchantments Alex had cast. She gathered them by the pattern of their vibrations, which she could see, sense, and hear. Sirenī created the three pyxides: small dark gray cubes two inches on a side. They were blank when Sirenī made them, but as Imara embedded the spells she'd gathered from Alex into each pyxis, magical symbology etched into the sides in shimmering rainbow-hued patterns.

It took four hours to complete the repairs on the canal. The changes hadn't yet propagated fully along the entire length and width of the corridor—that would take several more hours. Imara saw the wave of change moving steadily along the walls of the canal, flowing away to her left and right.

She turned to Sirenī and grinned. "Well, that's it."

Her partner smiled and nodded. She turned to Amlodd and held out her hands with the three pyxides resting on her palms. The cubes hummed with internal power, and Amlodd's eyes widened as they lifted and floated to him. He took them gently as if they might break.

"I cannot thank you enough," Amlodd began. "This is the most amazing thing! To witness it firsthand is even more incredible. Why, we never even imagined such power existed, never mind thought any of us would see it firsthand."

The Three glanced at one another, then Sirenī rested a hand on Amlodd's forearm. "You're very welcome, Amlodd," she told him warmly. "If you direct people to place one of these boxes as close to the central edge of one of the walls of each canal as they can get, then the spells will activate. This will prevent more subsidences from damaging the walls in the future."

Alex huffed, but Imara could tell he was pleased. "These canals will outlast the continent," she said.

Amlodd laughed a little hysterically, but he nodded and was obviously happy. He looked around while clutching the three small boxes in his arms. "Uh…" he started.

Imara saw him flinch when Alex raised his hand, but he snapped his fingers before Amlodd could say anything else. The canal drained away from them, and their hotel room flexed inward. It seemed to bow and flutter as the walls, floor, and ceiling snapped around them. Air rushed away from them and fluttered the leaves and flowers of the foliage to either side of the couch.

"That's a, uh, unique way to travel," Amlodd mumbled. He shook his head and pulled himself together with a respectful bow before he turned to leave. "I'll get these to the governor and have them distributed immediately. Oh, and you can shut off the video display by pressing your palm against the remote."

The door shut behind him. They looked at one another and burst out laughing. Imara went to the remote and pressed her palm against the top without picking it up; the embedded wall display deactivated immediately.

She turned to her partners. "Shall we break in the bed? I feel… energized." She stretched luxuriously and shook her arms and neck to loosen everything up.

Sirenī nodded eagerly. "I'm feeling naughty!"

Imara laughed, and Alex practically sprinted ahead of them to the bedroom. Sirenī hooked her arm in Imara's and laughed at his enthusiasm, but she wouldn't have it any other way.

"I'm bringing my olisbos out," she called after him in a singsong voice.

Alex peeked around the bedroom door with a considering look on his face. The women reached him, and he tapped Sirenī's nose.

"Fine."

Sirenī's jaw dropped, and Alex laughed and swaggered to the bed. She looked at Imara. "Did he just agree to let me fuck him with my strap-on?"

Imara nodded, looking amused. "Yes, he did. Go get him while he's still receptive," she urged, ushering her forward.

With a gleeful whoop, Sirenī ran into the bedroom.

Nineteen
Undeviginti

Three weeks after the incident with Patrine, a bored Eric decided to take a walk down the long driveway. He returned in a rush and told Carter someone was at the barrier who wanted to talk with him.

Carter was relieved that he'd revoked everyone's ability to pass through the shield after he'd fought the undead, since Eric could have accidentally wandered past the protective field effects while chatting with whoever was there.

Granting and revoking permission required a brief exertion of his will for each person, but the simplicity was unexpected. He'd always thought advanced magic was more complicated, but it turned out to be easier to use—at least where the Three were concerned.

Carter strode down to the barrier and saw a somewhat familiar face. He slowed when he reached the end of the drive, wondering what the Zalcent tech wanted with him. The man was thirtyish, lean, a few inches over six feet, and wore a baggy winter coat with the Zalcent logo embroidered on the breast. He nervously shifted from foot to foot as Carter approached.

Thurley, Carter thought as he recalled the man's name.

Thurley had zipped up his blue, boxy jacket to deal with the cold. Carter no longer felt the temperature, and he no longer needed to sleep. To occupy his nights, he'd taken to reading in the manor library. He'd idly picked out a few books of low-level spells and rituals. In them, he'd found a treasure trove of concise, practical knowledge such as personal thermal regulation, methods to beguile, and a variety of alternatives for casting common spells.

Carter found some of the variations useful now that he was more powerful. *I wonder what my Grade would be if I took the Auditum Peritiae Arcanae today?*

A part of him desperately wanted to retake the Registry's assessment to see how he scored in the audit, but the rest of him was too nervous. Not that it mattered: he couldn't do it since he was on Earth.

And Kāmla dismantled the Registry, anyway.

He stood at the end of the drive with his thick, hairy arms crossed over his broad chest and looked at the technician. "Your last name is Thurley, right?"

The man gave a nervous nod.

"What do you want?" Carter demanded.

Thurley gulped and looked over his shoulder toward the surveillance shack tucked into the woods across the street. Carter expected soldiers—and other Zalcent employees—were watching their interaction.

"Uh, yes, I am Thurley. Good memory." He chuckled nervously and wrung his hands, then forged on beneath Carter's squinty gaze. "My employers, Zalcent International…" he pointed helpfully to his jacket where the name and logo were embroidered, "…want to open a dialog with you and your, uh, companions."

Carter cocked his head, flexed his arms slightly, and leaned forward. "Whatever for?" he growled.

Thurley looked even more flummoxed as the soldier stared intimidatingly at him. Then he blinked behind his glasses and blurted, "Damn, dude, you're jacked!"

Carter's amusement overwhelmed his exasperation; he guffawed, uncrossed his arms, and said, "Did your employers tell you to mention I was… What did you say? Jacked?"

He put his fists on his hips and flexed slightly to strain the sleeves of his T-shirt even more. The fabric pulled across his chest and shoulders.

Thurley's eyes traced the lines of his muscles with unabashed admiration; when his gaze dropped to Carter's crotch, the soldier chuckled and titled his pelvis forward suggestively.

Carter didn't realize at first that he was flirting with the Earthen man. When it clicked in his head, his grin broadened.

Well, well. Are these "the vibes" Richard keeps talking about picking up from people that I never seem to notice?

He cleared his throat and asked, "Like what you see, Thurley?"

The other man turned beet red and said, "I'm very sorry. That's not what I'm supposed to talk to you about. Let me start over."

Before Thurley spoke, Carter stepped through the invisible barrier. They'd shaken hands after the fight with Patrine, but he extended his again to the younger man. Thurley shook somewhat weakly, but the soldier knew not to expect an iron grip from previous experience.

"I'm Jack Carter, but everyone just calls me Carter."

The tech nodded after the handshake. "I'm John Thurley; everyone calls me John. Or Johnny, but that's mostly just my mother and sister." He laughed, blushed, and muttered, "I'm making a fool of myself."

"In what way?" Carter prompted.

John looked past the soldier's left shoulder. "I'm very shy, socially awkward, and usually only date online." He flinched and met Carter's dark eyes, adding frantically, "Not that we're dating… Oh, god, I'm such an idiot!"

Carter laughed and glanced past John to the blind across the street. He was sure the soldiers and techs were listening in on them.

"It's fine," he waved away the comment, "I realize we aren't dating." He grinned. "And if we were, wouldn't that get you in trouble with the United States government and your bosses at Zalcent? Fucking a foreign national cultist, or some such garbage?"

John laughed and nodded, some of the tension defusing with Carter's words. "*So* much trouble," he said.

You're an intriguing man, John Thurley. "What did your employers want you to pass along to me?"

John cleared his throat and squared his shoulders, which did not make them appear any broader but helped the technician focus on the situation. "My employers want to open a dialog with you and whoever else is in your…place. They want you to know they bought Grace Manor and have removed all police and federal authorities from the premises. They're interested in administering several noninvasive medical tests, with your permission, and, barring that, at least discussing information about your unique skill set since you're a fucking real-life superhero." John quirked his lips.

Carter shook his head. He was only familiar with the reference because Eric had coaxed his father, Carter, and Richard into watching the entire Marvel Cinematic Universe, which comprised about a million movies and TV shows. Carter was lost the whole time since they didn't have cinematic productions like that on Gaea.

They had plays, operas, music, radio shows, organic crystal displays, and movies that tended to be short with specific themes underpinning them. There were no three-hour-plus movies or long, convoluted TV shows with twists, turns, and surprises.

However, if John was comparing Carter's recent combat demonstration to a superhero, Carter decided to take it in the flattering spirit in which the younger man had meant it.

"Can they hear what we're saying over there?" Carter asked.

John pressed his lips together and glanced over his shoulder. "Yes, but they know I'm a total dork, so it's hardly like any of my inane mumblings are surprising."

Carter found the self-deprecation a typical Earthen response for those who felt alienated. People of Earth could be cruel toward anyone and anything that didn't fit into their consensus realities of "normal," especially when it came to sexual orientation and religion.

"Give me a second," Carter told John.

The man nodded then watched with wide eyes as the soldier held up his hand and began to chant one of the spells he'd recently discovered he could cast. It was called Kalypto Hesykhia, in honor of the ancient sorcerer obsessed with quiet. She experimented with spells that produced blankets, cones, and field effects of noise nullification or cancellation.

The Kalypto was Hesykhia's most-enduring spell because it was highly effective and easy to cast for upper-level sorcerers. John's expression became more dazed as the cloak of silence blanketed them. The Earthen man could feel the magic working; the spell caused a tingling buzz that crawled over his skin and made his teeth ache slightly.

"Holy fuck! Did you just cast a spell? That's fucking amazing!"

Carter liked John and his sense of awe. He said, "It is magic, which is commonplace where I come from. I created a blanket of silence over us because I wanted to talk to you without your employers being able to hear us. They can't discern lip movements, either. The spell blocks the manifestation of all words from all forms of perception."

John became serious and spoke in a whisper. "Don't trust them. Zalcent is a dangerous, powerful corporation, and they'll fuck you over as soon as they can. The head of the company, Anar Iskariótés, is pure evil! They want your DNA, plain and simple."

Carter had already known Zalcent couldn't be trusted. He'd seen how these corporations worked on Earth and had spoken about it at length with his Earthen friends. In turn, they'd shared some of the business Zalcent was involved with—situations that governments worldwide had suspicions about. They didn't have any proof of wrongdoing, so nothing ever happened. Carter was never going to trust any of the all-powerful corporations of this world.

"Thanks, I figured they were shit," he rumbled. "Why'd they send you?"

John shrugged. "People way above my pay grade record everything in the blinds; I doubt we can take a shit without them watching. Anyway, they've monitored your property with drones and mapped out the barrier down to a few centimeters of variance, and they saw that every other adult on the property is paired off except you. The creepers sent me because somehow I'm the only gay man around, and someone, somewhere, must have analyzed body language and figured out you don't dig chicks." He hesitated, then added nervously, "If that is the case, of course. I mean, I don't know. If you're, um, really from another world, maybe you're all bi or something."

Carter was confused by John's rambling. "We don't eat chickens or any animal products. Why would I prefer chicks?"

John burst out laughing and shook his head. "No, no. I meant they think you aren't into women, so they sent me. We call women 'chicks' sometimes. I'm not sure why, it's not very polite. Anyway, the point is, they're trying to manipulate and watch you."

Carter studied the other man's face and saw only innocence and sincerity. He snapped his fingers, and the spell dissipated with unfamiliar ease.

"Thank you for speaking to me." He extended his hand, and John fumbled in his pocket for a second before shaking it again. "Maybe I'll see you around."

The young man's face lit up, and he nodded eagerly. "I'd love to see you again. Well, for the first time… You know, properly."

Carter went back through the barrier. He turned once he was safe inside and narrowed his eyes, staring into the woods at the well-hidden blind. His mind raced as he considered the interaction—both personally and situationally.

Does this affect our safety?

Because of his preoccupation, it took him a moment to realize that he held something in his hand—John had slipped it into his palm when they shook. Carter turned away from the blind and walked along the drive. Before he went into the house, he studied the paper, which was nothing more than a scrap. Scribbled on it were ten numbers which Carter understood to be a phone number.

He tucked it in the pocket of his snug jeans and entered the house. He wanted to find Jordan, Richard, Brent, and Drëndi to discuss what happened. Their insight would be invaluable and help him determine what to do next.

A part of him, lonely and horny, wanted to take John up on his interest just to let off some steam. He'd have to meet the Zalcent tech outside the barrier or authorize him to come in; either way, it could lead to trouble. Still, he could think wistfully about the comfort and fun it would provide.

No harm done.

Jordan and Drëndi disagreed utterly with Carter's assessment as they talked over the incident in the sitting room.

Drëndi's point of view was astonishingly vulgar while being practical on several levels. She said Carter should encourage John's interest.

"What?" she said in amused exasperation when Brent and Richard looked at her in shock. "He's the only one here who isn't screwing like crazy, so after he pumps John, he can, you know, pump John."

Jordan laughed but nodded as she and Drëndi gave each other a high-five. Then she calmly looked at Richard's and Brent's disapproving faces, and Carter, who stared at them in surprise.

"What? Things didn't work out with José, then everything went down with the blockade. Imara, Sirenī, and Alex left. You didn't think Carter would be bored and lonely?" she asked tartly.

"No, it's not that. I mean, this guy is an employee of the devil corporation that controls most of the world. Wouldn't Carter be risking his soul or something getting involved with him?" Richard asked.

Jordan rolled her eyes and patted his thigh. "No, Carter would finally have someone he could fool around with, and we'd have someone we could question about Zalcent. I don't know how much he knows about their projects—probably very little—but it would still be more than we can find out through their online portals."

Brent shook his head. He held up his fingers as he listed points off. "We live inside a barrier. The United States government is still after us as terrorists for aiding and abetting foreign nationals. The PID is currently suspended as a branch of Homeland Security." He dropped his hand. "We must be careful, and I'm not sure sleeping with the enemy is the best choice."

"Well, I don't like that Zalcent is involved or that they bought Grace Manor. I think they want to weaponize your magical skills," Drëndi said when her partner finished. She sipped at her wine while everyone nodded in agreement with her words. "Surely, one technician is hardly a threat, though. You could magic him somehow to make sure he's being truthful, right?"

Carter nodded. He couldn't believe the turn this conversation had taken. Against his better judgment, he was intrigued.

Jordan shrugged and looked at Richard and Brent. "See? We can control everything if we do it right."

"Why don't we see what Carter thinks before we put him in bed with someone we don't even know he's interested in?" Brent said somewhat parochially.

Everyone but Carter stared at him.

The special agent blushed slightly. "Well, I mean…" His voice trailed off. He turned to Carter, silently begging the other man to bail him out of the hole he was digging.

The soldier laughed and waved it away. He didn't have the sexual hang-ups the men of Earth carried around. "Regardless of my nonexistent sex life since I came to Earth, there is merit in finding out what we can from John. When I cast the silence spell to give us a couple of minutes to talk freely, he insisted that we do not trust Zalcent at all."

"Any good spy would," Brent reasoned. He held up a hand when Drëndi opened her mouth to argue. "No, you know that's true. Anyone worth his salt as an agent would say exactly that to establish initial trust."

"True," Drëndi agreed reluctantly. "However, we control everything on this property." She looked at Carter. "What spells can you conjure?"

"There are truth spells. I'll do some research."

He stood, reached into his jeans pocket, and retrieved the paper with John's phone number.

"*Well*, you got your second set of digits," Drëndi congratulated.

She took the small scrap and held it up so everyone could see. She turned her sparkling blue eyes on the soldier and studied him. She felt a personal interest in making sure Carter dated. She liked him and wanted him to have someone in his life like the rest of them. Besides, who wanted to live without sex? By comparison, the partnered dyads in the house were more libidinous than ever, with all the rest and tranquility that came from knowing they were safe behind the barrier. With no need to work to survive, they'd all adopted a more biorhythmic sleep cycle. They ended up unintentionally following a more ancestral routine, which unexpectedly improved their overall health and well-being.

"This could be your first serious date on Earth." She smiled. "In any case, we have options and can explore them more. I'm afraid I don't think we should include Paul and Sue in any of this just yet. They aren't as invested as we are, and I'd like to continue monitoring how they're handling this situation—just for a short time while we feel things out."

Everyone agreed.

"On an unrelated note," Brent said, "can we leave the property now? It's been a few weeks since you fought the līc. There are a few things Drëndi and I would like to take care of that we can't do over the phone."

Everyone looked expectantly at Carter.

He nodded slowly. "Yes, people can leave the property, but I want everyone back by sunset, if possible. We don't know what's going on out there. We also can't trust Zalcent at all, and I'd rather minimize our risks all around."

The group discussed it a bit but ended up agreeing with Carter's suggestion. They went on to talk about matters unrelated to Zalcent International's diabolical aspirations.

Even though they all knew something terrible was happening in the world as the corruption slowly but inexorably spread from its nexus in the Middle East, they also felt safe. For the first time in their lives, they had everything they needed.

It was a novel experience.

Jordan took Richard's hand and led him to the couch after they went upstairs to their room. She leaned against him, rested her head on his shoulder, and placed her hand on his chest. She felt his heartbeat for a moment. He kissed the top of her head, and she tilted her face to meet his gaze.

"What do you think about having a baby?" she asked tentatively.

He stared at her for a second, then chuckled. They both wanted kids, and they'd talked about it several times since they got together.

"I mean, with everything happening," she continued, "with us being on the property and my age... I could take my copper IUD out—"

"Yes," Richard interrupted. She blinked at him, uncertain she'd heard correctly. He nodded. "Yes, I'd love to have kids with you. We've already talked about it. Let's do it."

She shifted and crawled onto his lap. He grinned and cupped her ass, and she stared at him, searching his face. He met her gaze. He looked serious, and she knew he wanted kids. She kissed him deeply.

"I love you very much, Richard Eric Bryson," she whispered.

"And I love you, Jordan Maire McInerney."

Twenty
Viginti

Mount Lauremanda erupted just past the two-day mark. It belched smoke and gases into the sky in a towering pillar visible across the ocean for fifty miles.

The Three were dozing in the twilight sleep of the amṛta when someone knocked frantically at their hotel room door. They'd spent the night passionately fucking as, for some reason, their energy levels remained high after they fixed the canals.

Imara slipped out of bed at the insistent pounding on the door. She waved a hand and draped herself in blue jeans, a burnt orange blouse that perfectly complemented her complexion, and low-heeled boots. By the time the songstress was halfway to the door, her hair was in a neat ponytail, and Sirenī was out of bed.

She garbed herself in a just-below-the-knee skirt of luxuriantly tropical colors with abstract floral patterns stitched across it in a dark red. At the same time, a brightly colored, solid shirt in the style of Omejis flowed across her torso. It fell slightly off one shoulder and nicely across her lush curves. High-heeled, open-toed shoes with straps that climbed halfway up her calves encased her feet, adding four inches to her height.

Alex slid out of bed and blithely waved on his usual outfit just as

Imara opened the door to reveal a frantic Amlodd. The panting official wrung his hands in a dither. Imara knew what it was about as they'd come from a future where all these events had already happened.

"What is it, Amlodd?" Imara prompted.

He started, then stopped, and started again. "Mount Lauremanda in the Bitter Islands is erupting, and we had no warning. I'm afraid we'll be unable to evacuate people to the other islands to keep them safe before things cut loose. Can you possibly help? We'd be eternally grateful."

The Three looked at each other, making a show of considering his words. They only took a few seconds, just long enough to make it look good, then Imara looked at Amlodd.

"Of course, we'll do everything we can."

He practically sobbed in relief and gasped, "My daughter and grandchildren live in Lauremanda City! I don't know what I'd do if—"

"It'll be fine."

Alexander smiled as Sirenī interrupted Amlodd before he could catastrophize. The official closed his mouth and nodded gratefully with hope shining in his eyes. Sirenī patted his arm and then looked at Alexander.

He nodded and snapped his fingers. He already knew teleportation would fail because the bookstore proprietor told him they'd used the Gatehouse to go to the Temple. The magic worked two days ago but failed now.

The kṛtyā bījā has taken root, he thought grimly, and said, "We must get to the Gatehouse."

Imara and Sirenī agreed. They understood the volcano's eruption and the corruption were linked somehow. Alexander gestured, and Imara and Sirenī hurried out of the room with him on their heels. Sirenī ushered Amlodd ahead of them. When they reached the lobby, she pushed him toward the reception desk and the woman on duty.

"Make sure we have unobstructed access to the Gatehouse. We're going to use it to get to the Islands!" Sirenī yelled as she ran to the exit in her heeled shoes.

Alexander was behind her and saw the clerk on duty blink as she watched Sirenī's effortless lope. Amlodd looked at him and shouted, "Ask for Eirianedd! She's the governor of Lauremanda!" as they went by.

Alexander waved a hand in acknowledgment and followed his partners. They ran through the shadowed streets in the early dawn; the sun wasn't high enough to shine down into the canyons formed by the buildings spread among the hills of Rilladwen.

They quickly reached Gatehouse Hill and took the stairs two and three at a time to the top. The guards stood to the side, alerted by Amlodd in the short time it took them to run there. The armored figures waved them on, the urgency of their stance and gesturing underscoring the severity of the catastrophe.

Alexander reached out when they were nearing the top of the stairs. The Gatehouse activated, and a holographic pane flared into view. Simultaneously, the pyramid sank into the cube, and the walls folded out and buckled inward. He focused on the Nephilim Temple in the Bitter Islands, and the display changed to reflect the choice. The red curtain flowed into the air, hazy and translucent, emanating from the Darhavil script ringing the transportation platform.

Imara and Sirenī went straight to the platform while Alexander paused at the display. He tapped the icon to select the Temple and joined his partners. The light flared and hardened, then sluiced down into the dais inside the superancient building.

"Why couldn't we teleport?" Sirenī asked in Demurrian as they stepped off the platform inside the brightly lit Temple.

Alexander scowled. "The kṛtyā bījā has activated. The eruption and the dark flower must be related."

Imara said, "Of course they are. There is no coincidence, just synchrony. We know this all too well from our past experiences and the history of Gaea. Too often, magical forces have pulled together the disparate pieces of the solution in the most unforeseeable ways."

Alexander led the way to the exit, and the colossal circular door began to slide up the exterior of the Temple. "Indeed. I would even hazard the guess that the celestial beings in the next density of the prāṇamaṇḍala have influenced events. It seems odd, but I feel it is true."

Imara put a hand on his left arm, and he looked at her. "You've had a relationship with Valas Amris for decades," she stated. "Do you believe the Celestial Bird is guiding you?"

The sorcerer hesitated only a moment before he confessed the truth with a sharp nod. "I do. A long time ago, Valas Amris told me to find you. A couple of months ago, he told me it was time for us to reunite."

"Why didn't you tell us that? I thought you pushed for our reunion because of your visions of the corruption?" Sirenī asked.

"That is correct," he confirmed, "but Valas Amris told me to act because I was hesitant."

"You were hesitant?" Imara scoffed. "I need to thank it for getting your ass in gear."

Alexander laughed and took their hands in his. "I am grateful, too."

The Three walked through the open door into the early morning light of the Bitter Islands, which were in a different time zone than Rilladwen. Sirenī snapped her fingers and engulfed them in an impermeable field. She lifted them from the ground, and they flew through the superancient shield protecting the Temple.

They rose above the lip of the caldera's walls and spotted the great column of smoke spewing from the top of Lauremanda. They began to fly toward it and swept out over the ocean. They passed Temple City a third of the way up the mountain. They saw shuttles lifting off landing pads from all over the conurbation girding Temple Mount, but they were just small personal fliers. None of them were large enough to evacuate thousands of people. Similarly, boats launched from their moorings at docks and anchors all around the seashore to head across the low chop of the ocean toward the imperiled island.

"The synchronicity here is obvious," Alexander remarked.

He turned his attention from the meager evacuation attempt already underway and looked at his companions. They raced toward Mount Lauremanda as panicked citizens filled the streets.

The sorcerer frowned and looked at Imara and Sirenī. "I believe it is critical to find the dark seed, and we must also retard the eruption to buy time to get the people to safety."

Imara concurred and thought about how they could best manage this situation. They already knew they were successful because of the future, but they didn't know how they would achieve their goals. She chastised herself because she hadn't written details like that in the journal. She assumed whatever they decided would work because of the nature of time—history couldn't be altered because it was already the past for most people, even though it was the present or future for those few who messed with time travel.

She took a deep breath and addressed her companions. "There are three tasks, and three of the most powerful mages who've ever lived happen to be traveling to the scene of the crisis." She smiled wryly and said, "Sirenī, you handle the lava and pyroclastic events."

Sirenī knew Imara had insider knowledge, so there was no need for further discussion.

Imara turned to Alex and said, "You help get the people down to the shore and establish a Tanager-Rosen bridge to Temple Mount. We can evacuate more people that way while the ships and shuttles take who they can."

Sirenī said, "I heard Amlodd say to look for the governor of Lauremanda City. I didn't catch her name."

"Eirianedd," Imara supplied.

"Yes," Alex said. "And what will you be doing, my love?"

Imara smiled predatorily and said, "Testing a theory."

Alexander pointed to a building towering over the others. It was four stories tall and fronted by a huge plaza where many people gathered.

"That looks like an official building. Drop me there," he told Sirenī.

She nodded and swept the bubble to a brief halt fifty feet above the indicated plaza. Without a word, he stepped through the boundary of the impermeable field and floated to an easy landing in the square, which still had clear space. People gawked at him, eyes widening in shock at what they witnessed, momentarily distracted from their panic by the spectacle of the flying people and the floating man.

The sorcerer looked up and waved to Imara and Sirenī; they waved back and departed. He watched Sirenī send her impermeable sphere hurtling up the mountain. The ground shook violently, and a profoundly ominous roar emanated from the volcano's burning, molten heart.

Alexander cleared his throat and augmented his voice. "I need to find Eirianedd!" he shouted.

His words carried over the people's voices as they streamed into the plaza, the roar of the trembling ground, and the sputtering of the angry volcano. A second after he spoke, a woman held up a hand. She was tall and slender, with long white hair hanging to her waist in a sleek cascade. She strode over to him, her olive skin gleaming brightly with the sweat of her fear.

"That's me!" she cried over the noise.

He nodded to indicate he'd heard her. The rumbling ground subsided, and Alexander gestured toward Temple Mount. "Get everyone down to the seashore. Boats and shuttles are coming from Temple City. I assume the shuttles can land on the beach?" At her nervous nod, he continued, "My partners and I are from Gaea. I will create a magical gateway between this island and Temple Mount. People need to make their way to the beach so we can evacuate them."

Eirianedd nodded at his words, stunned but capable. "We're very lucky magicians from Gaea happened to be here right now," she called out.

Alexander nodded and was about to reply when the top few hundred feet of Lauremanda exploded, sending a titanic plume into the sky and launching pieces of the volcano and molten rocks from the interior into the atmosphere. The cloud swelled upward, and the stones arced up and out over Lauremanda City. The people in the plaza screamed and cowered, and Alexander's heart thundered in his chest as he watched Sirenī's bubble disappear into the pyroclastic cloud.

The debris flow slowed, then stopped, with chunks of stone and molten rock hanging in midair high above the city. People pointed, eyes wide at what seemed a miracle. He knew it was Sirenī and her phenomenal psychokinetic power: she'd halted the fall of the cloud and debris, but there was a limit even to what they could do with the amṛta. He needed people to get down to the beach.

He looked at Eirianedd. "Get them moving. *Now!*"

She nodded. She turned to two men standing behind her and shouted instructions to them. They nodded and spoke into shoulder mics, hurriedly issuing orders to a coordinated and discreet group of people who began urging the civilians to move to the beach. Alexander amplified his voice further and sent his words rippling across the city girding the volcano.

"Get to the seashore! The evacuation efforts will begin there. Help the people around you who are having a harder time. We can save everyone, but we need you to get to the beaches!"

He put a touch of compulsion in his voice. The gentle magical force influenced the feelings of the people, soothing them somewhat and helping them focus. The citizens began to flow like water through the streets and down the mountain's slope toward the pristine white beaches. They were calmer than he expected, even with his magical support.

The sorcerer joined the exodus along with Eirianedd. She quickly shouted herself hoarse, exhorting her people. As he jogged along with the crowd, Alexander summoned to mind the spellforms of the Tanager-Rosen bridge since he had never cast the enchantment.

Thankfully, he remembered every spell he'd ever seen, whether cast by someone or diagrammed in a book or written on a scroll or anywhere else, so he knew the basics. However, new spells could be tricky, with complex phrasings, particular actions, or motions needed to set the forms into action. He inhaled and allowed the geometries of the magic to flicker to life around him, startling those nearby into backing away, which gave him some space in the crowded streets as he evaluated the mechanisms of the spell.

He shook his head, slightly annoyed that he'd be casting this complex and beautiful magic for the first time under emergency circumstances. Still, he was confident in his ability to pull it off—and not just because he had more than enough power to cast the Grade Five magic.

No, he was sure because he was Alexander Eldred, and Eldreds didn't fail.

Ävidä smiled as he felt the birth of the kṛtyā bījā across the targeted worlds of the Ring. Tethers formed active connections between the seeds of the dark flowers and the row upon row of pyxides in his citadel inside the pocket universe he'd anchored to Byrne. He rubbed his hands together in glee, his granite face splitting in a malicious smile of joy as the magic empowered.

All over the Ring of Worlds, the seeds began to feed. They'd already drained the resources of the human mulch in which they grew. When they bloomed, the flowers would spread the miasma worldwide in magical waves and rippling washes of poisonous energy.

Nothing would be safe: vampire, shapeshifter, mortal, magician, ghūl…all would feed the corruption and send vital energies along to the līc and their magical reservoirs. Buildings, structures, and feats of engineering on every world would fail—collapsing, crashing, or crumbling into ruin, creating fear and chaos.

The dark flowers bloomed in their own time; the seeds would take several years to mature and grow. Ävidä was patient: what was a decade to one who had already lived for centuries and would live forever?

He only feared one thing, or rather, three things: Alex, Imara, and Sirenī. They were imprisoned in their respective homes, separated by governmental decree, and Kāmla Vicchāya did everything she could to keep them apart forever. The archlīc knew magicians as powerful as they were could reunite whenever they wanted, and they were unstoppable.

He was no fool; he knew they'd saved Gaea, which meant him, too. He'd been alive then, of course, and he'd even done his part to stop the Tèng Empire from bringing Sogma into the world. No one with any sense could stand on the sidelines of that battle for the fate of Gaea.

Even then, he'd already started to put his plans in place, but he'd taken a break from his ambitions to fight on behalf of his homeworld. When Alex cast the devouring spell, the magical wave traveled across the entire planet. Ävidä had trembled in fear at the power he felt—no one should have been able to cast that spell. Adrienne Vorpahl couldn't have done it, and Ävidä Saclendra was self-aware enough to know he couldn't, either.

It didn't matter that Alex, pushed beyond his limits, hadn't been able to complete the spell because just casting the Dawntime magic should have been impossible for a modern mage. The magic washed over the world and pulled energy from everyone and everything. When it returned to Alex, it was an unstoppable tsunami of power. As shocking as it was for Alex to cast the spell, it was as astonishing that Imara Inanna finished it: she wielded more power than Ävidä would dare, and she shattered the Abyssal Gate and sent the Empire's plans crumbling into ruin.

If the Three moved against him right now, Ävidä knew he would lose. He'd fought two of them once before and failed. All three of them would make quick work of him. He was under no illusions that they'd destroy his phylacteria, too.

Ävidä drew in a breath he didn't need and sighed it out. The only way to defeat the Three was to avoid them until the kṛtyā bīja took care of them: time and entropy would do what he could not.

Twenty-One
Viginti Unus

The day after Carter spoke to John, he celebrated his first Thanksgiving. It was a strange custom to him, coming from a planet without holidays. People threw parties around the solstices and equinoxes, but that was the extent of any "holy days." Earth had too many for him to count from a myriad of religions, and he'd been surprised to discover that countries also celebrated days of importance, the births of leaders, and other sundries with holy days.

When his friends asked him about famous people on his planet, he rattled off a list of names. He explained it would never occur to anyone on Gaea to "celebrate" any of those people by establishing a national or planetary holiday. It all seemed strange to him, but he enjoyed eating with everyone.

Since the blockade was gone, he allowed people to leave the property during the day but insisted they be back by sunset. He, Jordan, Sue, and Drëndi went to the local Hannaford a few days before Thanksgiving and bought supplies.

Along with Brent, the women cooked a massive meal with entrées, side dishes, snacks, and desserts. Carter picked up the beers Richard, Paul, and Brent listed, the women grabbed several bottles of wine, and then he grabbed what Drëndi assured him was a higher-end whiskey.

They overate, drank too much, and slept in the next day. Carter and the kids got up at the usual times, but the other adults crept around, pained and ill-looking, thanks to their hangovers. Carter waited a bit, then took pity on them and used his trusty healing spell to bring them back to life. He treated Jordan, Richard, and Sue first—they'd come out of their rooms—then tracked down Sue's crumpled husband.

He looked like death warmed over and lay on the couch in their bedroom with a cold washcloth over his eyes. He begged Carter to kill him when he strolled into the room, but the soldier only chuckled and chanted the healing spell.

Paul groaned in relief when Carter finished. He got up, clapped the beefy soldier on the shoulder, and shook his head. "You're a fucking lifesaver, Jack Carter," he said thoughtfully. "I only wish I'd known you in my twenties, but I was drunk through most of them, so I wouldn't remember you if I had."

Carter laughed and clapped him on the back, then went to rescue Brent and Drëndi. They were still in bed and groaned in pain when he slipped into their room. They blinked in amazement when he cast the spell, and their agony subsided. He grinned and welcomed them back to the land of the living.

After midnight on December 1, Carter shut the book he'd been reading. He'd finished researching truth spells in the books he could understand. Some were so complex he couldn't follow the spellforms, and many were written in Saṃskṛta or Greek, which he didn't know. But he found what he needed.

Armed with the new enchantment, he felt ready to reach out to John. He felt some nervous anticipation, which was a novel and annoying experience that he'd never had before. Nervousness wasn't typically his problem; an overabundance of balls was. He didn't always stop to think about what he was doing, and he'd taken dangerous risks that weren't necessary to complete missions, but something about reaching out to John Thurley made his palms sweat.

Carter sat in the library and drummed his fingers on the cover of the book in his lap. He thought over the Grade Five truth spell he'd just memorized—the Verum Iacet.

Well, this is the perfect time to be honest.

His feelings about sleeping with John were complex—he found the man attractive in a boyish and goofy way. The soldier was blisteringly horny, too, which made the prospect of sex appealing.

He released a sigh and thought about how fun some sex would be—those thoughts were interrupted by thoughts about the Three. Why they kept coming into his mind eluded him. He couldn't see a connection between his feelings or thoughts for them and John, who he didn't know but wouldn't mind exploring further.

Carter knew he'd come to care for Alex, Imara, and Sirenī not just as friends and compatriots of his homeworld but as a family in exile. They were more important to him than everyone he'd left on Gaea except for Tricia Welter, his best friend.

His thoughts didn't quite ring true, but he wasn't sure why. On Earth, religions told people what kind of relationships were acceptable. On Gaea, no spiritual authority told people that this was good or that was bad—everyone agreed that adults could love and fuck who they wanted. It was no business except that of the people doing the loving or fucking.

He'd found Richard attractive as soon as he laid eyes on him. That was a no-go for many reasons. Since then, he'd come to love Jordan and Richard and considered them dear friends.

Carter's internal code wouldn't permit him to make a move on a friend's partner. He'd throw himself in harm's way for the people he loved, as when Adam and Bohuslava assaulted Jordan. He knew he couldn't defeat the undead without weapons or magic, but he couldn't sit back and do nothing—there was no bend in his code of conduct, and there had never been.

That was one of the reasons he was such a good soldier.

His thoughts ran in circles. He kept thinking of John and wondering if the other man was up for sex—but then his mind tracked back to Alex, Imara, and Sirenī. The contrast in his mind made no sense, but it did dampen some of his enthusiasm for carefree fun because he felt so confused.

After a couple of hours of circular thinking, he stood up with a growl and paced. It was proving harder than he'd expected to be utterly truthful with himself. He considered himself an uncomplicated man, but his situation had turned complex. He finally gave up trying to figure it out and grabbed Drëndi's phone off the desk where he'd been reading. She'd loaned him her phone the evening before since she was eager for him to move forward with John.

It was four in the morning, but he shot off a short message to John anyway. The soldier thought he'd have to wait until later to get a reply, but one came within seconds. He'd invited John to meet him around sunset at the same place they first spoke. John agreed.

Carter sprawled in his chair and put his hands behind his head. He wondered if he was letting his cock and balls lead him into trouble. If so, how would he get out of it without someone getting hurt? It wouldn't be the first time his dick got him into trouble, but it felt like more was at stake than an awkward fling.

Carter got to the spot where the līc attacked the blind about twenty minutes before he expected John Thurley to arrive. He wore his armor since he didn't know what he might find. His mind supplied several options: a squad of Zalcent paramilitary operators, private military contractors, Undying, necromancers, or plain-old annoying assholes.

None of those were waiting when he got there, but he scouted the area anyway. The remnants of the surveillance shack were gone, with evidence of the fire intelligently and cleverly swept away. He toed through the leaf cover artfully arranged over the most extensive burns and exposed blackened earth, fabric fragments, and melted plastic the cleanup crew had failed to remove. He *tsked* at the sloppy work.

Cover-ups only worked if you eliminated all the evidence.

He prowled around for a few more minutes, then headed back to the barrier and stepped through. The soldier loved feeling comfortably warm as he stood outdoors in the cold air. He leaned against a tree, obscured with magic, with his thumbs hooked on his belt.

Carter's eyes constantly moved as he surveyed the environment, alert to every little thing. He saw a flicker of iridescence and assumed it was the enormous moth he'd seen a few weeks ago, but he stayed where he was; he didn't want to miss John's arrival. He felt tingling anticipation. His stomach fluttered, his palms sweated, and he resolutely avoided thinking of his absent friends.

The sun set so early in December that it felt like midnight to him instead of early evening. There wasn't any snow on the ground. Richard told him that twenty years ago, there were usually a couple of feet of snow in the foothills by this time of year. He idly wondered what it would be like to be snowed in at the manor. That led him to wonder about spells to manage snow; plenty of places on Gaea got copious amounts, and people didn't move it by hand.

He broke off those thoughts when he heard heavy footsteps and muttering. "Christ, how was it this far away? I thought this blind was closer to the street. Why didn't I think to bring a flashlight? He fucking told me to meet him after dark! Ugh! What did I trip over? What the fuck?"

John grumbled as he blundered through the leaf litter and dried branches. Carter straightened, an amused smile curving his full lips. Several seconds later, the other man appeared: he held out his phone, using its multiple LEDs to illuminate the ground before him. He kept muttering and cursing as he turned toward where the blind had been, flashing his light over the area and seeming impressed despite himself at the cleanup.

"Hey," Carter called.

He canceled the Obscuratus with a mutter and stepped through the barrier. John Thurley jumped a foot off the ground, shrieked in surprise, and dropped his phone. Carter sauntered over and bent down to grab the electronic device. If this man was a spy, he'd fooled the soldier's well-honed bullshit detectors: Carter didn't believe anyone could be that good an actor.

He handed John's phone back to him. "Uh, sorry about my badass scream. I know it's intimidating," John quipped, grinning sheepishly. "I, uh, didn't see you."

"I was obscured, so you wouldn't have." Carter grinned.

"Right. 'Cause everyone does that on a first date," John replied with a smirk. "So, while you seem totally comfortable in the cold, my hands and toes are freezing, and I need to eat like every three hours, or I turn into a rage monster. You know how it goes, blood sugar and all that."

Carter didn't know, but he let it slide. On impulse, he stepped a little closer and saw John swallow at his proximity. "Can I touch you?"

He watched John's eyes flick to his gloved fingers. "Wow, you have huge hands and fingers. That's a little scary." He chuckled and squinted. "So, uh…right here?"

Carter dropped his hand. "Right here, what?"

"You want to touch me right here? I'm fucking freezing, man."

Carter realized what John meant. He laughed and shook his head. "I'm not asking you to take off your pants, John. I want to test out a theory." He held out his hand. "Just your hand, please."

John laughed; Carter could see the flush spread over his cheeks above his sparse beard. He licked his lips and shyly put his hand in Carter's. The soldier took a deep breath and exerted his will to temporarily extend his thermal regulation over the other man. He saw the spell work on John, and the other man grinned as he stopped shivering.

"That's fucking awesome," he said excitedly. "How'd you do that?"

Carter felt himself blush and was grateful that his skin tone hid it. "It's a fairly simple set of spells that provide a balanced personal environment. The magic counteracts hot, cold, rain, and shine as the effect travels through my aura until it's completely neutralized and fully regulated in my body."

John chortled in glee and looked at their hands.

Carter enjoyed holding John's hand, but he let go anyway. "Shall we go up to the house?" he asked. "So long as we stay within about five feet of each other, the magic will hold."

John looked slightly disappointed as their hands parted. They turned toward the barrier. "I'm blown away that I'm not freezing my ass off. You should hear everyone at Zalcent and the military; they're saying you've got some kind of unknown technology producing these bizarre effects." He chuckled. "Anyway, can I, you know, touch it before we step through?"

Carter's mind supplied a couple of things John could touch, but he kept those thoughts to himself and nodded amiably. He hadn't granted John access to the property yet, which would be temporary in any case, so he nodded toward the space before him where the field effects divided the property from the rest of the world and gestured.

Animals, birds, and vegetation could pass the barrier, but not machinery or people unless permitted. The younger man stuck his hand out and laid it on the curved surface, which was so expansive it seemed almost flat. John shined his phone light around, then slid his hand up and down.

"It's slippery!" he crowed. "I'm handling this rather well, if I say so myself." He grinned at Carter, who smiled back, amused by his companion's delight in things. "I mean, Christ, this is completely unbelievable! Wait until I post about this. Can we do a selfie here before we go through?"

Carter cocked his head. "What do you mean?"

John held up his phone, accidentally shining it in Carter's eyes. He glanced away from the harsh white light with a wince.

"Sorry, man," John said immediately. He explained selfies and then waved his hand to encompass the two of them and the barrier. "So, can I take a photo with my phone, maybe leaning against the barrier?"

Carter shrugged. "Sure, why not?"

What harm can a selfie do? he thought.

John stared at him, wide-eyed again. "Man, this is incredible. What's it like, the place you come from?"

Carter opened his mouth to answer; John whipped his hand off the barrier and held up a finger to stop him. "Wait, don't answer that. Selfie first, conversation second." He frowned, then timidly asked, "Can you like, make light or something? So I can get a good picture? The phones are still terrible when it comes to night photography for portraits or selfies."

Carter laughed. Witch lights were easy—he'd been able to cast them before taking the amṛta. He'd practiced these and a few other simple enchantments in his bedroom and had learned to do it with a snap. He did that now, and a yellow ball strobed into existence above the two men. The warm, lemony light shone down on them.

"Fuck. Me. Sideways."

John's awestruck words reminded Carter how different things were on Earth. Paul and Sue had told him that magic was incomprehensible to them, but for some reason, Carter had never quite believed them. Everyone with any magic could make witch lights—children learned to create them almost as soon as they could speak.

If you went to a nighttime event anywhere on Gaea, you'd see all the little kids throwing witch lights around like baseballs. The adults would create more sedate lights to illuminate the proceedings, but they were commonplace and difficult to imagine living without. The little things drove home how different the human stocks on Gaea and Earth were.

"This is perfect," the technician said breathlessly.

He urged Carter to move closer and pressed his hand against the barrier, fingers splayed. John snapped several photos, crowed in delight at how good two of them were, then posted them to his Presence account with corresponding hashtags.

After the selfie, Carter led him through the shield. The witch light followed them, floating fifteen feet above the ground and directly over the two men as they strolled through the trees to the Lower Forty and the Gatehouse. Carter saw John videoing everything and realized he should have made him strip and change at the barrier and leave his phone behind. It felt like it was too late, and he hadn't brought a change of clothes for the other man, anyway.

What harm can it do? he rationalized.

He'd made good friends on Earth, but he hadn't met anyone that was his friend, first and foremost. The desire for companionship made him reckless, but it wasn't like anyone from Zalcent could gain permission to cross the barrier through recordings on someone's phone.

John told Carter that he was livestreaming to his Presence account and was gaining viewers and likes by the moment. People were tuning into the fact that something extraordinary was happening in the

Western Foothills of Maine, and it wasn't because of a cult or nuclear threats.

"You might go viral," John commented happily. He pursed his lips and squinted at the soldier. "However, does it strike you as strange that all this stuff has been going on in this area, but no one has come to view it firsthand? Normally, crazy happenings in America draw tourists and gawkers faster than water running downhill."

Carter shrugged. "I have no idea why people aren't coming to the area. Maybe they don't know what's been happening."

John nodded and shrugged. "Well, they will if I have anything to say about it!"

When they reached the end of the path from the garden to the manor, Carter asked John to shut off his phone and hand it over. John understood: recording his new friend's home was too intimate. They weren't there yet, but he hoped they might get there. Something about Jack intrigued John—beyond the fact that he was absurdly hot.

He agreed eagerly, even though his central nervous system shrieked alarms at the thought of being without his phone. He was a gamer, tech nerd, and social media addict: he lived through his phone. He hurriedly typed one last post, shut his phone off, and handed it to Carter.

Their hands brushed, and John felt an electric zing even though Carter wore gloves. So far, John had managed not to drool over the other man, but he was losing his self-control.

He was also agog when he saw that his livestream on Presence had garnered twelve thousand viewers. That was more than he'd ever had, and he'd been on social media his entire life. He'd captured plenty of photos of Carter and posted them, along with hashtags about how sexy he was. He saw that plenty of people agreed because men and women were liking and commenting like there was no tomorrow.

John watched Carter stash his phone in a pocket of his armor, then followed him to the front door of the vast mansion. He stared at it, eyes wide, and wondered how rich these people were. He'd seen drone footage of the spacious, symmetric manor, but standing front and center before the three-story structure was a different experience. They'd breezed past the circular drive with its elegant stone rostrum, but it didn't hold a candle to the beautiful house.

"How the hell did you build this…" he began. He stopped and held up a hand to forestall Carter's answer. "Let me guess. Magic?"

Carter laughed. "My friends Alex, Imara, and Sirenī built it."

"Awesome. Can I meet them?" he asked eagerly.

"No," the soldier replied.

"I get it. I'm a security risk," John said quickly. He was disappointed, but he understood.

"No, it's not that," Carter replied. "They're…away."

John blinked. "Okay. Like…offworld away, or they went down to Boston for the week?"

"I don't know where Boston is, but they're farther away than that."

John laughed at the evasive answer but let it go. He was with Jack, and they were about to enter this incredible house. The other people from his world were anecdotal, even though he was supposed to pump Jack for information. He'd been coached on the questions to ask, and the harridan overseeing this whole shitbag operation, Rudine Ellswyth, had told him to get a DNA sample.

She doesn't want the kind of sample I do, John thought lustfully. The foreigner was a walking wet dream. *Spank me, Daddy!*

He blinked and realized Carter had said something. "Sorry, I missed what you said."

"Shall we?"

The other man gestured to the front door.

"Hell, yeah!" John crowed.

Carter laughed at John's naïve enthusiasm and gestured toward the front door. The soldier enjoyed John's captivation as he stared in awe at the tasteful opulence and decor of Gaea: it was similar to Earth décor from the fifties and sixties of the last century but different enough to stand out. Anyone could see that the manor was built by and for humans, but it didn't seem quite right to the people of Earth. It wasn't solely because of the sprawling size and magically enlarged rooms.

Sue had summarized the feeling to Carter in one sentence: "It's just different enough to be weird, but not weird enough to be uncomfortable."

John looked around the sitting room for several minutes, studying everything. Carter saw his hand twitch toward his pocket like he was going for his phone, but he caught himself before reaching. He shook his head and turned to Carter with his eyes shining—he seemed a bit euphoric and almost danced in place in his excitement.

"This is *the* most amazing thing I've ever seen," he beamed. "I'm a dork, and this makes my inner nerd bust a nut."

The soldier laughed and gestured. "Why don't you wait here while I put on some regular clothes? It'll only take me a few minutes."

John nodded and took a seat. Carter hurried up the stairs to his bedroom. Thankfully, when his armor flew off his body, he was sweat-free since he hadn't fought any lic.

He yanked on jeans and a T-shirt and checked his appearance. He grinned at his reflection, feeling cocky and rather good-looking. He padded back downstairs, barefoot, and peeked into the sitting room. John smiled at him and gave a little wave like it had been hours instead of minutes.

"How about we get something to eat?" the soldier suggested.

John jumped to his feet and followed Carter down the hall to the kitchen. The soldier directed him to sit at the huge table. John stripped off his winter jacket and tossed it over the back of a chair while Carter went to the fabricator.

His friends had agreed there was no need to share the device outside the core group, so he ordered various foods and brought it all back to the table a little at a time. He pretended he was retrieving them from a larder, and John didn't appear to care where they came from or even what the dishes were, really.

After setting the plates down, Carter asked John what he wanted to drink.

"Whatever kind of beer you've got, good sir," he said pithily. "I'll drink pretty much anything. I wouldn't mind a joint, too, if you have any of those in your magic larder."

Carter laughed, but he didn't understand John's reference to a joint. *A joint of what? Meat?* Maybe he meant human joints of some kind? Or restaurants, clubs, or businesses? Perhaps it was some colloquial sexual innuendo, and in that case, Carter had a "joint" he'd be happy to give the other man later on.

John seemed more relaxed when the soldier disappeared and returned with two bottles of beer. According to Jordan, their labels were "exotic" with their Latin text and retro-sophisticated artwork. The other man studied the bottle some more and then looked at the cap, seeing it was a pop top and wouldn't unscrew.

John glanced at the utensils on the table. "Bottle opener?"

"We don't have one. Give it to me," Carter offered.

John gave him the bottle with a bemused expression. Carter held it in his left hand and used his right thumb to pop the top off, then repeated the same trick for his beer while the Zalcent employee stared at him wide-eyed.

"Dude, what's with the Thumbs of Doom? Is that a normal thing where you come from?"

John shook his head and laughed. He studied the top of his bottle and the two caps on the table like they might reveal some great secret about his dinner companion.

Carter guffawed and shook his head. "No, but surely men on Earth can pop the top by hand? It's just thin metal."

"I'm sure some men can," John replied dryly. He smiled, held up his bottle, and offered a one-word toast. "Cheers!"

Carter clinked his beer against that of the other man; they each took hefty swigs and tucked into their food. John sampled every dish. For a skinny guy, he efficiently packed away a surprising amount of food and two more beers.

Carter had seen the type: slim and rangy but with an appetite like an ox. The soldier once had that kind of appetite, but since taking the amṛta, it had stopped like someone flicked a switch and turned off his need for food and drink. He could eat, but he never felt hungry or full.

It wasn't a bad trade, though, considering all the other benefits he'd gotten from the nectar of immortality.

Twenty-Two
Viginti Duo

Imara and Sirenī flew up the face of the mountain. Imara focused on perceiving what she knew was out there—the kṛtyā bījā. She was positive the eruption was linked to the dark magic.

A cave caught her attention halfway up the volcano; she directed Sirenī toward it. To her sight, the void had the unmistakable emanations of dark magic wafting from the black opening as if thick, fell vines clawed their way from the entrance. Beyond that, she perceived a maze of lava tubes that terminated in a cavern a quarter of a mile into the mountain's body.

Sirenī stopped the impermeable field when they reached the cave and looked at Imara. The songstress kissed her partner on the lips and stepped through the wall of the bubble to drop to the ground. She landed lightly, waved to Sirenī, and strode fearlessly into the darkness. She'd always been brave, but she'd been frightened when she went blind. Now, with the Epiphany of Light guiding her eyes, she feared nothing.

The ground trembled, and the volcano grumbled like a giant with severe acid reflux. Imara grimaced and stumbled a bit, wishing for Sirenī's perfect balance. When the rumbling stopped, she made her way through the lava tubes as directly as possible and strode into the cave. Her hair spun into a Battle Bun while her blouse tightened to fit more snugly to her figure—she didn't want anything loose that an enemy could grab in a fight.

She saw four figures in the cave as she navigated the tubes. They had no idea she was coming; she was sure of it. They stood idly about, gazing at the hideous spectacle of the dark flower. It had a short, stubby stalk with a pustulous bloom squatting atop it. Even though the flower was closed and had only spread its poison to Lauremanda, it was already fully established. She knew it wouldn't die without a fight because dark magic never did.

She decided this would be a short, brutal battle—there was no time to wait. She stepped into the cave, already singing, with her arms outstretched. Strobing bolts of multicolored combat lightning flashed from her fingertips. They incinerated three of the four līc, instantly destroying their animate forms as thunder boomed and rolled through the confines of the mountain. The entire place trembled from the combination of the imminent eruption and the thunderclaps; the two forces made the situation momentarily worse.

The remaining līc screamed in rage and turned on her, beautiful blonde braids swinging about its desiccated skull as the undead shouted the words of a fire spell. Hot winds blistered the air, and flames blasted Imara like the stream of a flamethrower. The fire dissipated after several seconds, long enough for most sorcerers to be burned and seriously injured, if not dead outright.

Imara strode determinedly forward, spectral shielding flickering as her embedded defenses deflected the attack. She reached out and clenched a hand of iron around the throat of the līc and lifted them right from the ground while they shrieked and hissed and clawed at her flesh with dark, crusty talons that scraped harmlessly across her kinetic wards.

Imara turned and hauled the shrieking creature to the foul flower that grew out of a pile of corpses. It was revolting; her stomach turned when she saw thick pulsing roots moving inside the bodies, feeding on their physical nutrients after siphoning off their spiritual energies. One of the corpses was a younger man; his crotch shifted as if the rotting body were getting an erection. She knew that wasn't the case, but the horrifying bulge instantly drew her gaze.

A grotesque root burst from the front of his pants and stretched toward her like a blind serpent, wriggling as it probed the air and extended into space. The songstress watched it with revulsion and opened a hand; energy pulsed in a multicolored throb. The root exploded, and the blossom atop the stalk shuddered and wailed as she injured it.

Instantly, the corpse mulch began to buckle and bulge as the dark flower reacted to her attack. Filthy, weeping roots burst from every conceivable place a human body could spare, writhing as they twined and oozed toward Imara. She suspected the semi-sentient flower sensed her tremendous power, and the diseased magic wanted it.

Just try it, fucker.

"Who is your maker?" she asked the līc.

She let her vocal magic compel the monstrous creature, and the līc squealed. They keened and shook in her grasp, but before they could burst into flames like the one Sirenī compelled outside Glimmerwick, Imara began to sing. She hung a short phrase in the air about her and the līc, disrupting the immolation wards embedded in their animating magic. She shook her arm, and the creature flailed like a rag doll, wailing in terror now as they realized how outmatched they were.

"Who. Is. Your. Master?" she shouted, letting her power flood the room.

Multicolored radiance engulfed them, and they rose into the air. The creature in her hand wilted into compliance as Imara entranced them with her voice.

"My father is Ävidä," the creature whispered in a frail voice. "He made me one hundred and ten years ago. I lived on Gaea and wanted more power than I had, so I took it from the living. My dark father found me and helped me become Undying!"

The creature began to writhe and keen as soon as they finished speaking; Imara knew they were determined to resist further compulsion. The filthy, blackened nails scratched weakly at her flesh but couldn't touch her. Imara growled, her voice trembling with multiple harmonics that grated through the air with a gravelly roar. She spun and threw the līc at the dark flower. They hit the short, thick stalk, and the plant wailed again in its creepy way. A dozen of the questing roots whipped around and sank into the necromancer.

Although the līc had no physical nutrients to provide, they did have powerful magic—and the flower consumed it. The glistening, black roots burrowed into the squirming, shrieking corpse as ugly green energy began to drain through the tendrils. Imara hovered, watching the līc grow weaker over a couple of minutes. They grew still as the dark flower sucked the magic out of the animate figure. The skeletal form crumbled as the roots withdrew, hungering for more prāṇa.

Imara realized her mistake and began to back away, drifting through the air and settling on the cave's floor. "Shit," she snapped, angry with herself.

The energy contained within the līc—and possibly even the reserves in their phylacterium—had fed the flower faster than the living it was sucking dry. As she watched, the dark plant shot up from three to five feet tall; the vile bloom opened into a toxic black sunflower. It twisted hungrily on its stem and searched for her like a bloodhound.

She had to admit the magic was ingenious. This mysterious necromancer Ävidä was powerful indeed to have created such vile constructs with a limited, subsentient awareness to help them thrive.

She was drumming a foot on the floor while running through her catalog of spellsongs when the air compressed within the lava tubes, shoved by a tremendous force deep within Omejis. The air mass slapped into her, and Imara blew backward as Lauremanda's top blew clean off. She looked through the mountain and saw titanic boulders arcing into the sky; they hovered at their apogee for a split second before gravity snatched them from their flight and dragged them toward the city below. Shocked but unharmed, she lay on her back and cursed herself for a fool. She'd thoughtlessly accelerated the eruption.

"You moron!" she shouted as she rose easily to her feet.

The power of her voice blasted through the lava tubes and made the stupid mountain tremble even more.

Imara saw the pyroclastic flow and raging magma lake fill the caldera and begin to expand. The catastrophe spilled over the sides of the shattered volcano in a poisonous miasma of superheated gases, rock, and debris. It would destroy everything in its path as it plunged inexorably toward Lauremanda City.

Distracted by the eruption and worry for the people the Three were trying to save, she felt more than heard the arrival of new figures. The songstress spun; she already had her hands out and caught the fireballs thrown by two more līc. Their aurae were linked, and they were casting more spells—one shouted the words to a firebolt and the other to multicolored combat lightning.

Imara smiled grimly and unexpectedly ran toward them, her voice raised in spellsong even as she twisted and lashed out with a psychokinetically-enhanced kick. Mages never expected physical attacks—that gave Jack Carter an advantage against the sorcerers he'd fought on Gaea. He was magically weak, at least before the amṛta, but he was physically mighty. She took a page from his book and sent the firebolt caster into the nearest wall twenty feet away.

The blow broke their concentration, and they miscast the spell. Magical energy crackled across their body as they hit the wall and rebounded to the cavern floor with a howl of rage. She knew she'd broken the creature's ribs, not that it caused them pain. She turned in time to snap out a hand as the other līc finished casting the combat lightning. Scintillating blue, red, and green bolts arced between them while thunder boomed and shook dust and grit from the cavern's ceiling as she absorbed the attack.

"Nice try, blondie," she taunted.

She pointed her fingers at the downed līc, and the spell she'd just absorbed leaped from her fingers in a braid of electricity, the plasma machining the corpse and slicing it into pieces that bounced into the air. Their head flew past her, wreathed in the lattices of necromantic power as they disanimated. She laughed and held out her hands; her voice rang in a pulse of energy that swatted the remaining līc off their feet. They scrabbled away from her but remained careful to avoid the pile of corpses and the questing roots of the kṛtyā bījā.

Imara wanted more information but doubted she'd get anything more out of this one than the last. She and the līc squared off, and they warily watched her with empty sockets set beneath a crown of glorious golden hair.

Sirenī released Alex where he wanted to go, then did the same for Imara. She was worried for her beloved companions but trusted that they could handle what lay before them. It was synchrony: three problems, three magicians, as they'd already discussed.

After releasing Imara before the entrance to the cave, the daughter of Medusa flew up the mountain more slowly so she could evaluate what she saw. Unlike Imara, who could see through the universe and solid matter or whatever else, Sirenī was limited to her eyes and psychic sight. Those were both keen instruments but nowhere near as robust as the Epiphany of Light.

She smirked as she considered asking for a pair of autolenses, but it was a silly, fleeting thought. They were awesome, but they weren't for everyone. When Imara had told her and Alex what she went through adapting to them, any lingering interest Sirenī had in them disappeared.

Nausea? Dizziness? Perception versus sight and seeing everything all the fucking time? Thanks, but no.

She was jerked from her reverie as Lauremanda's cone blew apart, and the pyroclastic cloud billowed over the shattering walls of the caldera while boulders the size of modest homes flew into the sky. She knew some might arc into the ocean, but many would land on the volcano's slopes or in the city girdling it and roll to the beaches below. They'd crush everything in their path.

Who the fuck builds cities on volcanoes?

The debris expanded from the wreck of the caldera, and she narrowed her eyes. This would be a serious test of her amṛta-augmented abilities.

Can I hold back the eruption of a volcano?

Psychokinesis had always been easy for her, even as an infant. Her parents had to proof their home against her powers after baby Sirenī accidentally ripped the door of her room off its hinges when she fussed. They'd had the house enchanted by a powerful mage so that Sirenī couldn't snatch anything with her psychokinetic grip. She'd gained control of her abilities by the time she was six, and Cassandra and Uday were able to have the enchantments removed.

Every toy she had as a child was soft, shapeless, and smushy so she couldn't hurt anyone if she angrily flung one at them. She felt bitter about it until she smashed through the sorcerers protecting the Abyssal Gate when they stopped Sogma from entering the world. After that, she began to appreciate how dangerous her untrained skills were when she was an infant and toddler. She could have killed people, smashed houses flat, and caused great harm during a temper tantrum.

Her parents had been stressed about her for years, and her fatal beauty was a constant source of terror for everyone. Sirenī dreaded it until Alex and Imara helped her learn to control it. She heard Alex's words as she sailed into the debris cloud, *"Every power lies within our control. There is no ability we cannot master, no power we cannot refine, and no situation without a solution."*

She extended her arms, centered in her impermeable field, and reached. The cloud slowed its advance down the sides of the mountain, and the boulders slowed their arcs through the sky, but it wasn't enough. Sirenī needed to stop the flow, to hold it back while Alex got everyone down the mountain, and Imara did whatever she was doing.

With a grimace, she exerted her will with greater determination. The cloud stopped, but the boulders only slowed further. They still crested their arcs and threatened to slip from her psychic grasp any second.

No, I am stronger than this!

She dug deep inside herself, and something did happen with her power, but it was the one thing that terrified her more than anything else—Medusa began to rise. Bitter, acidic jealousy billowed within her as violently as the lava within the volcano. Sirenī screamed—at herself, her fatal beauty, and Medusa's vengeful, self-destructive rage from ages ago.

"Enough," she snarled. "What purpose do you serve?"

I. Am. Rage! the power inside her roared back. *Everything will fall before me! I will be seen! I will be heard!*

"You are seen, you crazy bitch!" Sirenī shrieked back. Her corona burned bright blue with her fury. "But all you do is destroy. I saw you, but you hurt me and those I care about. What is wrong with you?"

She felt a brief hesitation before the rage surged hotter. Medusa's jealousy was a caustic flame in her throat.

No, I was never seen! the monster roared. She wrested control of Sirenī's body and finished the sentence aloud, "I loved him, but he never saw me."

"Oh, come on!" Sirenī howled back.

She stood in the impermeable sphere amid the pyroclastic flow as rocks the size of houses toppled toward the ground. They began to slip from her control. *This can't happen—I know we're successful, that we save these people. Come on, you fucking bitch bag, work with me instead of against me,* she thought furiously.

"That was ages ago! You died, bitter and alone—I get it, I do, but if you can't be useful, then go away!"

"I am useful. I saved you!" Medusa shrieked back.

Blue lightning crackled across the surface of her impermeable field as they battled for control. "Saved me? You tried to harm the people I love and who love me. They accept me unconditionally and love all of me—even your crazy ass!"

Tears of anger and bitterness at her failure poured down her cheeks. The cloud began to flow out of her control, billowing and deforming as she lost control.

Maybe the past can be changed. Perhaps I can fail, she despaired.

"What?" Medusa gasped. "I didn't know!"

Sirenī scoffed. "Because you're blind with rage, Medusa! It's been thousands of years. Please, work with me, not against me," she pleaded to the monster within.

There was only silence. She felt the power of her distant ancestor subside, and she slumped in exhaustion. Medusa took everything out of her and gave nothing back. She felt wrung out, but she still had to try to save the people of Lauremanda City. She growled, straightened, and thrust her chin forward belligerently.

"You will not defeat me!" she yelled at the volcano.

She reached out with her power and tried to gather the pyroclastic cloud and the sluggishly falling debris, but she felt unbalanced for the first time in her life. Something inside her was different, shifted after her short, violent argument with Medusa.

She hollered and strained, but her powers weren't going to be enough. Seconds passed that felt like an eternity. Sweat soaked her shirt and matted her hair to her face. Medusa returned, blazing inside her head, and she groaned. "I don't have time for this!"

Medusa waved her anger away. "You say you are loved? That they return the adoration you feel for them?"

Sirenī blinked at that. "Yes, you foolish woman," she whispered. Her control slipped further, the strain crushing her beneath an impossible pressure. "They love me so much it hurts to think I might ever do anything that causes them pain."

"Did we cause them pain?"

"Yes, Medusa," she said tiredly. "We did when you took over. You shut me down deep inside and ignored my screaming for you to stop."

Thankfully that only happened twice! she added mentally.

She knew Medusa heard her thoughts. The alternate personality or power was intrinsic, like her fatal beauty. She couldn't think, say, or do anything without Medusa knowing. She'd never communicated directly with Medusa before now, though—this was a novel experience, but it was absolutely the worst time for it.

There came a thoughtful pause, a stilling of the turmoil inside her. Sirenī took a deep breath, and as she exhaled, something burned white-hot inside her core. Strength surged through her like a storm, rising and whipping about, coursing through her body like fire. She screamed and wondered distantly what new abuse Medusa was laying upon her—but the pain began to subside as fast as it appeared. Behind it lay stillness; Sirenī fell into the revelated space, and her exhaustion disappeared between one heartbeat and the next.

Her impermeable sphere began to gleam with a ferocious cobalt glow. Bolts of lightning arced off the surface and slammed into the side of the mountain, machining deep, cherry-red molten furrows. Power blazed through the spiritual channels in her subtle body. Her nāḍī ignited, and energy rose, and rose and rose, leaping to obey her command.

"*Beauty is not your only power,*" Medusa whispered.

Her gravelly, angry voice was gentle as it faded. Sirenī knew this time was different and that Medusa wasn't going to sleep back in that place where she hid. She'd surrendered to the truth and purity of Sirenī's love for Imara and Alex and theirs for her. As the bitter spirit of her ancestress laid down the burden she'd passed along to all her descendants, her distant daughter's magical and mystical powers syncretized.

Alexander reached the beach and ordered everyone to make room. A few shuttles had already landed on the sand. People boarded in an orderly fashion, but the aircars couldn't depart with the umbrella of debris hanging over their heads.

More people came to the beach every minute, ushered by the local constabulary or whoever Eirianedd's assistants were. Of course, those on this side of the mountain could easily reach the designated evacuation zone despite the catastrophe, but those on the sides and around the back of the volcano had little chance of making it.

Alexander shoved away his concern and refocused on the spell he needed to cast to establish a wormhole to take people to safety. The modern term, Tanager-Rosen bridge, had an older name: *Ásbrú*. It was the method by which the ancient Norse sorcerers, the Æsir and Vanir, traveled between Gaea and the vacuolated realm they created when they began to become unconcerned by external matters.

They'd disappeared about two and a half thousand years ago and never showed themselves again, but much of their peculiar magic was still known across the centuries. Being a student of obscure magics, Alexander naturally knew the forms of the Ásbrú. Heather Tanager mathematically codified the physics of wormhole functions as a mental exercise, but she never finished the equations. Nathan Rosen—a mathematician and physical engineer—formalized the equations at a later date.

The two geniuses figured out how the Ásbrú worked; thus, the bridge was named after them. How it worked was less interesting to

Alexander than the spell itself. The only problem was that he needed to sight the endpoint, or it could slip and spew people all over the place, including places where space, time, and reality might not exist.

He stared across the miles of water with his psychic sight until he located the beach on Temple Mount. People were already there to help those evacuated from Lauremanda. He found the space he needed and studied it until he saw it clearly in his mind.

Alexander concentrated and began to chant the words to the spell. His corona surged brightly around him, more crimson than orange. He'd noticed his aura was changing color and wondered abstractly what it portended, but he hadn't given further thought to it. Like many things, it waited for calmer days.

A pinprick of light burned in the air five feet before him; he knew an identical aperture had formed on the beaches at the foot of Temple Mount. He continued chanting as the ground trembled violently and more debris blew out of the top of the mountain. The shaking ground quickly became distracting, and he levitated above the sand. He shouted the last words of the spell, and the pinprick before him sluiced backward. It fell away within a perfectly circular membrane ten feet in diameter.

Alexander confirmed he'd seated the terminus properly at the other end. He returned to the ground and gestured for two wide-eyed people to transit the wormhole. They did so, mumbling their thanks as the ghastliest explosion yet rocked the island.

He spun, ready to throw up a shield, only to see a strident blue glow ignite within the debris cloud that drifted down the mountain. Electrical discharges arced out, machining the mountain's flank, which caused more slippage of the caldera as the powerful bolts vaporized stone and exposed lava tubes, inadvertently releasing pressure.

He watched the blue glow rise higher and brighter. It created an unnatural cobalt daylight beneath the expanding umbrella of debris. Someone screamed, and people started to panic as lava surged out. It poured down the side of the volcano and slammed into an invisible wall.

Then began to flow up the mountain.

People gaped as they stared at the reversed flow of lava in awe and hope. Alexander let out a whoop as the blue star in the sky rose into the clouds. The house-sized boulders began to curve through the air in long arcs around the island's far side from where he'd established the Ásbrú. The lava kept flowing up against gravity's urging, the molten red glow outlining the curves of an invisible bowl. He grinned as the pyroclastic cloud swirled and spiraled around the peak of the erupting volcano.

A funnel formed, sucking the rocks, pyroclastic debris, and molten magma away from the mountain in a long, graceful arc. The admixture splashed into the ocean in a churning froth as boulders sent massive waves from the impact site. The pyroclastic debris spread in a thick slurry that formed a coarse effluvium on the sea's surface.

Sireni seems to have things under control.

Alexander wondered what Imara was up to, but he had too much on his hands to give it any more thought. He waved in shuttles and boats, gesturing them close to the beach now that the sky was clearer. The Ásbrú would continue to work until he canceled the enchantment so he could use his magic to help the people struggling down to the beach.

He began to cast again. Lines of light surged out of his hands—first five, then ten, then twenty, then forty—each line tracing to a nearby boat, shuttle, or aircar. The lines of light expanded beneath the water's surface and rose, flaring into sight above the waves to form shimmering platforms that people could walk upon.

"Go!" he bellowed.

He'd never cast more than one platform spell, and although the magic was only Grade Three, forty of them at once was a considerable strain. He gestured urgently as sweat beaded on his forehead. People began to run along the paths, but there were too many. More shuttles and boats pulled up, and people gathered on the beach, fearfully looking at the volcano as they clutched crying children. Some had pets in their arms or on leashes, and the animals cowered in terror or squalled in fear.

He let out a growl and created more magic platforms, and people began to run along them. The spell included amendments to prevent stumbling and slipping, so people seemed unusually sure-footed as they raced to the waiting ships. When one was full, it would pull away, and another would motor up. People who waited on the magic docks for their turn would dive into the next vehicle until it was at capacity, then the pattern repeated.

On the beach, those with animals and children stepped through the Ásbrú in anxious but orderly groups. Alexander grimaced with the strain of maintaining nearly eighty magic pathways that stretched hundreds of feet over the ocean.

Is it enough?

He didn't know how many thousands of people lived in the sizable city encircling the mountain, but there was no way to get them to the beach in time.

Twenty-Three
Viginti Tres

Carter enjoyed himself as John told him funny stories and facts about himself. The meal was among the most enjoyable Carter had had since he came to Earth. His Earthen friends were conspicuously absent, hanging out at Jordan's place, eating and watching a movie. However, he knew Paul and Sue would be back with their kids before too long.

He, Jordan, Richard, Brent, and Drëndi agreed to keep Paul and Sue out of the first few interactions with John. Richard had told Paul that Carter had met someone and was having a date at the big house, and Paul had ribbed Carter mercilessly about it right up until Sue dragged him out the door this afternoon. Carter took it in stride—he was usually the one doing the ribbing, but he could take it as well as dish it out.

When Eric asked who Carter was meeting, Paul told him it was a man. They didn't hide his sexual interests from the kids; the Earth of 2031 was more blasé about LGBTQ+ relationships, even though plenty of people still weren't accepting. Before moving onto the property, Eric and Cassie went to school with several families with two moms, two dads, or other identities. Blended families looked different than they had in the previous century, and they would undoubtedly continue to change and evolve in the next.

Twenty-Three

After eating the last bite of a slice of chocolate chiffon cake, John sat back in his chair with a groan. He crossed his hands on his stomach and adopted a contented look.

"That was delicious. I haven't had so much fun in years." He paused to think it over. "Yep, since college, I think. I've got a great buzz going on. Your beer is rockin'." He burped and excused himself. "Still, are you sure you haven't got a joint anywhere?"

He looked around as if one was on the table somewhere.

Carter laughed and leaned back. "What do you mean when you say 'a joint?'"

John raised his eyebrows and gave it some thought. *How do I provide an executive summary of marijuana to someone from another planet? I'm sure they won't have weed there, but they'll have something similar.*

It occurred to him that he'd just thought about someone coming from another world as casually as he thought of going to the store to buy a pint of ice cream. He was pleased with how well he'd handled that detail. Before, he'd wanted to believe but was skeptical. Where were the visitors from other worlds if they really were "out there?"

Well, it turned out the visitors were humans, so you couldn't tell when they came to Earth because they looked like everyone else! In Jack's case, they came equipped with a droolworthy body and magical powers.

It was a lot to take in. John enjoyed the beers—they had a helluva punch—but he really wanted some dank weed to calm his nerves. He settled on the best way to describe cannabis and launched into a quick but detailed description of the plant, its many uses, methods of consumption, and the highs it produced.

"It helps with my nerves," he concluded. He squinted at the three empty beer bottles. "But that helped with my nerves, too, because I'm really relaxed right now."

Carter laughed, looking amused. "Well, we have drugs on Gaea, but I'm not sure marijuana ever took off. Maybe it did in Persia before Unification, but it's not widely consumed now. Lotus, however, is pretty popular and gives a nice mellow high. You feel like you're floating for days but only out of it for a few hours with a hit."

John's eyes widened. "Wait a second! You said Persia—but Persia's on Earth."

Carter nodded. "And Gaea. The planets are very similar." He held up a hand when John made to ask him how that was possible. "You'll have to ask Alex someday. I have no clue."

John blinked and changed tack. "Well, in that case, do you happen to have any lotus to hand? I'd love to try some."

Carter hesitated. His chemicals of choice were beer and hard liquor. He debated fabricating a small dose for John to try, but the younger man would be out of it for the rest of the night. That wasn't the direction the soldier wanted things to go. Before he could say he didn't have any, John waved a hand to dismiss the notion.

"You know what? Screw it. I've got some other things in mind to top off this amazing evening, and getting wasted on lotus blossoms isn't how I see it going," he declared.

He looked at Carter with a gleam in his eye. The soldier knew that look—he'd seen it on every male face at one point or another, whether the men were putting the moves on each other, women, or vampires.

He smiled and raised his thick, dark eyebrows to invite further explanation of the things John had in mind to finish off the evening. He'd heard the front door open a while ago while he and John were still chatting and eating, but Paul, Sue, and the kids were long in their rooms. John had chattered on, apparently not noticing their return. Carter was shocked at how long they'd been talking. He'd collected John at sunset, which came early in the Maine winters.

He was sprawled comfortably in his chair. He waited, letting John make the next move; the other man worked up his courage and leaned forward. He stood slowly, then cautiously approached Carter like he might be dangerous. The soldier straightened slightly as John stepped over; he looked up with what he hoped was a welcoming expression.

The Zalcent technician bit his lip and carefully straddled Carter's muscular thighs. He gingerly settled his weight as if Carter might break, but the soldier barely even felt it.

Why does it look so romantic on TV? Damn, this is uncomfortable.

John didn't want to move because being so bold was also incredibly arousing. He was pleasantly buzzed, but had he lost all sense of scope with his personal safety?

What if they are terrorists? a small, nervous voice whispered in the back of his mind. It sounded reasonable. *They could kidnap you, kill you, or do awful things with their magic. You know they're the real deal. He fought something with flayed skin done up in loops like a bad hairstyle from the sixties. Do you really want to risk fucking this guy?*

John kept his thoughts from his face as he recalled the conversation with his boss' boss' boss before he gave Carter his phone number so they could set up this date. It was all part of a plan in which John had reluctantly agreed to be involved, but he'd struggled with his feelings about it from the outset….

"You'll be able to connect with him and *probe* him for information," the supervisor told him in a private meeting.

She made air quotes and smirked when she used the word "probe."

They sat in her enormous office in Texas, where she gazed speculatively at him as if he were an insect. Rudine Ellswyth was a powerful executive in Zalcent and was challenging to get along with. She saw everyone and everything as an asset owned by the company. In true corporate fashion, she believed money solved all problems. When Rudine continued speaking, she confirmed everything he'd heard about her.

"I'm sure a pansy man like you likes to bottom." She waved a hand and dismissed his masculinity completely. "And this thug will be likelier to share things if you let him fuck you senseless."

She spoke with a snidely vulgar crassness that left John's mouth gaping in shock at what she said. He couldn't believe anyone would speak to him that way. What was the point of the social justice movement in the early '20s if people like Rudine still had the same horrid, hateful beliefs and willingness to act on them?

And doesn't she have to attend the same sensitivity training as the rest of us? Fucking A!

He was flabbergasted.

This wasn't how I thought this meeting was going to go! he thought angrily. Color flushed his face an ugly, blotchy red while he clenched his fists in his lap. "Did you just suggest pimping me out for Zalcent so I can get information from people you claim are from another world? What the hell, Rudine!" he snapped. "I'm not some toy for this corporation to pass around!"

Blood roared in his ears, and his heart pounded. He shouldn't have called her by her first name, but he was pretty sure *Rudine* was better for his career than *Raving Bitchface*.

It didn't matter. She stared at him like she didn't understand why he was upset. She dismissed his words with a moue of distaste and came in with her solution to all problems: money. She didn't understand human feelings and valued only what she could get out of people, not who they were or what made them unique.

"Don't worry, John, we'll pay you extra to give up that pasty white ass of yours," she said with her typical insensitivity. John stared, but she ignored him. "You know, we wanted to send in a trained operative, but there's no way we can risk it. This man is dangerous, and our security consultants selected you based on everything we've been able to uncover about the terrorists. Of course, that's limited to the people they've radicalized, but it gave us a baseline."

She pushed a folder across her enormous, polished mahogany desk. John reluctantly opened it; he scanned the pictures attached to single-sheet summaries of the people involved in the bizarre cult on the "energetically protected property." He read the names—Jordan McInerney, Richard Bryson, and Paul and Sue Arsenault—and shook his head as he pushed the folder away.

"I, uh, don't even know what to say about this, Rudine. I'm not just going to have sex with a stranger *you* claim is from another world."

He put as much scorn into his voice as he could. It wasn't much, but it made him feel better. The conversation left a sick feeling in his stomach.

She cocked her head and stared at him, apparently confused by his reticence. After several seconds, she shook her head. "Watch this." Rudine picked up her cell phone and swiped on it a few times to cast a video to the screenwall on the righthand side of her office. The display was made of woven optical fibers embedded into a bioelectric substrate.

Amazed at her spiteful obtuseness, John turned from Rudine to study the screenwall. A short video played in ultra-high fidelity on the obscenely large display. It showed an overhead view of the property in Steadfield recorded by one of Zalcent's satellites as it passed over the area. He saw from the colors of the leaves that it was autumn. There was a garden with a curious stone building in the center.

A redheaded couple walked down the path to the building and paused, and it was clear from the man dropping to one knee and fumbling in his pocket that he was going to propose. John glanced at Rudine, but she imperiously gestured back to the video; he looked back and saw the couple stand, alarm writ on their faces as lines of red crawled up the sides of the building and slid across the pyramid that capped it. The top sank into the cubical bottom, and his jaw dropped.

What the…

The pyramid's disappearance revealed a blackness so deep the screen had trouble rendering the imagery. The sides fanned out, twisting and buckling to slide into the base of a platform that faded into view through the darkness like a three-dimensional model being rendered in real time. A curtain of red flared in a thin-looking outline around the circular dais in the center.

The red light solidified and flicked out of existence, revealing four people: two women and two men. John leaned forward as the satellite zoomed in. The four were dressed in clothes like one would find on Earth, except the details weren't quite right. One of the men was the same one he'd met outside the surveillance shack though he was cut up pretty badly. John could see that his armor was damaged.

The video froze on the image, and he turned back to Rudine.

Bitchface studied him with calculation in her emotionless eyes. He shifted, suddenly uncomfortable because, despite himself, he was fascinated by what she'd shown him.

"Did you have me profiled?" he asked.

She smiled thinly. "Of course. According to my team, you'd do anything to meet people from another world, including letting me pimp you out." She cocked her head. "I honestly hope you're willing to let that fag fuck you so we can get what we want." She spread her hands and leaned back. "It's a win-win."

He glared at her, his anger surging at her twisted expectations and obvious homophobia. *Who talks like that in real life? Christ, what a bitch!*

"Honestly, John, this is quite a bump for you. You're a level-two technician: we'll upgrade your security clearance and give you a massive raise if you do this." John thought her smile looked almost real for a woman with no soul. "I'm sure you—and your family—can use more money," she patronized.

John thinned his lips but didn't protest. He couldn't believe he was agreeing to this scheme, but he was. They were travelers from another world. There was no reason for him to assume he'd be peddling his ass for this hag; they couldn't know for sure the soldier who'd defeated the flayed woman was gay, no matter how good the surveillance and profiling were.

He took a deep breath, and Rudine laughed in triumph. She was despicable.

She magnanimously gave him an obscene bonus on top of the pay raise. She told him she'd give him ten times as much if he collected DNA from the target. "I'll leave it up to you how you want to acquire it. You can certainly use a condom, but our lab techs aren't squeamish—they'll collect it from you just as readily as from a rubber."

John was mortified and angry—but two could play this game. He'd tell Carter *everything* and let him decide how to handle the situation. If something developed between them, well…so be it.

His face broke into a smile. Rudine thought she'd won, and he let her believe that.

John smiled and squirmed to get more comfortable. "So, I find you very, very attractive." He reached up, removed his glasses, and set them on the table. "I know you're all supposed to be terrorists, cultists, and crazies, but you seem okay to me."

John wasn't usually courageous when initiating sex and was terrible at hookups despite their prevalence in the modern world. He wasn't assertive when it came to things like this, which he traced back to the miserable experience high school had been. It taught him to be quiet, unobtrusive, and invisible.

Despite the progress Earth had made in the last couple of decades in acceptance and equality, some things seemed destined to remain the same, especially being a nerd in a big public school. Being smart enough to graduate high school early made him a target for jocks. Even after going on to MIT and getting dual majors in computer science and machine learning, he found he intimidated people who were just plain dumber than he.

Jack Carter seemed authentic, and his genuineness made John feel atypically brave. The buzz from those heavy-hitting beers also helped; he didn't mind a bit of liquid courage now and again. Typically socially awkward, John thought he'd been reasonably witty and relatively coherent after the embarrassing misstart in the woods.

Still, despite their conversation that evening, he knew next to nothing about Carter.

"I find you very attractive, too," Carter said.

That statement made John suddenly feel shy. The light in Carter's beautiful brown eyes made John's knees weak. Thankfully he was sitting on his lap, or he might have fallen over.

He nodded and licked his lips. Carter put his hands on John's lower back and rubbed them slowly up and down his spine and flanks, sending pleasurable zings through his body. The tingles localized in his pelvis and gave John a raging boner that made him ache to be free of his boxers.

"In the interest of honesty, it's been a while since I've been with anyone," the soldier added.

His deftly roaming hands indicated that abstinence hadn't made him rusty.

John squirmed, trying to get his cock more comfortable in his pants. It was impossible, of course. "How long are we talking, my man? A couple of days? A couple of weeks? A month?" He faked a gasp of horror. "Years?"

His expression was shocked as he put his hands on Carter's chest and bravely caressed it through his T-shirt. *Jesus, his muscles have muscles.*

Carter smirked and shifted his hips; John glanced down and saw the tent in his jeans.

And, we have a very nice bulge.

"Months," the soldier said with a bit of a growl. "But I've kept in touch with my hand this whole time."

That bulge looks commando.

"What's 'commando' mean?" Carter asked.

"Jesus, did I say that out loud?" John laughed. "Uh, you know, no underwear?" He pointed southerly to the other man's obvious erection.

"Why the fuck would I wear those? Earthen men seem fixated on packing their cocks up, but I like my freedom," Carter replied.

John giggled then was horrified. *Oh my god, did I seriously just giggle?* Out loud, the technician changed the subject. "Well, also, in the interest of honesty: a few months is less than me. I've also kept in touch with my hands, but I'll still be rusty." He blushed. "I'm not the best at—"

Carter leaned forward and kissed him, silencing John's unnecessary explanation. When they broke apart, John was panting, and the soldier had a hungry look on his face. It was intense, a little scary, and made John feel like he was playing with fire. Carter wrapped John in his arms and stood, holding him off the floor like he weighed nothing.

"Fuck me," he breathed at this manly demonstration.

"I'd love to." Carter kissed him again.

John surrendered to the unfamiliar experience of being carried by someone; Carter's muscular arms made him feel good in a way he'd never have predicted.

Several hours later, feeling more relaxed than he had, Carter looked over at John. The other man was sprawled on his stomach in the soldier's enormous, comfortable bed, sleeping soundly after good food, beer, and a couple of orgasms. The soldier grinned contentedly and zoned out into a twilight doze.

Around four in the morning, John stirred next to him and woke up. He slipped from the bed and stumbled into the bathroom; the room was light enough to see without tripping over anything. When John came back to bed, Carter rolled onto his side. John sidled up to him, and Carter slipped his hand under the sheet and caressed his way down to the younger man's hip.

"Good morning," Carter murmured.

"It certainly is."

John tried ineffectively to push the muscular soldier onto his back; Carter laughed and went with the motion. John grinned as Carter mock toppled away from his feeble "shove," then crawled over the soldier's hips to straddle him.

"Sorry for the morning breath," the technician said sheepishly. He kissed Carter lightly with his lips closed, then sat back and reached behind his pale, bare ass to find Carter's dick. "Ah, yes, just as I remember," he said with a purr. His grin widened as he gently stroked the soldier's uncut wood.

Carter looked at him with a hungry expression but waited for John to make the next move. John hesitated, unsure if Carter was a strict top—he was so manly—or if he'd be amenable to bottoming....

Before he could get all knotted up in his head, he timidly asked, "Last night, you said we could do anything I was comfortable with. Were you being serious?"

"Of course," Carter replied. "What do you want to do?"

John thought he might like a good spanking but figured he'd wait to throw some kink into the mix.

"Uh, well… Can I be top? I've never done that before." John blushed. "I've always been, you know, too hesitant to push the issue, but if you're okay with it, I'd really like to…"

Carter shifted beneath him. "You were on top last night."

He sounded puzzled. John realized this was a colloquialism issue. "No, not 'on top,' *the* top." He saw the soldier shake his head, so John leaned down and whispered into his ear.

Carter laughed. "Sure, but why didn't you just say you wanted to fuck me?"

"Uh, well, some guys are strict tops, others prefer to bottom. I didn't know if you were versatile, you know."

"Tops? Bottoms? Don't men on Earth just have sex?" Carter asked.

John could see he had some explaining to do. "I'll tell you all about it," he promised.

Carter put his hands on John's back and sat up. They kissed, and the soldier reached down to stroke John's cock, which stood proudly out of his well-manicured bush. John had been slightly surprised by how hirsute and ungroomed the other man was once he took his clothes off.

It was unusual on Earth to see a man au naturel, especially one with such a beautiful physique. Ripped men tended to remove all their body hair to better show off the hard work they'd put into their gorgeous bodies. It took him about five seconds to decide he loved Jack's hairiness.

"We can do anything you like, as often as you like. Just tell me what you want," Carter urged him.

"Are you for real?" John mumbled.

He was equal parts elated and terrified. Carter's only response was another kiss as they began to fool around again.

Twenty-Four
Viginti Quattuor

The sorcerer dug deeper into his power—the ecstasy of his magic morphed from pleasure into pain. It felt like the final spell he'd cast against Sogma, and the shame of his failure to finish that enchantment drove a spike into his brain.

He'd failed, and Imara had suffered the consequences of his weakness.

Alexander let out a bellow of effort as he summoned more magic platforms. People raced down the planks of light as other shuttles and boats efficiently pulled up to collect the evacuees.

A young woman ran up to him and gasped, "Thank you," with such sincerity that he forced himself to nod even through the strain of what he was doing.

Then she grabbed the free hand of a young man carrying an infant, and they were gone through the Tanager-Rosen bridge. His world momentarily narrowed to the couple with the infant—a child like his would someday be. In the future, the bookstore owner had told him, they'd saved everyone, including pets and wildlife. That wouldn't happen unless he pushed past the obstruction formed by the dark flower. He needed teleportation to save everyone.

He struggled to find more power and screamed with effort as he dug deeper into his core, tapping reserves of magical power he didn't know he had. His corona burned so brightly people couldn't look at him as they ran past him to the platforms and the Ásbrú. Power flowed into him; it poured in from the universe as he dug deep into the prāṇa that flowed out of the ākāśa, which formed the substrate of the prāṇamaṇḍala.

He wanted to keep screaming, but there was no time for his pain. He reached out to locate people and animals all over the island. He began to teleport them in clusters of two, three, and five as blood ran from his nose.

Sirenī felt immense power whipping around her. It created a vortex of wind and rapid pressure differentials that wanted to tangle her hair around her face. She exerted the tiniest sliver of her power to tame her curls into a coil at the nape of her neck.

She floated inside her impermeable field. Streamers of blue lightning flickered as they strobed from her body and outstretched arms to the inside curve of the bubble and then discharged in tremendous arcs.

She had never felt so good. The energy was phenomenal and intoxicating. The absence inside her, the emptiness where Medusa had always rested, made her feel light and free. She felt transformed with the syncretization of her powers as Medusa sublimated and dissolved into her consciousness. The legacy of her angry ancestress flowed freely into her subtle body, transformative and profound.

She grinned fiercely and created a funnel, her will commanding another impermeable field to suck up the boulders, pyroclastic debris, and some of the magma. She sent it arcing out to sea so that it splashed down a mile offshore. Sirenī saw it form a slurry, mixing with the cold, mineral-rich waters in a floating mass.

She imagined it flowing onto the beaches and covering them in toxic, caustic waste.

That won't do.

She exerted her will and grimaced as she held more of the growing mass of lava englobed near the top of the mountain while simultaneously pulling the rocks and debris away from the island. She created another funnel in the ocean so that it sucked down the slurry and diffused the caustic mixture through the limitless water.

She strained for the next several minutes until she gained the upper hand. Now, only smoke emerged from the volcano's shattered caldera as lava poured from a great rent in the side. The boulders and the first wave of pyroclastic debris were gone, sent safely out to sea. She gained traction on the eruption; it was a force of nature so powerful and deadly that the fact she mastered it with her magic was astonishing.

She took a deep breath and flew to the top of the volcano. She looked into the caldera and saw seething magma bubbling and churning as it flushed out of the volcano's guts. She knew Mount Lauremanda had slept peacefully for centuries, but the dark flower had awakened the slumbering titan. The people who lived among its beauty didn't deserve to die.

Certainly not because some necromancer asshole in the Ring of Worlds wants more power, she thought righteously.

Sirenī grimaced and expanded the globe around the lava flow until it covered the top of the mountain like a massive, inverted fishbowl. She tuned the impermeable field so that pressure and heat could escape, but solids would be contained. She tied off the power flow by anchoring it in the planet's power bournes, letting the electromagnetic fields of Omejis sustain the magic. She surveyed her handiwork and felt triumphant. She snapped her fingers to refresh herself. She'd sweat through her clothes when she confronted Medusa, but within seconds she looked freshly showered. She smiled and spun about.

She flew to the beach and saw the island's population as it ran into the throat of the Tanager-Rosen bridge. She saw dozens of people hurrying along the magical platforms to boats and shuttles. They piled in, and the vehicles pulled away. Sirenī blinked when she swept her gaze over a group of people and saw five disappear.

That's teleportation. How? Oh, no!

It only took her a moment to figure out what was happening; Sirenī's heart leaped into her throat as she understood that Alex was pushing himself too hard. Even with the nectar of the Nephilim in his body, he took on too much, just as he had during their fight against Sogma. Sirenī quickly floated closer to him. He was on his knees, head sagging, as he held his arms out at an angle from his chest while a strident corona of blazing red light burned around him.

She'd seen his corona because of its brightness but hadn't realized what it signified until she saw him on his knees. She floated down to the beach and saw his terrible state. The blood ran in thick rivulets from his eyes, ears, nose, and mouth, staining his white shirt a blotchy crimson. There were bloodstains on the front and back of his pants, too.

She cried out and touched down near the crowd hovering outside the blazing whirlwind of his magic. Her impermeable field disappeared with a cobalt flash, and she stood in her heeled shoes on the sand. She ran effortlessly across the sand and ducked between the people, slipping among them with magical grace. She stepped fearlessly through the burning curtain of his magic and knelt beside him.

She leaned into him, gently grabbed him with her power, and helped him to his feet. She felt his heart from where she leaned against him. He looked at her, his blood-filled eyes glazed with pain.

"I've got you, my love," she whispered. Although she worried about him, she was proud of his accomplishments. "You're not alone, Alex. Let me in," she commanded.

He stared blearily at her. Over the noise, the commotion, and the rumbling ground, she heard people continue to disappear from the beach as Alex pushed himself. She nodded encouragingly and tentatively reached out, doing something she'd dreamed of since she was seventeen.

He trembled and reached out a hand to cup her cheek. His knees buckled, and she held him up. Tears ran in beautiful, luminous trails down her cheeks. "Do you feel that, my love?" she whispered.

He nodded weakly but accepted her invitation as they linked aurae. She felt her power twine with his in an action that was thrillingly intimate for her since she'd never been able to connect aurae with her partners. Their energy expanded exponentially in a blast that knocked the people around them to the ground and sent fine white powder sheeting in all directions.

She knew that was unusual and was worried for Alex, but remained gleeful about what she could now do.

Few people understood what the Three had accomplished when they fought to save the world from Sogma. Those who did were floored by the power of the two young women and the scion of the Eldred line because they'd done something everyone thought was impossible. Imara and Alexander could always link aurae, but Sirenī had never been able to because of Medusa.

That obstacle was now gone.

Alex's gaze sharpened, and he blinked as his power expanded, easing his burden. His eyelids were smeared with blood as he stared at her, astonished, and Sirenī saw the understanding appear on his face and glow in his luminous eyes. She grinned and nodded at his unspoken question. Alex stared at her with love and relief as his pain eased. Together, they reached across the island and snatched people, pets, and wild animals to safety on Temple Mount.

Imara incinerated the last līc inside the cavern and planted her hands on her hips. She looked around with a frown on her pretty, stern face. She studied the dark flower from a safe distance as the ground rumbled and the cavern heated. Her magic continued to regulate her personal environment, even in an erupting volcano. She wasn't hot, but she had a distant awareness of the increasing temperature.

The songstress wondered how to destroy the dark flower. She was confident it would absorb any spells she threw at it since it fed on magical energy. Sure, it consumed the physical nutrients from the corpses, but it really devoured their vital energies. Her lips thinned as she recalled Gaea, the rift grenade, and the…word.

If I can even call it that, she thought.

She drew a deep, centering breath to the bottom of her lungs before slowly letting it out. The situation replayed itself in her mind, and she felt a tiny shiver of vibration, a sympathetic resonance that responded to her memory of that moment. The sensation thrummed so deep inside her that she could barely discern its existence. She traced it, lost it, found it again, followed it through the inner landscape of her beingness, and finally stood before it. The cavern, eruption, and crisis faded as her awareness went inside.

Imara felt as if she were in a room. She stood before a mirror, but nothing about the space was defined. Her reflection looked like her but different, too, almost reptilian. She cocked her head. The mirror image raised its eyebrow and put its hands on its hips instead of copying her actions. Imara flinched, and the image smirked.

The songstress straightened and scowled at her likeness. She stepped closer, and her likeness donned a challenging expression. It reached a hand forward and beckoned to her. Imara had a sense of someone throwing down the gauntlet in a challenge.

"Okay, Bitchy Imara," the songstress said to her mirror image. "Challenge accepted." She stepped forward and passed through a membranic field effect of some sort.

She floated in the sky above a storm-lashed ocean. Lightning flashed, and the waves towered hundreds of feet in the air. This was no world she knew, but it felt familiar. She hovered above the chaotic sea, safe and dry, as the vision unfolded above the black waters of the deeps.

She looked about through her autolenses, intrigued. She saw waves smashing against rocks that jutted above the surface a few miles away. A great cliff's beaten face rose from the tumultuous black waters a mile beyond those. Her attention was drawn back to the waves beneath her —they rose and crashed as rain fell in torrents, lightning flared, and thunder boomed.

Was that…

She stared and perceived a light rising from the depths of the sea. It floated, or rather swam up, from a fissure in the ocean bed. The ravine plunged miles deep into the world's crust. The light grew closer, and a form took shape within. It was serpentine, with a lumpy, misshapen back and a stupendous length. The creature continued to rise from the ravine, but it was at least a half mile long—larger than any living creature she'd ever heard about. It finally got close enough to the surface that she drew back, wanting to watch the monstrous being move in its entirety.

An aquiline snout breached the briny surface. Two massive nostrils punched into the air, and water rained from them in grand cascades. Colossal jaws covered in luminous aqua and ultramarine scales cleaved the sky. Great cataracts of water poured from the shimmering edges of the giant scales, forming endless rivers that draped over the muscular form.

As she watched, the weather calmed, and the waters stilled. She understood there was no weather front on this ocean. The creature was the storm—a force of nature so profound it whipped the sea into a frenzy for miles as it rose from the deep.

The head continued to emerge, and she saw ridges, scales, and horns of varying sizes. When the eye passed her, it flicked its gaze over her. The massive slash of the pupil narrowed, and then it was beyond her, held by a column of thick, sinuous muscle in the form of a long neck. This was no sea serpent or dinosaur but something beyond her preconceptions.

Finally, the misshapen back crested the surface, revealing massive shoulders and a thick chest. Two long, supremely muscular arms depended from the shoulders, and she saw the lumpy back wasn't malformed. It proved to have something extraordinary attached.

Wings!

They were folded tight to what could only be a dragon's spine, held that way to permit swimming through the ocean. However, as the body continued to rise, those impossible wings began to open with a creak of muscle and tendon that sounded like the firing of heavy artillery. All the while, a seemingly endless deluge flowed from the ridges and horns, the scales and fringes.

The wings creaked outward to either side until they covered a span more than a mile across. The creature was so large that it couldn't exist, never mind fly, but the wings began to beat with a tremendous snap, displacing tons of water and masses of air. The tsunami raced away, spreading in deceptively low undulations as the creature lifted into the sky.

At last, the hind legs, the taloned feet, and the long, serpentine tail flared free of the ocean. Water now fell from the creature in a gentle rain as it flew away. Imara tuned her eyesight to watch the majestic dragon rise from the planet's atmosphere. She stared, slack-jawed and wonderstruck, as it sailed into space, no longer flapping its wings but accelerating under some unknown power.

She blinked, and her vision changed. She floated next to the rocks that rose from the ocean near the dragon's emergence. Imara saw a figure on the stone, holding on with one muscular, draconic arm. It was an undeniably female form, with long twisted hair and scales that covered her strangely lovely features. The reptilian figure opened her mouth, and the most ethereal song burst forth beautifully from her hinged jaws.

Listening to the wordless aubade offered to the dragon who'd flown away, Imara understood. Just like that, she was back in the room before Bitchy Imara. The reflection stared at her still, with the same look of challenge. Her mirror image asked with her snarky expression if the songstress could comprehend what she'd witnessed.

Imara smirked. "Yes, that was the first Seiren. My ancestor."

She'd understood immediately. The dragon had slumbered for eons in the ocean, somehow influencing the development of a line of bipedal, wingless draconians. For some reason, the Seiren had a voice like the heavens—ethereal, transcendental, and utterly compelling to any who heard it.

Through all the long ages, however it happened, Imara inherited that power, just as Sirenī inherited fatal beauty from Medusa. Her reflection nodded approvingly at Imara's swift grasp of the situation—not that she ultimately cared. Standing there considering, the songstress could easily see in Bitchy Imara's features the essence of the draconic creature from her vision, clinging to the wave-lashed rocks.

Her ancestor was beautiful and strong, unafraid, with a voice that could stop a man's heart or inflame him to the heights of passion, as her distant ancestors were known to do...often before eating the unfortunate sod. That thought led to another, and she scoffed, amused.

"I see—I'm descended not just from the Seiren, but even further back, from that dragon in the vision?"

She said it to her reflection and sounded disbelieving because the creature who flew away was too big to live in any world she could fathom. Such creatures had certainly never lived on Gaea. There were no dragons in the historical records, and though there was evidence of their existence, no one knew on which world they lived in the Ring. The reflection nodded as Imara grasped the fullness of her vision. Between one instant and the next, she was back in the cave.

The roots of the dark flower were inches away from her, having crept slowly closer while she was absorbed. She flinched backward, scowling as she realized how risky that vision had been. The roots pulled back a couple of feet but didn't retreat into the pile of corpses. She frowned, keeping an eye on the tendrils while considering the vision. It revealed something about her bloodline that potentially explained the word of power she'd spoken on Gaea. Imara wasn't entirely human because that ancient Seiren had arisen from the dragon somehow.

She at least understood she hadn't spoken in a human language.
Perhaps it is the language of the Seiren?
She quickly searched inside herself but found nothing. The songstress narrowed her eyes and glared at the dark flower. It could absorb any power she threw at it, so a direct attack was out unless she made it physical.

Then she realized she didn't need the language of dragons to accomplish her goals. Her laughter rang off the cavern walls.

"Let's see you deal with magma."

Imara raised her voice in song as a multicolored aurora formed around her. She directed her voice at the structure of the lava tubes and cavern. The spellsong expanded and echoed through every tunnel, every fracture, every crack in the basalt. The ground began to tremble. The dark flower sensed the danger and let out a distressed wail. Its roots retreated as molten rock welled from cracks in the floor and the chamber's back wall.

Imara watched smoke and steam belch into the cave from several lava tubes. The kṛtyā bījā closed its hideous, sunflower-parody head and hunkered down on its stalk as the reddish glow of magma began to gleam in the tubes' throats.

The songstress stood near the entrance and watched molten rock well into the cavern and inch across the floor. The kṛtyā bījā began to scream unbearably as the lava flowed onto the corpses and over its root system. Imara's grin widened but quickly faded as a strange, black lattice emerged from the stalk. It grew like crystals and enshrouded the flower in a dark chrysalis.

The songstress cursed, turned, and hurried from the room. The mountain began to tremble again, preparing itself for another blast. She quickly negotiated the lava tubes and went out the same way she came in. She emerged into the cool afternoon light. A weak sun shone through a halo of fine particles dispersed in the atmosphere from the eruptive plume.

Imara looked up and gasped, astonished at Sirenī's handiwork. An inverted fishbowl filled steadily with lava. She looked around and perceived her partners on the beach. Alex leaned heavily against the much shorter Sirenī, but the two were alone on the clean, white sands. She briefly wondered why the beaches weren't black from all the basalt, but she dismissed that thought and hummed herself into the air.

She could tell that the evacuation was successful. She flew down to the beach on a wave of sound, soft and harmonious, and settled onto the sand. She was careful not to turn her ankles as she approached her partners. Unlike Sirenī, who stood on the beach in high-heeled shoes, Imara would twist an ankle if she stepped wrong.

"What were you thinking?" she cried at Alex when she saw blood all over him, gory and half-dried, mixed with sweat.

No dust clung to him because of his intrinsic wards, but he still looked horrible. He smiled, his teeth white and clear despite the blood on his face. She groaned in relief at the expression and hugged her companions; they tiredly returned the gesture.

"We saved everyone—even the animals," Sirenī explained. She glowed happily.

Imara let out a joyful cry as she saw that Sirenī and Alex had linked aurae. "How?"

Sirenī grinned. "I'll explain everything," she promised.

"You'd better," Imara declared. She looked at the mountain, then back at her companions. "The dark flower is in a cave—I flooded it with magma. The kṛtyā bījā erected some defense, maybe cryptobiosis. I suspect we can curtail the corruption here if we collapse the volcano and encase it in rock. I don't think it will die, at least not for a long time, but who knows."

Imara glanced at Alex; he looked better than when she'd first arrived, but he was still ragged.

"We'll take care of this," Imara told him.

Alex cleared his throat and said sternly, "No, we can link aurae now. I will not do much, but I refuse to sit this out."

He's stubborn, Sirenī said telepathically.

Tell me about it, Imara agreed. *Still, he won't have to do much since we're linking aurae—*

"I know you are discussing me," Alex interjected sulkily.

The songstress looked at him and spoke aloud. "Yes, Grumpy, we are, but we've agreed to let you help." She couldn't resist smiling. "So long as you do as little as possible."

He chuckled and nodded, then straightened. Imara made sure he wouldn't fall over, then took a breath and opened her aura. She extended psychic energy to Alex, with whom she'd linked before. He accepted the connection, and she felt her accessible power expand. The flow was strong but steady. Then she reached out to Sirenī, who'd never been able to link because of Medusa.

Imara's eyes widened, and she gasped; Sirenī echoed the sound a moment later. Energy swept through them like floodwaters, rapid and raging. The tumultuous flow was overwhelming, and Imara floundered, unsure of what to do next. She'd never used her full power and hadn't even discovered her actual limits, yet here she was, immersed in magical currents that felt like the ocean of her vision.

"Let me take control for a moment," Alex said.

Imara relaxed and felt the flow of energy smooth. She perceived his mental actions, saw him align their energies, and watched the raging tumult settle into a deep, mighty river. He nodded and released control back to her; she took it and let the power flow around and through each of them, getting a feel for handling that much energy.

"That was intense," Sirenī declared.

Imara laughed nervously and said, "Yes, much more than I expected." She took another breath and looked at the mountain. "Are we ready?"

"Yes," Alex replied. Sirenī nodded.

They stepped into their accustomed position. Imara held Alex's left hand in her right; Sirenī held his right hand in her left, and the women clasped their free hands together. Their coronae flared, multi-colored for Imara, crimson instead of orange for Alex, and cobalt for Sirenī. Imara noticed Sirenī's corona was much more intensely colored than before. She couldn't wait to hear her tale.

Imara guided their magic. Because of her autolenses, she was the only one who could see the mountain. Sand whipped around them as their magic created a hot, balmy wind, sending fine dust everywhere.

"Squeeze the impermeable field you created and push everything downward," Imara told Sirenī.

Her partner closed her eyes and focused.

Imara saw the mountain shudder as the invisible bowl full of molten rock compressed, squeezing in and down. The top third of the volcano splintered with a stupendous cacophony; rock rained down the sides of the mountain. Imara winced as the rocks shattered like glass, the sound assaulting her ultrasharp hearing.

She grimaced as the grating continued but pushed her discomfort aside and began to sing. Power flowed through her so strongly she felt a trifle delirious. The sheer volume of energy made casting the spellsong almost effortless as she gathered falling rocks from around the mountain. The stones, most of them large, some of them massive, rose into the air and began to smash together.

She hung the spellsong she'd been singing in the air so the ethereal sound vibrated around them. It made the beach sand shudder and shift. Then she sang another song of heat and density. The stones began to smolder, turned cherry red, and then fused into a long, conical plug. She spun it and shaped it until it had a sharp point. Then, inspired by their working at the damaged canal, she changed her song. She'd have smiled if she weren't singing as the rocks turned the dark gray of nanocarbon.

"Excellent choice," Alex complimented.

She winked at him and kept singing.

Sirenī had pushed as much of the magma back into the volcano as she could. Once it was out, the planet didn't want it back, at least not yet—maybe in a few hundred or a million years. Imara chuckled at her thoughts and told Sirenī to hold the magma where she had it.

Her partner nodded. Imara waited a beat, then shout-sang a word of power. The spear of stone plunged into the volcano's throat with a deafening crash.

Twenty-Five
Viginti Quinque

"Can you fuse it?" Imara asked Sirenī.

"Yes," Sirenī said.

She let go of their hands and spun in place. She chanted the same transmutation spell Alex had used to create the nanocarbon. She amended it to remove the heat from the lava and fuse the mountain into a solid mass.

Imara watched the transformation propagate through the volcano. She was sure their actions would seal Lauremanda for thousands of years—undoubtedly long past anyone on Omejis caring about it.

She reluctantly let the link with her partners dissipate. They studied the mountain and looked at the ruins—Lauremanda was a third shorter than before the eruption. The eruption, quakes, and collapse of the top had wrecked Lauremanda City. Imara assumed that once Alex and Sirenī worked together to get everyone to safety, they'd stopped trying to keep the boulders away from the city, which shattered marble, crystal, and concrete with equal disregard.

Once they were sure the situation was contained, Imara felt emotionally exhausted. She knew they had much to share but could only say wearily, "I think we're done here."

"I concur," Alex said.

He sounds ragged, but at least he looks better, Imara thought.

Sirenī created an impermeable field and lifted them into the air. They hurtled toward Temple Mount and the evacuees. Imara watched the ocean blur by beneath them for a few seconds. Then she looked at her partners and said, "You've both got some explaining to do."

Ävidä slammed his hand on Kāmla's desk. Virulent green energy crackled around it and burned a handprint into the enormous, expensive surface. Unlike most things, this was not a product of the Magical Utility Grid but instead handmade. Kāmla had traded MECs to get it, and she didn't appreciate having it ruined.

Suppressing a sigh, the Minister considered how much magic she'd have to expend to repair the damage. Her new secretary was too good to kill, so Patrice would not do as a power source. After a moment's consideration, she let out the sigh she'd held in and met his flinty gaze.

"What happened?" she demanded.

He'd appeared in her office in a rush of displaced air. He'd been ranting but hadn't told her what prompted the vitriolic diatribe. It took him a few moments to get control of himself enough to speak.

"My children's skins were destroyed on Omejis!" he bellowed. He would have spat if he'd been mortal and had saliva. He took a deep breath, fists clenched as flickers of dreadfire lapped over his hands and singed the cuffs of his sleeves. He continued in a moderated tone. "A sorcerer confronted them and obliterated them. That's not the worst part, though."

That an unknown sorcerer on Omejis could defeat six līc was frightening.

I thought the Three were the only magicians of that caliber, Kāmla thought with a frisson of worry.

"What is?" she prompted.

Ävidä's green eyes narrowed, and he said, "I've lost touch with the kṛtyā bīja there."

Kāmla stared at him blankly. "I don't understand. How?"

He threw his hands in the air. Thankfully, he didn't throw dreadfire around the office with the flapping motion. "I don't have a fucking clue!" he growled. "I didn't even think it was possible. Only Abyssal flames or hellfire can destroy the chrysalides protecting them."

He paced and shook his head. "Yllundi and Hrdlička have already taken new skins. They described a woman who looks improbably similar to Imara Inanna."

Kāmla's eyes widened, but she smoothed her expression. Strong contractions of the facial musculature led to fine lines and wrinkles. Weathering looked good on Ävidä, but women were held to different standards. She took a deep breath and stood, her breasts swelling beneath her skintight dress.

Ävidä's eyes snapped to her curves. Even in his fury, his male desires were so predictable. She enjoyed it; it was so easy to manipulate men. She stepped around the desk, touched the handprint, and traced it with one long, blood-red fingernail.

"That's impossible, as you well know. Imara is a blind old hag living in Louden. The perpetually lovely but dumb Sirenī Adamma is in her natal home in Glendale, and that fuckstain Alexander Eldred hides in his mansion in Timil Deeps."

Kāmla's voice was glacial as she recounted the locations of her nemeses. They'd never met her—well, Eldred had once, in passing—but they were the bane of her existence.

The necromancer's rage cooled slightly at her logical words. "Timil Deeps is your hometown, is it not?" he asked. His eyes glittered with malice.

The minister smiled and played his little game. "Yes, Ävidä, it is. Why do you ask?" she asked sweetly.

She watched for any reaction, but he gave nothing away.

"The Three are trapped," she continued when he remained silent. "Imara is watched day and night, and the blind bitch can't get to the Columbia Gatehouse, go to Omejis, and come back without her monitors knowing. I'll never let the Unified Government forget the threat they pose."

Ävidä crossed his arms. "How, then, do you explain someone of such power?" he demanded belligerently. "Yllundi fought with the Three in the Empire. She recognized Imara. Hrdlička is reliable, unlike the other members of their twisted little family. They took inferior skins to tell me this."

Kāmla stared at him, and she scrunched her face momentarily. She picked up the phone on her desk. It barely rang in the anteoffice before Patrice answered.

"Get me Major Jack Carter of Zeta Force. Immediately," the minister demanded.

The girl hung up to obey.

Kāmla and Ävidä waited three minutes in grim silence before the phone rang.

"Minister Vicchāya," the brooding voice of the swarthy Zeta Force commander said in a forced tone. "How can I help you?"

He got results, so she tolerated his disrespectful attitude. He was an orphan, trash, and desperate to prove himself. She couldn't manipulate him like she could Ävidä since he favored men, but he wanted approval so badly that he overachieved with a vengeance.

Someday, though, he'll outlive his usefulness.

"I need an update on the Three." She put the phone on speaker.

"Alexander Eldred hasn't left the manor in months, but we confirmed with his monitors that Skawen'na'há:wi of the Kanien'kehá:ka continues to visit for two weeks every year." Carter paused. When she said nothing, he continued, "Imara Inanna lives alone in Louden, essentially a shut-in since her son was killed helping the Unified Military expand the Grid in Persia along the borders of the Tèng Empire.

"Sirenī Adamma lives in Glendale, throwing parties and going to the spa. The vampires monitor her day and night, two at all times. She's got a housecat." Carter paused. "That's it, ma'am."

"And there is no chance one of them disappeared or went elsewhere?" Kāmla pressed. "Imara, maybe?"

"Elsewhere, ma'am? The blind one?" The soldier's scathing tone questioned her sanity. "There is no 'elsewhere.' They're monitored all day, every day." He paused a beat. "Ma'am."

"Thank you, Major Carter."

She hung up without giving him a chance to reply.

Ävidä thought about what they'd just heard. "Then we have an entirely new and unforeseen problem. Gulielmus Occamus expanded upon the probability of such things six centuries ago in his writings on logic. I'm certain you're familiar with his *lex parsimoniae?*"

Kāmla did not appreciate his patronizing tone. "Everyone is, fool," she snapped. "The law of parsimony states that entities should not be multiplied without necessity. The likeliest explanation is not that there are more sorcerers as powerful as the Three roaming around the Ring of Worlds. At the same time, we know they are all here on Gaea."

She knew Yllundi and Hrdlička had no reason to lie, and only Councilmembers were powerful enough to defeat more than one līc in a duel. She doubted anyone besides the Three—even the Consiliarii—could singlehandedly defeat a curse of līc.

It doesn't make any sense.

"Can you order their surveillance reduced?" Ävidä asked suddenly.

She narrowed her eyes. "I fail to see how that proves anything."

He grinned. "If they can escape somehow, they will be likelier to do so if they have less oversight, right?"

"I can see that," she admitted. "It will take years for this. As you know, nothing happens swiftly in the Unified Government or the Ministry."

"We have the time," he assured her.

She drafted the orders and signed them that day.

The Three sorted everything out with Eirianedd and the refugees, who were so grateful for their help that their appreciation became overwhelming. Alexander, Imara, and Sirenī escaped the thankful horde and returned through the Temple to the Gatehouse in Rilladwen, and from there to their hotel. They met with Amlodd, who brought the governor of Rilladwen, Grummore, to their room.

The two men were just as grateful and profusely thanked the Three, assuring them they could do whatever they wanted on Omejis for however long they stayed. Grummore said the government would cover any costs they incurred and stated there was no way to repay the debt the citizens of Omejis owed. He wanted to host a worldwide celebration with parties in the streets and parades, but the Three frantically declined such demonstrations.

Grummore reluctantly conceded. A moment later, he erupted in a new round of praise for their help with the canals. "Thank you again," he enthused. "I haven't forgotten about it."

The Three thanked the officials for their supportive words and assurances. They explained they needed time and a place to stay near the Temple. The bureaucrats assured the sorcerers that they'd arrange for a home in Temple City within a few days.

Alexander decided Grummore was an earnest fellow, diligent and sensitive. The politicians of Omejis seemed to be a uniformly patriotic lot—serious, intellectual, and obsessed with the best interests of the people under their care—quite a departure from the rampant narcissism of the individuals governing Earth.

"We appreciate everything you're doing for us," Imara told them. She sat on the couch to Alexander's left, her usual spot, while Sirenī sat to his right. The two officials were seated in armchairs opposite the sofa, which they dragged into place for this meeting.

"You've been kinder to us than we ever hoped," Sirenī added.

Amlodd and the governor beamed at their words and chatted idly for a few more minutes before departing.

When they were alone, the Three relaxed in the emptiness of the hotel room and savored the quiet. Alexander watched Imara walk onto the balcony running the room's length. She tilted her face up to the lovely heat of the tropical sun.

"We can travel back to Temple Mount in a few days," Alexander suggested.

He already looked better and felt halfway back to normal. He had no doubt that was down to the amṛta. He required months to recover from the events at the Abyssal Gate, and he'd used more power at Lauremanda. The difference was dramatic.

The episode at the Bitter Islands had changed them all. Imara discovered her draconic bloodline in a vision, and Sirenī argued with Medusa before the monster willingly surrendered itself. Alexander discovered more power inside himself, and his corona had become almost pure crimson. He didn't know what the changes portended, but he looked forward to seeing how things developed.

He thought of dealing with volcanic eruptions on a routine basis, but the mere thought seemed overwhelming in his weakened state. He turned instead to the near future when they'd work together to harness the magical and the mystical forces.

Imara and Sirenī had already confirmed the babies were okay. Using magic was fine during pregnancies, though transmutation and shapeshifting were contraindicated. What the women had done at Lauremanda was unique and might have unexpected consequences, but they'd assumed the amṛta would keep the fetuses safe, and it had.

Besides, there wasn't anything they could do if something adverse had happened. The Three knew they had helped with the island's evacuation because they'd already done it. They wouldn't have willingly left people in danger even if they hadn't known about their past actions.

That was why Alexander healed the people of Grace Manor and provided them with the transportation device to continue their work. He, Imara, and Sirenī wanted to help others. There was more need on other worlds, especially Earth, with billions of people and a capitalist society that kept at least half the world in debt and scarcity.

On Earth, a small handful of people held all the wealth. Alexander, Imara, and Sirenī had resources of a different kind they could share. When they saw a need, they acted. They didn't always do things correctly because they couldn't hope to see or know every facet of a situation, but they did what they could when they could.

Alexander was content knowing that his mistakes came from actions in alignment with his principles. He'd always believed that having the courage of one's convictions was its own kind of power. *And someone who has nothing but acts with the understanding that they might lose what little remains to them is genuinely inspiring and courageous.*

"Alex?"

Imara's questioning tone cut through his reverie. He looked over to see that she'd returned to sit on the couch on his left side, and he'd been so preoccupied he hadn't even noticed. He blinked and smiled.

"Yes?" The songstress cocked her head with a curious look. "I wandered down a mental path and got lost," he joked lightly.

"Ah. Sirenī and I agree we should go to the Nephilim Temple without too much delay."

"I should fully recover in a day or two," he said.

Sirenī tightened her arm around his and leaned to look at Imara. "This is off-topic, but it's been on my mind. You stopped your cycles when you went blind, right?"

"That's right."

"We took the amṛta, which reversed our biological appearance to what I would say is our early thirties. Then, I delved into your aura on Earth, and we figured out how to restore your normal cycles. Then, you and I conceived, and now we know the babes are okay because we delved them, too...."

"And?" Imara prompted when Sirenī paused.

Thanks to the journal's Spartan content, Sirenī and Imara knew they would be in their first trimester for eight years. They'd devised a way to introduce the idea of a prolonged pregnancy to Alex so he'd be prepared for the long delay. After all, he'd be expecting to meet his children in eight months or so, but that wasn't going to happen.

"Well," Sirenī began, "do we know how long Nephilim women were pregnant?"

Alex and Imara gave her a stunned look.

Imara's good at this, Sirenī mused. She kept her face composed as she continued to expound upon her "idea."

"We took amṛta, and that's the Nephilim's nectar of immortality, a relic of the Dawntime. The Nephilim age was a long time ago, and we know next to nothing about it. So, maybe this will change our gestational duration; we don't even know what their biology was, but we agree the amṛta protected the babes from our extensive power usage. It could change everything, and we won't know ahead of time."

Alex stared at her, aghast. Imara gave her a thumbs up from behind his shoulder and then supportively rested the same hand on Alex's shoulder.

"I hadn't even thought of that," Imara said. "The Nephilim are an ascended race. We don't know anything about them. Why—Nephilim women could have been pregnant for years. We'd never know if no one thought to write it down."

"It is true," Alex allowed. "We cannot know the length of their gestational cycle. I assumed it's similar to our human stock, but your logic is inarguable, Sirenī." He looked at her, flummoxed, and then regained his composure. "We must take nothing for granted with either of you."

He shifted between them and put a hand on their bellies; his face suffused with a quiet, luminous joy. They put their hands over his and smiled happily. The Three sat in peaceful silence for a time and thought about their future family.

They recuperated for two days and nights and left on the third morning for Temple Mount. They used the Gatehouse since they couldn't teleport without exerting tremendous power. It seemed excessive to do that casually, given they had another means of effortless transportation.

Grummore had sent a letter with a bouquet of beautiful tropical blooms. Imara thanked the delivery girl and showed the flowers to her partners. "Thīaterīka would have loved to snack on these," she joked.

She read the letter and paraphrased it. "Grummore has arranged a home for us in Temple City. He's also set up a shuttle and pilots to ferry us anywhere we'd like to go around the Bitter Islands."

"How…unexpected," Alex remarked.

Imara smiled and shrugged. "They're grateful."

"Indeed," he replied dryly.

When they stepped through the superancient shield protecting the Temple, one of their pilots was already present and waiting, an eager grin on her face as she unnecessarily saluted them. She stepped forward to clasp their hands.

"Thank you so much. My parents and siblings were in Lauremanda City; without your intervention, they'd have died." Gratitude shone from her eyes. "My name is Aeronwen, and I'll be alternating as your

Twenty-Five

pilot with my brother, Sulwyn. We volunteered to help you for as long as you need, no matter what you ask."

Alex smiled at her, bemused, and when Sirenī grinned at her, Aeronwen stared, the young woman's jaw dropping open in typical fashion. Imara rolled her eyes and shot her partner a look. Sirenī winked at her, shutting down her fatal beauty. Aeronwen came to with a start and blushed at having stared so openly at the beautiful woman, even though she'd had no choice. She recovered quickly from her embarrassment and ushered her passengers aboard the shuttle.

Sulwyn turned out to be as chirpy and bubbly as his sister. The siblings were fair and blond in contrast to the darker-skinned occupants of the aggressively tropical supercontinent. The native islanders were almost the first fair-skinned people the Three had seen in their time on Omejis.

Only a fraction of fair phenotypes developed on Gaea, with Sirenī's vampire friend Darren being an example of someone from that grouping. Most groups had black, olive, red, or yellow tones. On Earth, they had primarily seen White people during their stay in Maine, but their contact with the local population was minimal.

On Omejis, they'd seen a few fair-skinned people wandering about Rilladwen, but most were Black, and the Three looked like locals. Imara spoke like she'd grown up in Rilladwen; only Sirenī and Alex's accents betrayed their foreignness. Amusingly, Aeronwen and Sulwyn's names in Cymraeg meant *golden* or *pale*.

The ride to their accommodations in Temple City took fifteen minutes, and the shuttle landed on a private pad beside the small home granted to them. Eirianedd had wanted to gift them a mansion with staff, the biggest on the island, but they'd demurred since that would poorly suit their needs.

As soon as they arrived, people began coming by their accommodation with gifts. Their appearance didn't bother the Three in any way —except they left so many items to show their gratitude that the entrance to their abode became obstructed within hours. Aeronwen and Sulwyn took it upon themselves to manage the collection of foods, trinkets, notes, and keepsakes to prevent the street from becoming blocked and to keep the Three from undue inconvenience.

Alexander hoped to shave time off the learning for his partners. The first shock came about three weeks in—Sirenī had already achieved the syncretic results.

"It has to be from when Medusa sublimated and gave over," she declared. They were in their accommodation in Temple City. "When it happened, I felt terrible pain; I remember screaming it hurt so much. Then I felt such a surge of power. It was breathtaking."

"How nice," Imara groused.

Alexander nodded, grimacing as he remembered the pain he'd felt. He'd almost died, but Skawen'na'há:wi had used her mystical power to help him.

The songstress sat there looking glum; she smiled only when Sirenī took her hand with a sympathetic expression.

"No, it truly is nice," Imara declared. Her smile faded quickly. "I'm just unaccustomed to struggling like this. I can't even feel the energy Alex is talking about. At least Medusa's remaining energy, or whatever it was, could act independently within you."

"That's true," Sirenī agreed. "Which means the Medusa energy must have been rooted in the mystical side of things. That might explain why I could never control it, and the two times it came through, I was completely helpless, stuffed down so far inside myself I could do nothing."

Alexander shook his head while Imara shivered. He contemplated those two frightful episodes but could only imagine how awful it was for Sirenī.

"What a terrible burden," Imara empathized.

Sirenī seemed to shake off the memories with a slight grin. "It was, but now there are two of us to help you," she said positively. "It might be that if we both tell you what we understand of the process, we could speed it up for you." She looked at Alexander with a slightly apologetic smile. "I love you, dear heart, but your descriptions of things are rather, well, male."

Alex chuckled. "You are entirely correct. My tendency to be literal does have its occasional drawbacks."

Sirenī pretended to gasp in amazement at his ready agreement; he scowled in mock umbrage. Alex grabbed her and swept her in a circle. Sirenī laughed and flung out her arms, letting him spin her about. He set her down and dropped his face to hers, kissing her. She returned the gesture with enthusiasm. Sirenī leaned into Alex's arms and looked at Imara when they broke off.

Are you okay, love? she asked.

It will take me eight years to figure this out, Imara replied. *I need to be patient. I hoped things could work differently, but this is our history, even though we're going through it for the first time.*

Think of it this way: you'll practice syncretizing the forces for four days, and then we get to take six days off together. For the next eight years. Without worlds ending, government decrees, or undead assholes trying to murder us. It's more time together than we've spent since we met. I'm looking forward to that more than anything! Sirenī exclaimed.

Imara grinned and walked over to them. Alex moved his arms and shifted to include her in their embrace. *You're correct. I need to look at it that way and not worry so much about mastering the mystical forces.*

Sirenī chuckled against Alex's chest; he shifted to look down at her. "I'm talking with my woman," Sirenī told him tartly.

He rolled his eyes and then kissed the top of her head.

You're incredibly competitive, Imara. You need to relax. Even if you work as hard as possible, you know exactly how long this will take. Sirenī's mental voice was gentle. *You can't rush this, and pushing yourself won't accomplish anything.*

Hmm, you're correct, Imara replied. She kissed Alex but continued to communicate with Sirenī. *I'll have to try to temper my impatience. I'll figure it out when I figure it out, and not a moment sooner.*

Afterword

I hope you enjoyed *The Vergence of Time,* Book Three of The Ring of Worlds series. If so, consider leaving a review on Amazon, Bookbub, and/or Goodreads.

You may also join my mailing list to receive short stories and information about my upcoming novels. Join here: csharrisbooks.com

Keep scrolling to read a sample of the next book in The Ring of Worlds series.

— Chris Harris

The Consiliency of Lines Sample

The Consiliency of Lines Sample

ONE — Unus

Imara picked her head up and dropped her pen in the crease of her journal. She heard footsteps approaching the door on the walkway outside the house, then a heavy knock. Her mother, Theresa Inanna, opened the door and greeted the visitor.

A male voice answered.

Imara perked up at her desk and cocked her head. With her magical abilities, she heard them talking as clearly as if she stood beside them.

"Hello. Can I help you?" her mother asked.

"Greetings. Indeed you can, Mistress Inanna."

The man's voice was smooth. Imara's curiosity surged at the sound.

"I am here to speak with your daughter, Miss Imara."

"About what?"

Theresa's voice hardened. Imara pictured the scene with her mother's lips thinning into a firm line as she leaned back from the stranger.

"And just who might you be, sir?"

"My name is Alexander Eldred."

Alexander Eldred! Here to see me?

The Eldreds were the strongest magicians on Gaea. The family's scion was well-known, but he didn't socialize much. She'd read about him in the gossip mags, but he didn't sit down for interviews. Everything she'd seen was speculation.

Imara shut her journal. She slipped silently to her bedroom door and peeked down the hall. She padded to the head of the stairs and hoped she was out of her mother's sight.

Peering around the banister, she saw her mother standing in the doorway, blocking Alexander. Imara saw him around her mother's petite figure: mature, distinguished, with luminous blue eyes and short, curly dark hair lightly threaded with gray. He had a well-groomed beard that was also speckled with iron. He wore a white button-down shirt, black trousers, and an elegant jacket that hung to his knees. It was old-fashioned but suited him well.

She traced the planes of his cheeks and the shape of his jaw with her gaze, and he flicked those intense eyes from her mother's face toward her. Imara felt something jolt her as their gazes met, and he quirked his lips in the smallest of smiles. Seeing that, Theresa turned and scowled reprovingly.

"Since you're eavesdropping, you may as well come down and greet our visitor," she said crisply. Imara joined her mother. "Mister Eldred, my daughter, Imara," Theresa said by way of introduction. Her tone was still disapproving.

Their visitor nodded his head.

"It's nice to meet you, Mister Eldred," she said.

She was slightly breathless with excitement at meeting the powerful wizard. She cleared her throat and drew in a deep breath to center herself as if she were preparing to burst into song. Once she had herself under control, she continued to speak.

"What brings you here to see me?"

"Why don't we sit down before we continue this conversation?" her mother suggested.

She sounded resigned.

Alexander nodded, and Imara preceded her mother into the living room. Their visitor followed. Imara sat on the couch, and their guest sat in an adjacent chair. She rolled her eyes when her mother disappeared from the room with an admonishing look at the wizard, and he grinned.

Unwilling to sit in complete silence, Imara made small talk with Alexander while her mother made a pot of tea. She brought three cups and a platter of sugar cookies into the living room. She set everything on the coffee table and sat on the couch to Imara's right, conspicuously between her daughter and the magician. She served the fragrant wūlóngchá and cookies before speaking.

"What brings you to our humble home, Mister Eldred?"

The Inanna-Ó Gallchobhair home was posh. It was handmade since it predated the Doctrina Unitatis set forth by the Council of Wizards. Imara's parent's families had been well-to-do before Unification, and their bloodlines produced mid-Grade magicians. That gave their name some cachet in the world.

Imara felt inexplicably drawn to the magician. She assumed it was his celebrity and the raw, primal magic she sensed around him. The vibration of it made her want to be alone with him so she could listen to his master harmony without distractions.

Alexander smiled slightly and looked past her mother to Imara. "I have had a vision of a great crisis." He looked back at Theresa. "In that vision, without Imara's help, the world will be destroyed."

The words hung in the hollow silence that followed them. Imara's mother stared at Alexander and glanced at her daughter before turning back to the magician with a skeptical look.

"I'm really not certain why you came to me with this, Mister Eldred. There's no way I'm allowing Imara to go anywhere with you. Why, you must be a century old, at least!" she scoffed. "I'll see you out."

She gestured toward the door. Alexander ignored Theresa and turned to Imara. "I did not come to you with this, Miss Inanna, nor did I come to your husband, Ciarán Ó Gallchobhair. I came to Imara with this information. While I understand your position, I will not risk the world because of your parental instincts."

His words hung in the air. He'd spoken calmly and without any attitude, but his words were still shocking. Imara felt her eyes widen and she looked at her mother, wondering how she'd handle this. Theresa stared at Alexander, and then she spluttered, appalled and offended.

"My daughter is entirely unsuited to going on an adventure with anyone, never mind someone we don't know!" she ground out. "Get out of my house immediately!"

Theresa pointed to the front door. She looked from Alexander to Imara and back. Imara withered beneath her mother's enraged gaze. She stood as their visitor rose to his feet and nodded. He held Imara's gaze for a moment before he turned and walked past her mother without a glance.

Theresa followed the magician to the door and slammed it behind him. She whirled to face her daughter. "Don't go getting any ideas after this little episode!" she announced as if Imara ran off regularly. "You will not go anywhere with that man. A vision of the world's destruction, and he needs your help to stop it. Preposterous!"

Imara felt her face heat with embarrassment and ran upstairs to her room.

What if my power could save the world?

She threw herself onto her bed, mortified by her mother's actions. After a couple of minutes, though, her pragmatism reasserted itself. Alexander Eldred did have it coming, at least a little bit. On the other hand, Theresa didn't have to be so dismissive of Imara's abilities, either.

The air in the room shifted. Imara pressed her lips together and pulled herself upright. She moved to the edge of her bed, smoothed her dress, and waited. A moment later, her door swung shut with a whisper of sound. Imara cocked her right ear toward the corner and smiled.

"Mister Eldred."

She spoke softly so her mother wouldn't hear.

The sorcerer leaned against her bedroom wall with his arms crossed over his chest. He smiled when she looked at him. He snapped his fingers, and a shroud of silence blanketed the room, sealing them within its magical field effects. She recognized the Kalypto Hesykhia even though she couldn't cast it.

He came to her bed and sat on the edge near her. "I know your mother is only saying and doing what she thinks is best for you, but I saw a world in ruins without you at my side." His words were soft but filled with absolute conviction. "And this will not happen in ten years, or fifty, or a hundred. It happens soon. We do not have much time."

She held up a hand. "Let me listen to you. Then I will know whether you are telling me the truth." She smiled. "No one can lie to me, Mister Eldred."

He nodded without hesitation. She closed her eyes. Everything became louder: the beat of her heart, the flow of blood through her veins, and the air moving through her ear canals and nostrils as she breathed.

Imara heard a harmony right away and listened to it for a moment. Then she turned her magical hearing away from her master note and listened to his. First, she heard the steady thump of his heart and the crackling sounds of his joints as he shifted. She felt him study her as she listened to him.

She continued to breathe. She listened to blood pump through his veins, heard the peristaltic contractions of his gut, and the shift of his scrotum as he moved his thighs. She caught the subtle change in his blood pressure and synovial fluid as he tensed and relaxed his hands. She inched slightly closer and listened past his body to the music of his aura and magic.

Her lips parted as she heard a song unlike that of anyone she'd ever listened to before. Imara felt her memories stutter like a reel of film hitting a snag, jolting her out of the memory. Before she could do more than acknowledge the disruption, everything settled, and she was back in the memory.

Alexander's unusual master harmonic faded into the background and images flickered in her mind: worlds, kingdoms, cities, and stars rose and fell before her. A city flew through space, covered by a translucent barrier. Plasma discharges burned through a nebula, igniting fires bigger than worlds inside clouds larger than a thousand suns. A black oval towered over a battlefield beneath a wheel of fire raining destruction on the ground.

He is Alex. That's what I call him, what I've always called him, she marveled. *I've known him for so long. How?*

There was no answer to that question, so Imara opened her eyes. He studied her with blue eyes so bright they almost seemed to glow. She drummed the fingers of her right hand on her thigh and shook her head, wrestling with herself.

"What you ask is no small thing," she said at last.

"On the contrary, I know just how great a thing it is," he countered. "I sense you know it, too."

She rolled her eyes as she thought of what she had to tell her parents. "I will help you, but I will not run away from home. Give me three days."

Alex nodded. A relieved smile crossed his handsome face. "I will return in three days at this same time." She looked at the clock to confirm before nodding. "Thank you, Imara Inanna."

She smiled a little mischievously and nodded. "You are welcome, Alex."

He chuckled and swept his hands out, then clapped them together, teleporting out of her bedroom as the air whooshed inward to fill the vacuum his departure created. The Kalypto Hesykhia dissolved.

Imara sat for a moment, feeling like she'd just woken from a dream.

Did that really happen?

Her mother knocked on the door and startled her. Theresa didn't wait more than a second before she leaned into Imara's room. After a quick survey, she stepped inside.

"Did you say something, dear?" Theresa sat on the bed in the spot he'd occupied. Imara shook her head. "You know, I didn't say what I did to Mister Eldred out of doubt about your capabilities. I realized what I said and how mean it sounded, but that wasn't my intent at all."

Imara cocked her head in thought, pragmatic as always. "I don't think I thought that, Mom, but thank you for saying it." Theresa nodded and looked relieved. "But at the same time, do you think someone like him would come to our house with this story and not be serious?"

Theresa hesitated. "I believe that someone as powerful as those in the Eldred lineage would believe completely in what they say. I also know that visions are uncertain, so who knows what it really means? Besides, I'm not allowing you to go off with a man decades older than you—you're a beautiful young woman, Imara dear, but you're too young for a man as old as he." Imara's mother searched her face. "You know he's old, right, despite his youthful looks?"

Imara nodded thoughtfully but was already plotting how to win this argument. She'd never used her vocal powers for selfish reasons. She believed that manipulating others with magic was improper. In this instance, though, she had such a deep, heartfelt connection with Alex that she would if she needed to.

If I do use my power on them, will I feel bad about it someday? she wondered.

She sat with her mom, and they chatted about other things. It took her a while to realize she wouldn't feel bad—especially if she saved the world.

Alex Eldred returned to Imara's house at precisely the appointed time three days later. He knocked once on the front door. Imara answered. She stood at the bottom of the stairs with a small suitcase by her side. She wore blue jeans, a loose-cut blouse in grays and browns, sensible boots, and had her hair in a ponytail.

Imara smiled at him and saw his eyes light up. He opened his mouth to speak, and it was years later. They were having sex. His lips were pressed to hers as he moved on top of her. She twined her legs around his waist and broke off the kiss, pushing against his chest to make him lift his weight. He looked down at her as he stopped thrusting.

"Are you uncomfortable?"

She watched him search her face. He was well endowed and had to be careful when they fooled around, but that wasn't her problem. She shook her head and thought back to the first few times they'd made love. It was all so awkward: the initial penetration, the breaking of Ävidä knew of blended families with a human father and a ghūl mother. For some reason, ghūl males were sterile; even though they could fuck, they could not produce progeny because semenarkhe never occurred for them. Menarkhe did occur in the females and, as such, ghūl women could get pregnant and carry a human hybrid to term.

Such children were humanistic until puberty and then became full-fledged ghūl within weeks of the onset of adolescence. No one knew how the rotters got their start, but it was certainly easy enough for them to procreate. Unlike the other Undying, there was no risk of true death in the process of turning; it just happened with ghūl.

Ghūl were lucky, in some ways, that they turned once menarkhe or semenarkhe occurred and only aged into their mid twenties or early thirties past that. They had eternal life and eternal youth, as it happened, but they subsisted mainly on week old corpses. Fresh foods and non-human meats were simply not nourishing enough to sustain them.

If they starved they began to go crazy with hunger, just like vampires, and would kill indiscriminately until they had fed enough to make up whatever deficit they accrued. Go long enough without food and ghūl could wither and die; it took some time to get to that point, but once the line was crossed, the deleterious effects escalated rapidly.her hymen, the irritation and bleeding.

Sex had become more fun, but it was taking its sweet time.

"I'm fine. I love you so much it scares me," she told him, taking a shuddering breath. "I feel like I have for centuries!"

He smiled, shifted his weight to one arm, and caressed her face. "I have loved you since I was younger than you."

His voice was husky with emotion.

No matter how Imara pressed him, he wouldn't elaborate. She pushed his cryptic words out of her mind and hooked her ankles together to pull him closer, taking him deeper. He groaned in the unbearable pleasure of the movement and trembled. She loved having power over him this way. He was the mightiest sorcerer in the world and quivered helplessly at her command.

She tugged his face down for a kiss. "I never want this to stop," she breathed through the contact.

"I would make that possible if I could," he panted as he quickened.

Imara arched her back beneath him, surging to an upright position and shielding her eyes. She was caught amid a catastrophe as flames thundered and roared in a blazing wheel overhead. The burning ring had eight spokes. It was five thousand feet across and blanketed the battleground in a rain of devastation.

The Trochos tou Hephaistos was one of Alex's two signature spells. The fiery construct shed a rain of thick, viscous flame across the warzone below, where enemy combatants drew the plummeting fireballs like magnets. They ignited into shrieking, incandescent columns that winked out in seconds. Hot winds scoured the ground from the conflict of battle magic, and greasy ash and grit blew everywhere.

"I know this place..." Imara breathed.

Lightning and thunder clashed in a maelstrom around the wheel of flame as magical forces twisted, whipped, and writhed. Daggers of energy lanced down to snipe people on the battlefield. The bolts struck them dead or crashed into personal shields and exploded harmlessly in showers of sparks. Radiating aurorae flushed and strobed over the battlefield as the combatants' spectral defenses flickered and flared.

The conflicting magical tides produced plasma arcs, carving deep furrows in the ground. The bolts threw chunks of molten earth and rock skyward in plumes. The discharges also cut through anyone unfortunate enough to be in their way.

Small groups of rebellious Tèng sorcerers fought against the loyalists. Hundreds of feet away, fuchsia and cerulean pyxides powered the Abyssal Gate and began to glow brighter. The master pyxis flared, the blood-red jewel at its heart throbbing with energy as the loyalists tried to provide the prāṇa gradient necessary to fully activate the superancient gateway.

Inside the frame of slippery-looking black metal, smoke swirled and fluttered. A hungry and malicious eye fumed a fiery red while it peered avariciously out of the partially-formed gateway at the material realm.

Those magicians loyal to the Emperor continued to chant. They remained singularly focused on their task even though it would destroy Gaea. On the other side of the inchoate portal, Sogma waited impatiently for the magicians around the gate to complete the spells that would bridge the Abyss and Gaea.

It would form a permanent nexus between the astral planes and the material realm. If the Tèng Empire succeeded, an infernal denizen would be able to manifest its fullest power in a physical way. Gaea would be the first of many worlds the demon king would drag into chaos.

Imara scrubbed her hand across her burned and stinging face. She waved a hand to sweep her snarled hair into what Sirenī called her "Battle Bun." The chaos of the magical energies surrounding the conflict kept knocking her hair free, and the stray wisps were like an incessant buzz or a bug that wouldn't leave her alone.

Sirenī stood to her left and sustained the most powerful impermeable field anyone alive had ever seen. The daughter of Medusa had created a flat cross-section at the bottom of the englobement, and the Three stood on it. She'd levitated the bubble twenty feet above the ground so they could see the battlefield in all directions. It required all her concentration to maintain the field, so Sirenī couldn't use her magic in the main battle.

Alex stood to Imara's right. He held his hands out while he chanted in Darhavil. He was casting one of the most powerful spells from the Pāskendińoldor. It came in two parts: one to summon the magic, the other to direct it. It was the kind of magic that could save or destroy worlds. Only Alex, Imara, or Sirenī were strong enough to cast the enchantment without linking aurae to augment their strength.

Imara's throat stung from the caustic brume over the battlefield. She smelled burned human flesh, sulfur and brimstone, blood and feces, and the stench of pain, fear, and despair. She cleared her throat and spat to try and clean the taste from her mouth. When that didn't work, she diverted a trickle of her power to calm her throat and lungs.

Three thousand Empire sorcerers were arrayed against a few hundred combatants from around the world. Imara, Sirenī, and Alex spearheaded the resistance, accompanied by rebellious members of the Empire who rejected the Emperor's alliance with Sogma. Almost two thousand Empire sorcerers were trying to empower the Abyssal Gate. Whatever its creators had used to turn it on had not been found when the Empire discovered the artifact.

All over Gaea, others supported the Three and the Tèng rebels. Sorcerers across Albion, Āryāvarta, Demurria, Glacialis, Ifriqiye, and Kaná:ta helped however they could. Those nearby bombarded the shield protecting the ancient artifact and cast spells to strengthen the Grid. The battle was worldwide, but the focal point lay with the Three. They'd fought for months to reach this point, to stand before the Gate and destroy it.

Imara smiled grimly. The day she'd met Alex, she'd been writing in her journal and wishing she could do something meaningful with her life.

Look at me now!

She and her companions were exhausted. Before they reached the battlefield, they'd recuperated on Earth for several weeks with a woman named Maria McInerney, but it wasn't enough: they'd faced an arduous struggle to get to the battle site, and they still had to overcome the enemy forces and destroy the Abyssal Gate so no one could use it again.

Sogma glared at the scene before the portal while Imara stared across the three hundred feet between herself and the Abyssal Gate. Alex's corona flared to her right in a crackling gleam of orange-red light; Sirenī's glowed an intense azure. Imara drew deeper on her magic, and her rainbow-hued aura flared brightly. She listened to the agonized symphony of the battle and prepared to project her voice.

She cleared her mind as best she could in the chaos and focused on her innate power. She shifted from humming to singing; she began to sway with the harmony. Her voice rose and rang across the battlefield in a wordless spellsong. The sound cut through the thunder and lightning, the screams, and the wheel of fire's endless roar.

Imara opened her psychic sight, and the world turned into a static-laden landscape of pulsating waves. The patterns of reality lay bare before her, revealing how prāṇa appeared to become matter thanks to the influence of the guṇa. Her song's electromagnetic waveform flowed across everything.

She saw massive currents of power swirl as they were snatched up and twisted by the will and the chanting of the sorcerers all around them. Behind her, the Trochos tou Hephaistos glowed blisteringly bright, while before her, the Abyssal Gate's magical fields crackled and surged in orange and charcoal chaos.

Imara looked left and right, glancing at the blazing pillars of light that were her lovers. They glowed with so much power that the prāṇa bled into the astral planes. Field lines radiated in arcs from their bodies, shimmering as their magic flowed.

Sirenī fanned her magic into the protective sphere englobing the Three. Alex just continued to grow brighter as he gathered more power in his aura. The arcane geometries and symbology of the superancient spell from the Dawntime blurred the air with a haze of awakening energies.

She turned to the Abyssal Gate and looked at Sogma. The crimson eyes of the demon lord glared back at her, and Imara shook her head. No matter what happened, even if she died in the effort, she would stop Sogma from coming into Gaea.

It was the deepest, most unremitting desire of many of the formless creatures born in the astral realms to acquire a physical form. They took them by possession of the living, by the occupation of dead bodies, and by making deals with mortals.

Demons couldn't manifest a physical presence in the material realms for long, so the wizard who summoned them needed to provide a body of some sort. These usually looked human but were just blank canvases with generic features and sexless figures, but demons wanted it all: a tongue to taste food and wine, a heart that could pound with excitement, sex organs to provide pleasure, and everything else a body offers.

They couldn't have this on their own because they were born in a realm where bodies were mental constructs, swift and mercurial. While the mind could endure in the astral planes, the flesh could not. Sogma wanted to change that; his legions would follow once he entered the world and took physical form.

Imara and her companions knew eudaemons from the Abyss: Lägrimä and his mate, Mélisandre. They'd helped the Three on Earth and warned them of Sogma's plans. He wouldn't stop with Gaea but would use the Infernal Gate system of the Nephilim to cross to the thousands of planets in the Ring of Worlds.

Imara was more determined than ever to stop the demon lord of the Abyss.

TWO — Duo

"She can't die, right?"

The anxious words tumbled through Imara's mind, mixing with the memories of battle and destruction.

"I do not believe so. The amṛta should prevent any lasting harm," someone replied. "However, Skawen'na'há:wi's words to me feel as appropriate this time as they were then."

There was a pause. Imara groaned. She was distantly aware that she'd fallen down and was writhing in pain and confusion. Part of her realized she was disoriented, but she felt that awareness like a dream. The second voice pushed itself into Imara's confused existence. His words coaxed her gently.

"If you do not embrace the power of your heart now, you will die, my love."

Imara wrenched her gaze from the Abyssal Gate and glanced over her right shoulder. A hole in her memories formed like an oculus, and two figures peered through the void. Their images were distorted but deeply familiar. Imara shuddered and fell toward the inflection point. The battlefield shattered like a sheet of glass, and the shards cut into her. Pain blossomed throughout her being.

Imara sat up with a gasp as the dream of their battle against Sogma faded.

Sirenī knelt beside her. Surprised, she swayed back at Imara's abrupt movement. Alex squatted near her shoulder and fell on his ass when Imara lurched upright. The songstress would have found his graceless sprawl and surprised expression comical at any other time, but she was in too much pain.

Her entire body pulsed with waves of agony that rolled from her head to her fingers and toes. She trembled and labored for breath while her hands shook atop her thighs. She tried to shake the pain off, but the discomfort continued.

Imara's heart pounded with adrenaline. *What happened to me?*

She couldn't recall how she ended up in the grass, but the images of Sogma and their final battle were ultravivid. Imara used the breathing techniques she'd practiced for decades as a singer and got her heart rate down. The pain began to recede as she calmed her nervous system.

She felt better after a few minutes of focus, but something was different. She couldn't put her finger on it, but the more she thought about it, the more obvious it became. She pursed her lips and looked at her companions.

"What happened?" she asked. Her lyrical voice sounded rough. She swallowed and spoke again, "Why am I on the ground?"

Sirenī pushed herself up from her knees and held out a hand. Imara took it, and her lover helped her stand. Alex got to his feet beside them. Even though they'd all been in the grass, none had any dirt or stray blades on their clothes.

"You did it, Imara." Sirenī's face shone with a subtle light in her joy. "You syncretized the mystical and magical forces."

The songstress looked at Alex. He nodded. "You have succeeded, my love."

She stared at them. What they said made no sense…until the memories rushed back. She recalled the agony when her nāḍī tore open, and the mystical power began to flow alongside her magical energies.

The subtle channels of the aura conducted magical power in sorcerers and the power of the heart in those who practiced mysticism. They'd all believed that no one used both simultaneously until Alex successfully harnessed them. He'd needed the help of the world's strongest mystic, Skawen'na'há:wi of the Kanien'kehá:ka, who had trained him for two weeks a year for more than four decades. Imara mastered the process much faster than he did. The training had been grueling, but eight years was better than forty.

The songstress stared at her partners. "I dreamt of the battle." She didn't need to say which one as her partners stiffened in reaction. "We were there when Sogma came through."

Alex reached out, taking her right hand with his left. He took Sirenī's with his other while the women joined hands. They shifted, coming into their customary stance. The position formed a delta, or triangle, with each person standing at a vertex where two sides joined.

"Tell us about it," he urged Imara. "We have not talked about the battle since our reunion."

She, Sirenī, and Alex had been separated for forty-eight years. A vision prompted Alex to defy the government decree that kept them apart. They'd reunited almost nine years ago, fleeing their homeworld of Gaea to seek sanctuary on its sister planet, Earth. They'd only been there briefly when they realized there wasn't enough time for Imara to fuse the magical and mystical forces. Imara cast a spell to take the three of them back in time, and they'd spent the last eight years on Omejis while she mastered the skill.

They planned to return to Earth just a few weeks after leaving. So far, everything had worked out as planned.

Imara took a deep breath, gathering herself. "I'll do better than talk about it."

Sirenī nodded as the songstress opened her mind. Both women could communicate telepathically; it had come naturally to them early in their relationship. Alex could use telepathy but wasn't as facile with the skill and had to work hard to use it. He opened to Imara, completely trusting, and she gathered her beloved partners in a tender, mental embrace and shared her memories with them.

Imara focused her attack on the sorcerers around the Abyssal Gate. They'd linked aurae to form a continuous, powerful flow of magic. They poured it into the pyxides that controlled the power-hungry artifact, and Imara knew they must be exhausted. Their power wasn't limitless, even linked as they were.

The storms of magic created a foul pall over the region. The conflicting field effects leached the color from the world so that the

Trochos tou Hephaistos, lightning, and multicolored magical fields began to lose their vibrancy.

Sogma's crimson eyes looked out of the portal and focused on the Three. Imara knew the demon lord recognized them. Their magical aurae were the most powerful on the field, marking them as the greatest threat. Sogma focused his first attack on them, and Abyssal flames surged out of the aperture. They streamed in black, vaporous jets over Sirenī's impermeable field.

The Abyssal flames tapered off, and Sogma let out a howl when he saw they were unharmed. Imara sang the notes for combat lightning. Flickering, many colored bolts leaped across the gap and plunged into the portal. Electricity flashed along the glistening black frame of the Abyssal Gate and grounded out.

Imara hadn't expected the thunderbolts to do much—it merely revealed that the gate would absorb lower-level spells into its power-hungry interstices. She turned her attention to the loyalists trying to power the device. She listened to the harmonics of their magic and began to nod in time to the rhythm.

She hung a melody in the air and let it vibrate. She adjusted the frequency until she created a standing wave. She gathered her power and made it stronger. The air warped and shimmered as the energy built, and then she sang a single word to unleash her power.

A pulse of energy radiated out and slammed into the loyalists. It broke the flow of magic they channeled, and strobing purple field effects blazed brightly. Imara held up a hand to shield her eyes as the two forces clashed, the horizon where they met burning with blistering brilliance. Her standing wave collapsed the enemy's enchantment.

Energy burst outward in a shimmering fuchsia explosion and rocketed across the battlefield. Rebels and loyalists staggered as the power swept over them. People fell over, unconscious. Dozens of the Empire loyalists around the gate burst into brief-lived pillars of violet flames. Those who survived screamed as spellburns crawled over their bodies in angry red swatches. Their flesh puckered and peeled as the miscast magic grounded itself through their bodies.

Sirenī's impermeable field kept them safe from the blast while Alex continued to chant in Darhavil. Imara gathered herself and focused on

Sogma. He lurked on the other side of the portal, glaring as he waited to come through. She readied another spellsong as Sogma let out an unearthly roar.

The sound blasted from the Abyssal Gate and dragged on. The entity didn't have vocal cords or lungs, so he wasn't bound by physics and breath. Once he took a material form, he'd suffer from its limitations. She realized she couldn't fathom the body he'd create, so maybe he could scream like that even with organic pipes.

Sogma thrust a long, undulous tentacle through the gate. The loyalists had succeeded in creating a stable bridge. The appendage stretched toward their impermeable sphere, and black lightning frothed from the tip. Imara flinched as it spattered the shield with a crackle like a million angry bees. It rippled and scratched at the barrier, making it flicker and flash.

Imara turned to Sirenī when she heard a grunt. Her companion's beautiful face became wrathful, and her eyes flashed red as the attack continued.

Oh shit, not now.

Imara held her breath, dreading Medusa's appearance, but Sirenī got herself under control. The songstress let out a ragged sigh.

"You know what, Sogma?" Sirenī hollered. She used a flicker of power to amplify her voice. "Shove that tentacle up your fat, formless ass!"

With that, she thrust out a hand and focused her prodigious psychokinetic skill. Imara saw the electricity cut off like someone had thrown a switch. The tentacle accordioned and compressed on itself. It exploded and showered the Abyssal Gate in a pulped mist of flesh, gore, and gray blood.

Sogma shrieked and pulled back from the portal, giving them a moment's respite.

"Yeah, how's that feel, motherfucker?" Sirenī yelled.

Imara laughed and spun to face her companion, who grinned back. "You showed him."

"Yes, I did!" Sirenī agreed. Then she grimaced from the strain. "Now, it's up to you two. Close that gate so we can get out of here."

Imara nodded. "Right."

She faced the portal as Alex finished chanting in Darhavil. He clapped twice to manifest the magic. Imara looked at him, her ears ringing as he unleashed the enchantment he'd put so much effort into casting.

The arcane geometries around Alex expanded in a scintillating pulsation. The spellforms coalesced into a complex interlocked pattern of lines and sigils. The parts rotated into alignment, and a tremendous pulse of power flared into the visible spectrum as an ultramarine wave. It swelled across the battlefield with bone-jarring force.

Every spell fizzled out as the field effects flowed past. The ancient spell absorbed the lesser enchantments as it expanded and moved beyond the area. The Dawntime magic gathered power as it traveled, growing stronger the further it moved from its source.

Even though Alex had successfully cast the devouring spell from the Pāskendiñoldor, the battle wasn't over because the portal was stable. Sogma began to come through, heaving his energetic bulk into the material world. Imara saw he was still made of formless smoke and dark, glittering light, but he'd be embodied soon enough. The demon lord of the Abyss roared in ecstasy as his mass began to flow out of the aperture in reality.

Imara heard a groan and spun. Alex had fallen to his knees. His skin was gray with exhaustion, with deep, bruised circles around his eyes. Low-level spellburns flared across his skin, leaving blistered, angry weals on his flesh. He toppled sideways, spent. Blood began to ooze from every orifice in his body, staining his pants and shirt.

"Alex!"

She knelt at his side. She couldn't defeat Sogma with her magic alone; they had only minutes before he cleared the Abyssal Gate. Once he was on Gaea, he'd be almost unstoppable. Alex looked at her with bleeding eyes, the blue irises wrapped in ruptured blood vessels. Blood bubbled on his lips, giving him a horrifying crimson smile.

Their efforts to reach this point had caught up with them. Alex had expended the most power through their journey and reached his limit. No one else could have recalled and cast the spell he'd used, but he could go no further.

Imara knew what she had to do.

No matter the cost.

She took his shoulders and rolled him onto his back. She smiled at her lover even as Sogma's roars of triumph grew stronger. More of his energetic bulk poured into Gaea, and she couldn't stop it unless she completed the spell.

She knew Alex could die at any moment. He'd used so much power that his master harmonic was barely audible. She flicked a glance to Sirenī. Though her face was etched with strain, she looked radiant. Not the slightest hint of soot rested on her skin, and her clothes remained perfectly draped over her full-figured form like she was out for a walk rather than in the worst battle in thousands of years. Sirenī caught Imara's glance and looked from the songstress to Alex and back. The concern in her eyes was unmistakable.

We have to end this.

"I can't help," Sirenī said.

Her voice was tight, but she did exactly what she needed to by keeping them safe. Imara had already known Sirenī's part in this was keeping her and Alex safe. The songstress wasn't looking for Sirenī's aid; she wanted to look at her lover one last time in case she didn't survive.

It's up to me now.

Imara took a deep breath and hummed the melody of Alex's master harmonic to bolster it. He shuddered and twisted his head to look at her.

"The spell…" he mumbled. He stopped and tried again. "The spell… will return on itself. It must be captured. I can…" He coughed blood, and his head lolled. Imara began to panic, but he rallied. "I can't do it, Imara. I'm too weak. I'm sorry."

She heard the self-recrimination and self-loathing in his voice, but she was more alarmed that he'd used contractions. They sounded so foreign and somehow filthy coming out of his mouth. He always spoke every word, fully and precisely, with perfect diction and elocution, as his mentor Galen had taught him.

"Tell me the words, my love," she commanded.

He stared at her as the magic he'd summoned traveled around the world and grew stronger with every second. He nodded weakly. She leaned close, and he breathed the phrase to conclude the enchantment.

"If you don't catch the wave, it could destroy the world…" he whispered.

His face went slack. Imara's heart thudded painfully, but she couldn't take the time to see if he was still alive. She stood, ignored the tears that ran down her cheeks, and stepped to the front of the platform.

Sogma was a tremendous hulk of tentacles and appendages, some ending with twisted, hideous heads, others with claws, and still others with vile, obscene growths that slurped, sucked, or oozed foul liquids. Imara shuddered in revulsion as the mist continued to pour from the portal and congealed into the mass before the gate.

Ultramarine light glowed at the edge of Imara's perception. She thrust out her hands and waited while the Dawntime spell returned to its point of origin. As it traveled, it pulled magic from the planet, taking energy from the Tanager Grid and the countless spells and enchantments used worldwide. It was a leviathan that devoured everything before it.

Imara's rainbow-hued corona flared brightly as she shouted the phrase that would give her command of the power of the Dawntime. The light swelled from the ground to the sky in all directions. She drowned in ultramarine glory as it crashed down upon the impermeable sphere.

From within the blaze, Imara heard Sogma scream in rage. She pictured him trying to force himself out of the astral realms and into Gaea, but it was too late. Pain such as she'd never known seared her body and mind. The power was too much for a human body. The Nephilim designed it, but they were gone. There was only her.

Imara screamed and flung her head back. Beams of light blazed from her eyes and scorched through the atmosphere. The power emitted a deep, bellicose gale of sound. She gritted her teeth, clamped down on her scream, and forced her head down to turn the magic upon the demon lord and, beyond him, the Abyssal Gate.

The beam destroyed his inchoate form in a flash of incandescent destruction. Then it slammed into the portal. The Abyssal Gate absorbed the power, but it poured in too fast. Black lightning flashed and crackled around the wrought metal of the superancient artifact. The frame began to glow, the black metal reddening as the power built. Hot, molten runnels of metal ran down the oval frame, and the whole thing started to buckle and twist on itself.

Imara shuddered as the magic poured out of her for several more seconds before it dwindled. The pain receded, and she fell to her knees. Her agony faded into a dull, whole-body ache. She toppled to the floor a moment later, like her strings had been cut. She sprawled bonelessly beside Alex, her head by his feet, and darkness subsumed her.

"That's all I remember until we woke up in the triage tents after the battle," Imara finished.

Sirenī nodded sympathetically as she looked from Imara to Alex. He looked dyspeptic. Sirenī knew he was upset at seeing his weakness from Imara's perspective. Decades after the fact, he still chafed at collapsing at the end of the battle despite doing things no one else on Gaea could have matched.

Except for Imara, Sirenī thought.

Once again, she was amazed at Imara's abilities as Sirenī relived her past through Imara's mental gifting. She hadn't realized she'd sent that thought to Imara, but linked as they all were, she wasn't surprised.

It wasn't just me. It was all of us. We each had our roles to play, Imara sent back in their particular way. Aloud, she added, "Now, it's your turn. Show us what happened at the end."

Sirenī nodded and took a deep breath, gathering her memories to share.

Sirenī hurriedly lowered her impermeable sphere to the ground. She ignored the collapsing artifact and knelt by her partners. Imara was unconscious but breathing evenly. Alex, however, looked dead, but he was holding on.

There's no time to waste.

Sirenī pressed her hands to Alex's chest. A vivid azure glow flared around her as she summoned her magic and chanted a Level Four healing spell. The enchantment began to work immediately, but it took twelve minutes to recite fully.

As she cast, Sirenī sensed something happening with the Abyssal Gate. She half turned, and her eyes widened in horror as the pyxides ringing the artifact began to flash purple. The effect dazzled her eyes, and she knew the enchanted devices would explode. They'd absorbed too much power, and now no one was managing the flow.

"Fuck!" Sirenī hollered. She tapered off the healing spell to prevent a miscasting and stood. "I'm so done with this shit."

She was the only person standing on the battlefield. Everyone else was down, dead or unconscious.

She realized Alex had cast the spell to destroy the gate. Imara completed it. Now, Sirenī needed to save them all.

Three sorcerers. Three problems to solve. We each had a role to play, she thought tiredly.

Sirenī thrust out her hands and screamed her defiance. The melted ruin of the Abyssal Gate glowed brighter, the purple flicker of unconstrained magic slithering across the wrecked structure. Her face contorted with strain while her hair whipped about her head in serpentine coils. She seemed to grow taller as she erected an impermeable field around the apparatus.

She unleashed a roar of effort that bordered on inhuman. She held the shield for seventeen minutes until the last flickering glow faded.

Then she passed out, too.

They stood in silence as Sirenī's gifting faded.

Imara shook her head and blinked away the painful memories. They no longer had the sting they once held, but that battle was the worst in living memory for the people of Gaea. The Tèng Empire had never recovered from the fiasco. She knew the country would need to open its borders and accept the Grid soon, or it would collapse from within. A high-ranking ambassador for the Unified Government, Thalatte, had worked tirelessly for the last three decades to facilitate the transition.

Alex let go of her hand to reach up and cup her cheek. She leaned into the caress. "You did it, my love. Now, all three of us have syncretized the two forces."

The songstress nodded. She'd tried to unify them every month for the last eight years. Her intrinsic magic was connected to her supera-cute hearing and musical sensitivity. She'd never needed to feel for her power because she heard it. The mystical power of the heart eluded her because it didn't ring with a detectable sound, and she was so set in her ways that learning to feel it had felt like an impossible task.

Over the last two months, things had changed. Alex's constant exhortations and the countless ways he and Sirenī tried to explain the process to her crystallized. She'd felt the pieces fall into place that morning when a subtle vibration tingled behind her eyes. She let it move independently and refused to give in to her desire to control it like she would her magic.

When the sensation reached her heart, it happened. She felt a thrum that was unique and unfamiliar in every way. She carefully reached out to it without moving a muscle or letting her thoughts drift. The sensation became a river that swept her away as the mystical force ripped her nāḍī apart.

Imara grinned at her partners. She leaned in and kissed Sirenī, then Alex, unable to keep the pleasure from her face. Their happiness banished the terrible memories of the battle at the Abyssal Gate, pushing the trauma back into the box where it belonged.

They stood outside the Temple on Omejis. The golden shimmer of the ancient shield protecting the structure filtered the sunlight, lending a warm, lemony glow to the air. After they kissed, Imara looked at Sirenī out of the corner of her eye.

Even though I knew it would take eight years, I felt it would never happen! I didn't know what the key was to the process or how I discovered the method of it all, she confessed.

Sirenī sent a sympathetic vibe along their telepathic connection. *I've been keeping track: today is eight years to the day since we traveled backward in time. We've already arrived on Omejis through the Gatehouse. We'll be here soon.*

We need to get out of here, then. Imara kept her concern from her face and turned to Alex. "Sirenī just mentioned that today is when we arrived through the Gatehouse in Rilladwen. We should leave."

Alex nodded. "I thought our arrival was imminent. I did not keep track of the time well enough to know it was today."

The Three needed to leave the Temple before their past selves arrived to travel back in time and live through the preceding eight years. They hadn't run into themselves in their history, so she knew Future Them wasn't at the Temple when Past Them arrived.

As they moved to leave, Alex laughed in delighted relief. Imara knew it was because she'd finally succeeded at syncretizing the two forces. He let her tug him and Sirenī along, amused by her impatience.

The Three crossed through the shield for what Imara hoped was nearly the last time. They walked toward the edge of the caldera where the Nephilim Temple rested and joined the ever-patient Sulwyn at the shuttle. The fair-colored and cheerful young man had grown in the eight years they'd known him.

He had two kids, and his sister Aeronwen had one. They were lovely little things, and being around the babies had repeatedly reminded Imara and Sirenī that their pregnancies seemed to be on pause. They hadn't progressed past the first trimester. Imara didn't know why things had stalled out, but the babies sounded fine when she listened to their harmonics.

The children seemed to hover in a sleepy twilight, quiescent but healthy. Neither Imara nor Sirenī could imagine what might end their gestational hiatus, but they trusted it would happen. They and Alex assumed the amṛta, the Nephilim's nectar of immortality from the Dawntime, had something to do with the delay.

Imara settled into her seat in the aircar. She held Alex's left hand while Sirenī snuggled against his right side. She shifted and leaned her head against his shoulder, and he kissed the top of it. She felt a dreamy smile cross her face as Sulwyn lifted off, using the almost-silent electromagnetic drive to fly them back to their accommodations in Temple City.

THREE — Tres

Alexander recalled thinking something about the Nephilim Temple on Omejis felt familiar when they arrived. That was eight years ago, of course, but it was also today. The sorcerer smiled and watched the pastel evening light paint Temple City in blues and purples as the sun sank into the ocean.

The sorcerer couldn't pinpoint his initial feelings at Temple Mount after Imara recovered from unifying the two forces. Some kind of vibration tickled his senses, but he realized he was feeling magic only after they left the Nephilim Temple.

His own magic.

He felt the energy of his time-traveling self intersect with his present-day being. The reaction was called sympathetic resonance. While the feeling was interesting, it didn't mean much since they'd gotten away from Temple Mount in time to avoid their past selves, and now that version of the Three was safely in the past. Alexander knew that he, Imara, and Sirenī could return to the Temple to travel back to Earth.

Before doing that, however, they needed to smooth things over in Rilladwen: this was the day they'd arrived on Omejis after rescuing the queen celerity moth, Thīaterīka, from her hopeless situation on Byrne. Amlodd had welcomed them when they exited the Gatehouse and checked them into lodging in Rilladwen, the capital of Omejis.

That same day, they had to rush from the city to stay in alignment with their time-traveling plans. Now, the hotel room was unoccupied after they'd slipped away. Alexander solved the problem with a half-assed solution: he sent an electronic message to Amlodd, the chief of the Gatehouse Transit Authority, to apologize for his, Imara, and Sirenī's abrupt arrival and equally sudden departure.

He didn't offer any real explanation, merely an apology. Alexander couldn't think of any reason that made a lick of sense for why he and his partners would go to Rilladwen from Temple Mount and then leave so abruptly…so he hoped the lingering goodwill Amlodd felt for them would cover any oddness.

After all, we are the mysterious sorcerers from Gaea who fixed the great canals and saved the people of Lauremanda. Perhaps that will be sufficient for Amlodd to simply assume we are eccentric and leave it at that…

Alexander didn't waste any more energy worrying about it and returned his thoughts to the situation at hand: the necromancer threatening multiple planets across the Ring of Worlds. Alexander was certain they'd be capable of tackling the challenge of the corruption spell afflicting the Ring of Worlds now that Imara had unified the two forces. They'd also have to defeat the sorcerer who'd created the corruption, who they knew to be an archlīc of great power.

Imara had gleaned a name for the necromancer eight years ago when they saved the people of Lauremanda City from the eruption of the volcano: *Ävidä*. Alexander was convinced this līc was too powerful to be anything other than the offspring of Adrienne Vorpahl, whom he helped defeat decades before he met his partners.

Another līc might have risen to power, filling the vacuum her death left behind, but it seemed unlikely. His mentor, Galen Ohahakehte, used a Kanien'kehá:ka ritual to restore Adrienne's spirit to the Vincula Mortis, the Chains of Mortality. That act forced her spirit to continue its birth-death cycle. Decades later, Alexander used the same prayer to defeat the two līc that attacked them on Earth, whose names he hadn't learned.

The sorcerer stood on the balcony of his, Imara, and Sirenī's home in Temple City on Omejis. He took a deep breath of the crisp evening air…smelling salt, water, and the rich flora of the Bitter Islands. He looked from the setting sun to his right toward the volcano's slope on his left.

Alexander felt a hand come to rest on his arm. He turned to smile at Sirenī.

"What are you thinking?" she asked.

He didn't answer but instead took her in his arms. She was seven inches shorter than him in her bare feet as she stood now, so he had to lean down a bit to kiss her. She melted into him quite readily, and his dick stiffened immediately.

Feeling his erection through their clothing, she grinned mischievously. He smiled ruefully—there was no chance they could sneak away for sex right now—and held her close. The slight swell of her belly altered the shape of their embrace.

After a few moments, he pulled back, looking down at her stomach. He touched it tenderly, smiling as he felt the energy of consciousness within. As yet, he could discern nothing of the babes in either woman beyond their presence. Despite being pregnant for eight years, they appeared only a few months along.

He, Imara, and Sirenī had taken amṛta before he got his partners pregnant. It appeared the nectar of immortality had altered their gestation, but at least neither woman had any symptoms. Eight years of morning sickness would have been unbearable.

A few days ago, Imara got out of bed and remarked that if she was only in her first trimester, she wasn't keen on being pregnant for sixteen more years. Sirenī laughed at the comment but sobered quickly when she realized she'd be pregnant just as long.

Sirenī brought his mind back when she slid her hand into his pants. The touch of her soft, powerful fingers on his cock made him grunt like an animal in desire. She deftly shifted his stiff pole to the side so his hard-on was less evident in his slacks.

"This is a time when underwear would be helpful," she remarked.

The sorcerer scoffed. "I am not ashamed of my manhood," he told her. "I see no need to constrain myself like Earthen men."

She grinned and winked at him. He realized she'd expected just that response and smiled ruefully. She glanced critically at his trousers and shrugged. "Imara and I will happily address that later, but for now…"

She gestured gracefully to the interior of the house. He nodded, adjusted his equipment to make it more comfortable and discreet, and returned to the group that had gathered to say goodbye.

Alex, Imara, and Sirenī had used their time on Omejis well. They'd traveled to Rilladwen, the world capital on the planet-circling supercontinent, Ednyfed. They'd eaten delicious food, met many wonderful people, and enjoyed their stay on the panthalassic world.

Before Mount Lauremanda erupted and they saved everything alive on the volcanic island, they'd repaired one of the grand canals on Ednyfed. Four such waterways transected the supercontinental landmass and allowed the two oceans of Omejis to mix. When the Three arrived on the planet, one of the canals was damaged from a subsidence in the seafloor. They used their magic to repair that, then created three pyxides that anyone could activate at the other canals to stabilize them against future collapse.

The government of Rilladwen appreciated their actions with the canals, but when Lauremanda blew its top, they rushed to rescue a hundred thousand citizens in Lauremanda City and every animal on the island. They hadn't told the people of Omejis that the volcano only erupted because a kṛtyā bījā, a dark flower of corruption, had bloomed. Imara had encased the flower in magma, hoping the molten rock would kill it.

Their actions at Lauremanda garnered so much approbation from the public that they'd submitted to a public ceremony. They'd flatly refused awards but conceded to stand on a raised stage in a sports arena and wave to ten thousand cheering fans while the spectacle was broadcast worldwide.

Alexander knew he had an enormous ego but felt oddly uncomfortable with the enthusiastic praise. Imara had nudged him and leaned close, projecting her magical voice so he could hear her over the crowd.

"Give them some magic," she urged.

"It's what they came to see," Sirenī reminded him as he balked.

He grunted but acknowledged the sense of his partner's words. With a charming smile, he stepped slightly forward and held up his hands. The crowd swiftly grew silent. He swept his arms through exaggerated gestures he wouldn't be caught dead using to cast an authentic spell, but he wasn't above a bit of theater.

He felt people's anticipation grow as sparkling reddish light flashed around him, slowly swirling out to flicker in lines and patterns around the stage. He began to chant nonsense in Latin, reciting silly rhymes he recalled from childhood.

The sorcerer didn't dare look at Imara or Sirenī; he'd burst out laughing if he did. Instead, he swept his arms toward the sky. Multicolored lightning flashed from his fingertips. Thunder clapped, startling the crowd. Their eyes naturally followed the lightning like metal filings to a lodestone.

The bolts twined and warped in long, arcing streams, bowing and looping back on themselves as shimmering aurorae flickered and flashed. Animals cavorted through the lights: a herd of horses jumped over a fallen log made of auroral flares, transforming into dolphins diving into a rainbow sea. A whale breached the surface, spinning and crashing back with a spray of luminous froth, only to become pegasi that flew through coils of electricity as they soared away.

The magical display lasted a few minutes before the glowing lights dwindled. The crowd sat there, mesmerized, for several seconds longer. Then they were on their feet, cheering and screaming, and the Three bowed, waved, and slipped from the stage.

Alexander smiled nostalgically. Their time on Omejis had been lovely, but it was over.

He focused on Imara, Sirenī, Aeronwen and her husband, her brother Sulwyn and his wife, and the former governor of Lauremanda, Eirianedd. She'd flown to Temple City from Rilladwen this morning for the goodbye celebration. Their friend, Amlodd, couldn't make it, but he did make a video call, joined by Grummore, Rilladwen's governor. Amlodd was the chief of the Gatehouse Transit Authority and the first person they'd met on Omejis.

The eternally jovial man remarked that he was happy to have run into them so recently when they visited Rilladwen. He made no mention of Alexander's apology, and the Three laughed and thanked him for his kindness to them through all these years.

Amlodd waved it away. He grinned, said he hoped he would see them again, and wished their further travels were as fruitful as their time on Omejis. When the gathering broke up far past midnight and all too close to dawn, he, Imara, and Sirenī celebrated in their own way.

*****

It was midday when they wrapped up their affairs.

Eirianedd reiterated that the home they'd been using was theirs.

Over the years, they'd received many gifts that they couldn't take with them, so Alexander cast a preservation spell over the entire building and its immediate surroundings. The sorcerer didn't know the future but hoped to return someday. The planet was beautiful, and he wondered what Carter would think of Omejis.

He would enjoy himself here.

After taking one final survey of their home, they boarded the shuttle. A crying Aeronwen turned the controls of this last flight over to her brother. Sulwyn barely held it together but successfully flew them to the superancient shield in the caldera of Temple Mount.

The group had flown to the Temple so many times that the siblings could make the run from the house in Temple City to the top of the volcano in their sleep. Never once in eight years were they grumpy with their self-appointed task. In turn, the Three used their magic to ease the siblings' lives, helping with injuries, the births of their children, teething, and sundry other things.

Once they landed outside the shield, everyone stepped from the skimmer. Aeronwen sobbed and hugged each of them. Sirenī cried but looked glorious while she blubbered thanks to her fatal beauty. In contrast, Imara turned blotchy and puffy, and her eyes reddened like she'd taken a fistful of sand and ground it into them. Alexander's eyes welled. Tears ran down his cheeks, but they were quiet and spare. His emotions ran so deep that only his partners ever saw them in their fullness.

After Sulwyn hugged them and tearfully said his goodbyes, the Three walked through the shimmering golden shield and stopped before the Nephilim Temple. They waved to the siblings as the massive circular door rose up the front of the structure, then stepped into the cool, shadowless white interior. The door descended to seal the entrance.

Alexander didn't waste time but strode toward the circular dais toward the rear of the vast chamber. A line of Darhavil script ringed the edge of the low transit platform, and from it, a shimmering curtain of red light sprang toward the ceiling. The gauzy field effects undulated slowly, clearly visible in the Temple's shadowless white interior.

The sorcerer concentrated, and a solid rectangle of red light flickered into view before him at chest height. It was covered in lines of Darhavil script. When Imara and Sirenī summoned photonic displays, everything appeared in Demurrian Latin, their natal tongue. It seemed his proficiency with Darhavil meant the interface he worked with was written out in the ancient Dawntimer's script.

Alexander turned and smiled at his partners. They smiled back and stepped past him onto the dais, passing through the red haze. He joined them and staggered as the Temple shook on its foundations.

Sirenī's eyes widened, and she looked at Imara. "Is this it?" she gasped as she swayed gracefully with the trembling floor.

Imara grabbed onto Sirenī even while she nodded and smiled reassuringly. The songstress turned her gaze to Alexander, her features stern. "You have to trust me. Look in your left pocket—"

"What do you mean?"

"—when you get home. Everything will make as much sense as it can. I'll see you both soon," she finished.

Alexander wanted to demand an explanation for her stark words, but the floor dropped beneath him, and he crashed to his hands and knees. The red haze around the dais shot up to the ceiling as the Infernal Gate activated. He lifted his head as every color of light he could imagine flooded into the space and blotted out his partners. He blinked, momentarily blinded by the brightness.

The light dwindled swiftly, leaving sparkling motes in the air that hummed with a distant, familiar resonance that he couldn't place. Alexander stared, astonished, and looked around the empty Temple.

He was alone on the dais. He hadn't traveled to the Gatehouse on Earth as he was supposed to. Something, whatever that light was, had taken Imara and Sirenī.

Or they traveled as planned, and it took me. This may not be the Temple on Omejis, he thought somberly as he got to his feet.

He turned around to look toward the entrance and saw the circular door through which he and his partners had entered. It was indeed the Temple on Omejis—or another structure with a circular door, but he had a feeling that was unique to the panthalassic world.

Alexander assessed his situation and remembered Imara's words. He reached into the lefthand front pocket of his slacks and felt a crinkle of paper. He frowned and pulled out a thick piece of paper from their house in Temple City. It was folded over several times. He didn't know when Imara had slipped it into his pocket, but clearly, it happened after he manifested his usual clothing for the day.

His hands trembled slightly as he unfolded the paper and looked at two distinct sections, one each in Imara and Sirenī's handwriting. Imara's was small, neat, and pragmatic, while Sirenī's was flowing and graceful. Both were easy to read.

Alexander took a deep breath and read Imara's note since it was above the fold of the single page:

Alex,

I can't tell you how I know what I know, but I have knowledge of the last eight years and a little bit of our immediate future. We'll only be apart for a short time, I'm not sure exactly how long, and then we'll be together again.

The babies are fine. Sirenī and I will be fine, but you have to let us go for now. Don't search for us. Remember how much I love you. I know we swore we'd never be apart again, but these past eight years were a blessing, and this separation is nothing in the time ahead of us.

I want to apologize for getting pregnant and keeping it secret from you for as long as I did. It's been weighing on me these last few years. I know you're as happy as I am to have this baby, but I shouldn't have done what I did. I should have talked to you first. I kept meaning to say that I was sorry, but somehow, it just never felt like the right time. I guess this letter gave me an opportunity to share those feelings.

All my love. I'll see you soon.
Imara

Alexander sighed at her words. All that mattered to him was that he, Imara, and Sirenī were together again. After forty-eight years without them in his life, he didn't mind if they had fifty kids together and he was the last to know, so long as both women were there with him. He dropped his gaze to Sirenī's note, which was much shorter.

Dearest Alex,

You know I'm not one for long goodbyes or making a big fuss. I love you. I don't know anymore than you do about what's happening because Imara wouldn't tell me, either. I'm sorry Imara and I talked about having kids and got pregnant without involving you. It was kind of thoughtless, but I also know you don't worry about things like that. You'll probably be worried about us being apart, but Imara assures me we're all safe, according to her source, and we're back together again in no time. Well, a short time. Not sure how short, but you know what I mean.

Lots of love!

Sirenī signed her note with a swirly drawing of a heart, which brought a smile to Alexander's lips. He snapped his fingers to manifest a chair and sat heavily in it, worried despite the words his partners had written. He reread the note several times and scanned it with his psychic senses. It was just what it seemed, with no hidden message or magical properties.

So…do I do what Imara says and wait? Or do I look for them?

Alexander hadn't adhered to Imara's directions to wait until he got home, but he didn't think that counted in the scheme of things. He knew that Imara's innate magic allowed her to hear the melodies of creation, the sounds of the universe, and the echoes of space and time. She'd heard herself casting a time travel spell before they left Earth, and that event triggered their time travel eight years into the past.

Alexander also restored Imara's sight by giving her locrunite autolenses etched with the most powerful spell known, the Epiphany of Light. The spell allowed the caster to see across space and time to anywhere they could imagine without limitations. She'd mastered the incredible vision the lenses gave her, but Alexander couldn't imagine everything she saw with them.

His reasoning made sense to him. Everyone talked about how powerful he was, but Imara and Sirenī were also prodigies. Imara was a Seiren, distantly descended from a race of beings on another world who'd developed a unique relationship with some kind of draconic being. Imara had seen it all in a vision when she fought the līc inside Mount Lauremanda.

Her aural powers were profound.

Sirenī's fatal beauty came from Medusa's powerful bloodline. It was a magical power Sirenī could control with absolute precision, but she also had mystical powers. Those allowed her to transform into a ten-foot-tall monster that could smash boulders and turn people to stone with her wrathful gaze.

Sirenī had fused Medusa's mystical power with the magic of her fatal beauty and controlled the eruption of Mount Lauremanda. Neither woman knew the extent of their powers. Alexander wasn't sure he knew his own limits, but he was certain Imara and Sirenī hadn't come close to theirs.

"I will trust you."

Alexander spoke aloud for his benefit, to clarify his thoughts and bring his focus to what he needed to do next: return to his friends on Earth. There was certainly nothing more for him in the Temple or on Omejis, but Carter and the others were waiting on his adopted homeworld.

Alexander stood and dismissed his chair. He summoned another holographic display as the hazy curtain of light sprang from the dais. The transit system's destination was still Earth, so he tapped the screen to confirm it and stepped onto the platform. The light hardened and snapped to the ceiling, then retracted back into the script ringing the dais.

Alexander stood at his destination without any awareness of time or movement. He turned in a slow circle, then stepped down from the "front" of the Earthen Gatehouse platform. The wintry garden surrounding the superancient building was covered in light, crunchy snow. As soon as he was far enough away, the sides of the Gatehouse extended out from the base, unfolding and untwisting before they fanned upright and formed a cube. The pyramidal top slid up from the cube, and the building was again dormant.

Although he, Imara, and Sirenī spent eight years on Omejis, he calculated that his return should only be a few months past the time they left Earth. The panthalassic world had a slightly longer day and a few days extra per year, averaging to what he calculated as the passage of eight years and three months or so on Earth.

Alexander wanted to go to the manor and check in with his friends, but a tingling alarm tickled his awareness. He frowned and reached out with his senses, discovering anomalies along the barrier. He snapped his fingers to teleport to the end of the manor's driveway, but nothing happened.

The sorcerer sighed. He, Imara, and Sirenī had assumed the corruption was active on Earth and however many other worlds the necromancer had selected, but they didn't know the extent of it all. An inability to teleport without using excess power was a clear sign of the corruption's presence, though.

Alexander walked briskly across the Lower Forty to cut through the trees toward the road. The snow was marginally deeper in the wooded area. He traipsed along in his customary white button-down shirt with the sleeves rolled up to his elbows, black slacks, and shiny shoes. The snow flattened out and away from each step.

Alexander's mind drifted to his partners while he walked. He wondered why the three of them seemed fated to be torn apart. He didn't believe in destiny or predetermination. Anyone could play his role if they were inclined: he was a resonance in the greater prāṇa-maṇḍala, and that vibration could manifest in countless ways as an infinite number of people.

For him, though, Imara and Sirenī were irreplaceable.

Perhaps I should ask Valas Amris for insight.

Alexander had always had a connection with the Celestial Bird. He knew the ascended being would obliquely answer his questions if he followed that path. With that thought, his agitation settled some.

He blinked to open his psychic sight when he reached the barrier around the property. He perceived a strange, immaterial growth climbing the outside of the barrier. It consisted of thick, trunk-like structures at ground level spaced every twenty feet, each pulsing with the dark, virulent green sparkles and shimmers of necromantic magic. About twenty feet from the ground, the trunks began to branch, first in two, then ten feet later into four, and so on, until they formed a strange, twining band that girded the curve of the barrier about halfway between the ground and the peak.

He raised an eyebrow as he beheld the corruption. He wondered how fast it moved to be so well-developed on the barrier—surely this wasn't the progress of just a few months? He hadn't even sensed the corruption before leaving Earth with Imara and Sirenī. He stepped up to the interior perimeter of the barrier and looked across the street. He didn't see anything beyond the shield.

Is this part of the spell? Does it specifically attack sources of magical energy?

Alexander pursed his lips, but there was no direct way to know unless he found a copy of the spell somewhere. As awful as it was, he did admire the artistry and mastery of the archlīc who'd created it. It was a complex, multilayered piece of magic with numerous amendments and filters built into it. He hadn't seen the dark flower on Omejis, but he would have loved to study it since it was a nexus for the corruption spell.

Alexander closed his eyes and projected his avatar onto State Route 26. The asphalt was clear of snow but had a thin layer of ice. Above, the sky was uniformly overcast, but the clouds were silvery instead of dark. He realized the moon must be full, with a thinner cloud cover. He quickly looked in both directions along the road and returned his attention to the barrier.

The sorcerer gestured with his left hand, fingers spread, and summoned a revelation spell using his willpower alone. Arcane symbols appeared before him as the magic confirmed what he suspected: the virulent growth was a product of the corruption. He targeted various areas of the manifestation and recast the spell, but the results remained unchanged.

The sorcerer dismissed the spell and his avatar. He opened his eyes, turned away from the street, and walked through the woods on a line that would take him to the manor. He knew Carter would be there and awake, no matter the time.

He inhaled deeply to ease the pain in his chest that came from being separated again from Imara and Sirenī. Despite his resolve to trust them and focus only on what he could manage, his heart made it plain that his logic was easily refuted when it came to them.

To continue reading, order your copy of *The Consiliency of Lines* on Amazon.

Also by C.S. Harris

Fulfilling a Vow
A Ring of Worlds Prequel

Reunion of the Three
The Ring of Worlds, Book One

The Sorcerer's Gambit
The Ring of Worlds, Book Two

The Vergence of Time
The Ring of Worlds, Book Three

Acknowledgments

My adventures in the Ring of Worlds started as an unexpected astral projection, a vivid vision of a world where things are like Earth but simultaneously different. The stories that evolved out of that experience wouldn't be in print without crucial assistance from many other people.

My wife, Jen, through every lifetime.
The capable crew of The Authors' Assistant: Mindy, Danielle, Danylle, and Laurie.
Rhys Davies, for the map of Gaea used in my books.
Joseph W. Windsor, for invaluable help with the Ôrënos language.
My family, friends, and readers, for your enjoyment and support of Alex, Imara, Sirenī, and Jack's ongoing adventures.

I've always believed that support is the key to a would-be writer becoming an author. Never underestimate the power of your encouragement.

Languages in the Ring of Worlds Series

I like languages. It's important to me to understand how to pronounce words when I see them, whether we're talking Earthen tongues or invented languages straight from the author's mind. Accent marks are a key element to understanding how to pronounce words, real or imagined.

You'll spot a smörgåsbord of diacritic-laden words from around the world and across the centuries in my books. You'll also find a lot of accent marks in my conlang, Ôrëńos, which I co-crafted with Joseph W. Windsor. It's a viable, naturalistic language, and every diacritic denotes a specific pronunciation that seldom varies.

You can find Ôrëńos details at **www.theringofworlds.com/conlang,** and you can further explore your conlang cravings at **www.conlang.org**.

If you're yearning for a glossary for the Earthen languages from the Ring of Worlds instead of my conlang, then you're in luck. Head to **https://www.theringofworlds.com/glossary**. I keep adding to it as new words come up.

Are the accent marks bugging you? By all means, ignore them. Your enjoyment of my work trumps any kind of pronunciative pedantry I may have implied. If you don't find the stories fun, then what's the point, right?

I strove for accuracy and completeness in these books, but if I've missed anything or botched something, please help me correct my blunders. After all, 10,000 eyes are better than ten or twenty. Drop me a line by email at **chris@theringofworlds.com**.

About the Author

In his early childhood, Chris embarked on his creative odyssey, armed with a box of crayons, a penchant for painting, and a quirky typewriter. Today, he shares his Maine abode with his wife and a mischievous gang of cats who think they're the true authors of the household. While he savors Maine's charm, Chris dreams of chasing the sun to a locale where sunscreen is a daily essential, all in the name of art and adventure.

Learn more about Chris at csharrisbooks.com and theringofworlds.com.

Made in United States
Cleveland, OH
04 May 2025